HUNTED

THE BANNING SISTERS TRILOGY

Shameless

Irresistible

Scandalous

OTHER TITLES BY KAREN ROBARDS

Shiver

Sleepwalker

Justice

Shattered

Pursuit

Guilty

Obsession

Vanished

Superstition

Bait

Beachcomber

Whispers at Midnight

To Trust a Stranger

Paradise County

Ghost Moon

The Midnight Hour

The Senator's Wife

Heartbreaker

Hunter's Moon

Walking After Midnight

Maggy's Child

One Summer

Nobody's Angel

This Side of Heaven

Dark of the Moon

KAREN ROBARDS

HUNTED

**Doubleday Large Print
Home Library Edition**

GALLERY BOOKS

New York   London   Toronto   Sydney   New Delhi

This Large Print Edition, prepared especially
for Doubleday Large Print Home Library, contains
the complete, unabridged text of the original
Publisher's Edition.

G

Gallery Books
A Division of Simon & Schuster, Inc.
1230 Avenue of the Americas
New York, NY 10020

GALLERY BOOKS and colophon are registered
trademarks of Simon & Schuster, Inc.

Cover design © Lisa Litwack
Cover image © Dougal Waters/Getty Images

Manufactured in the United States of America

ISBN 978-1-61129-060-8

**This Large Print Book carries the
Seal of Approval of N.A.V.H.**

This book is dedicated to my editor, Lauren McKenna, who has been absolutely fantastic as always and has gone above and beyond with this one. It is also dedicated to Louise Burke, with profound appreciation for her support, and to the entire staff of Gallery/Pocket Books. And, finally, it is dedicated to my husband, Doug, and my sons Peter, Christopher, and Jack, with love.

CHAPTER ONE

It was the kids that got to him. Every damned time.

Even now that Social Services had taken the little girl away, New Orleans PD homicide detective Reed Ware couldn't get the crumpled, tear-stained face of the mop-haired five-year-old who had just watched her mama get shot to death out of his mind.

He needed a drink. Several drinks. Hell, a whole bottle of Jack Daniel's, hold the glass.

For a moment, he craved the smoky smoothness of whiskey on his tongue.

Then he reminded himself that he didn't drink anymore.

And refused to allow himself to remember the reason why.

Do not go there.

It was just after 3 a.m. on December 23. Two full days to go before Christmas, and the seasonal crime wave was in full swing. Something about the holidays—the pressure of dealing with family, the loneliness of those without family or whose families were broken, the expectations, the disappointments, and in New Orleans especially, the booze and drugs—added up to a measurable uptick in the number of murders and violent crimes as people looked forward (or not) to the arrival of good old St. Nick.

Peace and goodwill toward all, anybody?

The cracked brick sidewalk Reed was standing on was shrouded in shadows that were kept from being dangerously dark only by the gassy yellow streetlights that dotted the French Quarter. Despite the lateness of the hour, even this out-of-the-way area near Canal Street was not quite deserted. A couple of onlookers huddled together across the street, faceless in the dark as they watched the comings and goings of the investigation. A few more people slunk along the sidewalks, oblivious or uncaring. Somewhere not too far away, he could hear a street musician on a violin playing what sounded like "O Holy Night."

The irony of it didn't escape him.

He was just coming off his shift, which had run way longer than expected because he had been, what else, investigating a homicide—the homicide of that little girl's mother to be precise. It was horrible. And it was the job. The job that paid for the dinged-up six-year-old Ford Explorer—his personal vehicle—waiting for him at the curb and the dinged-up two-bedroom cottage with the dinged-up microwave dinner in the freezer waiting for him a dozen blocks away in Bywater.

He hadn't chosen to become a cop for the salary. Or the perks. Or the hours. Or the, well, anything. Except once, a long time ago, a cop was all he had ever wanted to be.

Look at him now: thirty-five years old,

no family, precious few friends, not even a cat to go home to. Living the dream, he thought wryly.

Laissez les bons temps rouler. Let the good times roll.

"Merry Christmas, huh?" That weary remark came from his new partner, Bob Terry, as he caught up to Reed in front of the run-down apartment building where the murder scene was still being processed. Terry had actually been his partner for a little over a year now, but Reed called him his new partner to differentiate Terry from his old partner, Elliot DeBlassis, who'd moved to Boston at the insistence of his new wife, Helena, who was from there. She had gotten sick of the heat and humidity that were as much a part of the city as gumbo and jazz—along with, of course, the crime and the gangs and the never-ending violence and threat of danger to her husband that was part of being a cop in New Orleans.

She's the smart one, was what Reed had told DeBlassis at the time. Parting from his longtime partner and closest friend would have been hard, except by then he'd become so emotionally numb that nothing had really bothered him any-more.

"Yeah," he replied to Terry. Terry was thirty-three, about Reed's own height of six two, husky and blond where Reed was lean and dark, and at the moment packing an extra twenty pounds or so from sympathy eating while his wife, Mia, had been pregnant. The infant was three months old now, and Terry was looking haggard from lack of sleep. "You go on home. I'll do the paperwork."

That was the thing about crime: it always came with paperwork. Reams of it.

Terry was a good guy. He even hesitated a minute. "You sure?"

Reed waved him away. "Tell Mia she owes me one."

"Will do. Thanks." Terry took off down the line of police vehicles that had parked alongside the curb toward his own seen-better-days Honda Accord.

Reed watched Terry leave, then got in the Explorer and headed toward the Eighth District Station House. People moved along the sidewalks in ones and twos, little more than black shapes in the darkness, most of them holding the plastic cups in which they were allowed to carry alcoholic beverages on the streets as they flitted from bar to bar. The bars had no closing time, and the people who frequented them all had about the same amount of restraint, or lack thereof, which led to a lot of booze-related crime. The Christmas decorations were up, twinkly festoons of greenery hanging from the wrought iron balconies, wreaths on the doors of every other shop, red bows on every other post. Like the Quarter itself, the decorations looked slightly seedy, shabby, raffish. So late at night, the atmosphere was straight out of Dickens. Or **Interview with the Vampire**.

He was just turning onto Royal Street when his cell phone rang.

A glance at the name on his screen made him frown. Elizabeth Townes? He didn't know anybody by that name, as far as he could remember.

Suspicion narrowed his eyes. Only a very few people had his personal cell phone number.

"Ware," he answered.

"Hey, Dick, you want to see what I'm talking about, you get yourself over to Grandma's House and come on down that alley back there." Even if the **dick** hadn't been a dead giveaway—it was a smart-ass way of shortening **detective**—Reed would have recognized the voice instantly, despite its current barely audible whisper. It belonged to Hollis Bayard. Holly was an eighteen-year-old street tough whose rap sheet ranged from theft (stealing things like cell phones from unsuspecting tourists), to underage drinking, to marijuana possession, to assault on a police officer. All of which, fortunately for him, occurred before he had turned eighteen two months before. Since the magic birthday that had made him a legal adult, he'd managed to avoid being picked up. Reed had zero confidence that Holly's luck would last. "Shit's popping **right now**."

The whisper was the giveaway: Holly was close to whatever was going down. If he knew Holly, he was too damned close.

Reed felt his gut clench. For whatever unfathomable reason, he felt a small amount of responsibility toward the kid. The Quarter was one of those places where minding your own business was prized. You didn't, you could get yourself killed.

Lately, minding his own business wasn't Holly's strong point.

Grandma's House was slang for the headquarters of the 110ers gang, a murderous bunch of drug and gun traffickers that even the cops were afraid of. If Holly got in their way, he'd be floating facedown in the muddy brown waters of the Mississippi before morning.

"You haul ass out of there," Reed ordered. He was already hanging a hard left and putting the pedal to the metal. Luckily, at this time of night, vehicular traffic in the Quarter was almost nil. "You hear me? Whatever it is, I'll handle it. I'm on my way."

"Holy fuck," Holly muttered, not in response to anything Reed had said, and the phone disconnected. Reed listened to the buzzing sound with a combination of alarm and wrath. He'd known Holly and his family since the kid was maybe ten years old, when, as a vice cop, he'd busted Holly's prostitute mother, Magnolia. He'd discovered her two little kids—Holly and his then five-year-old brother, Anton, universally known as Ant—curled up asleep in the propped-open trunk of the beat-up Saturn where she'd been turning tricks.

Holly was a pain in the ass, one of those kids who found trouble like water found low ground, but he wasn't bad at heart. Over the years, as Reed had busted Magnolia multiple times and then, after he got promoted out of vice, been around as other cops had busted her, he'd gotten to know Holly and Ant pretty well. He'd found himself looking out for them a little, doling out advice and warnings, to which they mostly didn't listen, trying to steer them away from getting involved with the gangs running rampant in the city, providing protection if he was around and they needed it, offering them the occasional meal, and handing over a few bucks when one of them particularly needed something, like shoes. Six months ago, Magnolia had been shot to death along with her drug dealer boyfriend. It hadn't been Reed's case, but he'd informally looked into it anyway and saw no reason to disagree with the findings: they'd been the victims of a rival pusher, who'd since bit the big one himself, as the result of more street crime.

Holly had a bee in his bonnet, a crackpot theory, about who had killed his mother. Unfortunately for the kid's peace of mind, it didn't jibe with the official version. It was, in a word, wrong, but Holly had been slinking around, listening to rumors floating on the streets, sticking his nose into places he was better off keeping out of, trying to prove otherwise.

From that phone call, Reed had little doubt that Holly was at his amateur sleuthing again.

You're going to get your idiot self killed, was the furious thought Reed sent winging Holly's way as he jerked the Explorer around on practically two wheels to make yet another tight corner.

What it came down to was that Holly, and Ant, too, were still reeling from their mother's death. Magnolia had had her faults, but she had been a fiercely protective mother who had loved her two sons. Against long odds, she'd managed to keep both boys in school, and when she'd died in June, Holly had been on track to graduate high school in one more year, while Ant had just finished up fifth grade. Since then, Holly had pretty much gone to school when he'd felt like it, which Reed suspected hadn't been all that much. Ant was doing better about school attendance, but only because Holly, in classic "don't do what I do, do what I say" mode, stayed on his case about it.

Magnolia might not have suited every-one's idea of what a good mother should be, but, in Reed's eyes, and more impor-tant in those of her children, she'd been a good mother nonetheless. The way the two boys had hung together since her death was a case in point: she had raised them to love each other. And they had loved her. As Reed had gotten to know her, he'd respected her for that. "I got to put food on the table," Reed had heard her reply once to a bar owner who was giving her grief about setting up shop too near his establishment. "I got to put a roof over my kids' heads. Ain't nobody else gonna take care of them if I don't." She was always getting and losing minimum-wage jobs, but as she'd put it, "I can work forty damn hours for what I can earn in four hours turning tricks. And while I'm out there scrubbing toilets for diddly-squat, who's going to keep my boys out of trou-ble?" Which she had done her best to do.

Reed still remembered seeing her take a broom to members of the St. Mary Mafia, an offshoot of the 110ers, when they had shown up outside her apartment building to try to get Holly to go somewhere with them. Wielding that broom like a baseball bat, she'd charged out of the building and whopped upside the head three or four of the meanest young toughs in the city, sending them scampering away like rats. Then she had turned around and whopped Holly upside the head with her broom, too, for going outside to talk to them. "You ain't getting into that shit," he'd heard her yelling at Holly even as, weapon in hand, Reed had stepped out of his car—he and DeBlassis had been cruising through the complex looking for a suspect—in case the vanquished punks had decided to turn back around and mother and son had needed more protection than just Magnolia's broom.

The small apartment that Magnolia, Holly, and Ant had shared—lost, now, in the wake of Magnolia's death—had been for the most part a happy place. In the last year or so of her life Magnolia's twin weaknesses—feel-good drugs and no-good men—had begun to take a toll. Every loser who had passed through her life had been a bad influence in one way or another, and with the last one, the drug dealer with whom she'd been killed, she'd spiraled as low as Reed had ever seen her. She and Holly had been fighting pretty much non-stop over her escalating drug use and her scumbag boyfriend in the days before she had died, and Reed suspected that guilt over that was mixed in with Holly's grief. Whether or not that was the case, Magnolia's death had hit Holly—and Ant—hard. It was still a constant presence in their thoughts, their lives, their dreams. They were still in denial, still going through those useless **if only I had done this or that differently, it wouldn't have happened that way** scenarios in their minds.

Reed understood. He'd been there himself. Sometimes, although with lessening frequency now, he found himself back there. He was pretty sure that that was one of the reasons he'd bonded like he had with Holly and Ant over the last few months: he knew what it was like to lose the person you loved most in the world. He knew what it was like to feel like you were slowly bleeding to death inside.

Three years before, he'd lost his own

young son in a car accident that had also killed his ex-wife. The world had been a different place for him ever since. What had once been brightly colored and full of warmth and life was now gray and cold and dead. From the time of his son's death until Magnolia had died, nothing and no one had been able to penetrate the icy barrier of grief and regret that had encased him. But in Holly's and Ant's anguish, he'd seen a reflection of his own. Those boys had needed someone, and for lack of any alternative, that someone had turned out to be him. The three of them had somehow managed to grab hold of one another in the darkness, and now, for better or worse, they were connected.

He didn't particularly like it, but there it was: they turned to him when they needed help, and he looked out for them when he could.

Since Magnolia's death, Ant had been placed in a foster home, from which he'd promptly run away to rejoin Holly (nobody in officialdom seemed to care), who crashed with his girlfriend Edie's large family in a tiny apartment on Port Street when they would have him, and on various friends' couches when they wouldn't. Several times lately, Reed had gotten home in the middle of the night to find Holly and Ant sacked out on his front porch. He'd taken them in, let them sleep out what was left of the night in his spare bedroom, fed them breakfast in the morning, and then, the daylight and full stomachs making them cocky, the boys had been on their way.

So far, Holly had even managed to refrain from stealing anything from Reed, which, given his predilection for small electronics and the fact that Reed's house contained a lot of them, was something.

To Reed's mild surprise, Grandma's House—a seedy storefront on the wrong side of Elysian Fields—was dark as a grave. Nobody on the sidewalk out front. Not a wino, not a punk, not a pusher, not a hooker. No activity at all. No sign of Holly or anyone else. Just mist wafting like smoke down the sidewalk, illuminated by a fragment of moonlight from the not-quite-full ghostly circle hanging high in the onyx sky. The narrow mouth of an alley yawned black as a tar pit to the building's left. Cursing under his breath, Reed parked and got out.

No sign of Holly. Too much to hope that the kid had listened to him for once and left the scene. No, Holly was down that alley, in the thick of whatever he'd summoned Reed to see. Reed knew it as well as he knew his own name.

Goddamn it.

He could smell the dampness of the river, the smoky, boozy essence of the Quarter, and a hint of ripe garbage, too, as, gun drawn, he headed down the alley. He moved fast but cautiously, his footsteps quiet on the uneven cobblestones. A couple of paces in, and the darkness swallowed him up. Two- and three-story brick buildings formed a solid wall on either side of what was a narrow, uneven canyon. As his eyes adjusted, he saw that the walls were windowless. Metal garbage cans, most of them missing their lids, stood in clusters around recessed doorways. All was quiet except for the hum of distant noise from elsewhere in the Quarter and a steady drip of water somewhere nearer at hand. It made Reed think of the swamp he'd grown up in, how you could always tell when a predator was nearby because all the birds had flown away.

Something's wrong. His pulse rate quickened along with his step. He was on high alert now, scanning the shadows with care even as he focused on the lessening of dark at the end of the alley, which, if memory served him correctly, opened onto a small church with a surrounding cemetery.

Whatever's going down is probably going down there. Even as he had the thought, he caught a glimmer of movement out of the corner of his eye. A split-second later, something leaped out of a doorway and rushed him.

His heart jumped.

"Dick!" The cry was no less heartfelt for being scarcely louder than a whisper.

Not Holly: Ant. Jesus Christ, a man with less steady nerves would have shot the kid. Unlike Holly's, Ant's usage of Dick was entirely without malice: it was simply what he'd learned, from a young age, to call the police detective who'd been a fixture in his life for as long as he could remember. Thirteen now, skinny and undersized, black hair buzzed and big eyes shining in the darkness, he grabbed the sleeve of Reed's sport jacket and bounced up and down on the balls of his feet with agitation as he pointed toward the end of the alley.

"Holly's down there. Some guys came—I think he's watching them rob some people." Ant sounded breathless.

Doing his best to tamp down the curses that crowded to the tip of his tongue, Reed was already moving again—faster but still deliberate—in that direction, with Ant, having let go of Reed's jacket, trotting beside him.

"You follow him here?" he asked Ant in a growly undertone, because to Holly's credit, Reed knew that if he'd thought something bad was going to go down, he wouldn't have brought his little brother anywhere near it. Ant shrugged guiltily. Reed had his answer: **yes**. "My car's out there on the street. Go crawl under it and wait for me."

In Reed's experience, even in the deadliest of street confrontations, even if the bullets were flying and the bad guys were mowing each other down like weeds, nobody ever looked under a vehicle for potential targets. Therefore, especially at night and for a kid Ant's size, having him take shelter beneath a vehicle was way safer than, say, passing over the keys to the Explorer and telling him to hide in the backseat. Everybody always looked in the backseat.

"What?" The look Ant gave him was disbelieving.

Reed's answer was short. "Do what I tell you."

"But I don't—"

The rest of Ant's words were lost as a woman screamed. The terror-filled sound sliced through the darkness like a knife, making Reed's muscles tense and the hair on the back of his neck catapult upright as his gaze snapped toward the sound. A split second later the sharp **pop pop pop pop** of gunfire exploded through the alley. It was close, loud, and almost certainly coming from the cemetery just a couple of dozen yards ahead.

Shit.

"Go get under my damn car," he barked at Ant as he broke into a dead run and, at the same time, yanked his radio from his belt. Out of the corner of his eye he watched Ant melt back into the shadows.

Damned pain-in-the-ass kid—would he do as he was told? "Officer needs assistance at—"

He had just finished giving the address as he burst out of the alley into streaming moonlight, then pulled up to orient himself, pressing his back against the flat wall of the side of the last building. Juiced by adrenaline, blinking against what felt like a sudden onslaught of brightness, it was all he could do to stop himself before he possibly got in trouble, to give himself time to let his eyes adjust and conduct a lightning survey of the scene. An ancient wrought iron fence edged the cemetery that was just a couple of yards away. The fence surrounded an overgrown lot, which housed a church in the middle—equally ancient, no more than a chapel really, a one-story brick shoebox with a crooked steeple. Behind it—he had exited the alley at the back of the church, which faced out on a narrow residential street—monuments ranging from knee-high marble arches to six-foot-tall stone angels leaned mostly out of plumb and cast long shadows over weed-infested plots. A slamming of doors and a squealing of tires made him look sharply toward the street in front of the church, although he couldn't see the vehicle in question because the church itself was in the way. The buildings across from the church were dark and deserted: not a soul in sight. A whooshing sound, and he knew the vehicle was gone.

Movement nearby brought his focus instantly back closer at hand.

Holly stepped out of the shadow of one of the stone angels. Five ten, lanky in the way of a kid who hadn't yet filled out, wearing his uniform of jeans and a hoodie, he impatiently pushed his too-long black hair back behind his ears as he struggled with a small object that he was holding up in front of his face. A phone, Reed identified a second later. Elizabeth Townes' stolen phone, almost certainly. Holly was focusing the phone, as well as every bit of his attention, on something that appeared to be on the ground in front of him. Something that the darkness, and the shifting shadows, and the monuments that semi-blocked his view, prevented Reed from seeing.

Holly was taking pictures with the phone. Of what? Reed couldn't yet tell, but the quick answer was, it couldn't be anything good.

Reed thrust the radio back into position on his belt, tightened his grip on his gun, then took a running step and vaulted the thigh-high fence.

"Holly." His footsteps were soundless in the overgrown grass. His voice was quiet as he came up to the kid. Holly cut a glance at him. Visually probing the darkness all around, Reed identified no threat. But danger and violence hung in the air: like any good cop, he could feel them in his bones the way some people feel rain.

"I saw 'em! I told you! They acted like they wanted to make a buy, and then they shot them!" It was an emotion-packed whisper. Holly's hands shook. His eyes were wild. "I got pictures. I think. This damned phone—"

"Yo. Everything okay?" Ant slunk up behind them.

Holly turned on him. "I told you not to follow me!"

"I told you to get under the damned car!" Reed growled at almost the same moment. Of course Ant hadn't done as he was told. By either of them. That was Ant.

Ant threw up his hands in a gesture meant to be placating. "I thought you all might need some help."

"From you?" Holly countered scornfully.

Reed missed the rest of that brotherly exchange, because by then his eyes had adjusted enough to find what he was praying he wouldn't see—victims, sprawled in the shadow of an above-the-ground crypt maybe thirty feet away.

His gut tightened.

"Fuck." Reed felt more tired than he could remember feeling in a long time as he started toward the motionless figures. He had little doubt that they were dead, probably as Holly had said, the victims of a drug deal gone bad, just a few more casualties of the escalating, gang-related violence that was tearing the city apart. So many murders provided him with job security and all that, but truth was this shit was getting old. Even he, hardened to violent death as he was, was beginning to be sickened by all of it.

Not for the first time, he wondered if he was in danger of getting burned out.

"It's the same thing that happened to Mom." Holly's whisper was urgent as, with

Ant trailing him like a shadow, he followed Reed. Crouching to check each victim in turn for a pulse—there were four of them, two adult males, an adult female, and a boy who looked like he was about Ant's age—Reed registered the raw meat smell of fresh blood with a grimace. What looked like oily black halos leached into the grass around each victim's head. He placed two fingers beneath the ear of the youngest victim. Like the others, he had a bullet hole between his eyes. Nice and neat. Death would have been instantaneous. No pulse, big surprise, although the boy was still warm. His wide-open eyes were already glazed and vacant as he stared sightlessly up at the night sky.

Another goddamned kid. Two minutes earlier, and I might have been able to save him.

Reed could feel the pounding of his own pulse in his temples.

"You listening to me?" Holly demanded, and Reed frowned up at him. The teen was standing over him, waving the stolen phone practically in his face. Holly continued, "This time I saw them. For real. I even took pictures. I mean, if I did it right. Anyway, it's like I told you: it's the five-o."

By five-o, Holly meant the cops.

"Would you give it a rest?" For an instant, as he held Holly's gaze, a graphic mental picture of Magnolia's corpse flashed in front of Reed's eyes. A once-pretty woman aged prematurely by the life she'd led, she'd had a bullet hole drilled through her forehead, too, just like all four of these victims did. Thing was, though, as every officer who went through the police academy learned, torso shots were the high percentage shots. A couple of rounds from a 9mm pumped into a chest would stop pretty much anything. Head shots like these were the trademark of gang members, not cops. "No way in hell were they cops."

"**Way.**" Holly darted a glance in the direction of the fast-approaching sirens that were growing louder with every second, and shifted nervously from foot to foot. "What, you think I don't know what I saw? I'm telling you the truth."

"Give me that phone." Reed stood up abruptly and took the phone from Holly's hand, ignoring the kid's indignant "Hey!" in response. The victims were beyond help: there was nothing Reed or anyone else could do for them except find out who had killed them. As an eyewitness to the murders, Holly would be invaluable to the investigation—with or without a phone full of pictures—and he would also be dead, just as soon as the perps found out about him and what he had seen. Holstering his gun, Reed slid the phone into his pocket, pulled out his keys, and wrested away his house key from the others.

"Go to my house. You and Ant. Let yourselves in, and stay put until I get there. Don't talk to anybody about this or anything else. Do not tell anyone that you were at the scene of these murders. Hear?"

"What am I, stupid?" Holly asked with disgust. He caught the key Reed tossed him without argument, which told Reed that he knew just how deep he was in the shit. Casting another wary glance in the direction from which the sirens were shrieking now as the posse Reed had summoned closed in, Holly thrust the key into the front pocket of his jeans, then looked at Reed again. "I ain't lying. I swear. It was a bunch of cops. Like, four."

"We'll hash this out when I get home," Reed told him. **"Go."**

"Yeah." Holly grabbed Ant by the arm. "Come on," he said to his brother.

Lips compressed, Reed watched Holly and Ant scramble over the fence and vanish into the dark as, lights flashing, a pair of squad cars slammed to a shuddering halt in front of the church.

CHAPTER TWO

The thing about the steamy heat of New Orleans was, sometimes it had a tendency to seep into its residents' brains. Where it drove them all kinds of crazy. Mix that with the holiday season, include a full moon on Christmas Eve, add in plentiful amounts of booze, and the city was ripe for trouble. What you got was the proverbial Bad Moon Rising, which it was, big and yellow as a tennis ball right over the smooth black waters of Lake Pontchartrain.

At about fifteen minutes before midnight, all hell broke loose.

"Where is he? Is he going to shoot?"

"He has a bomb!"

"Liza! Has anyone seen Liza?"

"Run! Keep going!"

That last bellowed order came from a cop. It sent adrenaline surging through the veins of Jefferson Parish Police Sergeant Caroline Wallace, who was shooting that malevolent moon a grim look even as she ran toward the mansions fronting the lake. It punctuated the panicked voices that somehow managed to reach her ears above the bedlam created by the intermingling of wailing sirens and shouts amplified by bullhorns and hovering helicopters. Sprinting for the Mobile Command Unit—a white van parked at the curb directly in front of the crime scene—she threw a quick, harried glance in the direction of the voices to check things out. An explosion of women in glittering ball gowns and men in tuxedos rushed down a long driveway and across the wide street just a few dozen yards away. The harsh glow of police floodlights illuminated the fear in their faces. The uniformed police officers running with them, protecting them, hurrying them along, looked agitated.

Survivors were being evacuated from

the beleaguered mansion situated on two waterfront acres directly in front of her. Sixty or more, according to her lightning count.

Which left one burning question: how many remained inside?

When she had arrived on the scene just a few minutes before, the block already had been cordoned off and the perimeter team was sealing off any possible escape route. The perp was trapped, which was both good and bad news: good because he wouldn't be going anywhere, and bad because, like trapped animals, surrounded humans were always the most dangerous. Her instant conclusion when her pager had gone off with Code 923, which meant hostage situation in progress, was that she, the hostage negotiator on call, was racing to a domestic, because that was most common this close to Christmas. But by the time she'd slammed her cruiser into park on a manicured lawn just down the street that was already thick with official vehicles, she had known that tonight was going to be anything but typical.

Tonight she was going to have to rock and roll.

Jefferson Parish's top brass, including the sheriff and the council chairman, as well as New Orleans' superintendent of police and mayor, were among the hostages being held inside the mansion, as she had learned via radio on the way over. That made it personal. That upped the stakes by about a thousand. That made it just that much harder to maintain the necessary distance, that much harder to do her job.

See, the sheriff was her boss. And the NOPD superintendent of police? That would be her dad.

As she ran, she was tightening up her body armor, which she'd learned the hard way not to show up at a crime scene without and which she kept in the trunk of her car, along with various other job-related necessities, for just this kind of occasion. The flak vest was state-of-the-art, designed to be thin and lightweight, yet it was still uncomfortable, still felt big and bulky on her slender, five-six frame. Along with her duty belt that held, among other items, her Glock 22 in its holster, she wore the vest beneath a black windbreaker with JPPD emblazoned across the back. The skirt she'd been wearing on the date the pager call had interrupted was a couple of inches short of her knees, slim fitting and black, while the sleeveless blouse beneath the windbreaker was thin silver silk, with a collarless V-neck that revealed a hint of cleavage. Since she'd had no time to change, she was actually glad for the coverage provided by the collarbone-high rise of the body vest. All she'd had time to do was trade her blazer for the windbreaker, kick off her high heels, slam her feet into the black sneakers that she also kept in the trunk, and grab her gear.

Be prepared. It might be the Girl Scout motto, but it worked for Caroline as well.

Her heart pounded, either from the dash from her car or the thought of what she faced. Deepening her breathing—the air smelled of fresh-cut grass and, faintly, of the wide lake stretching out like an expanse of flat black glass behind the houses in front of her—she tried to concentrate on mentally chilling out and easing into professional mode. What she was going for was cool, calm control.

Ice, ice, baby. That was her reputation. That was how she rolled.

As usual, lives depended on it. Tonight the lives of some of New Orleans' most powerful people might depend on it. Her father's life might depend on it.

Caroline wasn't sure how she felt about that.

"Yo, Wallace! Chop-chop! Need you to get busy pouring some oil on the water in there." The voice yelling at her out of the dark belonged to her good friend Lt. Jorge Esteban. He ran one of the TELS units, which told her that snipers were on the scene. She spotted him through the shadows, standing at the base of a cherry picker hoisting a basket with its cargo of one black-clad police sharpshooter high in the air. With the houses as far apart as they were, and given the nature of the exclusive neighborhood, which was as well manicured and flat as a golf course, she was guessing the logistics of getting off a kill shot were going to be difficult.

It was her job to make sure a kill shot didn't become necessary. As in, to pour oil on troubled waters until she got them smoothed out.

"On it," she yelled back as she passed, and finished snapping the rubber band in place around the ponytail she had just scooped her thick, shoulder-length coffee brown hair into, then tucked the tail up under her black JPPD baseball cap. Her eyes, artfully made up tonight to bring out the green tinge in her hazel irises, were busy darting every which way as she tried to gather as much information as she could before the ball bounced into her court.

Sometimes the smallest detail could be used to establish a connection with the perp.

In this case, rich envy was a no-brainer. She could definitely use that, see if he would bite, see if she couldn't get him feeling like he and she were on the same, poverty-stricken side of the fence. That was key: to make him—hostage takers were almost universally male—feel like she was his ally, like he could trust her. She didn't know who he was or what his motivation was yet, but that was an easy place to start trying to build some rapport. The palatial houses in this section of Old Metairie were so far out of touch with most people's lifestyles that it was hard to remember that these enormous structures—with their elaborate fountains, wide porticos, and multiple wings—were indeed people's homes. With many of them ablaze with Christmas lights, the neighborhood looked like something conjured up by Disney. Directly in front of her, the huge white southern-style mansion where the hostages were being held had been decked out to impress. Festoons of evergreen boughs intertwined with sparkling white lights adorned the three long verandas, one fronting each level of the three-story house. More sparkling white lights illuminated the wide staircase leading up to the front entrance. The small round bushes lining the sidewalk were aglow with lights. Farther out on the lawn (it would be almost sacrilegious to call an expanse of grass so well kept a yard), the small flowering trees had been wrapped in white Christmas lights, too. The revolving red flashes of light from multiple police cruisers that danced across the pillared facade could almost have been part of the holiday decor—if the holiday decor in this exclusive enclave had been real cheesy this year.

'Twas the night before Christmas . . .
And the owner of the house, billionaire

Allen Winfield, had been holding his annual black-tie ball. Only the rich, famous, and powerful were inside.

Where some of them—she had no idea of the exact numbers yet—were currently at the mercy of a crazed gunman. Who may or may not have planted bombs throughout the house, and may or may not be wearing a suicide vest with a dead man's switch that would blow the whole place sky-high.

As a hostage negotiator, it was her job to talk him into giving himself up without harming anyone. Or at least to keep him talking until SWAT could overpower him or a sniper could take him out.

"About damned time." JPPD Major Tom Dixon, command officer, greeted Caroline with a scowl as she pulled up, breathless, outside the van, before he turned back to continue the discussion that he had been in the midst of. He was in a huddle with senior officers from both police departments—Caroline knew most of them, at least by sight—because, while Jefferson Parish PD had jurisdiction over Old Metairie, the NOPD had a vested interest in what was happening considering that their superintendent of police and the mayor were inside. She knew Dixon well, having been in his chain of command until, after three years on the force, she had been accepted onto the Hostage Negotiation Team and whisked away for the initial FBI-sponsored training course. Given the high-profile nature of this event, she had been informed en route that the two departments were collaborating, with Dixon in charge, at least unless or until another, higher-ranking officer appeared on the scene. Despite the night's low-seventies temperature, she could see the sheen of sweat on Dixon's thick-featured face. Well, no surprise there. The burly, gray-haired fifty-five-year-old veteran officer was under a lot of pressure, Caroline knew. If this went down wrong, high-profile casualties were a virtual certainty. Old Metairie could be the next Colorado theater shooting. International headlines. The darling of the twenty-four-hour news cycle. And Dixon could kiss his fanny—and his career and his pension—good-bye.

"I think we should go ahead and send in a man with a dog. At least if the bastard's really gone and set bombs inside the mansion, the dog can sniff them out and we'll know where we are," Paul Villard said. A small, wiry man in his midforties, he was head of the JPPD bomb squad. Although Caroline had never worked directly with him, she had heard via the grapevine that he suffered from so-called little-man syndrome, with its compensatory tendency to be overly aggressive.

It wasn't her place to object to anything the big boys chose to do. She was the negotiator, not the playmaker. Still, Caroline automatically shook her head. Hostage negotiation Rule Number One: don't spook the perp.

"The last thing we want to do is get Mr. Winfield's house blown up," John Lagasse said uneasily. Average height and looks, muscular and balding, about the same age as Villard, he was in charge of the NOPD's Special Operations Unit.

"We get in there and find the bombs and disarm them"—Villard's voice was growly— "and we won't have to worry about the house blowing up."

"Yeah, but what if we don't get them disarmed in time? Or what if we miss one?" Lagasse scowled at Villard. "Forget the damned house: we get a lot of people blown up."

Dixon made an impatient gesture. "How about we let Wallace give it a try before we do anything else?"

The men turned and looked at her almost as one. Police work was a high-testosterone business, with no room for incompetence. She was the only woman on the hostage negotiator team, and, at twenty-seven, with two years as a full-fledged negotiator under her belt, she was the youngest and least experienced. Add to that the fact that she was the daughter of New Orleans' superintendent of police, and attractive enough so that she was more or less constantly fending off come-ons from her fellow cops, and skepticism as to her performance abilities had initially abounded. Caroline took pride in the fact that she had laid those concerns to rest. No, she had used them, harnessing them to fuel herself to be the best at her job that she could be.

Which was pretty damned good, if she did say so herself.

She had earned the respect of her fellow officers because she deserved it.

She said, "I'd like to try to establish a connection with the perp before anyone else goes in there. In case he **does** have the house set to blow."

The men looked at one another. Villard shrugged. Lagasse looked dubious. Dixon nodded.

"Okay," Dixon said. "Go ahead." To the others he added, "She's good." Then his eyes slashed back to Caroline and gleamed with sudden humor. "Don't make me regret saying that."

Caroline shot him a withering look.

"We got eyes in the house," a man's voice called excitedly from inside the van.

"Way to go, Isaacs," Dixon boomed back. He made a gesture for Caroline to precede him into the van. She did, ascending the fold-down steps into dim overhead lighting and walls lined with desks and computer equipment in a space about the size of a tin can.

"Hey." Walking forward, she nodded at the two technicians, Rob Isaacs and Kevin Holder, who were seated in front of the control panels. As Dixon stepped inside, behind her she found her attention riveted on the eye-level monitors. There was a row of them, fed by the telescoping antennas that stretched up from the van's roof like a bug's feelers.

They were showing scenes from inside the house.

"I was able to hack into the mansion's security system," Isaacs said to Dixon.

Caroline barely heard him.

On the monitor to her far left was her father, Col. Martin Wallace, in full dress uniform, not a strand of his snow-white hair out of place, his craggy face set in angry lines. He was seated in a chair in what looked to be a large, wood-paneled library or conference room. Men in tuxedos and women in ball gowns sprawled facedown on the floor in front of him. In a moment she would do a head count, check for visible injuries.

But for now, all she could do was look at her father's grim face—and at the handsome, black-haired man who held a gun to his head.

Her breathing suspended.

She knew him. More than knew him, in fact. She'd once had a hell of a thing for him.

Over long ago, of course.

One of the NOPD's own: Detective Reed Ware.

What the hell?

The shock she felt upon identifying him threatened to tip her world on its axis.

She'd be damned if she was going to let it.

"He's one of us," she said tightly. "What's the story?"

Scowling at the monitor, Dixon folded his arms over his chest. "No idea. Nobody's had a chance to talk to him yet. Only word we've gotten about what's happening in there is from people fleeing the scene."

"Who called it in?"

His eyes shifted in her direction. "Initial call went out on a silent alarm when somebody hit a panic button in the library. Since then, 911's been blowing up with cell phone calls. I'd say, everybody in the damned place."

First things first. "Anybody dead? Wounded?"

"None known so far."

Caroline felt a glimmer of relief. The situation had not yet totally spiraled out of control. "That's a plus."

"You all right to do this?" Dixon asked her. "I know it's hitting close to home, what with your father being involved. But at midnight on Christmas Eve, getting anybody else out here is going to take some time."

"I'm fine," she said, and she was. Absolutely. Even if her heart had started to beat a little faster, and her stomach had twisted itself into a knot.

That was normal, the result of adrenaline. That meant she was on her game.

She was a pro. Lives depended on what she did next. And what she was going to do next was exactly what she had been trained to do: her job.

Which was, first of all, to establish contact. Get Ware on the phone.

"We got a line inside?" she asked Dixon.

CHAPTER THREE

On the monitor, Caroline watched Ware's expression change as he registered the sound of the ringing phone. He stretched to punch a button on the instrument, which rested on the massive mahogany desk located at the far end of the room. To do that he used a single finger because, she noticed, both his hands were full—the right one with what looked to be his service weapon and the left one with—a dead man's switch? She couldn't be sure. Ware's leanly muscled, six-foot-two-inch frame had been perched, foot swinging, on a corner of that desk until he heard the phone. As he moved to answer it, his crow-black hair gleamed in the light of a chandelier hanging above the desk. Unlike Dixon, he didn't appear to be sweating, but his swarthy-skinned, chiseled-featured face was set in tense lines. Like the majority of the guests, he wore a tux. She guessed that was how he had managed to gain entry into the party, to which it was almost certain he had not been invited, because this storied bash was strictly for the rich and influential, and Ware was neither. Whatever, the elegant tux elevated his killer good looks to a whole new level of hot. Beneath the carelessly buttoned jacket, she saw no sign of a suicide vest. Which didn't mean that he wasn't in possession of a bomb, just that he didn't appear to be wearing it.

"Asshole," she heard her father say clearly, and realized that with one push of a finger Ware had put the phone on his end on speaker. Her phone was not on speaker, and would not be. Specially designed for use in hostage situations, the receiver she was holding was equipped with a button that you had to depress before you spoke into it if you wanted whoever was on the other end to be able to hear you. Otherwise, the handset did not transmit sound, which was the point. In hostage situations, there was generally too much going on in the Mobile Command Unit that the perp didn't need to hear.

"Shut the hell up," Ware replied almost amiably as he straightened to nuzzle the back of Martin Wallace's leonine head with his pistol. "Or I'll shut you up."

A muscle twitched in her father's cheek, which Caroline knew from experience meant that he was absolutely furious, but he didn't say anything else. No surprise there: contrary to his genial, glad-handing exterior, he was at heart cold and calculating, the opposite of rash. He would bide his time, wait for his opportunity, and strike back hard. Visibly on edge, he was seated in a leather-upholstered accent chair that looked like it was one of a pair designed to face the desk. It had been moved so that it was now directly in front of Ware, facing the room. Caroline recognized the self-control her father was exercising in the set of his shoulders and the thinness of his mouth. Ware's hand holding the pistol now rested negligently on the rolled leather back of that chair. The pistol's mouth was just a couple of inches short of the base of her father's skull. His wrists, she saw, were secured with zip ties to the chair's arms. A pair of bungee cords around his waist held him fastened in place. There was a bruise on his chin, and a small cut under one eye that had started to scab over. From the reddened scrape along Ware's left cheek-bone and the cut at the corner of his mouth, she surmised that her father, a bull of a man who at fifty-seven still took pride in his physical prowess, had put up a fight.

Only the injuries didn't look like they had happened within, say, the last hour or so. They looked older than that. Which meant they didn't fit within the time frame. According to what she had been told, this standoff had started approximately twenty minutes ago.

Something to puzzle over later.

She hadn't exchanged one word with her father in the last six months, and she wouldn't have talked to him six months ago if it hadn't been in the line of duty. They were the opposite of close. When he had lived with Caroline, her mother, and her two younger sisters, he had been a verbally abusive and sometimes even physically violent bully. When she was eighteen, he had divorced her mother, left the family, and married again. On most days, she would have said that she actively despised him.

But seeing him like this awakened all kinds of unsuspected emotions inside her, the simplest of which was a determination to get him, and the rest of the hostages, out of there alive.

I don't have to like him. I just have to do my job.

Her chest felt tight. She ignored it.

"If you've got something to say, say it," Ware said with a glance at the phone, and Caroline realized that he was talking to her.

Like the rest of Ware's too-handsome self, the voice was pure Louisiana Cajun.

She depressed the talk button on the phone.

"This is Caroline Wallace, Detective Ware," she said. "You want to tell me what this is all about?" Her father's eyes widened. It was the only acknowledgment of her he made. Even if their relationship had been different she wouldn't have expected anything more, given the situation. Revealing their vulnerabilities could only work in the hostage-taker's favor, and Martin would know that. The knowledge that her father would be listening to everything she said, evaluating her skills, judging her as he had always judged her, caused her stomach to flutter unexpectedly, and realizing that she was having that reaction annoyed the hell out of her. For the sake of the other hostages, the ones lying facedown on the obviously expensive Oriental rug with their hands zip-tied behind their backs, the ones whose fear she could practically feel through the monitor, she needed to keep her emotions out of it. To do what she had been trained to do to the best of her ability, and forget about everything else. With that in mind, she **almost** went personal. Almost called the perp Reed, as she had years ago. But she didn't: too many ears were around to hear, too many minds to speculate, too many memories to jog. Once upon a time, for a three-month period when the police superintendent's family had been under threat and Ware had been one of the officers assigned to watch over them and

keep them safe, she'd had the most enormous crush on him. Done her best to se-
duce him, which, to his credit, he hadn't
allowed her to do.

She'd been seventeen. He'd been
twenty-five.

Jailbait, he'd called her at the time.

Since then, she'd seen him around.
She'd grown up and gotten over him, of
course, but she had always been aware
of him. In a casual, heard-it-through-the
grapevine kind of way, she'd known when
he got married, had a child, got divorced.
She'd known when his ex-wife and child
had died in a traffic accident.

She'd gone to the funeral, one of a large
contingent of cops.

That was three years ago.

Now Reed Ware's eyes looked straight
into the monitor, as if he could see her. His
irises were so dark brown as to be almost
indistinguishable from the pupils. Framed
by sooty black lashes and straight black
brows, they were as steamy-hot as the
Louisiana swamps from which he had
sprung. Once, just having them look at her
in a certain way had been enough to make
her go all marshmallowy inside.

Once.

Not now.

She was all grown up now. And he—he was the perp she was getting ready to help take down.

How did this happen? she thought incredulously. **How did Reed Ware—a solid cop with something like twelve years of exemplary service under his belt—wind up taking all these very important people hostage?**

"Caroline." Ware spaced her name out: Car-o-line. Just like he had always done. She refused to acknowledge the shiver that sexy drawl sent down her spine. God, between his presence and her father's, this was going to be the job from hell, and she found herself wishing that anyone else had been on call tonight. But as the junior negotiator, she got the crappiest shifts, so here she was. Recalculating quickly, she had to throw the approach she had been planning to use with the perp out the window. Ware knew too much about her, too much about the way cops worked, too much about how hostage negotiation generally went down. She was going to have to go with her gut and what she knew about him, improvising on the fly. He continued, "Been a long time, cher."

Cher, which he pronounced **shah** as they did back in the bayous, meant dear or sweetheart. He'd called her that sometimes when she'd come down in the middle of the night to watch TV with him while he was on guard duty in the rented house where her family had been holed up; he'd called her that when he'd found her, trembling and upset, huddled on the staircase landing one night after her parents had had yet another terrible fight, and she'd ended up confiding to him the truth about how her father treated his family; he'd called her that on the night when she'd plopped her shorty-nightgown–clad self on his lap, twined her arms around his neck, and kissed him. He'd kissed her back for a hot, memorable moment, after which he'd stood up with her, carried her through the sliding glass doors to the patio, and dumped her unceremoniously into the swimming pool.

At the time, she'd been outraged, furious—and humiliated. Much as she hated to admit it, the memory still stung.

Luckily—unless he was the kind of guy

who bragged about his conquests, and she didn't think he was, or she would have heard—no one knew about that mortifying episode except the two of them.

No one knew that there had ever been any kind of personal relationship between them.

But it made what she was trying to accomplish here just that much more complicated. Firmly she pushed that tiny little bit of near-forgotten history out of her mind.

Here, tonight, she was a police negotiator and he was a perp, and that was it. Lives were on the line.

"Why are you doing this, Detective?" Her tone was brisk and businesslike as she rephrased her previous question slightly, made it blunter in hopes that she would get an equally blunt response. He'd located the camera, which was somewhere above him and to his left: she knew because he was looking directly into it. His dark eyes seemed to burn into hers.

He said, "First of all, I want this house cleared. Nobody in it outside this room. If I even think there's somebody else inside, we're going to have a problem."

"That's not an answer," Caroline replied. "Help me to understand so that I can help you."

Ware looked impatient. "You don't need to understand. And if you want to help me, just do what I tell you."

Knowing that pushing him could prove counterproductive and rebound on the hostages, Caroline didn't persist. Instead she released the talk button on the receiver and glanced at Dixon, who shrugged and said, "I got people checking him out. We know he's got a clean record. All I can tell you at this point is, something must have happened recently to send him over the edge."

"You know I mean it about getting the house cleared out, right, Caroline?" Ware's tone made it an implicit threat.

She pressed the talk button. "Yes, I know," she replied in her best conciliatory tone. "The house is being cleared. What else can we do for you?"

Ware's voice was hard. "A kid I know was arrested earlier tonight. I want him out of jail. Hollis Bayard."

Caroline shot a quick glance at Dixon, who shook his head: **don't know any-**

thing about who that is. He glanced at her receiver, she assumed to make sure that she wasn't still pressing the talk button—she wasn't, she released it whenever she finished speaking—and said into his radio, "I need information on a Hollis Bayard. Check the jails."

"Hope the little son of a bitch is worth it, because you just threw your life away for him," Martin snarled at Ware at the same time.

On the monitor, Caroline could see Ware's face tighten, see the way his pistol nudged the back of her father's head. Her heartbeat quickened. The last thing her father, or any of them, should be doing was antagonizing Ware. The situation spoke for itself: the man was armed, dangerous, and clearly capable of extreme violence.

"If I go down, you're going with me," Ware told him. "Count on it."

"I'd appreciate it if you'd let me handle this, Superintendent," Caroline said crisply.

Eyes widening a little, her father sat taller in his chair: the ultimate control freak, it was obvious that he was surprised by, and not particularly appreciative of, her intervention. A sardonic laugh came from Ware.

"That's right, that's your little girl on the other end of that phone, isn't it, Superintendent?" he said. "Play nice, and you two just might get to eat Christmas dinner together after all. Wouldn't that be nice, Caroline?"

"Yes," Caroline replied, lying through her teeth. Of course they had no such plans: the last Christmas Day she'd spent with her father had been the one before her parents had split up. He'd gotten drunk as a skunk and had an angry explosion over something, and the evening had ended with her little sisters hiding in a closet and Caroline standing between her parents, threatening to call the cops—**his** cops—if he came one step closer to her weeping, cringing mother.

Outside the family circle, nobody knew about that particular episode. Nobody ever had to know about that particular episode.

That the superintendent's first marriage had ended badly was common knowledge. The worst of the details were for the most part a shameful secret they all kept to themselves. Those details were also probably the reason she wasn't a particular fan of the institution of marriage to this day.

Love 'em and leave 'em: it might be a cliché, but that was how she conducted her love life. How she meant to keep on conducting her love life.

Seizing the moment, going with another rule of hostage negotiation that was to humanize the victims, she added, "All the people in the room with you would like to go home to have Christmas dinner with their families, too, you know. Why don't you let them go so they can?"

Ware laughed. Implicit message: fat chance. "Cut the crap, Caroline. You know I'm not going to do that."

"I can't believe you're really this stupid," Martin told Ware. "You're digging your own damned grave."

Ware's eyes narrowed. His lips thinned. "You don't keep your mouth shut, Superintendent, somebody's going to be digging yours."

Martin's eyes flashed.

"Detective, you want to tell me the name of the kid you want released from jail one more time?" Caroline said hurriedly before things could escalate. Her pulse raced and she found herself leaning toward the monitor as if she could somehow physically intervene between the two men. Much as she hated to admit it, the volatile combination of her father and Ware was unsettling her with its possibilities. If it escalated into violence, bad things could happen to all the hostages.

Keep your head in the game, she ordered herself fiercely. By her count, seven innocent people lay on the carpet: five women, two men. Add her father, and there were eight hostages in all. They were depending on her for their lives.

She did another quick visual sweep of the room as it suddenly hit her who she didn't see: Jefferson Parish Sheriff B. J. Cardwell, Council Chairman Leo Joseph, and New Orleans' mayor, Harlan Guthrie.

They'd been reported as being among the hostages. So where were they? She was afraid to ask. If they were dead, or hurt, she didn't want to remind Ware of it, and thus remind him, too, of how little he had to lose. If they were hiding somewhere in the house, she didn't want to alert him to that, either.

"Hollis Bayard," Ware replied, and spelled it out with a touch of sarcasm. "Anything happens to him, this is going to get real ugly, real fast. Might want to pass that on."

Caroline didn't need to: Dixon heard. "You'll pay for this," he muttered to Ware, who because she was no longer depressing the talk button couldn't hear him. "Just you wait."

Then he turned and exited the van.

"So if Hollis Bayard is released, you'll let the hostages go?" Caroline asked, assessing via the monitor as much of the room the hostages were in as she could see. It was on the second story, maybe eighteen by twenty feet, with artfully arranged bookshelves lining the long wall opposite the camera and, presumably, the one on which the camera was mounted as well, which she could not see. The veranda that ran outside it struck her as a possible staging area for a SWAT assault, if that became necessary. On another monitor, she saw that she was not the only one who had realized its strategic possibilities: a long view of the house revealed that as the exodus of beautifully clad guests continued through the front door, a ladder was being put in place that rose from the ground to the second-story veranda.

"Hollis Bayard's release is **one** of the conditions," Ware replied. Caroline was relieved to see that her father was sitting there with his lips compressed and a stony expression on his face. Apparently he believed in Ware's threat enough to comply with it. The realization that **Martin Wallace** was cowed into silence by Ware sent a cold chill down her spine: it told her how real he felt the danger to himself and the other hostages was. "I've got a couple more."

"And they are?" The thought that she was keeping Ware calm and occupied while all around the mansion the stage was being set for him to be killed loomed large in Caroline's mind. The horror of how in all likelihood this night was going to end made her stomach churn. She'd vowed to serve and protect, and she knew from experience that serving and protecting could be a bloody, soul-destroying business, but that didn't mean she was immune to bad things when they happened.

"Bayard's release is number one." Ware spoke directly into the camera. Directly to

her. "I also want a helicopter. And a pilot who's under orders to take me wherever I want to go. Have it land in the side yard, on that flat grassy area near the swimming pool. There's plenty of room over there. Oh, and I want a million dollars. Cash. Unmarked, untraceable, nonsequential bills. In a suitcase. In the helicopter."

Caroline's breath caught. "This is about **money**?" The question escaped before she could stop it. That was because she still couldn't fathom it: what could have occurred to make a good cop like Ware do something this monstrous? Quick answer, arrived at almost as soon as she considered the matter: probably not a sudden, overwhelming desire for a million dollars in cash. If a boatload of cash was what he wanted, there were easier, safer, more anonymous ways to get it, especially for an experienced cop like Ware. First thing **she** would think to do, if she desperately needed that much cash and was willing to commit criminal acts to get it, was shake down a few drug dealers. Or rob them. **Not** take half the movers and shakers in the city hostage. In fact, that was probably the last route she would choose: too dangerous; too public; almost zero chance of success.

Ware wasn't a stupid man.

"You have no idea what this is about," Ware replied. "Just get me my million dollars."

"So tell me," she invited, her eyes riveted on him as he stared down the camera. "**Tell me** what this is about. I might be able to help you."

He made an impatient sound. "I'm going to say this one more time: I don't want you to help me. I don't want you to **understand**. I want a damned million dollars in cash. Get it."

"That's a lot of money," Caroline responded cautiously, and thought, Okay, this is not about the cash. Then she immediately found herself worrying about where they were going to be able to get their hands on such a sum at such short notice anyway. A million dollars cash? In the middle of the night on Christmas Eve—or, rather, Christmas Day now? The department might be able to swing the other demands—although, face it, no way would any helicopter be permitted to take off with

Ware in it—but the cash was problematic. Then she remembered the billionaire homeowner, Allen Winfield, whom she had been told on the way over had managed to escape along with his wife in the general exodus and was at that moment being whisked away somewhere under the protection of his own private security: maybe he could arrange something. Reality hit a split second later: it didn't matter whether or not the money was actually made available. It only mattered that Ware thought it was.

Because he wasn't ever going to actually get away with the money. He was either going to be taken into custody or wasn't going to live long enough.

Ware had to know that.

If it wasn't about the money, then maybe it was about his first demand, although the same argument prevailed: there were a hell of a lot easier ways to get someone out of jail.

"Who is Hollis Bayard?" she asked him.

His face hardened. "If I wanted to have a chat, I'd be talking to a shrink instead of you. What I want is Hollis Bayard out of jail, a million dollars in cash, and a heli-copter to get me the hell out of here." His voice had an ominous ring to it.

Promise 'em anything: the negotia-tor's golden rule.

"I'll do my best," she said. Releasing the talk button, picking up the radio at her belt, she relayed his newest demands to Dixon, who snapped, "Tell that bastard he can have anything he wants," and clicked off.

"We're checking into getting Bayard, the helicopter, and the money for you," Caro-line told Ware, not promising that it would be done because another rule of negotia-tion was that you never wanted to give in too easily, and thought, **This is going to get bad**. Not that the impossibility of the demands was the reason: they would be met, although probably only insofar as was necessary to keep Ware thinking he actually had a chance of pulling this off. It was a foregone conclusion that he was not going to be allowed to escape. The truth was that hostage takers almost never got away. They were either captured or killed at the scene.

Since this was Reed Ware, thinking about

how this night was likely to end for him made her throat tighten.

He'd been good to her during that long-ago summer. Before he'd dumped her in the swimming pool, of course.

But he was the one who'd crossed the line tonight, Caroline reminded herself grimly, and nothing that was happening here, or was going to happen here, was anyone's fault but his. Still, she hoped he didn't have to pay with his life. And if she could help it, he wasn't going to. If she did her job right, he and everyone else in that room would be alive in the morning.

That was the happy ending she was aiming for.

CHAPTER FOUR

"Just as a heads-up," Caroline added, sounding far more casual than she felt, "a million dollars might be a problem in the middle of the night. Especially given that it's Christmas Day and all."

"The department can make it happen." Ware's tone was dismissive. He was looking directly into the camera again, and it was almost as if he could see her, although she knew that he couldn't. "You know that. I know that. Quit trying to jerk me around."

"I would never do that." She did her best to project sincerity down the phone line.

"We want to work this thing out. Get everybody out of there safely, including you."

"Oh, yeah?" He regarded the camera steadily. "Snipers in place yet?"

Caroline's lips compressed. "Not yet."

It wasn't quite a lie.

He laughed, the sound short and unamused. "Where are you, Caroline?"

"In a mobile unit parked in front of the house," she replied. Building trust was important here, and to that end she tried to tell the truth as much as possible: as a cop, he knew how things worked. He also would know how this night was going to play out for him, which raised the question once again: why?

For the first time, she wondered if maybe the reckless glitter in his eyes was at least partially attributable to drink or drugs, or some combination thereof. She remembered hearing a rumor, a few years back, that he liked to party. Maybe he was on something, strung out, high as a kite.

Otherwise, to have done something like this, he had to have totally lost his mind. If she couldn't talk him out of there, for him this night was going to end in his death, either by suicide when he detonated the bomb she hadn't yet seen, or by suicide by cop when SWAT or a sniper took him out.

He knew that. He had to know that. As she thought about it, the question that alarmed her most was, **Is** that **what he wants?**

If a perp was suicidal, the negotiator's job became infinitely more difficult.

Ware had lost his child, his ex-wife. Maybe he wanted to die, too.

She remembered him at the funeral. He had been bowed over with grief.

With that possibility in mind, Caroline tried to evaluate his present condition as best she could. Besides that hard glitter, his eyes were slightly bloodshot but seemed completely aware. His lack of other physical manifestations of stress—he wasn't sweating, his hands didn't shake, and his movements weren't jerky, as just some examples—might be attributable to the reality-clouding effect of drugs rather than the steely resolve she had initially assumed was the prompt behind his mannerisms, so unusual for the typical hostage taker. Cocaine, maybe? But in her experience, blow tended to make users hyperactive, and he showed no signs of that: if anything, he was unnaturally calm considering the circumstances. Heroin, which was enjoying a resurgence on the streets? But he wasn't showing signs of that, either.

The sound of the door opening made Caroline glance around. Dixon stepped up into the van, followed by NOPD Sgt. Sydney Miller, a short, barrel-chested, gray-haired officer nearing retirement who could generally be found manning the front desk at headquarters.

Surprised at Miller's presence in the van, Caroline raised her eyebrows questioningly at Dixon as he moved toward her.

Dixon grimaced. "I've got news about Ware. He got fired earlier today. Miller was on deck when it happened. I brought him in here so you could hear it from the horse's mouth."

"What? Why? Who would fire Ware?" The unexpected news made Caroline's eyes widen. Although the firing of a police detective wasn't official until it went through more channels than were available on cable TV, an officer could be relieved of duty and placed on administrative leave pending a hearing by any number of superiors.

But even as Caroline asked the question, she had a sinking feeling that she knew the answer.

"The superintendent," Miller said, confirming her guess. As he met Caroline's gaze he shrugged semiapologetically. "I was on the desk when I heard them shouting at each other. Hell, the whole building heard them shouting at each other. Ware was pissed." He paused. "My daughter's an administrative assistant in Internal Affairs. Scuttlebutt is Ware got caught taking a bribe."

"What?" Caroline's shocked reaction was instantaneous and instinctive. "No way in hell."

"That's the story," Dixon said. "Just to be sure, I gave John Hendricks in Internal Affairs a call to confirm it for myself. It's true."

Miller nodded vigorously.

Caroline shook her head. "I don't believe it." She did a lightning mental review of everything she personally knew about Ware. She thought of his years of service and his professional reputation, which was solid. Then she thought of all the things she probably didn't know about him, about the rumors of his partying, about the death of his ex-wife and child. Had any of those things been enough to turn a good cop bad?

"I don't believe it," she said again, but more slowly. Because the truth was, she couldn't be sure.

You have no idea what this is about, was what he'd told her. Could this—the bribery charge, his firing—be what he had been referring to? Caroline's attention was drawn back to the monitor by a sudden movement on the screen.

"You know they're out there prepping for a SWAT attack or something, right?" The shrill-with-fear voice, a woman's, came clearly over the phone, and had Caroline refocusing on the other monitors in a hurry. There it was: a woman in a green satin ball gown had lifted her head from the floor to hurl the question at Ware. As she continued, her tone teetered on the brink of hysteria: "The only way you even have a chance of getting out of here alive is if you let us go!"

The rest of the hostages were reacting. Several of them moved restlessly. Some dared to raise their heads and take surreptitious peeks at their captor. Caroline's heart stuttered. An ill-considered move by the hostages could get everyone in that room killed.

"Calm down, Ellen," Martin spoke sharply. Caroline registered that it was the first thing she had heard him say since Ware had threatened him if he didn't stay silent, even as she recognized the woman, a fortyish, reed-slim, perfectly groomed redhead, with a sense of shock: Ellen Tremaine, New Orleans' city attorney. Caroline had had no idea that she was among the hostages. Even if he lived through the night, Ware's future just kept getting bleaker and bleaker: from what Caroline knew of Ellen Tremaine, once she was released the woman would go after Ware with everything the legal system could throw at him.

He could be facing decades, maybe even the rest of his life, in jail.

Ware pointed his pistol at the attorney. "If you want to get out of here alive I suggest you put your face down and shut the hell up."

"Do what he says, Ellen," Martin snapped. Ms. Tremaine held Ware's gaze for a moment, almost pitiably defiant, then as he steadied his aim she grimaced and subsided back down onto the carpet, resting her cheek against the scarlet fibers so that only the top of her head remained visible to the camera. Martin's eyes shifted to Ware. "You know she's talking sense, Ware. You want to live, you'll let us go."

Ware bared his teeth in what could only be described as a snarl. "You ever think that maybe I don't want to live, Superintendent? And that maybe I'd be real happy to take all you people with me when I go?"

Caroline's mouth went dry. Her heart gave a weird little kick. If this was the answer, if he really was suicidal, the hostages were in even more danger than she had supposed. She could almost feel the anxiety level in the room rising right along with hers. If the hostages were to lose their nerve, try to rush Ware, or make a break for it, it could precipitate something catastrophic. The situation would deteriorate in a hurry. Which begged the question: how much time did she really have?

Pouring oil on troubled waters was her specialty, she reminded herself. **So get on with it.**

"We're working hard to get you all out of there," Caroline said loudly, hoping to be heard throughout the room. Whether she was successful or not, she couldn't tell: there was no visible reaction from the hostages, as far as she could see. Ware definitely heard: his eyes shifted toward the camera, and it was like he was looking right at her again. Her father heard, too: she could tell by the way his eyes also flickered in the camera's direction, and the deepening of his scowl. "We're committed to doing whatever it takes to keep everybody safe, so stay cool."

"Nobody's going to do anything stupid," her father answered. "Except for Ware, of course, who already has."

Ware's mouth twisted. "I thought I told you to shut up."

Caroline missed whatever Martin might have said in reply because her attention was distracted by the sudden movement of the SWAT team. The unit was getting into some kind of formation on the ground to the left of the house, apparently just awaiting word to ascend to the second story via the ladder: she could see them on a monitor. She knew that ideally they

liked to wait until the sniper team assessed the situation first, but whether a
sniper would even make the attempt tonight would depend on several factors, the
most important of which was whether such
an action might set off a bomb or bombs.
Her eyes ran over Ware again. He was
talking to her father now, his voice too low
for her to decipher the words, his expression as ugly as her father's was stony. It
was obvious that there was crackling animosity between the two. Again, if Ware
was wearing an explosive vest, as she'd
been advised he was, she saw no sign of
it. But from the way his left hand was fisted,
and the position of his thumb, she was increasingly convinced that he was indeed
holding a dead man's switch. Which meant,
of course, that there was indeed a bomb.

A cherry picker with a sniper in the
bucket was positioning itself so that, Caroline realized as she watched the action on
a monitor, it could potentially get a shot off
through the gap in the library curtains.

Her heart thumped in her chest.

"You still there, Caroline?" Ware asked,
his eyes shifting toward the camera again
as though he could feel her looking at him.

They were as shiny black as jet. His mouth was tight. He appeared to be growing increasingly restless and Caroline wondered if the hopelessness of his position might be starting to sink in. If so, and he was suicidal, that could be very bad news.

Looking at those gleaming eyes, she wondered again if Ware was on something.

"I'm here," she replied, trying her best to sound reassuring. What she said next was part of the game plan: stall for time. "We're still working on locating Hollis Bayard."

"There's a deadline on that," Ware said. "In case I forgot to mention it. You tell Dixon and whoever else is running the show out there that I gave 'em an hour. For all of it. Starting from the time I first told you what I wanted. Which means"—he glanced to his left, and from his next words Caroline presumed he was checking with a clock—"you have forty-five minutes left."

"That's not enough time," Caroline protested automatically, both because it was true and because that was the classic negotiator's gambit.

Ware said, "It's all you've got."

"I want to help you," Caroline said. "I'm

doing everything I can to see that this works out and you get what you want and everyone gets out of there safely. We all are. But you need to be realistic about how difficult this is, and give us a reasonable amount of time."

Again, Ware seemed to be looking right at her through the monitor. "You really think you can bullshit me, Caroline?"

Forgetting that he couldn't see her, Caroline shook her head. "I'm not trying to bullshit you. It's the truth."

"Well, you better figure out a way to speed things along. Because I'm starting to get a little antsy here."

With that Ware laid his pistol down beside him on the desk, leaned sideways, and pulled a wheeled leather desk chair into view. In it sat New Orleans' mayor Harlan Guthrie, his portly, tux-clad body secured to the chair with bungee cords and zip ties. A strip of duct tape covered his mouth. His pale eyes bulged angrily. The rest of his pudgy face was as red as a chili pepper beneath his shock of dyed black hair, which was usually worn in a pompadour and was now wildly disheveled. His brow glistened with sweat.

In his lap rested a big, black backpack.

Caroline's heart leaped. Dixon made a sharp sound.

She knew they were both having the same thought.

Bomb.

The sensation Caroline experienced was akin to having a cold hand grip the back of her neck. She shivered. Cradling the hard plastic telephone receiver, her palm felt suddenly damp. There was nothing—no protruding wires, no telltale bulge—that she could see to help identify what the backpack contained. But combine the dead man's switch, which she was now certain was what was in Ware's hand, with the expressions on his and the mayor's and her father's faces, and the very fact that the backpack had been brought into play at all, and she was pretty damned sure she knew.

They all were pretty damned sure they knew.

There's no way back from this. **No possible happy ending.**

The best she could hope for was that nobody would die tonight.

If that backpack really did contain a bomb, and every sign indicated that it did, all it would take would be one slipup from any of them and it could easily be game over for everybody in that room.

"I'd hate to see the mayor here—and your dad, and the rest of these people—get vaporized," Ware said, in what was an almost uncanny echoing of her thoughts. She'd missed it—too busy ogling the backpack—but he'd picked up his weapon and once again had it in hand. "But that's what's going to happen if I don't get what I want."

"You **are** going to get what you want. You just need to give us some time," Caroline assured him, as, cursing under his breath and shooing Miller before him, Dixon turned and strode toward the other end of the van.

Ware's eyes seemed to bore into hers. "Like I said, you got forty-five—no, make that forty—minutes."

"Do what he says, Caroline," her father said. He was breathing more heavily than before, and white lines bracketed his mouth. That look in his eyes—was he afraid?

Of course he was afraid. He would be a fool not to be afraid.

Caroline's chest felt tight with dread. She had barely noticed what cramped quarters she was in until now, when the walls of the van felt like they were closing in around her. The air seemed to thicken, making it difficult to breathe. For most of her life, she would have said that she didn't give a damn if her father lived or died. Now, she realized that wasn't true: for all their differences, for all the hurt he had caused her and her sisters and their mother, there apparently was still some vestige of family feeling there. During her training, she'd seen the effects of a bomb detonated at close range: in one hideous instant, bodies were reduced to shredded meat and blood spatter. If Ware carried out his threat, death would be instantaneous, and gruesome, for everybody in that room.

For the hostages. For her father.

And for Ware.

At the involuntary image that planted in her mind, she got momentarily light-headed.

Was Ware prepared to carry out his

threat? She couldn't be sure, but it might well be a deadly error to assume that he was not.

She took a deep, steadying breath.

"You don't want to hurt anyone, Reed," she said. To hell with stirring up Ware's memory where their past was concerned: the situation had just ratcheted up a couple of hundred notches on the desperate scale. Anyway, she doubted that he'd forgotten any excruciating detail of her teenage crush: she knew she hadn't. To anyone else who was listening, she hoped she would just sound like a hostage negotiator trying to establish a closer relationship with a perp.

"I don't want to," Ware agreed. "So don't make me."

Holding up his clenched left fist, he waved it at her almost casually. Caroline was sure, now, that what she was seeing was a dead man's switch: he had his thumb on the small flat disk that was the detonator, holding it down.

"Better call off your snipers," Ware added, and smiled at the camera. It was an almost malicious smile, and it caused Caroline to wonder again if he was quite sane.

"I take a bullet, and this whole place and everyone in it goes boom."

A voice beside her said, "Damn it," and with a sideways glance Caroline saw that Dixon had returned with Villard and that both men were staring at Ware on the monitor.

"He has a dead man's switch," Caroline pointed out, just in case they'd missed it.

"It sure looks like it," Villard agreed, then asked the technicians, "Can you get me a close-up look at that backpack?"

"Nobody wants you to take a bullet," Caroline said to Ware, maintaining her even tone with effort while the technicians worked to zoom in on the backpack. With the clock ticking, she needed to pick up the pace on winding her way up the behavioral change stairway, which was what negotiators called the process of building trust with a perp, until she reached the point where she could persuade Ware that surrendering was in his best interest. "We want you to come out of this alive, along with everyone else."

"I doubt your colleagues there agree with you." Ware's tone was sardonic. "In fact, I know they don't."

"You're wrong," she said. "Nobody wants you to die tonight."

His mouth twisted. "You don't know much about much, do you, cher?"

Caroline frowned. "It's the truth."

"You trying to fool yourself or me?" he asked.

"I'm not trying to fool you. I'm trying to help you," Caroline replied even as her eyes darted from monitor to monitor, trying to pick up clues about what was going on outside. Dixon and Villard were huddled together a little apart from her, conferring about the close-up of the backpack that the technicians had pulled up on one screen. "You can still walk away from this. All you have to do is release the hostages and come out. No one will hurt you. No one has to get hurt." She stressed that last part for emphasis.

"So I can just walk away like none of this ever happened, right?" The skepticism in Ware's voice was unmistakable.

"You'll face some charges." Her voice was steady. "But at least they won't include murder. And at this point, even the severity of the charges is on the table."

"Is there a rainbow out there anywhere?"

he asked. Caroline was mystified: the question made no sense at all.

"It's night," she replied cautiously.

"That's good, because the next thing I was expecting you to tell me was that if I saw one and followed it, I'd be finding me a pot o' gold."

Her lips re-formed in a thin line. "I'm offering you a way out."

"Are you?"

"Yes."

"Are you saying that I can trust you, Caroline?"

Caroline could almost feel the heightening tension surrounding him. Her own nerves were stretching to the breaking point. It occurred to her once again that she didn't really know Reed Ware at all, and she had no idea what he might be capable of if his demands weren't met. She had no means by which to judge whether or not he would do exactly as he had threatened. Her gut might tell her he wouldn't do it, but her gut could very well be wrong. For all she knew, he might be prepared to kill every single hostage in that room.

But even if she didn't fully trust him, she sure as hell needed him to trust her.

"Yes," Caroline said, and meant it, at least as far as it was possible within the parameters of the job and the situation. Even though she was prepared to lie to him, trick him, or do just about whatever it took to get him and the others out of there alive, what he could trust in was that she would do the best she could for him, for as long as she could.

Ware looked at her—at the camera, damn it—steadily. "Just how big a fool do you think I am?"

Fair enough. At least he was thinking logically enough to be wary. She decided to take the risk of upsetting him and probe into what was possibly the heart of the matter with a straightforward question.

"Is this about killing yourself, Reed?" she asked. "Because if that's what's on your mind, I'd like to talk to you about it."

He looked up at the camera, arrested. Then, unexpectedly, he smiled. It was wry, faintly mocking, and totally aimed at her. It made her breath catch.

"Are you asking me if I'm suicidal?" he demanded.

This was no time to beat about the bush. "Yes."

For a moment he stared silently into the camera. As hard as she tried, she couldn't read anything in his expression at all.

Finally he said, "Believe me, I'm prepared to do what I have to do."

Caroline's gaze cut sharply toward the men as a pager chirped: Dixon's, she saw as he pulled it from his belt and frowned down at it. Looking up to find her looking at him, he narrowed his eyes at her and made a slicing gesture with his hand that she interpreted as, **release the talk button**.

Until that moment, she hadn't realized that she'd still been holding it down. She lifted her thumb away from the button: Ware could no longer hear her, or anything going on in the van.

"Hollis Bayard's here," Dixon said.

CHAPTER FIVE

Caroline's eyes widened with surprise. Her first instinctive stirring of hope at the prospect of solving the crisis by giving Ware what he wanted was immediately dashed by what she saw in Dixon's face. Every instinct she possessed told her that there was no way they were meeting Ware's demands for any other reason than to pacify him until they could kill him. Talking him out seemed to be no one's priority except her own.

Her stomach tightened with tension. There was something about this that was just not fitting together properly in her mind.

"Who **is** Hollis Bayard? And what is he to Ware?" she asked.

"He's a damned street punk who was busted for felony possession a few hours ago. No judge available until the twenty-sixth, so he got tucked away in The Swamp." Dixon shook his head. "How he got mixed up with Ware I don't know."

"You really mean to let him go in there?" she asked.

Before Dixon could answer, Villard's cell phone rang. Digging it out of a pouch on his belt, Villard looked at the number and said on a note of triumph, "Aha. Here's our EMP expert at last," before answering the call and then listening intently.

Caroline remembered from her bombs course that EMP stood for electromagnetic pulse.

She looked a question at Dixon.

"Villard's got a guy who uses a device that emits EMP signals to disable the connection between bombs and their detonators," Dixon told her in a low voice. "He thinks he might be able to take out Ware's dead man's switch with it. The thing is basically a signal jammer, and it's been used successfully in situations like this a num-

ber of times. If it works for us tonight—"
He broke off as Villard said into the phone,
"Goddamn technology," and disconnected.

The disappointment in his face was obvious.

"What?" Dixon said.

"Turns out interrupting the EMP signal
is only going to work if we get up close.
There's too much interference," Villard answered with obvious disappointment. Then
he added, "Shit," and strode toward the
door.

Dixon looked at Caroline. "Looks like
the answer to your question is yes: Hollis
Bayard is really going in there," he said,
and turned to follow Villard. Caroline caught
his arm.

"What's really happening?" she asked,
because under the circumstances, believ-
ing that the powers that be had folded and
Ware was about to be given everything
he'd asked for, was right up there with be-
lieving in the Tooth Fairy.

"Here's the deal: unless we can come
up with another angle fast, we're going to
let the asshole **think** he's getting the whole
shebang—Bayard, a helicopter, a couple of
suitcases full of money." Dixon's expression

was grim. "Then when he's out in the open heading for the helicopter, we'll have our EMP guy in place, along with snipers to take Ware down if our guy succeeds in interrupting the signal. If he can't, if it doesn't work—and depending on the circumstances it's possible that we won't be able to take a shot even if it does—well, Ware still won't get very far. We're not planning to let him take off. If we have to—if he's got hostages with him, and we think he's serious about killing them—we've got a GPS tracker on the helicopter, and air support ready to pounce the minute it lands. Whichever way this plays out, bottom line is Ware has zero chance of getting away with this." Pulling away, Dixon followed Villard, saying to Caroline over his shoulder, "Go on and tell him Bayard's here. The helicopter and money, too."

"You're under ten minutes, Caroline," Ware warned, jerking her attention back toward the monitors.

Feeling slightly nauseated, Caroline registered the action on all the monitors with a glance. On one were Ware and the hostages. On another, she watched as the last member of the SWAT team made his stealthy ascent to the second-story veranda, where around seven team members already waited. On a third, she saw a small helicopter approaching the house, flying lower than the police choppers that were circling, shining its light over the side yard as it sought a place to put down. The smooth waters of the swimming pool gleamed bright blue in the chopper's strong light. Then the water started to ruffle, and the fronds of the ferns and the leaves and blooms of the flowers in the landscaping flanking the pool started to sway.

The helicopter was landing.

Was Ware's thinking really so disordered that he actually believed he would be allowed to just climb inside and fly away?

You have no idea what this is about. She could almost hear Ware saying it.

Caroline wet her lips.

"Hollis Bayard is here," she said into the phone. For a second there, she thought Ware looked relieved. Then, as she added, "So is the helicopter. And the money," Ware's face turned inscrutable while her father closed his eyes.

In that moment Martin looked incredibly old. And tired.

Again Caroline felt a stirring of unexpected feeling for her father. Harsh as he could be, as bullying and occasionally violent as he had been to her and her mother and sisters before his subsequent virtual abandonment of them, their relationship was still apparently not as dead as she had thought. Impossible as it was to fathom, on some level she obviously still cared about him.

I need counseling, was the acerbic corollary thought that popped into her head.

"I want to talk to Bayard. Get him in there, get him on the phone," Ware said.

Caroline nodded, forgetting Ware couldn't see her.

"I'll be right back," she said.

Putting the phone down, Caroline walked to the door and opened it. The fresh night air was more than welcome after the stale interior of the van. The rattle of a generator was the dominant note in the sea of sound that greeted her. So many klieg lights had been set up that it was now bright as day around the van, and she squinted a little and shielded her eyes as she looked for Dixon. He was standing with a small group beside a police cruiser

parked in the middle of the street. Someone opened the rear door behind the driver's seat, reached in, and, with a hand
protecting the top of the emerging person's head, pulled the backseat passenger out.

The emerging passenger was a young
man, Caroline saw at a glance, and if she'd
been about fifteen she probably would
have found herself thinking he was way
cute. Medium height, wiry thin in the way
of some still-growing adolescents. Black
hair long enough to curl around his neck,
a lean face with good bone structure, deep-
set dark eyes and a full mouth. Dressed in
jeans and a gray zip-front hoodie with a
Saints logo that was currently unzipped
to reveal part of a white wife-beater. A
tattoo—some kind of ornate cross—on
the side of his neck, small silver hoops in
his ears.

It was immediately obvious that he was
a prisoner: his hands were cuffed behind
his back.

Hollis Bayard, she had little doubt.

"Wallace," Dixon greeted her. He and the
others—Villard and Esteban were among
them—had broken off what had seemed

to be an intense conversation as she approached.

She kept her voice low enough so that Bayard, who was being watched closely by the uniforms, couldn't hear. "Ware wants to talk to him on the phone."

Dixon and the others exchanged looks. "That works," Dixon said. "You go on back in there and get Ware on the phone. Tell him Bayard's coming in to talk to him. And get those monitors shut down before Bayard can get a look at them. We don't want him telling Ware about our arrangements out here."

"Will do." Caroline gave a nod, and returned to the van. As soon as she glanced at the monitors, she saw that something was wrong. The monitor that had allowed her to see Ware and the hostages had gone dark.

"What happened?" she asked the technicians, tapping the darkened library monitor with a forefinger.

"Right after you left, the camera shut down," Isaacs said. "I'm almost certain Ware did it, but I was working on trying to get eyes inside other parts of the house and I missed exactly what he did. Then he must have noticed the opening in the curtains, because they got closed all the way and we lost that, too. Sorry."

"It's not your fault. Listen, Dixon wants the rest of the monitors shut down temporarily. Hollis Bayard's on his way in." Taking a deep breath, Caroline picked up the phone.

"Reed?" she said. "Are you there?"

"I'm here. Do you have Bayard?"

The sound of Ware's voice was so welcome that Caroline felt a flutter of relief. She realized that in some shadowy corner of her mind, seeing the darkened monitor had made her fear that he had been killed while she was gone. She realized something else, too: the reason she had felt such instant anxiety was because she was **expecting** him to be killed.

Nothing in Dixon's or anyone else's attitude made her believe that they wanted him to emerge from this alive.

Frowning, she replied, "Yes, he's here. He's on the way in to speak to you." Then she added impulsively, "You shut down the camera."

"Yeah, I did." He sounded unapologetic.

A sound at the door of the van told her that it was being opened.

"Reed, listen: you need to surrender. It's the only option you have if you want to live through this." She stopped talking as the creak of footsteps and the drone of voices told her that whoever had been at the door was now inside the van.

"You're living in la-la land if you think my surrendering would make any difference at all," Ware said.

Then Dixon and Bayard and the two uniforms escorting him crowded in behind her. Caroline glanced around at them in acknowledgment.

Dixon said, "Get Bayard up there."

Bayard was pushed forward just as Ware said, "If Bayard's there, put him on the line."

Bayard was standing next to Caroline now, looking sullen. He kept wetting his lips, and his eyes darted around suspiciously. His shoulders were hunched, and he swayed from side to side slightly as if he was too nervous to stand still.

"Detective Reed Ware wants to talk to you," Caroline told Bayard. "I'm assuming you know who he is."

For a moment Bayard held her gaze. She saw that his eyes were the color of caramel, that he was still young enough to have downy peach fuzz rather than whiskers on his cheeks, and that he was sweating bullets.

He's just a boy. And he looks scared to death.

"Yeah," Bayard said.

"Is the phone on speaker?" Dixon asked, and Caroline shook her head.

"Not on this end. On Ware's it is, just like before."

Dixon nodded. "We're going to be listening to everything you say, kid," he warned Bayard, who gave him a surly look. "You go spouting off, and the conversation's over, understand?" Bayard's eyes held his for a moment before his lids drooped over them. Then he gave a barely perceptible nod.

"Okay, then." Dixon gestured to Caroline. "Go ahead."

Caroline depressed the talk button and said into the phone, "Reed? I have Hollis Bayard for you."

As she started to pass the receiver to Bayard, she realized that he couldn't take it because his hands were cuffed. Holding it up so that Bayard could speak into it, Caroline reflected that talking to Ware without being able to see him was as disconcerting as flying blind. What was going on in the library that he'd felt he needed to conceal from the view of the camera? Merely considering the possibilities gave her the jitters.

"Holly?" Ware's voice filled the enclosed space.

"They can fucking hear every word you say," Bayard burst out fiercely, shooting Caroline a furious look. His glance then slid past her to encompass the others in the van. The chain linking his cuffs rattled as he jiggled from foot to foot. "There's like six of them in here. Fucking butchers. Fucking scum."

"Chill out," Ware ordered in a warning tone as the uniforms responded to Bayard's speech by taking nearly simultaneous steps closer to him. Ware continued, "What I need for you to do right now is just stay cool."

As he listened to Ware, Bayard looked at Caroline, who stood closest to him because she was holding the receiver. She could feel the nervous heat emanating from his thin body.

"Easy for you to say," Bayard told Ware bitterly. "You're a damned cop, too."

Ware made a sound that was impossible to interpret. "Are you hurt?"

Bayard's eyes flickered around. Nervously. "They picked Ant up not long after me. Edie got word to me in jail. They got Ant. You hear what I'm saying?"

Caroline noticed that he hadn't answered Ware's question.

"Goddamn it." The sudden anger in Ware's voice was unmistakable.

Bayard said, "He's just a little kid. I can't let nothing happen to him."

"I know," Ware replied. "Nothing's going to happen to him. I got this. Quit worrying about Ant for right now. What I need for you to do is focus on what's going on here."

"Yeah." Shifting from foot to foot, Bayard looked suspiciously at Caroline, then cast another uneasy look around at the others and added to Ware, "So what's the deal?"

"You come on inside the house here," Ware told him. "Come in the front door, up the main staircase, and the room right at the top of the stairs is the library, which is where I am. You come up here to me, and then you and I are going to head out to that helicopter waiting down there by the pool and fly on out of here." He paused. "Got it?"

Bayard's brows snapped together. He wet his lips as he gave Caroline another hard look and glanced around at the other cops again. "They ain't going to let that happen. They're gonna kill us, fool."

Bayard's assessment was so right on that Caroline had to work to keep her expression neutral.

"No, they aren't," Ware said. "I've got this under control. You just do what I tell you."

Bayard moved his shoulders nervously. "What about Ant?"

Ware said, "You leave me to worry about—"

Dixon interrupted by signaling to the uniforms, who grabbed Bayard by the arms and started pulling him toward the door. "That's enough," Dixon snapped. "Conversation's over."

"Hey." Sounding panicky, the kid yelled back at Ware, "They're taking me out of here."

Only then did Caroline remember to release the talk button.

"Hang in, Holly, it's going to be okay," Ware called back, then added, in a totally different tone, "That you I'm hearing, Dixon? Just so you know, I'm holding you personally responsible for that kid's welfare."

Dixon took the receiver from Caroline and spoke into it. His harsh expression was at complete odds with his voice, which was placating. "We're getting ready to have somebody escort him in to you right now. You're getting everything you want, so no need to go on making threats."

Ware said, "For everybody's sake I hope that's what happens. Caroline, you there?"

Dixon gave her back the phone.

"Yes." Caroline's throat felt tight as she watched Bayard being hustled out of the van.

"This is all going to be over very shortly," Ware said. "You've been doing great."

Ordinarily the praise would have warmed her, but the thought that everything really **was** going to be all over very shortly sent an icy slither of dread coursing down her spine. What were the chances that everybody would still be alive in, say, half an hour? What were the chances that Ware would be?

She felt sick thinking about it.

"Surrendering is in your best interest," Caroline told him. She was all too conscious of Dixon listening beside her: she couldn't do what she really wanted to do and drop all pretense of professionalism and outright beg. Still, her voice took on an urgent note. "Reed, think for a minute. No harm will come to you or Hollis Bayard or anyone else if you give up now. Just walk out with your hands up."

The look Dixon gave her was unreadable. He gestured to Caroline to indicate that he wanted to say something, and she held the receiver out so that he could speak into it.

"That's right," he said to Ware. "You do that, you walk out with your hands up, you'll make everybody happy."

Ware laughed, a brief, harsh sound. "I just bet I would." Then his tone changed. "Caroline, I want you to bring Hollis Bayard in to me." His voice hardened. "You hear that, Dixon? I want her to escort the kid, and it's not negotiable. She's the only one of you assholes I'm letting near me."

"I hear you." Dixon's face was grim as he looked at Caroline. "You game for this, Wallace?"

Caroline hesitated. Hostage negotiators had a saying: no cop ever got killed on the far end of a phone. She was supremely conscious of the risk of ordinary police work: her first stepfather, her mother's second husband (her mother was now on husband number three), had been shot and killed while pulling over a guy for speeding. A friend had been badly wounded responding to a convenience store robbery. Another had caught a stray bullet in the leg working crowd control at Mardi Gras. That was the reason she was so conscientious about always wearing a flak vest: in her line of work, when things went wrong they tended to go wrong bad and fast. Escorting Bayard inside the mansion would constitute putting herself in harm's way. If the situation went south—and the situation was inevitably going to go south—she could get caught in the crossfire. She could get shot. She could get blown up. She could die.

"Yes." Even as she said it, she knew that the driving force behind her decision was her hope that in the brief time that she could talk to Ware face-to-face, she would get him to see how hopeless his situation was and surrender. If she was forced to choose, the lives of the hostages had to come first, but she was going to do everything in her power to keep Ware alive, too. Not that she meant to let any hint of her intentions show in her face or her manner. She might be prepared to pull out all the stops and plead with Ware on the basis of their long-ago—what, friendship? flirtation?—but she wasn't prepared to share the fact that she meant to do so with Dixon or anyone else.

"If I do this . . ." she directed her words down the phone line to Ware. Her tone made what she said to him next a challenge. "If I bring Bayard inside, you owe me three hostages."

"Minute I set eyes on you and Bayard, I'll let three of them go," Ware promised.

"I'm going to hold you to that," Caroline said. The accompanying sinking feeling she experienced was because she knew in her gut that even if he lived up to his promise, it wasn't going to be enough to save him. Nothing short of his all-out surrender would do it.

"You do that. Come through the front door. From the way people were scooting out of it, I'm pretty sure it's unlocked. When you get inside, close the door behind you, lock it, and bring Bayard up to the library. Straight up the stairs, first door at the top. I'll be waiting. Oh, and Caroline? Come unarmed. Understand?"

"I understand."

"Good. I'm not talking on the phone anymore. This is it. I'm out."

"Reed—" Before Caroline could say anything more, the sound of a click was followed by the hum of a dial tone: Ware had hung up.

CHAPTER SIX

Dixon was already moving purposefully toward the door. Uncomfortably conscious of the increased drumming of her heart, Caroline followed him.

"Ware seems mighty friendly with you." Dixon waited for her as she descended the steps. "You got some history with him I should know about?"

Caroline looked across the sea of official activity at the beleaguered mansion and shrugged. "I've seen him around. He is—was—with the NOPD." Her tone implied that Ware's employment with their sister department said it all. It was not a lie. It was, in fact, the absolute truth.

Just not the whole truth.

"He's probably seen you around, too." Dixon's gaze slid over her, assessing her slender figure, her shapely bare legs. "Yeah. A womanizer like Ware—he would have noticed."

"Hey," Caroline protested as she followed him. "Think that might be a little sexist?"

"What? I can't tell the truth? You're hot stuff, Wallace, and that's a fact. Sometimes it's a pain in the butt. Sometimes, like tonight, we might be able to work it to our advantage. If it means Ware's willing to let you get close to him, that's a good thing. Come on."

Caroline opened her mouth to say something, anything, that would sum up her feelings at being assessed in such a way, but wasn't able to immediately come up with a retort with enough zing to it. Instead, she said, "What about you? Ware recognized your voice. You got some history with him I should know about?"

Dixon scowled at her. "We've worked together before. Guy's a prick."

She let the subject drop—for now—as they caught up with Villard, who was beckoning to them.

A few minutes later—standing in the middle of a semicircle composed of Dixon, Villard, and Jim Wasserman, who it turned out was one of the strangers she had noticed earlier and was also the EMP guy Villard had been talking about—she was shaking her head vigorously **no**.

"I think it's a bad idea," she said, though the words that had first crowded to the tip of her tongue, only to be immediately repressed, were, **Hell, no. I won't do it**.

"Here's the way this is going to go down," Dixon told her, blatantly disregarding her protest. She used the too-bright glow of the klieg lights as an excuse to pull her cap lower over her eyes for fear her expression would reveal too much, as in, her instinctive, complete disinclination to do what Dixon was suggesting. "We're going to give you the EMP device. As soon as you're within ten feet of Ware, all you have to do is push the button. Wasserman will be watching his monitor and will know instantly whether or not it worked to disable the dead man's switch."

"And then you'll—what? Have a sniper blow Ware's head off?" Caroline couldn't help the accusatory note in her voice.

"Or SWAT will burst in and take him out." Dixon gave her a hard look. "Whatever seems most likely to succeed at that time. Our mission is to rescue the hostages unharmed. **That's** the goal."

"We should be trying to save Ware's life, too, if we can," she argued.

"He's had plenty of opportunity to surrender," Dixon retorted. "Instead he's got a roomful of hostages in there that he's threatening to blow up if we don't give in to his demands. I'd say that means he deserves what he gets."

"It's our **job** to try to preserve his life," Caroline said. That wasn't just her aversion to seeing Ware get killed speaking. It was part of their serve-and-protect directive. "Remember the Law Enforcement Code of Ethics: all police officers will strive to preserve human life whenever possible."

"Actually, she's right," Wasserman said mildly. Tall and lanky, maybe early thirties, he had a long, lantern-jawed face and a brown, military-style crew cut.

"Yeah, yeah." Dixon grimaced, and waved a dismissive hand. "Fine, we will so strive."

Caroline wanted to continue pressing the point, but she knew any additional words she might come up with would make no difference.

"You don't think Ware's going to notice me aiming some sort of device at him?" she said instead, feeling nervous at the thought. She didn't like to think of Ware's possible reaction. "That might be all it takes to make him activate the dead man's switch. We won't be rescuing the hostages, we'll be the reason they're dead."

And I'll be dead, too. The memory of the shredded corpses in the videos from her bomb training class made her palms damp.

"You don't have to aim it," Wasserman reassured her. Caroline looked at him mistrustfully. "It's not much bigger than a gun. It comes with a holster, so you can conceal it beneath your jacket. You don't have to draw it to operate it: you only need to get within ten feet of the target and push the button. There's no flash, no sound. The perp will never even know you have it."

Caroline's stomach turned inside out. "What if I push the button and it doesn't work?"

"Then, nothing," Dixon said. "Ware won't know anything about it. It'll be like nothing ever happened."

"Here it is." Wasserman handed her something that looked like a miniature Dust-Buster. It was made of silver metal and a square black plastic button protruded from the top. The grip felt cool and smooth as her fingers reluctantly closed around it. "All you have to do is hit the button. Here, put the holster on."

Caroline took the black webbing harness reluctantly and fastened it around her waist. Since she already had given her duty belt and service weapon to Dixon, it fit smoothly over her flak vest. When she slid the EMP device into its holster, then let the windbreaker, unzipped for ease of access, fall into place over it, it appeared to be totally concealed.

"You see?" Wasserman sounded pleased. "Easy-peasy. He'll never so much as catch a glimpse of it. Practice pushing the button. Remember, you have to be within ten feet of the perp for it to work."

Caroline practiced pushing the button. "Like Ware's not going to notice me doing that?" She gave Wasserman a doubting look.

"With any luck, he'll be preoccupied with other things. Like Bayard's arrival, and getting the hell out of there," Dixon told her impatiently. "For God's sake, pick a moment when he's not looking at you and just do it. We'll take care of the rest."

"What if he frisks me?"

"If he has time to frisk you, it won't have worked. Remember, pushing the button is the first thing you're going to do. As soon as you're within range. Anyway, even if he should find it he almost certainly won't know what it is. If it comes down to it, tell him it's a radar gun or something. He'll be more interested in making sure you don't have your service weapon on you, I guarantee it." Dixon looked her over critically. "I can't see any bulge or anything. This is going to work fine."

"Glad you think so." Caroline's tone was sour. "I'd probably think so, too, if it wasn't my butt on the line here."

Dixon gave her a look, said, "Let's go," and herded her toward where Bayard stood, surrounded by another circle of cops. They were about halfway there when Dixon exclaimed, "Hell, the lights in the library are off. The SOB's turned the lights off."

Looking toward the mansion, Caroline saw the same thing: the library windows, which earlier had emitted a faint yellow glow through the curtains, were now as dark as the night sky.

"Maybe he's trying to make it harder for a sniper to hit him," she said.

Dixon grimaced disdainfully. "They've got night vision capabilities."

She had actually known that, and presumably Ware did, too.

"He doesn't want us to be able to follow him on camera," she guessed.

Dixon grunted. Translation: maybe.

As they neared the group surrounding Bayard, Caroline saw that TV crews from CNN and a couple of local channels were setting up in the street so they had an unimpeded view of the action. If the world wasn't already watching, it would be soon. The knowledge ratcheted up the tension she was feeling to a whole new level. Dragging her eyes away, she looked toward

Bayard, and was surprised to see that the kid was wearing a blindfold. Somebody had dug up a blue bandanna from somewhere and tied it around his eyes. Caroline looked at Lagasse, the Special Operations head who had been part of the group surrounding Bayard and who had just walked back to join her, Dixon, and Wasserman.

"We've got Bayard in a blindfold?" she asked disbelievingly.

"That's to keep him from seeing the operatives we have in place outside and reporting on our capabilities to Ware when he reaches him," Lagasse explained. "For our purposes, the less Ware knows, the better."

"If our plan works, Bayard won't have time to tell Ware anything." There was satisfaction in Dixon's tone.

"It ever occur to you that you're sending me into ground zero here?" Caroline groused. "You could try to sound less excited about it."

"You're the one that he wants. That means you're the only one who can do this, Wallace." Sweeping a look over the mansion, Dixon stopped walking abruptly.

"The whole house has gone dark," he said.

Stopping, too, and glancing in that direction, Caroline saw that he was right: where before the mansion had blazed with light from within, now every window that she could see was shiny black. Her stomach fluttered as she considered the possibilities: was this part of the plan?

Echoing her thoughts, Dixon frowned at Lagasse and asked, "Did we do that? Because I don't see how the hell Ware could."

Lagasse was frowning, too. "A panel controlling the house functions, including the lights and the security system, is located in the library. We saw it on the house plans. Apparently Ware's found it," Lagasse said. "If he thinks turning the lights off is going to help him, he's wrong."

"Let's get this show on the road." Dixon's expression had turned grim. "That bastard's had things his own way long enough. Ready, Wallace?"

Moments later, Caroline had a hand around Hollis Bayard's elbow as she half propelled, half led him down the driveway toward the mansion. Her adrenaline was flowing now, making it easier to ignore her misgivings. Although any way she looked at it, the chances that this would go wrong were way higher than the possibility that it would go right.

Consider the best-case scenario: Police save hostages. Bad guy taken out. That was how this was supposed to play out. That was the story her superiors wanted the TV cameras to cover.

The alternative—rogue cop blows mansion and everyone in it sky-high—was something she didn't even like to think about.

"Fuck it." Bayard stumbled as they reached the place where the stone pavers of the sidewalk joined the asphalt driveway, and Caroline's hand tightened on his arm. He'd been holding himself stiffly, and his steps had been on the slow and uncertain side, since they'd moved away from the group around the squad car. Not that that was surprising. Walking when he couldn't see a thing, with his hands cuffed behind his back, knowing that dozens of pairs of eyes and just as many weapons were tracking his every step, had to be unnerving.

"Careful," she said.

She understood the necessity for the blindfold, but that didn't make it any easier to steer him toward the wide stone steps that led to the palatial front door. Through his ratty sweatshirt, she could feel the wiry strength of his arm and the nervous heat of his body. He was also breathing way too hard for the amount of exertion he was putting forth. Fear and distrust practically oozed from his pores.

"This is bullshit," Bayard said angrily after he stumbled again, for what must have been the third or fourth time. As he caught himself and straightened up he added, "Look, I don't care what they're saying, I didn't have no dope on me. I didn't do **nothing**. Them cops had no business arresting me. I got rights. And speaking of rights, I don't think no damned police turds have the right to blindfold me, either."

"We don't have much farther to go." The last thing she wanted to do was have a debate with him on the merits of his arrest. Her chest was already tight with anxiety, and her nerves were starting to fray. Having lost her hold on him when he'd stumbled this last time, Caroline curled a hand around his elbow again, gripping it with grim determination. The kid tried to jerk away, but she hung on. She was supremely conscious of the gazes of everybody they'd just left behind burning into her back. Dixon and company were watching every step she and Bayard took, and much as she tried not to let the knowledge bother her, it did. If the kid decided to do something stupid like, say, pull free and take off running, it wasn't going to be pretty.

"They set me up," he said. "Them drugs they found? Fucking cop **planted** them."

That claim had been made so often by so many that Caroline scarcely heard it, and gave it no credence whatsoever.

"When this is over, I'll see that it gets looked into," she replied.

"That's bullshit, too." He stopped walking and turned his head as if to look at her, although of course he couldn't see her. "You don't give a shit, and we both know it."

"I give a shit." Tightening her hand on his arm, she urged him on. By this time it was about 1:20 a.m., but the klieg lights made it look like midday.

"They took my brother," Bayard said. "He's thirteen damned years old. A little kid."

"Ant?" she hazarded a guess, trying to push from her mind the close presence of Wasserman, who was following them through the yard on a roughly parallel course, carrying the tabletlike monitor that would allow him to see if and when she managed to deactivate Ware's deadman switch.

"That's right. If they fucking hurt him—"

"Who are we talking about? Who do you think would hurt your brother?"

"The fucking cops." He said it like she was an idiot for asking.

"No police officer is going to hurt your little brother," she replied firmly.

"Are you for real? What do you think they took him for?"

She couldn't help it: her heart was racing. She could see Wasserman out of the corner of her eye, an inescapable reminder of how badly this could end. "I have no idea."

"And you don't care, do you?" Bayard sounded bitter.

"I care. I do care. Of course I care. It's just that right now I'm more concerned with getting this hostage situation resolved without anybody getting killed," Caroline said, willing herself to ignore Wasserman. "But once it's over, I will look into your brother's situation as well as yours, I promise."

If we're both still alive. Of course, she didn't say it aloud. Bayard seemed totally oblivious to the danger he was walking into by joining forces with an armed man with a bomb, and she didn't feel like this was the moment to point that out.

"Golly gee, Ms. Cop, now I feel all better."

Caroline thought it better not to play into that bit of sarcasm, and Bayard lapsed momentarily into silence as they negotiated a curve in the sidewalk.

"What's going to happen once we get inside that big-ass house, anyway?" Bayard asked. "You ain't got some nasty surprise planned for me in there, do you? Like somebody waiting to blow a hole through my brains?"

That's **what you're worried about?** Again, she didn't say it aloud. "No surprises. I'm going to take you to Detective Ware."

"Then what? Is that when we're gonna get whacked?" Bayard's tone was truculent.

But the way he hunched his shoulders as he asked the question told her how vulnerable he felt.

"You're not going to get whacked." While one portion of her mind was busy worrying over various ways the coming confrontation with Ware might play out, Caroline experienced a reluctant welling of sympathy for Bayard. No matter what the kid had or hadn't done, he was just that, a kid. He was clearly scared to death, and with good reason. If they didn't get blown up, or shot, prison, possibly years in prison, loomed in his future. Clearly he wasn't all bad, if he was concerned about his little brother. His fears on that score were completely paranoid, of course. Maybe there were mental issues that could be addressed, which might influence a judge to look more leniently at his case? But that was an avenue to possibly be explored later if they both survived the night.

They were nearly at the end of the walk. As the house loomed, her stomach dropped toward her toes. Bucking up, she said to Bayard, "Maybe another six feet and we'll be at the steps. We go up the steps, across the veranda, and then we're at the door. As soon as we're inside, I can take the blindfold off."

His head slewed in her direction. "What about the cuffs?"

"We're coming to the first step. It's shallow: about six inches high. Step up," Caroline directed without answering his question, because the truth was that she wasn't going to take off his handcuffs. During their short walk to the house, it had occurred to her that if gunfire were to erupt, Bayard actually would be better off in handcuffs: nobody would be left in any doubt that he wasn't in a position to fire a weapon and didn't pose a threat. Thus no one would have any reason to shoot him.

As she and Bayard gained the top of the stairs and made their way across the wide front porch, her mouth went dry and her pulse raced as she faced the fact that the moment she had been dreading was almost at hand.

By the time they reached the front door, Caroline was sweating. She had butter-flies in her stomach. Her chest was tight with anxiety.

Possible scenarios for what might happen once she pressed the button chased themselves around and around in her mind as unproductively as a dog after its tail. Then a radical thought occurred as she turned the knob and pushed: what would happen if she **didn't** press the button? The massive oak panel swung inward with scarcely more than a **whoosh**.

Of course the door on a multimillion-dollar mansion wouldn't squeak.

For a moment she stood there staring into the darkness of the vast front hall while her heart picked up the pace until it was knocking against her ribs.

She could feel the whisper of air-conditioning on her face. An elusive, sweetish scent—potpourri? some kind of fancy furniture polish?—drifted out along with the cold air. Various small sounds—a hum, a creak, a rattle—from inside the house added up to an uneasy silence. Some fifteen feet beyond the open door, in the center of the hall, stood a large round table with a towering floral arrangement on it: the wedge of uncertain light spilling across the hall from outside revealed a massive pyramid of red poinsettias and white amaryllis. Caroline realized that the flowers were the source of the scent.

They smell like a funeral. The thought made her shiver.

Detach. Focus. Breathe.

"Yo, Ms. Cop, you get turned to stone or something?" Bayard asked. Then, in a tone that was slightly more uneasy, he added, "You still there?"

"Everything's fine." Pulling Bayard along with her, she took a resolute step inside and locked the door. The hall was not pitch dark, she was glad to discover as she turned back toward Bayard—a combination of moonlight and the outside lights streamed through the fanlight above the door—but it was dark enough so that she removed her cap and stuck it into her pocket to take advantage of every bit of night vision she could muster. Dark enough so that she was glad of the flashlight as she aimed it at Bayard. "I'm—"

She never got to finish what she was going to say: just as her flashlight found Bayard, somebody grabbed her hard from behind.

CHAPTER SEVEN

Even as he grabbed her, Reed inhaled the sweet, feminine scent of her shampoo and impartially cursed God, the Devil, and Fate, just in case he and the whole damned city of New Orleans were wrong about the existence of the first two, which was starting to seem increasingly likely in a world that just kept getting more and more unrecognizable.

If he hadn't had the foresight to clap his hand over Caroline's mouth the second he laid his hands on her, her scream would have wakened the dead. It would almost certainly have carried beyond the walls of the house, and possibly precipitated the very confrontation with the battalion of cops ranged outside—a number of whom he was now convinced actively wanted him dead—that he was doing his utmost to avoid. As he yanked her back against him, clamping her arms to her sides and covering her mouth, she let loose with a shriek that, muffled by his hand, came out sounding more like a squeal, and dropped her flashlight. The thing hit the marble with a crash, and went rolling away, throwing off bumpy stripes of light against the pillars and walls while she fought like a wild animal to get free.

Like him, she was a cop, fit and well trained. Still wasn't happening: in hand-to-hand combat, as in some other things he could think of, size really did matter. He was way bigger, stronger, better trained—and tonight he had too much to lose.

"Stop fighting, Caroline," he said in her ear as he did his best to contain her without letting either of them get hurt. She recognized his voice instantly. He could tell, because she quit struggling just as quickly as that. She hung in his arms, tense and panting.

"What the fuck?" Holly exclaimed. Jumping back, he came up with a **thump** against the table, and stood there jiggling from one foot to the other as he strained to see what was up, which he couldn't do because, Reed discovered with a surprised glance, someone had tied a blindfold over his eyes. The good news was the kid was breathing and appeared unharmed. From the moment he'd found out that Holly had been arrested, Reed had been in a cold sweat for fear that he was never going to see Holly alive again.

If Holly died tonight, it would be Reed's fault. He should have taken the kid seriously in the first place. He should have gotten all his ducks in a row—or at least made sure Holly and Ant were safely out of harm's way—before he did anything else. Having spent a good portion of the thirty-six hours following the cemetery killings conducting a rudimentary investigation of Holly's claims, he had been staggered by what had turned up. He should never have gone to Martin Wallace once he had decided for himself that at least one member of the NOPD, and possibly more, were involved in the shootings in the cemetery. But who the hell could have guessed that the superintendent would react as he had?

Who the hell could have guessed that the superintendent was **part of it**? The fact that Reed still didn't know exactly what **it** was didn't matter: not two hours after leaving the superintendent's office, he'd been called in to Internal Affairs, where he'd been stunned to find himself accused of accepting a bribe for letting a suspect in a drug-related murder walk. There were eyewitnesses, he'd been told, including a confidential police informant and one of his fellow officers, whom they refused to name.

Reed had been so shocked by the accusation that it had taken him until they'd demanded his weapon and badge to start putting the pieces together. Then he'd stormed out of Internal Affairs and gone straight to the superintendent. In the shouting match that had ensued, Reed had been fired, punches had been thrown, and, with all kinds of alarm bells going off in his mind, he had fled headquarters about two steps ahead of being placed under arrest.

Laying low until he could figure things out had been his intent, but then he'd gotten word that Holly had been busted for crack possession. Thing was, Holly might take the occasional toke off a joint, but to Reed's certain knowledge he had never done any harder drugs in his life. Magnolia's downfall was to thank for that: as Holly had told him not that long ago, no way was he ever going to let himself get that messed up.

That's when Reed had known for sure, just in case there had still been any doubt in his mind, any thought that what he had just been accused of could possibly have been no more than an honest mistake: he—and Holly—were being set up. By taking Holly's suspicions and his own confirming observations to the superintendent, he had walked into a hornet's nest, all unknowingly.

In the future—if he had a future—Reed promised himself that he'd be a hell of a lot warier about taking things, and people, at face value. Not that he was naive or anything: he'd known that the good guys weren't always good. But these people were his people: the NOPD was—had been—his tribe. This felt like—no, it **was**—betrayal.

Three years ago, he hadn't been able to save his own son's life. Tonight he was prepared to do whatever it took to save the lives of these two kids who were depending on him.

"It's okay, it's me," he told Holly. Then on his next breath, in a warning tone meant to make her understand that he was now the one in charge, he said to Caroline, "I don't want to have to hurt you. Don't make me."

Beneath his hand, she took a deep breath and muttered something. He took it for acquiescence.

"Holy shit, I thought I was a goner." Holly seemed to sag a little. "I thought they was gonna blow my head off for sure."

"Night's still young," Reed replied, easing his hold on Caroline just a little. She was stiff, wary, and he was careful not to give her enough room to try anything.

"So get us out of here already," Holly begged, taking a couple of uncertain steps toward him before stopping. Shrouded in shadows, Holly stood there in the middle of the hall swaying a little, his head craning in Reed's direction, clearly scared to death and discombobulated by not being able to see. "And get this fucking rag off my face."

Reed said, "Hang tight, I need to deal with this first."

"This" being Caroline. He could feel her continuing agitation in the heaving of her chest, in the shuddering breaths she was trying to take beneath his hand, but she was no longer making any attempt to fight free. That was good: he didn't want to hurt her. The Caroline he remembered had been sweet, sassy, sexy, in dire need of affection and protection, and she'd had a thing for him.

Of course, she'd also been seventeen. He might be making a mistake—a fatal mistake—if he assumed she hadn't changed since then.

It was a mistake that he couldn't afford to make. He'd already made enough of them over the last two days to nearly get himself and Holly—and now it seemed like Ant, too—killed.

"You can't scream," Reed warned her, tightening his hold on her a little to emphasize his point. She felt slimmer than he remembered, and stronger, too, in his arms. A grown woman now, not a girl. "Or give me any trouble. Understand?"

She gave a curt nod.

Cautiously he took his hand away from her mouth.

"You don't have a dead man's switch." Her tone made it a statement, not a question, and it surprised him. It took him a second, but then he knew exactly what she was talking about.

"It wasn't a dead man's switch." Sounding almost angry, she tried to look at him over her shoulder. "Was it?"

He realized that by having both hands free and available to grab her he had given himself away, because, clearly, if he'd had a dead man's switch, he wouldn't have been letting go of it. Not that it mattered now. The answer was that, no, the slim canister of personal-size pepper spray he'd been holding threateningly in his hand for the benefit of the hostages and the camera had not been a dead man's switch. But he had modified it just enough to make it look like one, and was mildly gratified to have further confirmation (besides his hostages' shuddering reactions to it whenever they had happened to look in its direction) of how well the bluff had worked.

Not that he was about to confess that it had been a bluff to Caroline. At this point, everything he did was on a need-to-know basis, and that she certainly didn't need to know. Instead of answering directly, he said, "I need you to hold still and stay quiet."

"Okay," she said. She was still breathing hard, still agitated. Given the direness of the circumstances, the surprise would be if she wasn't. She was clearly on edge, clearly afraid of him, and he regretted that. What seemed like a lifetime ago, he'd felt a lot of affection for the smart-mouthed, too-hot-for-her-own-good teen who had tried to disguise vulnerability with attitude. She added, "I'm here to try and help you, you know."

"You armed?"

"No."

"I need to check." He was wired, jazzed, running on pure adrenaline. He'd had almost no sleep or food since he had gotten a good look at the pictures on Holly's stolen phone and decided that there was indeed something there worth looking into.

The last thing he wanted to do was hurt her, though, so he handled her as gently as possible even as he did what he needed to do.

"Just tell me one thing: Why? Why are you doing this?" she asked as he pulled her arms behind her back—she didn't resist—and, holding them there by the simple expedient of crooking an arm around her bent elbows, began giving her a one-handed pat down. He knew she wasn't asking why he was frisking her. Rather, she wanted the **why** behind the hostage taking, the bomb threat, and the whole extremely criminal shebang in which he was currently engaged.

"I needed to get Holly out of jail." He gave her the short version. In a lightning decision, he rejected the idea of telling her about what Holly knew, what **he** now knew, about the deaths in the cemetery and Magnolia and the rest. He didn't know what she knew or whose side she was on. He didn't know if he could trust her. He did know that he and Holly might very well end up dead because of what they'd discovered. And if she wasn't involved—he was pretty sure she wasn't, but as previous events proved, his judgment in that regard didn't seem to be worth shit—he didn't want to chance putting Caroline at risk, too.

"You couldn't just **bail him out**?" Her indignation almost made him smile.

He couldn't resist. "Low on funds."

"You want to **hurry,** Dick?" Holly's voice was thin, and the way he was breathing told Reed just how nervous he was. "We don't got all damned day."

"I'm hurrying," Reed assured him.

"What have you done with the hostages?" Caroline craned her neck to try to look at him again.

"The hostages are fine," Reed assured her.

Checking the pockets of her windbreaker, he extracted a cell phone and set of car keys, which he thrust into his pants pocket. Then he ran his hand beneath the light-weight jacket and discovered a flak vest along with a mesh belt and holster holding one very weird weapon. One that he didn't have time to take more than a cursory glance at as he pulled it out.

"Fine?" Her voice was sharp. "Where are they?"

"Look, I'm done answering questions. Quit asking."

"Screw that. Where are they?"

He ignored her question in favor of asking one of his own. "What's this?"

He held it up for her to see. In the dark, the weird weapon looked like a DustBuster. Some kind of oversized stun gun, maybe? Whatever it was, he was 99.9 percent sure it wasn't deadly. Given that, at the moment he had scarier things to worry about than whatever the hell the thing was.

"Radar gun." Her grim reply came as Reed tucked the weapon into his jacket pocket. He didn't believe her and didn't have time to care, mentally labeling it a mystery to be explored later. Then he pulled the chest plate on her body armor out of the way and unzipped the flak jacket to make certain that the only things beneath it were soft curves of the natural kind. The shirt she was wearing was definitely not cop issue. From his vantage point behind her he couldn't really see it, but the top felt satiny smooth and sexy as all hell and her skirt, he discovered as he ran his hand down her thigh and encountered silky bare skin, was tight and short.

He was just registering that she was still as smokin' hot as he remembered, but definitely all grown up now, when Holly said, "Cops out there were saying you have this place all rigged up with a bunch of bombs. Where'd you go getting any bombs?"

Reed shot Holly a **shut-up** look—useless with the blindfold—and didn't answer.

"You don't have a dead man's switch," Caroline said slowly, and he knew that his nonanswer had resonated with her as she asked, "Do you even have a bomb?"

"You saw that big black backpack the mayor was holding, didn't you? What do you think was in it?" he countered, not yet ready to admit the truth even though she was now his prisoner and there wasn't a thing in the world she could do with the knowledge. Somewhat to his surprise, he had discovered that he wasn't a big fan of death, especially when it came pointing its fickle finger straight at him. And death was in the cards for both him and Holly tonight if he screwed this up.

For Ant, too, maybe. Jesus, would they really murder a thirteen-year-old boy? Reed had barely finished asking himself the question before he remembered the kid with the bullet hole between his eyes in the cemetery and had his answer: hell, yes, they would.

His gut tightened. His anxiety level rose and he felt his heart accelerate in response. He had to work to dial it back down.

"You don't, do you?" She sounded angry. "You don't have a bomb. What were you **thinking**? Do you realize **they're going to kill you**?"

"Not if I can help it," Reed replied, answering her second question because it was easier than the first, and completed his pat down by sliding his palm around the back of her trim waist as Holly exclaimed on a note of horror, "You were faking it about the damned bombs? How the hell are we gonna get out of here if there are no damned bombs?"

"You're not going to get out of here," Caroline said. Angry as she sounded, Reed could feel some of the tension leaving her body. He translated that to mean that she was no longer quite as afraid of him as she had been.

Holly groaned. "This blows, Dick. This really blows."

"How about you just shut up and stand there for a minute while I finish up here?" Reed said to Holly. He could hear the edge in his own voice, but he was absolutely not in the mood for Holly's shit.

Holly was undeterred. "You seen how many cops are out there? There's a fucking army. What've you got, one gun? We're dead. We need a bomb that's for real."

"Think about it: there's as much of a real bomb now as there's ever been," Reed growled, while at the same time Caroline tried one more time to look at him over her shoulder as she snapped, "What have you done with my father?"

Given what he knew about how she'd been treated by her father, Reed was surprised at the question.

"He's safe. All of them are safe."

"Safe?" Her voice went perilously shrill. She was looking all around, like maybe she thought he had them tucked away somewhere in the shadows. He wasn't mistaken: there was a definite lessening in her fear level, which for the sake of his plan probably wasn't a good thing. "Safe where?"

Before he could answer that—not that he was going to answer it—Holly chimed in with, "You got a plan to get us out of here, right? 'Cause Ms. Cop here wasn't kidding when she said they're going to kill you. And me, too. Like, any minute now. Red dot on the forehead and then **bang**."

Great image. Thanks, kid.

"Yes," he told Holly. "I have a plan. You could help it along by just **standing there and shutting up.**"

"So what's the plan?" Holly wasn't going to shut up—Reed had known Holly long enough that he hadn't had any real expectation that the kid would, although hope always sprang eternal—and as for standing there, he was twitching and grimacing and hopping from foot to foot with apprehension. Reed ignored him to concentrate on Caroline.

"What are you doing?" Caroline's voice was sharp. But she didn't resist as he quickly and prudently secured her wrists behind her back with the zip tie he'd extracted from his pocket. He might feel a little bad about it, but he couldn't afford to take any more chances. Until he had reason to change his mind, she was his hostage.

"Being careful," he replied, and let her go. She turned sharply toward him, glaring at him through the darkness.

"This isn't helping," she snapped. "Take it from me, you're out of time. Do you **want** to get yourself killed?" She nodded at Holly. "Do you want to get **him** killed?"

"Yeah, Dick, what about me?" Holly almost wailed.

"Not especially," Reed answered Caroline. She didn't have to tell him he was out of time. He could almost hear the proverbial clock ticking. But there were things he had to do, and they had to be done right if he and Holly were to have even a sliver of a chance of getting out of there alive. Grimly he focused on Caroline. "Sit. Right there on the floor."

Caroline looked at him with disbelief. **"What?"**

"Do it," he ordered her. "I don't have time to argue about it. Either sit or—" He left the rest of that blank, gave her a threatening look instead, and had his answer in her indignant huff as she folded herself toward the floor.

"Good girl," he said—he kept having trouble remembering she was no longer seventeen—and she responded by snapping, "This is the stupidest thing you could do."

"She's got the keys to the cuffs on her." Sliding one foot in front of the other like he didn't trust the floor beneath them, Holly came scooting toward him. Keeping a cautious eye on Caroline, who was clearly growing less afraid of him by the second, Reed moved to meet him. If she did something like, say, jump up and take off running, he didn't like to think what he was going to have to do. "You want to get 'em from her and get these things off me. And the blindfold. Like, **now**."

"I've got the key." Reed pulled the blindfold off Holly's head as he stepped behind him to free him from the handcuffs. God, he was jacked up on adrenaline. It was as if he could feel his nerve endings jumping under his skin. Every muscle in his body was taut. His blood raced through his veins. He was sweating, and he, born and bred in the sultry Louisiana swamps, almost never broke a sweat. Keeping his cool, keeping his focus, was a necessity, so he gritted his teeth, narrowed his eyes, and channeled his inner Zen master. Even as he inserted the damned tiny key into the damned tiny lock, more by feel than by sight, he did what he could to keep his body's instinctive response to the deadly peril it was in under control. Silently counting to ten, he rolled his neck to loosen it and shrugged his shoulders up and down to slow his breathing. Dixon and company had something in the works for him, he knew. They wouldn't have caved so easily otherwise. How much time did he have before whatever they had planned for him started going down? The closest he could come to an answer had to be, not much.

"He's better off with the handcuffs on," Caroline informed him. "When it hits the fan, he's less likely to get shot."

"We're gonna be out of here before then, right?" Holly tried to look over his shoulder at him as Reed succeeded in unlocking the cuffs. "Dick?"

"If we're lucky," Reed replied, then as

Holly said, "Shit," Reed added, "Edie tell you who took Ant?"

"She thought it was somebody from child welfare." Holly shook his head. "I don't think so."

The handcuffs fell away, and Reed stuffed them into his pants pocket along with the key. Later, they might come in handy. "Me neither."

Holly grabbed his arm so hard that Reed could feel each individual finger digging into his flesh through his jacket. "We got to get him back safe. You hear?"

"We will."

"You don't think they've done anything to him already?" Reed could hear the nervous strain in Holly's voice.

"As long as they don't have us, they won't touch a hair on his head. He's their leverage," he replied.

"Oh my God, you're not buying into what he's been saying about police officers wanting to hurt his thirteen-year-old brother!" Caroline exclaimed. "Tell me **that's** not what this is all about."

"You don't know shit about shit, Ms. Cop," Holly said.

Reed pushed out air through his teeth.

"Shut up, Holly. Drop it, Caroline. Right now we've got other fish to fry."

"Reed, listen: whatever your plan is, it's not going to work. You need to give yourself up to me." Caroline's tone was earnest.

She sat with her slender bare legs folded in front of her on the marble floor, and her upturned face looked pale in the moonlight. With her hair pulled back in a ponytail, the classic oval shape of it was apparent. It was a pretty, delicate face, slimmer of cheek and higher of cheekbone than it had been at seventeen. Her eyes were maybe a shade less innocent, but just as wide and luminous, and her mouth was just as lushly tempting. God, he'd wanted her that summer ten years ago! In a way, it was both his good luck and his bad luck that the negotiator they'd called in tonight had been Caroline. He hadn't foreseen it, and while it made things dicey in that he didn't want to hurt her and she wasn't as afraid of him as she should be, on the other hand if he'd been looking for the ideal bargaining chip, he couldn't have found one more perfect.

She continued, "If you don't you're going

to be killed. Him, too, probably. Surrendering to me, right now, is your only chance."

"You ain't gonna let her snow you with that, are you? We surrender and we're dead," Holly said at almost the same time as Reed told her, "Give it up, Caroline. Me surrendering isn't going to happen."

"You can't get away," she said urgently. "The house is surrounded. There are snipers. SWAT. The works."

"She's telling the truth about that." Holly rubbed the heels of his hands into his eyes. "Oh, Jesus, what are we gonna do?"

Reed heard the lurking panic in Holly's voice, but besides telling him, "I got this under control," there wasn't much he could do about it. He had to get a move on: at this point, every second counted. Every instinct he possessed told him that whatever was going to go down was going to go down soon. Even as Caroline said, "You don't have much time," Reed got on with implementing the plan he'd come up with when he'd heard that Holly had been taken. It had been modified on the fly a number of times already. Once he'd realized that Ant's life was in all likelihood on the line, too, it had also, with the addition of Caroline, gotten way more complicated than he liked. Still, it was roughly work-able. He hoped. Grabbing the backpack he'd brought down from the library with him, the one that he'd left waiting by the door, he pulled two windbreakers from it. They were standard black NOPD issue with SWAT emblazoned in big white let-ters across the front and back.

"Lose the hoodie. Put that on." He tossed one to Holly. While the kid looked at it in-credulously then made a face before he did as he was told, Reed stripped off his own tux jacket and bow tie. Dropping them into the big plastic garbage can he'd car-ried in earlier from the garage, he checked to make sure his 9mm was still secure but readily available in its shoulder holster, and shrugged into the second jacket himself.

"We gonna pretend to be SWAT? What're we gonna do, try to blend into the crowd when they burst in to kill us?" Holly practi-cally reeked of dismay even as Reed tossed him a black SWAT baseball cap with a terse, "That, too. Tuck your hair up under it."

Caroline, watching, said, "Oh, wow," in

a less-than-impressed tone that could have been an echo of Holly's.

"That's your **plan**?" Holly continued as Reed took his hoodie from him and dropped it into the garbage can. "Ah, hell, this ain't good."

CHAPTER EIGHT

"You'll get killed," Caroline warned. "Both of you. **Nobody's** going to fall for that. Oh my God, really, truly, this is not going to work. You have to believe me: surrendering is your only chance."

"They gonna drill us soon as they see us," Holly moaned as he slapped the cap on his head and started tucking his hair up under it as instructed. He was pale with fright. "No way are they gonna think we're SWAT."

"Reed, are you hearing me?" Caroline's voice rose perilously. "He's right: no way is anyone going to fall for this. If you surrender to me right now, I can walk you out of here. Nobody will harm you if you're with me. Either of you. I give you my word. **Please**."

"Oh, for God's sake." Just because they were giving voice to some of his own doubts didn't keep Reed from being fed up. "**You** need to trust me," he told Holly as he pointed a monitory finger at him. "Are you out of jail? Who did that?" Then he pointed at Caroline. "And **you** don't know a damned thing about it. So give me a break here, and lay off the surrender crap. Like I said, it's not going to happen."

He was busy taking one last size-it-up look at the garbage can, which was sturdy black plastic complete with lid, about forty-gallon size, and apparently new. Having come in through the garage, he'd noticed it in passing, thinking at the time that he might be able to use it to simulate the most terrifyingly big bomb ever, then accepted the fact that locating and isolating the people he needed to corral without attracting any undue attention might be a little difficult with a giant garbage can in tow. But then, when Holly had told him about Ant and he had realized that his plan needed to be adjusted to accommodate this new wrinkle, he'd remembered it. It was, he judged, perfect for the new use he had in mind for it. So he'd fetched it in the little bit of time he'd had after breaking off communications with Caroline, dumping out the miscellaneous sports equipment that had been stored within and lugging it into the hall.

"As long as you didn't do something terrible to the hostages, we can even still—" Caroline was saying as he confirmed the location of the lid with a glance and then took the two strides that brought him to her side. She broke off, looking up at him wide-eyed as he bent over her to scoop her up in his arms. He got the job done quickly but a little awkwardly—she was heavier than she looked, and he wanted to take care not to put too much pressure on her bound hands. She didn't struggle, but as he lifted her off her feet she sucked in air and her voice sharpened to a squeak: "What do you think you're doing?"

"I'm sorry about this, cher," he told her as he dumped her, feet first and sputtering, into the garbage can. The top of the can reached a little above her waist. There was, he saw with relief, plenty—well, enough anyway—of room for her to fit all the way inside if she hunkered down. He was pleased to discover that he had calculated correctly. Despite the fact that speed was increasingly of the essence, the sudden impulse to try to keep her as safe as he could made him lean over and zip her body vest back up.

Never could tell when or where bullets might start to fly.

"Have you lost your mind?" she demanded as she watched his hands at work on her zipper. Why she was wearing a slinky silk top low-cut enough to show some very nice cleavage, along with a snug little skirt that ended a pretty fair distance north of her knees, was something that he would have liked to ask about, but he didn't have the time. Just like he didn't have time to think about, much less enjoy, the electric zing that he experienced as his knuckles brushed up the front of that slinky top. "This is a trash can. You just put me in a trash can. You have to be insane. That's it, isn't it? That's the answer. You are totally, certifiably insane."

"Uh, Dick, I'm not seeing where you're going with this," Holly said uneasily while Reed, having finished with the zipper, tucked the reinforced front of her vest back in place and chucked Caroline under her chin by way of a reply.

She scowled at him.

"Look, Holly, just because he's gone nuts doesn't mean you can't save yourself." Caroline turned those big eyes of hers on Holly, who was breathing hard enough now that if Reed had been in possession of a brown paper bag, he would have passed it to him. "Even if he won't, you can surrender to me."

"Leave Holly alone, Caroline." Reaching into the backpack again, Reed grabbed the roll of duct tape he'd stashed away in there, said to her, "I need you to scrunch on down inside there," and tore off a strip.

"What?" She stared at him like he'd just grown a second head. "**No**. What is the point of—"

He couldn't have her yelling her head off or he and Holly would be screwed, and he didn't trust her enough just to order her to be silent and assume she'd obey. Sliding one hand behind her head, he did what he had to do and plastered the strip over her mouth.

"Mmm." Jerking away from his hold, she made an inarticulate sound while her eyes blazed at him.

"Scrunch down," he told her. She shook her head violently at him.

"Scrunch down," he barked. It was the harshest tone he had used to her yet, but he was getting a bad feeling here. His skin crawled, and that meant, if he used past experience as a guide and coupled that with what he knew of the present situation, something he wasn't going to like was heading his way.

He could almost feel that red dot on his forehead.

She shook her head at him again. The sudden jut of her jaw—he remembered that defiant jut of her jaw and what it signified the instant he saw it directed at him—told him that if he wanted her crouched inside that garbage can, he was going to have to put her there.

There was no way he was going to get physical with Caroline. But his other choices for getting her to do what he needed her to do were limited. In fact, they were **almost** nonexistent.

God, he hated pulling his gun on her. But needs must and all that, and he had Holly and now Ant, too, whose lives were on the line just as much as his. And it beat stuffing her down inside that can with his bare hands.

His one concern was that she wouldn't believe he would actually shoot her—well, he wouldn't, no matter how this played out, although it was best for both of them if she retained some doubt on that point—but he pointed his gun at her like he absolutely would.

And pretended not to notice Holly gulping in air like a fish out of water.

"Scrunch down," he ordered menacingly.

Glaring at him, she—thank God!—scrunched.

"Holly, hand me the lid," he said, not taking his eyes off Caroline. When Holly did, he restored his gun to his holster and stepped forward to seal her in.

She fit, barely, with her back against the plastic and her knees—slim pale knees on a pair of very nice legs, he noted once again in passing—wedged almost beneath her chin. Her face was tilted up to look at him. It was tight with anger. Her eyes shot sparks at him.

"Stay put and be quiet," he told her.

Her glare intensified. So did the jut of her jaw.

Holly was beside him now, looking down at Caroline, too. His face was a study in alarm.

"I'll get you out of there just as soon as I can," Reed promised her, just because he couldn't help himself. Her glare didn't soften one bit. "Hang tight."

Stifling his misgivings—if there was another way out, he hadn't been able to come up with it—Reed put the lid, in which he'd previously stabbed holes for ventilation so at least he didn't have to worry about her suffocating, on the trash can, fastened it in place, and tried not to think about Caroline shut up in there in the dark. Then he slung the backpack over his shoulder.

With Caroline secured, he needed to move fast.

"Help me pick it up," he said to Holly. "Grab the handle. Come on."

With Caroline inside, the can was heavy,

but not so heavy that the two of them, one on each side, couldn't move it with relative ease. They didn't have far to go.

"Stay right here with her," he ordered Holly as they set their burden down again. Except for a few thumps from inside the can, there had been no problems. He was breathing a little easier: this part of the plan, so far, was holding up. "Don't open the lid no matter what she does, and don't go anywhere. Got it?"

"Where are you going?" Holly asked, sounding and looking panicky.

"Do what I told you. I'll be right back. And, oh yeah, there might be some explosions. Wait for me."

He threw the words over his shoulder as he took off running toward the opposite side of the house. His objective was the utility room that was the smallest by far of about a dozen rooms that opened onto the pool area, where the helicopter and the money—and SWAT and a bunch of snipers and God knew what else—waited for him. As he ran, he pulled his Leatherman knife out of the backpack and stuck it into his jacket pocket. When he reached the utility room—it wasn't as dark as he would have expected; moonlight poured through the glass insert in the outside door—he drew his gun and unlocked the big closet that from its contents he'd discovered was used to store pool chemicals. Warily, in case a surprise was waiting, he pulled the closet door open.

Five of his hostages—the ones who'd been on the floor, minus Ellen Tremaine, whom he had judged to be too difficult to control—were crammed in there, seated on the floor, wrists secured behind them and ankles bound with zip ties, strips of duct tape covering their mouths. He knew none of them: they would be part of The Big Easy's high society, which meant they ran in radically different circles from him. There were four women and two men, both of whom were reasonably close to his size and build, both in black tuxes like the one he was wearing. In the dark, as the saying sort of went about cats, all men in tuxes looked alike, or at least alike enough to hopefully make for a few confusing moments.

The hostages glanced up at him almost as one, faces pale in the darkness, eyes fearful.

Their expressions didn't bother him, or at least only a little: he had already come to terms with the fact that from their point of view, he was a dangerous criminal. He'd made peace with it knowing that tonight his first duty was to Holly and Ant, and to himself.

"This is your lucky day," he told them as, knife in hand, he bent down to slash through the thin plastic strips securing their ankles one by one. "I'm going to let you go before I blow this house to kingdom come. On your feet. Get out of here. Hurry up."

They clambered awkwardly upright and spilled out into the utility room. Gesturing with his gun, he lined them up against the wall.

"You see that door?" He pointed at the door to the outside. Though he dared not get too close to the glass—he was wary of the snipers he knew were out there—he was able to see the glinting metal of the helicopter's body. The blades weren't rotating, which meant that there was going to be no quick takeoff. **That'll fix me,** was his sardonic inner response to what he recognized as his fellow officers' attempt to keep him on the ground. Then he added, "That's your way out. It's locked. All you have to do is turn the knob and it'll unlock. You turn the knob, pull the door open, and run like hell." Having their hands secured behind them would slow them down a little, which he was counting on, but it shouldn't present much of an obstacle. Just to be sure, just in case it was possible that he was dealing with a bunch of nitwits who couldn't figure it out, he thrust the knife into his pocket so that he had a hand free. Still holding his gun, he turned so they could see his back and, one-handed, demonstrated reaching for and turning an imaginary knob in a way that mimicked his hand being secured behind him as theirs were, waggling his fingers for emphasis. "Like this. Got it?"

Several of them nodded hesitantly.

"Good enough," he said as his gaze ran over them: they looked like they were ready to run for their lives. He decided to heap a little more fuel on the fire. "The house is set to blow in about one minute. If I were you, I'd head straight for that helicopter out there. That's the best path if you want to avoid the explosives I have set up outside. Good luck."

Then he left them, closing and locking the door to the utility room behind him just in case any of them should get it into their heads to try to take refuge in the house. He had no explosives outside, of course, the same as he'd had no bomb in the house. Just one more lie in a night full of them, this particular one designed to keep the hostages from running straight into the arms of the hidden battalion of law enforcement ringing the helicopter for as long as possible. Knowing that the moment of truth was at hand, that what he was about to do would cause all hell to break loose almost instantaneously and either get him and Holly out of there or get them killed, he took a deep breath, holstered his weapon, breathed a prayer, and grabbed two flash bangs from the dozen or so in his backpack. Then he set off at a dead run back the way he had come.

Boom! Boom! Boom! Boom!

By the time he reached Holly, he had tossed all the flash bangs he had with him and was basically deaf from the volume of the explosions, despite the twin facts that he had thrown the stun grenades as far away from himself as he could manage and had stuffed earplugs in his ears to boot. Even with what he could hear, it sounded like Armageddon. Explosions were still going off like popcorn, courtesy of the flash bang he'd lobbed onto the bag of M-800 firecrackers he'd left at the top of the stairs. The house was filled with acrid smoke. SWAT was no doubt at that very moment crashing its way inside, adding to the noise and mayhem, and the hostages he'd released should be hightailing it toward the helicopter as fast as they could go.

"Holy God, Dick, what the hell?" Holly was crouched beside the garbage can, Reed saw at a glance as he bolted back into the room, pulling out the earplugs as he came and dropping them into the now almost empty backpack, which he slung over one shoulder. To Reed's traumatized ears, Holly's exclamation was barely audible. The kid sprang to his feet as Reed ran toward him. Even in the dark, he could see how white Holly's face was, how scared he looked. He understood completely: his own heart jackhammered and his pulse raced.

He could almost feel death breathing down his neck.

"We got to go. Grab the can," he ordered Holly, skidding to a stop beside the garbage can and latching on to the handle on its side while ignoring the angry thumping coming from inside it. "We're going to run outside holding this can between us. All you have to do is hang on to the can, keep your head down, and run like hell. I'll do the rest. But we got to **move**."

"Oh, shit." Even to someone as hard of hearing as Reed currently was, Holly sounded terrified. But he did as he was told, picking up his side of the can just as Reed did—one hand on the handle, one hand on the can's bottom—and taking off on cue. Seconds later they burst through a door into the side yard on the opposite end of the house from the pool.

"Run," Reed growled at Holly, and they did.

The inky glimmer of the lake stretched out seemingly endlessly beyond the lush landscaping that marked the edge of the property. Lugging the can a little awkwardly between them, he and Holly galloped straight toward the cops who had been deployed around the mansion to form a perimeter designed to keep him—and Holly—from escaping. Behind them, explosions could still be heard coming from the house. Smoke billowed skyward in vast plumes of pale gray feathers. The air smelled of sulfur. Shouts and sirens and what sounded like gunfire (could still have been the M-800s for all Reed knew) and all kinds of other noisy commotion created an atmosphere of pure bedlam. The perimeter line, which Reed was certain had just a couple of minutes before been as stalwart and steadfast as any police commander could have wished, was now ragged. The cops had broken ranks. Some ran toward the house, weapons drawn. Others stayed in place, clearly uncertain where their duties lay, attention focused on the chaos unfolding in front of them. Pounding straight toward the onrushing cops and what was left of the perimeter line, acutely aware that he and Holly were coming under the scrutiny of many armed men whose job it was to catch them, conscious, too, of the weight of the garbage can and Holly's panting terror as he held up its other side, Reed sent one more prayer winging skyward and employed his last bluff.

"SWAT," he screamed. "Stay clear! We're carrying a bomb."

CHAPTER NINE

When the lid came off the garbage can, Caroline sat there for an instant blinking up at the deep soft black of the night sky. Her pounding heart was just starting to slow. Her racing pulse was just easing off a bit. There was a low-grade ringing in her ears. The moon—God, was it fitting or what, that almost the first thing that met her eyes was that big, fat yellow globe?—shone steadily down. The smell of brackish water, of mud, of decaying vegetation invaded her nostrils as she drew in a lungful of fresh air.

It beat the smell of plastic by a country mile.

"You okay, cher?" Reed loomed over the top of the can, no more than a tall, dark silhouette with the moon at his back, looking down at her. The relief of knowing that he was not a deranged would-be killer with a bomb was swamped immediately by a wave of anger. Unable to reply because of the **duct tape** across her mouth, she had to make do with a glare. It seemed to reassure him. "Come on, stand up."

Well, she actually would have stood up if she could have gotten her feet beneath her. But bent like a paper clip and wedged in as she was, there wasn't much room to maneuver. In fact, there was no room whatsoever. Space was so tight that the whole time he and Holly had been running with the garbage can and she had been getting jostled around inside it her chin had kept banging into her knees. At one point she'd even bitten her tongue, and it hurt.

Plus her hands were zip-tied together behind her back. Not having the use of her hands definitely hampered her ability to stand up.

Either her lack of compliance with his command, or the baleful stare she was giving him, must have clued Reed in to her absolute inability to do as he wished. Reaching in, he slid his hands beneath her armpits and pulled her upright. Grimacing at the discomfort inherent in being thus forcefully unfolded, Caroline swayed a little as, when she was upright at last, the blood rushed from her head toward her feet, which had gone to sleep.

Right along with her poor bound hands.

"She looks pissed," Holly observed as Reed wrapped a hard-muscled arm around her waist, slid the other beneath her thighs, and lifted her out of the can and into his arms.

Pissed? Really? She did? How surprising. Looking up at his handsome, familiar face, she discovered that she was no longer afraid of him. Didn't mean she liked him.

"Get the stuff out of the bottom of the can, put it in the backpack, and let's go," Reed told Holly as he strode with Caroline toward the water. She glared at his chiseled profile: the tension in his face was unmistakable, and she didn't care. Also, so the man was strong. So what? At the moment, as far as she was concerned, he could eat dirt. "As quick as you can."

"Like the speed of light," Holly promised. "Oh, man, I thought we was for sure gonna die in a hail of bullets back there. That was like Butch Cassidy and the Sundance Kid or something. Only we lived."

"Yeah, well, we haven't survived the night yet, so don't get cocky. The can?"

"I'm on it," Holly said, and, tilting the can, leaned down inside.

Caroline could have told him that there were several items at the bottom. Some of them were hard and uncomfortable, like the EMP device that Reed had stored in the pocket of his discarded tux jacket. She knew, because she'd been sitting on them. She was pretty sure their shape was immortalized by the bruising on her butt.

"That had to be uncomfortable," Reed said. He was looking at her now and sounding all sympathetic, which was a hoot considering that, oh, yeah, it had been and he was the cause of it. He had an arm around her shoulders and the other beneath her knees, which meant that she was curled against the solid wall of muscle that was his chest. She could feel the outline of his gun in its shoulder holster pressing against her upper arm. A turn-on? She knew a man with a gun was a turn-on for some girls, but, see, she carried one herself. Usually. Except when she was walking unarmed into a dangerous situation that her gut had told her from the outset was going to end badly, the point being that, for ignoring her instincts, she guessed she deserved what she'd gotten. A glance told her that her skirt had shimmied up. Way up. She was decent, but just barely. Her bare legs looked slim and pale curved over the solid black bar that was his arm in the misappropriated SWAT jacket. His large, warm, unmistakably masculine hand lay lightly along her uncovered thigh. It annoyed the hell out of her to discover that, despite everything, she actually liked the feel of his hand on her skin. In fact, the situation annoyed her on so many levels that she didn't even try to sort them out. Since she couldn't talk, she narrowed her eyes at him.

"I almost crapped my pants when those bombs started going off. There must've been a thousand of them. They were you, right? Yeah, they had to be." Holly was chattering, probably from nerves. His head had popped out of the can, and he was looking at the two of them—well, Reed really. "I thought you said you didn't have no bombs."

"They were flash bangs," Reed replied over his shoulder, which explained a lot to Caroline, who'd likewise had an extreme anxious reaction when the explosions had begun. To wit, her first, horrified thought had been that he'd blown up the hostages. She'd managed to rationalize it away before she'd had a complete nervous breakdown, but she still wasn't quite recovered from the trauma. "Noisy, disorienting, but harmless."

"That was awesome." Holly dived back into the can. "Man, them cops parted for us like the Red Sea."

Awesome wasn't quite the descriptive word Caroline would have chosen.

"The explosions didn't scare you, did they?" Reed asked her, apparently perceptive enough to read something in her face. "If I'd thought about it, I would've given you a heads-up, that they were only flash bangs."

The look Caroline gave him was positively evil.

His eyebrows contracted in response. His expression changed subtly, but she couldn't read it. The moonlight cast the hard planes and angles of his face in harsh relief. His eyes gleamed darkly down into hers. For an instant, as she took in his black hair and sensuous mouth, registered her own bound hands and the unfamiliar sensation of near helplessness she was experiencing as he schlepped her around like a bride on her wedding night, she was reminded of the pirate ancestry that ran heavy in the Creole bloodlines.

Thing was, there was no captive maiden ancestry in hers, which she meant to spell out for him first chance she got.

"We taking all this stuff with us?" Holly asked, causing Reed to glance around. Although she could no longer see him, his voice made it apparent that he had surfaced from the depths of the can again.

"Yes," Reed replied. "The fewer things we leave behind, the longer it's going to take them to figure out where we went."

They had reached the very edge of the lake, Caroline saw as he set her back on her feet. The ground beneath her was marshy and wet. She could feel the brush of weeds around her bare legs. Cattails were all around them, standing taller than even Reed, hiding much of their surroundings—and undoubtedly them—from view. The buzz of insects—or maybe that was still the ringing in her ears—seemed inordinately loud. He kept his hands on her waist to steady her, which was probably a good idea. She felt a little dizzy, a little light-headed. Her tongue hurt where she had bitten it. Her feet and calves tingled. So did her fingers.

And, yes, it was probably fair to say that she was pissed.

Tilting up her chin, she fixed Reed with what she was certain had to be the most speaking look she had ever given anyone in her life.

It wasn't saying nice things.

"If I take off the duct tape, you can't scream," Reed warned. "You can't even talk loud."

She nodded once to indicate her acquiescence. Leaning toward her, wincing pre-emptively, she presumed on her behalf, he began to gently peel away the tape.

It felt like a layer of skin was coming off along with the tape.

Pissed no longer even began to cover it.

Behind Reed's head, she saw a hazy cloud of smoke drifting skyward. The distant roar she had been vaguely aware of since the lid was lifted from her plastic prison began to differentiate itself from the ringing in her ears, which was gradually subsiding. She realized now that it was a medley of shouts, sirens, and the **thwump-thwump** of the helicopters she could see swooping around like dragonflies in the near distance. A searchlight from one of those helicopters swept down out of the sky over the roof—the roof was the only part that she could see—of the mansion from which she had just been hijacked.

Incredible as it was for her to process, Reed's scheme had actually worked. He and Holly had managed to get through a police net that was as tight as anything she had ever seen. Alive. And apparently undetected.

By using two stolen SWAT jackets and a garbage can.

What that said about the efficiency of her colleagues left her aghast.

Having been sent in to disarm the hostage-taker's bomb, she had wound up being kidnapped.

What that said about her own efficiency made her want to hang her head, and that in turn made her furious.

The last of the tape came off. Her lips felt dry and slightly swollen. The skin around them stung a little. She licked her lips, worked her mouth. Reed watched her, his expression impossible to read. They stood face-to-face. He had one steadying hand still on her waist. With the other, he was rolling up the duct tape between his fingers into a little ball.

"Better?" he asked her.

She looked him straight in the eye and snarled, "You **jackass**."

He blinked, clearly surprised.

She followed up with a fierce, "You brain-dead son of a bitch, what the hell did you do to the hostages?"

His eyes widened a little. Then his lips twitched, and he smiled. A real, genuine, amused smile. White teeth flashed. A dimple—she remembered that dimple; a long time ago she'd thought it was mega hot—appeared in his right cheek. His eyes danced. Okay, so the man was handsome. At this point she didn't give a flying—

"Locked them in a couple of upstairs closets. Except for the ones I let go. No real harm done to any of them. Unless somebody actually crapped his pants when the explosions started going off." He paused reflectively. "Which is a possibility. I left your father and the mayor with what they thought was a bomb."

"You've got to be absolutely bat-shit crazy." She was so mad her voice shook. "A lunatic. A reckless, selfish, stupid **jerk.** Some of those hostages could have had a heart attack. You could have gotten two innocent people—and by that I mean Holly and me, because you're sure as hell not innocent—killed."

"You **are** pissed," he said.

"You stuffed me into a garbage can at gunpoint." She was talking through her teeth now. "You bound my hands. You put duct tape over my mouth. **You scared the hell out of me**. And for what? You want to tell me? For what?"

"I had no choice," he replied, sliding a hand around her elbow. Even through the sleeve of her windbreaker, she could feel the size and strength of that hand. "About any of it. Like I said, you have no idea what's going on here. And keep your voice down."

She tried to jerk free. He wouldn't let go. **Fine**. With his long fingers fastened immovably around her arm, she stood her ground and verbally lambasted him. "If your Butch Cassidy thing had gone wrong, I could have been shot. Holly could have been shot. Of course, you could have been shot, too, but that would just be a matter of getting the inevitable over with. You know what you are? You're a dead man walking. You're going to get caught. You're going to get killed. You're—"

"Much as I'm enjoying this conversation," he said, interrupting, "we're going to have to save the rest of it for later." He looked past her at Holly. "Get in," he told Holly. "We've got to get out of here."

It was then, as she followed Reed's gaze to find Holly, who'd left the can behind to beat them to the water's edge, that she saw the boat. It was a small, flat-bottomed, open fiberglass vessel barely visible among the weeds. Having apparently just finished tossing things into it, Holly was clambering into the bow.

"Really? You think nobody's going to hear a boat?" Caroline's eyes snapped back to Reed as he pulled her toward it.

"It's electric. It's silent. It's used for bird-watching," he replied. "So, no."

"They'll see it. Helicopters, remember? They'll sweep the lake. And, by the way, you want to cut this zip tie off my hands?"

"They won't search the lake until they figure out we're not in the house. It's a big house, so I'm guessing we've got a little time. And I'll cut the zip tie off later. When I'm sure you won't dive overboard. See, I remember how well you swim." His eyes caught hers. In their sudden reminiscent glimmer she saw full evidence that he re-membered tossing her into the pool after she'd kissed him, then standing there watching as she'd surfaced and swum with swift, powerful strokes to the edge. He'd waited until she'd pulled herself out, prob-ably because letting the superintendent's daughter drown could not be considered a career enhancer, then said, "Don't try that again, little girl" in the teeth of her spluttering outrage. "Get in the boat."

"No." She shook her head. And planted her feet. And figuratively dug in her heels. "You've escaped. Not for long, probably, but that's for you to worry about it, not me. I've done everything I can to try to save your life, but if you're determined to commit suicide by cop there's really nothing I can do about it. Except to not be around to watch when it happens. And I want this zip tie **off**."

"You could still get your chance to save me." His tone was soothing. His mouth curved until it was dangerously close to breaking into another smile. "Who knows when I might need to hold you up in front of me as a shield?"

"You think that's funny?" She was seething. "It's not. You're in denial. It's pathetic. **You are going to get hunted down and killed**. But, bottom line, you are no longer holding any hostages, so you are officially not my problem anymore. I'm not going anywhere with you. If you'll cut this zip tie off—or even if you won't—I'll find my own way back."

He seemed to sigh. His hand on her elbow tightened. "Caroline, I know you're mad, and I don't blame you. But I really don't have time for this. I'll cut the zip tie off as soon as I can, I promise. For now, I need you to **get in the damned boat**."

"No."

They stared measuringly at each other. Then Reed solved the impasse by scooping her up off her feet again.

That caused her to leave pissed so far behind that it was like she was looking down on it from another planet.

"Where the hell do you get off manhandling me, anyway? You think you can just pick me up and carry me off and there won't be any repercussions?" Caroline growled, struggling, as he took two long strides and stepped into the boat with her. Screaming for help occurred to her, but the thought of the duct tape plus the maddening truth that she really, truly, when all was said and done didn't want to bring the hunt down on him kept her volume reasonably low. "Next time I'm with someone who wants to put a bullet through you, I'll give them a big thumbs-up. No, wait, screw that. How about I just save everybody a lot of trouble and do it myself, first chance I get?"

"Quit squirming or you'll tip the boat," he warned.

"This is kidnapping," she snapped as the boat rocked and she stopped struggling because she really didn't want to drown, which, if she went in the drink with her hands tied behind her, she just might. "A federal crime."

He laughed. "At this point, the feds will have to get in line."

"Careful, Dick," Holly warned as the boat rocked some more, and then Reed put her down on the narrow seat in the center of the boat. His arms dropped away from her and he sat down himself in the stern. Caroline looked at her long slim legs, bare to the tops of her thighs because her skirt had ridden up some more and she didn't have the use of her hands to pull it down, and felt steam figuratively coming out of her ears.

"They'll call in the FBI," she told Reed with relish as he used a paddle to push them away from shore. "The FBI will launch a nationwide manhunt."

He'd set her down facing forward, but she turned on the seat so she could see him, and watched as he did something— pushed a button?—that caused the engine to start.

The sound was a gentle hum, no louder than a cat's purr.

Caroline mentally harrumphed.

"Nobody's going to call the FBI. I guarantee it," Reed said with calm certainty as he worked the throttle and rudder so that in moments they were skimming along the water just a few yards from shore. "If they were going to call the FBI, they would already have done it and I would have been dealing with an FBI negotiator instead of you. See how well things work out?"

"You are delusional," she said. "Delusional, and **wrong**. Soon to be **dead** wrong."

He didn't reply. Glancing shoreward, she saw that houses lined the lake all along their path. They were considerably smaller in this area than the mansions that filled the section from which they had just come. A number of them still had some interior lights on despite the fact that it was the wee hours of the morning. Caroline was surprised at it until she remembered that this was actually Christmas Eve turned Christmas morning and there were likely to be sleepy parents up doing the Santa Claus thing. She didn't know whether she was more worried or hopeful that they would be seen, but there didn't seem to be much chance of that: the yards sloping down to the lake were big and there was a lot of vegetation in the way. Since the lake was smooth as black glass, the ride was only a little bumpy. The air rushing past felt cool, and Caroline guessed that the temperature had dropped to maybe the high sixties. At any rate, she was glad of her windbreaker.

"You really don't think they'll call in the feds?" Holly, in the bow, turned to ask Reed with obvious anxiety.

"No," Reed replied. "They want to keep this local if they can."

"They can't," Caroline said with relish. "Because, for one thing, you just kidnapped me. That rates an automatic call to the feds. Because it's a **federal** crime."

"Um, so why are we taking her with us?" Holly asked. Caroline saw that he had discarded the SWAT jacket and was once again wearing his hoodie, and remembered that it—soft cotton with a really sharp zipper—had been one of the items bouncing around beneath her buns.

"Good question," Caroline concurred. "I mean, since you've chucked your garbage can and you no longer need me to make part of a pretend bomb anyway, I'd think I'd just be in the way."

Like Holly, she was looking at Reed, but something about the quality of Holly's silence told Caroline that he agreed.

"I'm going to trade her for Ant," Reed said to Holly. Then he looked at Caroline to explain, "Holly's little brother. He's thirteen."

"I know that," Caroline snapped, while at the same time Holly exclaimed, "Dick! That's genius! It'll be like a prisoner exchange."

"His name's Reed," Caroline pointed out irritably.

"It's short for Detective," Reed told her.

Then the truth burst upon her. She stared at him. "That was why you wanted me to bring Holly in to you. You knew then that you were going to kidnap me and trade me for his brother. There I was twisting myself into knots trying to keep you from being killed and the whole time **you were planning to use me**."

The way Reed regarded her steadily for

a moment without replying told Caroline that she was exactly right.

"Not the whole time," Reed said, like that made a difference. "Only after Holly got there and told me about Ant. At that point, I had to improvise."

If she'd had a hand free, she would have smacked a palm to her forehead. "I cannot believe that I walked into that house. I cannot believe that I—that all of us—were that gullible."

"I mean to see to it that no harm comes to you, Caroline."

"You know what you can do with that," Caroline threw at him, and pointedly turned her face away. She was still furious, but knowing that he'd deliberately used her hurt, too. What bothered her the most was realizing that he'd remembered her ten-year-old crush on him and deliberately capitalized on it. Then she remembered the EMP device. She'd been prepared to disable his bomb, and to get close enough to do that she would have been taking advantage of their previous relationship, too. So, touché.

Looking behind them, she could see the mansion they'd left behind, or at least ascertain its location. Because of the multitude of lights around the house, it was enveloped in a pale glow that lit up that particular spot like a beacon. Smoke still rising from the scene looked like a hazy veil in the moonlight. The helicopters were easy to spot because their searchlights slashed through the night.

Caroline wondered how long it would be before Dixon and the rest figured out that Reed and Holly—to say nothing of herself—were not in the house. She guessed it would take a full search. And, as Reed had pointed out, the house was big.

Reed had turned the boat away from shore. They were at a narrow part of the lake now, and he was taking them straight across it. The small boat practically slid across the smooth surface. Caroline realized that they were going slower than she would have expected given the circumstances, and guessed that Reed was wary about kicking up wake. A ruffle of white in the midst of so much black water would make them easy to spot if anyone happened to look their way. Especially with how the moon was shining down on the lake.

Sooner or later, someone was going to look their way.

"Let me get this straight." She fixed Reed with a condemning gaze. He was scarcely more than a dark shape as they gained the other side of the lake and were enveloped by the shadow of the bridge they were passing beneath, but it was a large, broad-shouldered, very capable-looking dark shape. As angry as she was with him, the idea that he had put himself in this life-threatening position—and there was no going back from it that she could see—made her sick with aggravation and fear. Fear for him, damn it, as maddening as it was to admit even to herself. The question she wanted answered was, **why?** Why had he embarked on such a stupid, self-destructive course to begin with? Drugs and alcohol as an excuse were out: she was fully convinced that the man was totally straight and perfectly sober. Insanity? Now, that was still a possibility. "You got fired today—yesterday. For taking a bribe, I heard. I'm sure you're going to say you're innocent, but at the moment that's not the point. Then Holly got busted for drugs. He claims he's innocent, too, that

some bad cop planted the evidence on
him, but they put him in jail anyway. You
felt that the best way to prove your inno-
cence and get him out of jail was to take a
whole bunch of very important people
hostage and threaten to kill them if Holly
wasn't released and brought to you,
along with an escape helicopter in which
you wanted us to stash a million dollars in
cash. Now, in hindsight, I get that the helicopter and the cash were sort of a sleight-
of-hand distraction so that you could sneak
Holly away out a side door, but what I don't
get is why you did all this in the first place.
I mean, did you never hear of filing an ap-
peal? And how hard could it have been to
get Holly out of jail? Do lawyers, judges,
courts, bail bondsmen, and the entire legal and civil service systems just hold no
appeal for you?"

"Dick didn't take no bribe. He was set
up, just like I was. If he hadn't gotten me
out of jail, they would've killed me tonight,"
Holly told her starkly. "I was pretty sure
when they took me in, but then when I saw
where they was putting me, there was no
doubt. I know some of those dudes in

there, and I got the word: I was getting ready to get a back-door parole." Even as Caroline mentally translated that last to mean get murdered in jail and have his body-bagged corpse carried out of the prison via a back door, she shifted to look at him. He said earnestly to Reed, "I owe you, Dick."

"Yeah, you do. Big time. Don't forget it."

"**Who** do you think was going to kill you tonight?" Caroline asked Holly, struggling not to let her exasperation show.

"Damn, woman, I've told you a bunch of times: the cops," Holly responded impatiently.

"Shut up, Holly," Reed said, and from his tone it was obvious that he meant it. They were once more scudding through moonlight, going faster than before. The boat was kicking up wake now, but the bridge they had just passed beneath provided some concealment from anyone on the other side of it as the boat followed the shoreline into a small inlet. In the distance she could still hear sirens, but here in this quiet backwater the whirr of cicadas and other insects plus the croaking of the bullfrogs were equally loud. Reed added, "She's going back, remember? If she knows too much, she won't be safe."

Caroline looked at Reed. It was obvious that he believed every word Holly had just said. "You are in the advanced stages of paranoia," she told him, then included Holly in her glare. "You, too."

Holly started to say something, but Reed silenced him with a gesture.

"Quiet, both of you. We're here," he said.

As Caroline looked around to see where "here" was, her eye was caught by something she had never expected to see: the silhouette of a helicopter flying in front of the face of the moon. It was so reminiscent of the bicycle across the moon scene in **E.T.** that she stared at it for a second before realizing what it meant.

When she did, her breath caught and her stomach dropped clear to her toes.

"Reed," she croaked. "They're searching outside for you."

CHAPTER TEN

Both helicopters had peeled away from the scene of the crime and were circling over an ever widening area while their searchlights scoured the ground below. One appeared to be concentrating on the lake while the other combed the neighborhood surrounding the mansion. The white beams of the searchlights shot down through the darkness like tractor beams.

Now that she was looking in that direction, Caroline could also see red pulsing lights streaking away from the scene and racing along the road on the opposite side of the lake from where she and Reed and

Holly sat huddled in the boat. There were at least a dozen, one after the other. Heart in throat, she identified them as patrol cars, moving fast. Their sirens—yes, she could hear them as they drew parallel and flashed past. Though the sound remained thin and distant with the lake between them, the cars were definitely in full scream.

"I'd say you're right. Looks like they know we're not in the house." Reed's voice was so untroubled that Caroline shot a look at him. Her pulse raced and her stomach knotted from just the idea that all those police officers were hunting them. Which was ridiculous when she thought about it: the "them" being hunted did not include her. She should have been cheering the searchers on, because she was the victim awaiting rescue here. Reed, on the other hand, was the perp, the target of all that manpower, the bad guy who would be imprisoned for decades or killed in a firefight if—when—he was found. But if he was worried or scared, she couldn't tell it.

Caroline had a lightning vision of her father, freed from whatever makeshift prison Reed had left him in, learning that Reed had escaped with Holly and taken

her with him. He would be incandescent
with rage, putting the fear of God in those
on the scene whom he held responsible
for what he would consider an inexcus-
able failure, ordering a full-out manhunt
while he threatened everybody involved
with ruined careers.

Just the thought of her father coming
after Reed in that kind of white-hot fury
made her go cold all over.

The others—the sheriff, the mayor, the
city attorney—would be out for blood as
well. Reed's blood; nothing less would sat-
isfy them.

As she looked at Reed, Caroline felt a
thrill of despair. After everything he had
done, she could see no way out for him.

Something unimaginably bad had to
have happened for him to put himself in
such a position.

What? She frowned. Holly kept insisting
"the cops" had done this or that. Reed had
shut him up, like he thought there was some
substance there. The identities of the hostages had to mean something, too.

He wasn't going to tell her what was
going on, because he said knowing the
truth would put her in danger.

Frowning, Caroline turned the possibilities over in her mind. But she could come to no conclusion.

Reed had slowed down the boat, and was steering it through overhanging willow fronds that dipped so low they brushed the top of her hair. The rustle of the leaves combined with the gentle rippling sound of the water would have been soothing under less fraught conditions.

"They're going to set up roadblocks on all the exit points to the subdivision," Caroline said, her voice carefully even. She knew how this kind of manhunt worked. The warning emerged almost of its own volition. She was both a cop and a victim here, which definitely placed her not on Reed's side, and was mad as hell at him to boot, but—but—

Oh, admit it. You want him to get away.

"Good thing we're no longer in the subdivision, then," he replied. Fortunately for him—and Holly—Reed knew how this kind of manhunt worked, too, Caroline reflected, which meant that he didn't need her to tell him. He would know that the search would start with ground zero—the Winfield mansion—and work outward in ever-widening circles. Meanwhile, a perimeter would be established around the area. It was very possible that in the minds of her father and the others—oh, God, poor Dixon, he had to be going nuts about now—the lake would form a natural barrier to escape, and certainly they would conclude that any boat would be readily visible. The assumption would be that Reed had escaped on foot, because they would be certain that any vehicle attempting to leave the scene would have been instantly spotted and stopped. Still, the lake would be checked out just in case, and an alert would be issued advising officers to be suspicious of any type of moving vehicle. At this point, officers on the ground would be starting to search yards and outbuildings and unsecured vehicles, and blocking the roads. Next step, probably, door-to-door searches. Because Dixon and the others would not want to face the possibility that Reed, with her and Holly in tow, had gotten very far, it should be a while before the search expanded past Old Metairie.

A BOLO—be on the lookout for—with their physical descriptions would have been, or would soon be, sent out over the wire. It would be transmitted to every officer in the state, and was probably going out right about now, as a matter of fact.

The realization made her palms go all clammy with sweat on his behalf.

Not quite sure whether she was warning him or taunting him, she mentioned the BOLO to Reed. He nodded acknowledgment: his expression made it clear that the thought had already occurred to him.

"They catch us, they're gonna kill us." Fear plain in his voice, Holly stared up at the swooping helicopters as if fascinated by them. Now that the boat had passed beneath the willow-frond curtain, the helicopters were all they could see of the search. The racing police cars were blocked from their view, although the faint wail of their sirens could still be heard. Holly's face was pale in the moonlight, and he wet his lips as he looked at Reed. "Oh, Jesus, Dick, you think we're ever gonna be able to go home again?"

He said that last as if the words had been wrenched out of him. His eyes were so full of despair that Caroline found herself hurting for him. He was scarcely more than a kid, it was Christmas—

And she was very much afraid that the answer was **no**.

"I don't know. I hope so," Reed said, as calmly and matter-of-factly as if he were discussing the weather, and nodded at something in front of them that, because Holly was in the way, Caroline couldn't quite see. "When we get up there, jump up on the dock and grab this rope I'm going to throw you." He was talking to Holly. "We're getting off the lake."

"Okay." Holly took a deep breath. Caroline got the impression that Reed's response— not so much his words, but his imperturbable demeanor—had steadied him.

They pulled alongside a weathered wooden dock that looked gray as a ghost in the darkness. One long pier jutted out into the water. It had maybe twenty boats of differing types tied up on either side of it, and was obviously part of some sort of commercial operation. As Reed nosed into an empty space, Holly scrambled out. Reed immediately threw him a rope.

"Tie us to that cleat there," he directed

in a low voice as he cut the engine. As Holly obeyed, Reed got to his feet, staying low, Caroline presumed as the boat rocked, for balance. Water sloshed against the hull as the boat bumped the dock.

She stood, then staggered a little as the boat bumped the dock again. Reed was right behind her, wrapping an arm around her shoulders, steadying her before she could sit down hard, or worse. After that, she didn't make the mistake of trying to climb out unaided onto the dock, which was approximately two feet higher than the edge of the boat. With her hands fastened behind her, her balance wasn't all it could be and she had no way to catch herself if she should start to fall.

For which she blamed Reed.

"Grab her arm, Holly," Reed directed as he helped her out. Holly did, and a second later Caroline found herself standing on the dock. Reed stepped up after her, navigating the height differential with ease, the backpack slung over his shoulder.

"You want to cut my hands loose now?" she asked him. Her voice had regained its edge.

"In a minute. Come on, let's go. They've

got a night watchman. Supposedly." He caught her elbow again, hurrying her past the double line of boats toward the end of the dock. Holly walked ahead of them. Moving fast, they stepped off the wooden dock into a gravel parking area. The night seemed darker here. Caroline realized that it was because of all the tall trees ringing the parking area. The sound of their feet crunching over the gravel was all but drowned out by the piping of the tree frogs. To one side was a small, one-story frame building. It was dark and looked deserted. As they strode past it, Caroline read the sign in the large front window: Best Lake Tours and Boat Rental.

"You rented an escape boat?" she asked Reed in a hushed tone. Although why she was being so carefully quiet she didn't know: it all came down to her having trouble remembering whose side she was on.

"Place was closed when I got here. I borrowed it," he said.

"Stole it, you mean."

"I brought it back." He shrugged. "If I'd been stupid enough to drive a car to the party, we'd be in a peck of trouble right now."

"Speak for yourself."

A car waited in the farthest, darkest corner of the parking lot. It was a small four-door, inconspicuous, several years old. The shadows had kept Caroline from seeing it until they were almost upon it, and they kept her from discerning the make, model, or even the exact color now. Dark, was all she could tell.

"Every cop for miles around is going to have a description of your car, the license plate number, the whole works," Caroline pointed out as Reed pushed a button on the key ring to pop the door lock and the car beeped in response. The sound seemed abnormally loud in the quiet, and she shot an involuntary glance all around to gauge who could possibly have heard. Several smallish, warehouse-type buildings were nearby, and she thought that they must house more businesses. They were dark and seemingly deserted just like Lake Tours. Add in a number of parked vehicles and boats on trailers scattered around, and as far as she could tell the sum total of other humans within hearing distance was zilch. If there was a night

watchman, she saw no sign of him. Considering what night it was, it was reasonable to assume that he might have
been given some time off. Scoffing, she
continued, "You won't make it twenty
miles."

"What is he, stupid? That ain't his car,"
Holly said scornfully.

"You're in the back, Holly." His hand still
curled around her elbow, Reed tugged
Caroline around the vehicle, stopping when
they reached the front passenger door.
There he finally let her go.

"Whose car is it?" Caroline glanced up
at Reed in time to catch, by the flash of
the car's interior light as Holly opened the
door to slide into the backseat, him looking at one of the still safely distant helicopters that had just flown into view as it
continued to search for them. His expression was revealing, and she realized that
she had been mistaken earlier. The sudden harsh lines around his eyes and mouth
revealed both exhaustion and despera-
tion. She got the impression that he was
running on nothing but fumes, even if he
was determined not to show it. Sensing

her gaze, he looked down at her, and his face changed instantly. He was once again the determined, competent man she had been dealing with all night.

"My neighbor's. He's out of town until the middle of January, and I'm keeping an eye on his place. That includes his car. Hold still." He wrapped a hand around her wrist, and she felt the tug of downward pressure on the zip tie. A sawing sound gave her the answer: he was, she realized, cutting her free. A second later, her wrists were no longer bound, and she saw the glint of a knife as he folded it and stuck it into the front pocket of his pants. As her arms dropped to her sides, she felt the blood flowing back into her fingers and grimaced. Flexing them as they tingled and burned, she made a little sound of discomfort that came out sounding very much like a moan.

"Caroline." Reed picked up her right hand and carried it upward. She glanced at him in surprise. With the car door closed again, it was very dark where they stood, but she could see the gleam of his eyes, see his long, strong fingers gripping the slender paleness of hers, see that he was lifting her hand toward his face. To check for bruising? To see for himself if there were any visible marks on her wrist?

Even if there were, he wasn't going to be able to see them: it was just too dark.

"I really am sorry about this, cher," he told her in a low voice as she watched him, narrow-eyed. For a moment she could feel the whisper of his breath feathering over her skin. Then he pressed his lips to the inside of her poor chafed wrist.

Her heart stuttered. Her breath caught.

The feel of his mouth against her delicate inner wrist made her toes curl. It made her blood heat, and her body tighten deep inside. His lips were warm, and firm, and as they pressed against her quickening pulse she felt the hot slide of his tongue over the sensitive spot. It never even occurred to her to pull her hand away. All she could do was watch, and feel, and try to remember to breathe. It was the briefest of kisses, scarcely more than a butterfly touch, but she felt scalded by it. Branded by it.

Even as he let her go and opened the car door for her, Caroline came to a grim realization: the sizzling attraction he'd held for her all those years ago was still there, and was every bit as potent. The only difference was, she was all grown up now and knew exactly what it was that she wanted from him.

Shaken, she slid into the front passenger seat without a word.

By the time he closed her door and got behind the wheel, she had her breathing under control. Her heart rate was back to normal. The hot surge of wanting had cooled.

But the knowledge of how that barely there kiss had made her feel remained. It made her careful not to look at him, in case he should be able to see something she didn't want him to see in her eyes.

Or in case she should see something in his eyes that she was better off not knowing. Like, maybe, that he was crazy hot for her, too.

Sleeping with him is not happening. You are not that big a fool.

Much as she tried not to, she remembered the way her body had quickened when he had frisked her. His hands moving over her had been impersonal, the reflexive actions of an experienced and careful cop, and yet they'd made her soften with pleasure. They'd made her aware of him as a man. They'd made her think that under other, better circumstances, she might have turned in his arms and—

Well. Bottom line was, the last thing she needed now was for him to suspect that she still had a thing for him.

Even if she did.

"So what's the plan, Dick?" Holly asked as, with a brief reminder to his passengers to buckle their seat belts, Reed started the car. Lights off, tires crunching over the gravel, they pulled out of the lot. Caroline found herself actively welcoming Holly's presence. Until she was able to get a firm grip on her common sense where Reed was concerned, Holly served as a useful barrier between them. Out of the corner of her eye, she saw Holly flick a look at her as he added, "When are we going to trade her for Ant?"

Both were questions that she would like to have answered. Realizing just how very tired she was as the plush cloth of the bucket seat allowed her to relax for the first time in hours, Caroline discreetly opened her flak vest for comfort's sake as she looked at Reed, too.

"Once we get you squared away, I'll deal

with getting Ant back," Reed replied. A downward flicker of his eyelashes seemed to track the progress of her zipper. But then his attention was back on the road, and she wasn't sure whether or not he'd actually been watching her at all. The narrow country lane they were driving along veered away from the lake and turned from dirt into pavement after about half a mile. At that point, Reed turned on the headlights: he was right to do so, Caroline decided. The car was far easier to spot with the lights on, but there was no way to know who was inside unless they got pulled over. And if they were seen running without lights, well, the chase would be on. Although all she could now see of any ongoing search activity was the faint glow on the horizon that marked the mansion they were speeding away from, Caroline had no doubt that their continued freedom was a precarious thing. Her father would be breathing fire and deploying all available resources. Every law enforcement officer for miles around would be pulling out all the stops to find them. The mere thought of the manhunt that was being launched made her chest tighten with anxiety. If they

were stopped, she was as sure as it was
possible to be that Reed would resist arrest. And in the firefight that would almost
certainly ensue, it was very likely that he
would be killed. The mere thought of it
made her sick, so she did her best to ban-
ish the horrifying image from her mind as
Reed continued, "Then we'll see what we
can do to fix this mess."

"What do you mean, get me squared
away?" Holly sounded suspicious.

Reed flicked a look at him through the
rearview mirror. "I'm sending you . . . out
of town. Somewhere safe. I'll catch up with
you again when I get Ant."

"What? No!" The protest was accompa-
nied by the smacking of Holly's palm
against his door. The sharp sound might
have made Caroline jump if she hadn't
been so tired. "Hell, no!"

"I'm not asking you, I'm telling you."
Reed's voice was flat. "There's no room
for discussion. That's what's going to happen, so deal with it."

Holly leaned forward so that his face was
almost between the headrests, almost
even with hers and Reed's. He glared at
Reed. "Hey, Dick, guess what? You don't

got no right to tell me what to do. I'm a grown-ass man, and—"

"Hey, grown-ass man, who just saved your ass?" The sideways glance Reed shot Holly in return glinted in a way that told Caroline that this was a battle Holly had no chance of winning. "You want to be responsible for getting you and your little brother out of this alive? You do, say the word, and I'll be glad to stand back and let you have at it."

"I ain't running away. No damn way. It's my fault Ant's in this and—"

"The best thing you can do for Ant is let me get you the hell out of here," Reed replied. "As long as they don't have you, they won't hurt Ant. He's their insurance you'll keep your mouth shut."

About what, exactly? The question gnawed at Caroline. She narrowed her eyes at the pair of them, but didn't bother to ask. She knew there wouldn't be an answer. And she was growing more tired by the second. Way too tired to even try to think through the possibilities.

Holly didn't reply. The sudden droop to his eyelids and the sullen tightening of his mouth told Caroline that he knew when he

was defeated. His thwarted expression reminded her of how young he really was.

"So how you gonna **send** me somewhere?" he asked after a minute. "You
mean, drive me there?"

"By now the BOLO will be everywhere.
They'll be patrolling the expressways,"
Caroline reminded Reed, voicing the
warning simply because she couldn't help
herself.

"I'm going to get you there," Reed told
Holly. "Never mind how."

"I got a right to know what the plan is,"
Holly protested. "Especially since it involves
me. Ain't nobody else around here getting
sent **out of town,** and—"

"Would you stop going on about your
rights?" Reed gave Holly an exasperated
look through the mirror. "Caroline's going
back, remember? When I trade her for Ant,
I don't want her to be able to tell anybody
where you went. Or how you got there. Or
who might have helped you get there."

"Oh," Holly said, abashed.

"Yeah, **oh**." Reed was starting to sound a
little testy. Like her, Caroline reflected, he
had to be dead tired.

"Hey," Caroline said. She almost added,

"I can keep my mouth shut." Then she remembered: **I'm not on their side**.

I wouldn't tell me anything, either.

"Never mind," she added lamely.

They were nearing an intersection, Caroline saw as the car slowed. A single stoplight dangling from an overhead wire showed red. The road they were going to be turning onto was a four-lane highway. It was well lit but deserted, and the sight of it raised Caroline's anxiety level all over again.

It was just the kind of road on which they could expect to encounter a patrol car.

Glancing quickly at Reed, she reminded herself that he would know that as surely as she did, then reminded herself again that she was not on their side, and resolutely kept her mouth shut.

An expressway overpass with a cloverleaf of entry and exit ramps and, positioned to take advantage of them, a cluster of fast food restaurants, gas stations, and a truck stop, were located about half a mile up the highway. From their glowing lights, at least a couple of the establishments seemed to be open. She had just noticed them when Reed pulled onto the shoulder maybe a hundred feet short of the red light and stopped the car.

"What's up?" Sounding nervous, Holly asked the question that rose to Caroline's mind, too.

Reed's hands tightened around the wheel as he looked at Caroline. "I can't have you seeing where Holly goes. Which means I have a choice: I can handcuff you to a tree over there in that little wooded area and leave you all by yourself in the dark until I get back; I can blindfold you, tie you up, and throw something over you in the backseat and hope that nobody notices you; or I can put you in the trunk."

"What? Are you kidding me?" Caroline saw that he was dead serious and glared at him. "How about I just close my eyes and promise not to peek?"

Reed opened his door and got out without replying. By the time he reached her door, she was already all but certain that she knew what he had decided, and recognized, too, that it was the simplest and probably the safest choice.

Didn't mean she had to like it. Or him.

Which she expressed to him in no uncertain terms as he pulled her out of the car.

CHAPTER ELEVEN

"You gotta get Ant out safe." Holly couldn't stand still. He rocked back and forth on the AF1 high-top sneakers that were his pride and joy. His face looked haggard beneath the hazy glow of the halogen lamps that illuminated the parking lot. His arms crossed and uncrossed. He licked his lips. His eyes darted everywhere, touching on the nearby Dumpster, on the nearly impenetrable darkness of the field stretching off behind it, on the unlit golden arches of the closed-for-Christmas McDonald's next door. He was scared, and it showed.

Hell, Reed knew the feeling. Only he hoped that in his case it **didn't** show.

"I will," he promised. He'd almost said, **I'll do my best,** but he figured that there was too much truth in that for Holly to handle at the moment.

The two of them were at the truck stop, standing in the shadow of the eighteen-wheeler that was getting ready to take Holly all the way down to Tampico, Mexico, an eighteen-hour drive. Corbell Trucking Company was the name painted across its trailer. Tonight the rig was hauling farm machinery, but it just so happened to come equipped with a compartment in which, say, something that the border agents didn't need to know about could be tucked away. On this run, that something was going to be Holly. When Reed had made the arrangements, he'd thought he would be going down to Mexico in the truck to-night, too. That was after he'd come up with his plan for getting Holly out of jail and saving his own sorry ass, but before he'd heard about Ant. Since then, he'd been making it up as he went along. What it had come down to was, he needed to get Holly the hell out of there, but he couldn't just abandon Ant to his fate. So he was sending Holly alone, and going back for Ant.

After that, everything was on the table.

He'd thought that if he got Holly out, Ant, left behind, would be safe. He'd gotten the younger Bayard squared away, hidden in plain sight with Father Grayson's Kids at Risk shelter program at St. Anna's. It was one of the last things he had done before heading for the Winfield mansion. It had been hard saying good-bye to the kid for what he'd known might be a long time, if not forever, due to needing to get Holly out of jail before they killed him. Which Reed was as sure as it was possible to be would have happened before the sun rose. If they (and he still wasn't precisely sure who they were) had taken Holly, it was because they knew he had been at the cemetery, and leaving alive an eyewitness to four homicides just wasn't smart. Knowing that Holly wouldn't want to leave his brother behind and that Ant would be lost without Holly, Reed had even thought about bringing the thirteen-year-old with him to the mansion. But at the time, he hadn't been

sure he wasn't going on a suicide mission.
And even if he survived and succeeded
in getting Holly out, involving Ant in the
crimes he was preparing to commit just
wasn't something he could do.

Reuniting the brothers at a later date
had been a vague part of the plan. Nothing concrete, just an intention lurking in
the back of his mind to be acted on later if
circumstances permitted. What he hadn't
considered was that the bastards, whoever they were, would know enough to go
after Ant.

Miscalculation. But then, he hadn't had
a lot of time to think things through. After
finishing up at the crime scene at the cemetery, going home, and rigorously quizzing
Holly and Ant, then enlarging the photos
from Elizabeth Townes' stolen phone on
his laptop so he could get a better look,
he'd been intrigued enough to launch his
own private investigation just as soon as
he had snagged a few hours of sleep. The
pictures were too dark and the angles
were wrong: none of the faces were iden-
tifiable. But what he could see had been
electrifying. To protect Holly and Ant, he'd
kept things on the down low, telling no one

what he was working on as he talked to his tapestry of street contacts, checked surveillance cameras from establishments near the cemetery—which meant a couple of hours spent speeding through middle-of-the-night video from at least twenty cameras—and pulled the files of recent murders with the same MO.

Having uncovered enough to make him deeply concerned that the big bad that seemed to be going down involved at least one if not more NOPD officers, he'd done what he thought was in the best interests of the department and taken his suspicions straight to Col. Martin Wallace, the police superintendent. The one thing he'd been careful to do was keep Holly and Ant totally out of it: he hadn't mentioned their names, hadn't revealed their involvement to anyone, not even the superintendent. His discretion hadn't helped: somehow they'd smoked out Holly and, later, Ant. If he could do it over again—hell, he would have just left the whole damned case alone, whether it was the right thing to do or not. Then he thought of the bodies in the cemetery and sighed: averting his eyes and pretending the lives of four people hadn't been violently taken just wasn't something he could do. He was a cop, damn it.

Once Holly had finally succeeded in rousing Reed's suspicions that one or more individuals in the department might have been involved, there'd been no going back. Where he'd made his mistake was in going straight to the superintendent and revealing what he knew before he had nailed down the names, dates, and places, so at least he'd know who the key players were. As it was, all he knew was that he'd gone to Wallace and two hours later his whole life had blown up in his face. He should have waited, he should have made sure of what he was dealing with, and he should have gotten Holly and Ant safely out of the way. But then, hindsight was always twenty-twenty.

All he could do now was play the hand he had dealt himself.

"I can't just up and go. Ant don't have nobody but me." There was real anguish in Holly's eyes. He uncrossed his arms long enough to chew a ragged fingernail.

"He has me, too." Reed heard the grimness in his own voice. It was there because much as he hated to face it, he was telling the truth: sometime over the course of the last few hours, he'd mentally shouldered the full mantle of responsibility for Ant, and Holly, too. Whether he liked it or not, they were his problem now.

"I should've left it alone. If I hadn't gone poking around in things, this wouldn't be happening. It's all my fault," Holly said, his voice thick with remorse.

"Yeah, well, maybe next time I tell you to mind your own damned business you'll listen," Reed replied. Then he relented. "It's not your fault. Hell, if it'd been my mama got killed, I'd have done the same thing."

"Somebody must've seen me following those dudes to the cemetery. That's all I can figure out, 'cause I swear I never told nobody nothing about being there."

Walking over to the truck stop from the car, Reed had grilled Holly pretty hard on that point. After witnessing the killings in the cemetery, Holly had stayed the night at Reed's house and told him everything he knew, including every rumor he'd ever heard that might have the slightest bearing on what was going on. The only thing

Holly left out, Reed had thought at the time with an inward roll of his eyes, was the possibility that a UFO had descended over the city to drop off alien assassins. Holly insisted that he and Ant had kept quiet as clams and gone about their lives as usual.

He'd still been reeling with shock when they'd arrested Holly on that trumped-up charge. Reed had known then, if he'd still been harboring any doubts at all, that what Holly had been saying all along had at least some basis in fact: it was the cops (some cops? a rogue few? Couldn't be the whole damned department out there killing people, or else he'd been totally left out of the loop). The most conservative read on the situation said that somebody on the police force was involved in killing the four victims in the cemetery. According to Holly, cops had killed Magnolia as well. From what Reed had uncovered in his own very quick, very cursory investigation, within the last six months there had been at least four other murder cases involving at least thirteen victims with the exact same MO as Magnolia's and the one in the cemetery. Meaning that whoever had killed the four in the cemetery had probably killed Magnolia, her dealer, and the thirteen other victims as well. In other words, a cop or cops had been involved in the murders of at least nineteen victims. That he knew of so far. Why? Who the hell knew? Who exactly was involved? Who the hell knew that, either? Although Superintendent Wallace's reaction to what Reed had told him made it a pretty sure bet that he at least knew what was going on, which meant that this thing was more widespread, and went a lot higher up, than he would ever have believed possible.

He hadn't foreseen it, any of it. He'd been caught flat-footed, unable to do anything but watch and try to stay one jump ahead of the fallout as his life, and Holly's and Ant's, too, got blown to shit.

Reed said, "You sure you didn't catch a name on those cops who arrested you?"

Holly had already told him his version (sanitized, Reed was sure) of how it had gone down: he'd been hanging with a group of friends on Dumaine just after dark on Christmas Eve when a squad car had pulled over and ordered them all to the ground. They'd been searched, and one of the cops had held up a plastic bag with two crack rocks in it that he claimed to have found in Holly's pocket. That was just a straight-up, fucking-ass lie, Holly had indignantly told Reed, which he believed, knowing Holly's proclivities didn't run to crack. The cops had been rough and menacing, and by the time he'd wound up in The Swamp, Holly had been convinced that he was being set up to die.

Reed believed that, too. If he hadn't, he would have gone the lawyer route that Caroline had suggested.

"I guess they forgot to introduce themselves." Even under the circumstances, Holly's sarcasm made a corner of Reed's mouth twitch up into the briefest of unexpected smiles. "I told you: they was cops. Blue uniforms. One big, burly dude with dark hair. One big, burly dude who was bald." He shrugged. "That's all I know."

"They must have been looking for you." Reed had come to that conclusion the minute he'd heard what had happened, and Holly had further reinforced it by reporting that they'd let the others go. The names of the arresting officers should be in a number of places, including the arrest report and the jail admissions file. Reed vowed to find them: identifying those officers would at least be a place to start.

Holly tugged nervously on one of the silver hoops in his ears. His voice was full of remorse. "I should've stayed out of it. I should've listened to you."

"That's a first," Reed said, responding to the uncharacteristic admission. His eyes ran over Holly. The kid looked like he was on the verge of coming unglued. "Quit beating yourself up. You witnessed a crime. The fault lies with the people who committed it."

"Sounds real good, except you notice we're the ones out here running for our lives."

That acerbic observation left Reed with no counterargument to make. "You got me there."

"What if they kill Ant?"

"Like I said, the only way they're going to kill Ant is if they catch you and me and kill us first. Right now he's their ticket to keeping us quiet." Reed didn't share the thought that was worrying him most: if whoever had set the dogs on him and Holly had taken Ant—which he was all but

100 percent sure was the case—and they found out that Ant had been at that cemetery, too, Ant would become a target just as much as he and Holly now were. Never mind that he was a thirteen-year-old kid and as far as Reed knew hadn't even witnessed the actual murders. He assumed that their purpose in taking Ant had been to make sure he and Holly kept their mouths shut, but in the end it would be stupid to let Ant live. Ant might not have seen everything, but he had seen enough to serve as a corroborating witness for Holly. The thought made Reed's hands curl into fists. It was not, however, something he needed to share with Holly. "Which is why you're getting on this damned truck and getting the hell out of here. Now."

The big rig was parked between him and Holly and the back of the building, its position designed to block the security camera mounted on the corner of the convenience-store-cum-diner-cum-shower-facility from seeing anyone climbing into the passenger side, as Holly was about to do. The truck's driver, Julio Perez, was already behind the wheel, waiting for Holly to get in. Its engine was running, the sound a low-grade rumble. The smell of diesel exhaust tainted the air. Elsa Casta, the manager of the truck stop, waited nearby, staring off toward the McDonald's, absorbed in her own thoughts. Like a lot of people Reed came across in the course of his job, she had an elasticized view of what was against the law. Mostly, Reed had learned to leave the little fish alone and concentrate on the big transgressors. Elsa was one of those little fish, with her finger in many illegal pies but no violence or viciousness to her. Short, plump, and fiftyish, her black hair streaked with gray and pulled back into a bun, Elsa thought the sun rose and set on Reed since he had saved her idiot nineteen-year-old son from being murdered by the gang of drug smugglers he'd ripped off, then arranged for him to testify against the ringleaders in return for probation. Now twenty-five, the son was the manager of a grocery store in Houston and had never, as far as Reed knew, stepped outside the boundaries of the law since. A lot of criminal types—drug smugglers, gun smugglers, illegal immigrant smugglers, just to name a few—came through the truck stop, and Elsa knew them all. She had made the arrangements to have Perez and his truck waiting to pick them up after Reed, knowing that he and Holly were going to need a fast, anonymous way out of the country once he'd gotten Holly out of The Swamp, had contacted her earlier.

"Here." Reed handed Holly a wallet that contained, among other things, a fake ID—they were ridiculously easy to get if you knew where to go—and five hundred dollars in cash. Because the banks were closed on Christmas Eve and there was a daily cash withdrawal limit, the money was part of the two thousand that was all Reed had been able to get out of his bank account via the ATM when he'd strode out of police headquarters after his confrontation with Internal Affairs and the superintendent.

"When are you and Ant coming?" Holly thrust the wallet into the pocket of his hoodie. The way Holly's eyes clung to his, Reed was reminded that to Holly and his brother he had become the answer to all their problems.

The weight of their faith in him felt almost tangible.

"As soon as I can get us there. Not more than a couple of days, max." Reed pulled open the truck's passenger door and motioned Holly toward it. "Somebody will be waiting to pick you up at the other end. Go."

Holly hesitated, looked at him, and nodded. Then he got into the eighteen-wheeler's cab and Reed shut the door. A moment later, with a hiss and a rumble, the truck got under way.

As the rig pulled around the building on its way to the highway out front, Reed was already near the Dumpster handing over the thousand dollars in cash he'd promised Elsa. She might profess to love him, but she was also a businesswoman. Reed understood: that was how the world worked.

With Holly on the move, and with the groceries Elsa had put into a plastic bag hanging over his arm, Reed walked away into the dark, appreciating the obscuring shadows as they enfolded him, not wanting even Elsa to know too much about how he had gotten there and how he was leaving. Wary of the security cameras that were everywhere these days, he'd made a circuitous approach to the truck stop, which had involved pulling the Mazda into the field that ran up on the establishment from behind. He'd left the car parked there in the dark, with Caroline inside.

She was in the backseat, cuffed and belted in. No blindfold necessary because he'd come up with the easy solution of facing the car the other way around, so she was looking out toward a whole lot of nothing—more empty fields, woods, and swampland, all shrouded by darkness— rather than the truck stop. He'd had to put duct tape over her mouth again, though, just in case. He'd hated doing it, but he couldn't risk his and Holly's life on the hope that left alone she wouldn't start to scream her head off. She'd hated it, too, as she had made abundantly clear, but the bottom line was he just didn't trust her enough to stay silent if, say, a cop car should pull into view. He'd known that he wasn't going to be long, a fact that had mitigated some of his guilt, but when he'd shared that with her, it hadn't seemed to appease her at all. Last he'd seen of her, she'd been rigid with fury, but as he had told her, it was better than leaving her tied to a tree—who knew what kind of creature might come upon her in the dark? It was also better than putting her in the trunk of his car, which would have been quick and easy, and pretty tempting, considering the problem she posed. She would have been safe, and she only would have been in there for maybe ten minutes. But even for so short a period, the trunk would have been airless and cramped and miserable. Then he'd started thinking that if things went south, if maybe Elsa betrayed him or a stray squad car should spot him or anything at all untoward happened that ended up with him being incapacitated or dead, it might be a long time before anyone thought to look in the trunk of a nondescript car parked at the edge of a field.

She could die.

For the fraction of a second that he'd entertained it, that thought had stopped him in his tracks. **That** he wasn't about to chance.

At least if he got killed at the truck stop and she was fastened into the backseat, when the sun came up in the morning someone would see her there.

Like keeping Holly and Ant alive, getting

Caroline home in one piece was something that he was prepared to give his life to do.

Not many people meant much to him anymore. Holly and Ant did. Seemed like Caroline did, too.

The instant he'd heard her husky voice with its distinctive little rasp over the phone line, he'd recognized it. Even before she had identified herself, he'd been instantly transported back ten years. For a minute there, it had been as if he could see her: seventeen years old, succulent as a just-ripe peach, offering him anything he cared to take, nakedly hero-worshipping him.

For just a minute there he'd wished, fiercely, that he could be that brash young man again.

A lot had changed since then. **He** had changed since then. And she had grown up.

As he strode through the waist-high weeds that clogged the field, Reed found himself revisiting the impulse that had caused him to lift her hand to his mouth. It had been meant as a way of apologizing, of wordlessly saying sorry for any pain he might have caused her. As soon as his mouth had touched her skin, though, he'd known that he had made a mistake. Fleeting as it was, that brush of his lips against her wrist had turned into something different from what he'd meant—something combustible.

Jesus, she turns me on.

Not a news flash, he told himself drily. He'd known that for ten years now. He'd seen her around, after that long-ago summer. Found out that contrary to what he would have expected, she'd become a cop. Caught occasional glimpses of her, spoken to her a few times in passing. Been aware that the sexy, sassy, pretty girl who had tempted him had grown up into a beautiful, self-possessed woman. Heard the guys talk about the superintendent's hubba-hubba daughter, make crude jokes about how much they'd like to get it on with her. That last had irritated the hell out of him, every single time.

Bottom line was, he'd always been aware of her.

When he'd cut the zip tie, and she'd shaken her hands and come out with that tiny pained moan, he'd known he had hurt her and his conscience had smote him.

Even though he knew he'd only done what he had to do to survive, he'd still felt like the biggest bastard alive. The protectiveness she had engendered in him all those years ago was still there, he'd discovered, and still strong. So, too, was the sizzling physical chemistry between them that when she'd been seventeen he had forced himself to fight like hell. Now there was no reason to fight it except that his life, which he'd finally managed to halfway patch back together after the accident, had just spectacularly imploded. Whatever he might feel for Caroline, there was nowhere to take it. After tonight, if he even had a future, it wasn't anything that she was going to be able to be a part of. When being on the run for the rest of his life seemed like the best of outcomes, his future was the opposite of bright.

He'd forced Caroline to come with him tonight, meant to use her to get Ant back. He couldn't see that he had any other options, but that was as far as he meant to take it.

What he was putting all his energy into—what he had to put all his energy into—was surviving the night.

Knowing that she was as attracted to him as he was hot for her was what was driving him a little insane. It was something he needed to strive to forget.

Forgetting was damned hard.

He hadn't missed the way her pulse had jumped when he had pressed his lips to her wrist. Just like he hadn't missed the way she looked at him, or how her nipples had hardened and seemed to push into his palms when he'd run his hands over her breasts as he'd frisked her, or the sexy way her body had curled into his chest when he'd carried her in his arms, or how round and firm her ass had felt nestled against his crotch—

Goddamn it. Stop right there.

Slamming the mental door on that line of thinking, he cast his eyes up at the velvety black sky, eyed the full yellow moon that kept being partially obscured by a stampede of racing dark clouds, did a lightning review of all possible ways he might die in the next twenty-four hours or so, and finally succeeded in pushing the last erotic image of Caroline out of his mind.

Forget about sex. What he needed to

be focusing on was keeping himself, Holly, and Ant alive.

The question was, how to do that.

What about running to the nearest local TV station, or placing a call to CNN, and spilling everything he knew, or thought he knew, to some eager reporter, with the promise of a look at those pictures Holly had taken as a chaser?

For a moment, Reed brightened, seeing a possible way out. He had to be a hot topic on the news channels right now. Suppose he called one, or waltzed into a TV station, and offered them an exclusive about why he'd taken most of New Orleans' top brass hostage. Once the media heard about the murders, all hell would break loose. The NOPD would be investigated. Questions would be asked, and answers demanded, on what would probably balloon into a nationwide stage. With the spotlight turned their way, he and Holly and Ant would be safe.

Or would they be? The more Reed thought of running to the media, the more pitfalls occurred to him. First, whoever was holding Ant would almost certainly kill him the instant anything about this started to come out to the public. Why wouldn't they? If they killed the kid, they had only to dispose of the body and disavow all knowledge of him. On the other hand, if they didn't kill him and the media found him, Ant would sing like a bird, spilling everything he knew to the cameras.

If he were to put himself in the shoes of whoever was holding Ant, leaving out his own personal aversion for harming kids, the smart action to take was a no-brainer: kill Ant.

It was like Nixon with the tapes: if he'd burned them, he probably would not have been the first American president to resign, but instead would have ridden out the storm that was Watergate and finished out his second term.

Moral of the story for bad guys: when in doubt, dispose of the problem.

Reed was as sure as it was possible to be that after thinking things through for themselves, whoever was holding Ant would come to that same conclusion. Ant would be safe for precisely as long as his captors thought they had more to gain by keeping him alive.

With Ant dead, if Holly started to talk

before they could capture and silence him, they could paint Holly as a street thug, a gang member, a drug user with a rap sheet just trying to make trouble for the cops. Nobody would believe Holly. Hell, if Reed hadn't known Holly, and the situation, he wouldn't believe the kid, either.

Then there was Reed himself. Looking at it objectively, he knew talking to the media wasn't going to work any better for him. There was an excellent chance that whoever was calling the shots on this— right now, his money was on Superintendent Wallace, but he was open to other possibilities—would be able to spin it so that Reed, who had admittedly committed an impressive number of felonies in the last six or so hours, came out looking like a criminal, a nut job, a dirty cop with an axe to grind. They might claim he had Photoshopped the pictures. They might claim— hell, they might claim anything.

He might find himself arrested, tried, convicted, and thrown in jail for the rest of his life.

He might find himself shot on sight, or later, out of sight.

Holly had already been arrested for

possessing crack cocaine. Reed knew that was a lie. How many others would believe it was a lie, though? Would a TV reporter believe it? Would a judge and jury believe it?

Reed rated the odds that anyone would believe Holly was telling the truth as at best fifty-fifty.

Not great odds when you're gambling with your life.

So, going to the media as a solution was probably out.

What did that leave?

Not much.

His department? In the wake of the superintendent's betrayal, everyone was suspect. Even his partner, Terry—Reed couldn't be sure. He couldn't be sure of anyone anymore, or anything. Besides, they were all hunting for him now. Not just the NOPD, but all the cops from the surrounding parishes, too. After tonight, even the cops who were innocent of any involvement in the events in the cemetery would, best-case scenario, arrest him, worst-case scenario, shoot him.

Brows knit, glancing thoughtfully past the golden arches without really register-

ing them, Reed could see the expressway,
see the concrete cloverleaf curving up toward it. An eighteen-wheeler chugging up
the entrance ramp caught his eye. Impossible to make out any identifying marks at
this distance, but Reed was almost positive that it was the one Holly was in. He
watched it gain the top of the entrance
ramp, pull out into sparse traffic, and accelerate away, keeping his eyes on it until
he couldn't see it any longer. Then he blew
out a long, slow breath of relief. **Go with
God, kid**. With Holly now almost certainly
speeding out of harm's way, the situation
became slightly less dire. One rescued,
two (including himself) to go. By tomorrow
night, the kid should be safely out of the
reach of the not-quite-long-enough arm of
the New Orleans law. Reed felt some
of the tension that had been keeping his
muscles as tight as wound springs start
to ease.

For now, the broad outline of the plan
was to get his hands on Ant, get himself
and Ant away from New Orleans, and at
some point try to figure out exactly what
the hell they'd all gotten mixed up in.

Whatever this was, it was too big for

him to tackle alone. He was going to need help. The problem was where to find it.

Two days ago, when he'd gone rushing out of headquarters after his fight with the superintendent, when he'd known he had trouble on his hands but had not yet realized just how extreme it was going to get, he'd thought of hightailing it straight to the FBI with what he knew.

The problem with that had struck him almost immediately: the local feds were tight with a lot of the NOPD guys.

A little too tight for him to chance it, he decided.

But if not the media, or the feds, then who? Who was left? Who could he turn to? **What it boils down to is, who can I trust?**

It was like a game show. Catch was, get it wrong and you and people you care about die.

He'd already gambled on DeBlassis, e-mailing his former partner copies of the pictures Holly had taken, along with a brief summary of the facts as he knew them, asking him to get the pictures enlarged and clarified and then just sit tight: he would be in touch. For caution's sake, he'd used his neighbor's computer and e-mail account, because he'd known that one of the first things anybody looking for him would do was check his e-mail and phone records.

Possible issues with what he had done abounded: DeBlassis wouldn't recognize the sender's name, and might not open the message for a while; not being one to keep in touch, he hadn't sent an e-mail to DeBlassis since the guy had moved to Boston, which meant he had no idea if DeBlassis might have changed to another e-mail address; and since it was Christmas, he couldn't be sure that DeBlassis was even home or checking his e-mail.

And those were just the problems he could think of off the top of his head.

Reed was sifting through a mental list of other people he might possibly be able to turn to for help when he saw what looked like a dozen squad cars streaking into view up on the expressway, racing west from the direction of the city. The strobo-scopic bursts of red light hit his eyes a split second before he heard the first faint shrieks of the approaching sirens. Horror pumped a fresh jolt of adrenaline through his veins.

The cars were speeding down I-10 in the same direction in which the truck carrying Holly was traveling.

Were we spotted? Did Elsa sell us out? Did the driver sell us out? Jesus, are they going after Holly?

Or maybe the cop cars were heading for the truck stop, coming after **him**.

If so, he didn't have much time.

Breaking into a dead run as the volume of the sirens escalated into a full scream, he dodged around the enormous pile of dirt that came complete with a backhoe parked on the edge of it that stood between the car and the truck stop—he'd parked behind the dirt pile as an extra precaution, both in case Caroline should somehow manage to swivel around enough so she could look out the rear window, and in case random headlights from a vehicle pulling into or out of the truck stop should pierce the darkness of the field and illuminate the Mazda—and was almost upon the hazy patch of denser darkness that was the Mazda before he was really able to see it.

For a second, as he peered at the car, he couldn't quite make out what he was seeing.

Then as he sprinted closer he realized that the front passenger door was open, and the slender pale things emerging from it were a pair of long bare legs.

Caroline's long bare legs.

She was escaping, just as two shrieking cop cars separated themselves from the pack on the interstate, peeled rubber down the cloverleaf, and, bubbletops revolving wildly, raced toward the truck stop.

CHAPTER TWELVE

Caroline was so mad she could spit.

Her hands were cuffed behind her back. As he'd clapped the bracelets on her, Reed had explained—not particularly apologetically—that he was fresh out of zip ties.

The cuffs were actually more comfortable than a zip tie, which she was going to remember for future reference in case she ever had a choice of restraints when arresting someone. At least this time her hands hadn't gone numb.

Didn't matter. She was still pissed.

If Reed thought she was going to take

being held as his captive in stride, he was wrong.

He'd dragged her around to the rear passenger door, given her a chance to shed her flak vest and windbreaker, which for comfort's sake she had done, then cuffed her hands behind her back, sat her down, and belted her in. Then he had driven for several more minutes, cut the lights, pulled into a pitch-dark field, and after bumping across it for a couple of hundred yards, parked. He was being careful, even unscrewing the interior lightbulb so opening the door wouldn't create a flash. After he and Holly had gotten out, he'd shed the SWAT jacket he had been wearing and turned it inside out, hiding the bright white lettering. Then he put it on again, so it looked like a plain black jacket. She guessed he needed the jacket to conceal his shoulder holster, which she glimpsed bisecting the gleaming white of his shirt. That done, he had reached inside the car and yanked on her seat belt so it tightened into rigidity, pinning her against the seat. Then he'd told her to sit tight, he'd be right back.

And she'd told him to stick it where the sun don't shine.

Which had made him smile—right before he'd plastered a strip of duct tape over her mouth.

Which had made her madder than she already was. Call it mad times ten.

She really, really hated having duct tape over her mouth. More than she hated being handcuffed. More than she hated being clamped by a locked seat belt into immobility. More than she hated being **kidnapped**.

Duct tape tasted like plastic and glue. It made her lips dry. It made her skin burn. It made her anxious. It hampered her breathing (or at least, it could potentially hamper her breathing, so that was pretty much the same thing). Having her mouth sealed shut made her think of all the things that could go wrong while she only had one orifice through which to take in air: What happened if she choked? What happened if she had an allergy attack? The possibilities for something to go wrong struck her as endless.

So when the opportunity to escape had presented itself, she had seized it. That had happened after she had tried wriggling in an effort to give herself more room, which had only made the seat belt cinch even tighter. Furious, frustrated, and now actively uncomfortable, she'd had a **to-hell-with-this** moment and vowed to free herself from the damned thing or die trying. Scooting sideways an inch at a time, she'd strained to reach the seat belt latch and finally succeeded. After that, she'd only had to stretch her fingers out over the plastic casing and push down—

Hah!

Once the seat belt released its stranglehold on her, the rest should have been easy, right? Not so much. Caroline tried opening the back doors with no luck. It had taken her a moment to realize that Reed must have engaged the childproof locks.

Which left the front doors.

Turns out, climbing into the front seat was surprisingly awkward without the use of her hands.

She managed it.

By this time, she was hell-bent on getting out of the damned car.

Besides giving Reed a figurative one-fingered salute, the object was to persuade him that he could trust her. She was going to wait for him, sitting on the car's hood.

Message: **I could have escaped if I'd wanted to. Instead, I stayed. That means you can trust me. So tell me what's going on and let me try to help you, you dolt.**

For however long she had before something terrible happened, she was going to work to persuade him to give himself up.

Mad as she was at him, she didn't want him to die.

She was horribly afraid that was how this was going to end.

Her reasons for staying weren't just personal, either. Bottom line was, she was a cop. She wasn't entirely certain what Reed and Holly and Ant had gotten themselves mixed up in, but she was as sure as it was possible to be that a grave injustice was going down. She didn't believe Reed was a dirty cop or that he'd taken a bribe, and she didn't believe that he would have done something as spectacularly criminal (and boneheaded) as take a good number of the city's VIPs hostage without an extremely compelling reason. If she walked away and left Reed to his own devices, it was unlikely that justice would ever be served because the truth would die with Reed.

She could not just stand by and allow him—and Holly and his brother—to be killed.

Not if it was in her power to prevent it. From where she was standing, it was looking like she was the only chance they had.

She'd sworn an oath to serve and protect, and for what it was worth she'd meant it.

So she was going to stay and get to the bottom of whatever the hell this was.

The first step, obviously, was to persuade Reed to confide in her. Which she was hoping her non-escape would facilitate.

Once she was safely in the front passenger seat, Caroline became aware of the distant wail of police sirens. The sound caught her attention, perked her up, made her heartbeat quicken, because as much as she reminded herself that she wasn't on Reed's side, her body didn't seem to get it. It reacted with an instant jolt of adrenaline to the specter of pursuit. She knew that as the victim, she was being searched for, but it **felt** like she was being hunted. Breathless from the exertions involved in actually getting from the back to the front seat, she curled her legs beneath her for height and squirmed around until she could grasp the door handle. With a real sense of triumph she finally got the door open. Without the cushioning effect of the car around her to block the sound, the scream of sirens split the air. A shiver ran down her spine as she registered how close the police cruisers had to be. They sounded like they were no more than a block away and flying directly toward her . . .

Staring fruitlessly in the direction from which the sounds were coming—tall, back-lit black shapes including a hill of dirt approximately ten feet high and an abandoned backhoe blocked her view—she swung her legs out of the car.

Maybe Reed and Holly had been spotted. Maybe they had been captured. The prospect was electrifying, and not in a good way.

No shots had been fired. Or at least, if they had been she hadn't heard them.

She was willing to bet money that no way was Reed going down without a fight.

In a screwed-up way, realizing that was almost calming: if he'd been captured or killed, she would have heard gunfire.

Standing up, nostrils flaring as she sucked in the night air that felt still and almost heavy now, as if rain were on the way, Caroline craned her neck toward the onrushing wall of sound that was the sirens as she tried to guess what was happening. Her brow furrowed in reaction as the wailing screamed closer and closer— then stopped abruptly. She blinked in surprise. Somebody had cut them off. **Why?** That was the question that made her stomach tense. It was followed almost instantly by another, even more urgent one: **Where are Reed and Holly?** Were they running? captured? hiding? None of the above? Of course from where she was she couldn't see anything that might give her a clue. Pushing the door shut with a hip, she turned to squint in the direction in which Reed and Holly had disappeared. She was frowning toward the pale glow of the lights of the businesses that were blocked from her view by the dirt hill when she saw, out of the corner of her eye, a blur of movement as someone—something—came racing toward her through the dark from only a few yards away.

Her heart jumped. Her eyes went wide. Skittering backward, she would have screamed if she could have. Instead she turned to run, only to have hard arms grab her around the waist and shoulders and yank her back against a strong male body.

Reed! She knew him the instant he touched her, had known his identity almost from the instant she'd seen the blur of movement, really, she realized. Her first surge of fright at the charging unknown figure had been instinctive, and now it gave way to surprise and anger—and, yes, more than a little relief.

At least he hadn't been captured. Or worse.

"Mmmm." Her expression of outraged protest at being grabbed was muted by the tape.

"Don't make another sound," he growled in her ear, dragging her farther back into the darkness behind the dirt hill. From squirming impotently in his hold, Caroline went perfectly still as his urgency transmitted itself to her. The sirens added up to cops nearby. Holly—she couldn't see Holly.

Where was he? Had the kid been arrested? Had Reed gotten him safely away?
The duct tape made it impossible to ask,
so all she could do was speculate wildly,
and worry.

Whatever Reed might have done, Holly
was innocent of the crimes that had precipitated this.

"Squad car," Reed muttered, hauling
her with him into the shadow of the backhoe left beside the dirt hill. A plastic bag
filled with hard items hung over his arm.
The bag crackled faintly as whatever was
inside knocked against her hip: cans, she
thought. With Reed's arms wrapped tight
around her, she was pressed so closely
against him that she could feel the heat of
his body—and the too-rapid rise and fall
of his chest. She could feel his tension in
the rock hardness of the muscles impris-
oning her. The unmistakable outline of his
gun dug into her left shoulder blade. The
backs of her thighs were wedged against
the powerful length of his; his tuxedo pants
felt cool and smooth against her skin.
Knee-high weeds brushed her bare calves.
The insect chorus was loud; the smell of
damp earth was strong. Less pervasive

but still detectable was the scent of fabric softener—must be his shirt—and man.

Even before she saw the twin beams of light pierce the field, she knew danger was at hand.

Of course, the danger wasn't to her. But still her heart pounded.

Reed continued, whispering, "Two of them came off the expressway and started cruising through the parking lots of the businesses out front. Looks like one of them is checking out the field."

The twin beams were headlights. One of the squad cars had obviously parked facing the field. The sound of a car door being opened and closed was followed almost instantly by another. Caroline pictured it: two uniforms, out of their patrol cars. When two more, smaller lights started playing over the field, she mentally put flashlights in their hands.

Her stomach dropped toward her toes.

As a kidnap victim, what she should have done, of course, was throw a kick back into Reed's kneecap, tear herself out of his arms, and run headlong toward rescue.

What she did was go quiet as a mouse

in his arms, waiting, praying that they—
they—would not be found.

Her being a cop was not going to matter
under these conditions.

Cuffed, with duct tape over her mouth,
she would have no chance of intervening
in the first few crucial minutes of a show-
down. Whatever was going to happen
would occur without her being able to do a
thing, or say a word, to stop it.

Damn Reed anyway for trussing her up
like this.

The smaller beams of light started criss-
crossing the field.

Locked in Reed's arms, Caroline stayed
perfectly still, except for her heart, which
was knocking in her chest, and her eyes,
which followed the slow crawl of the lights
as they played over the weeds. Holding
her breath, she watched the lights move
toward the dirt hill, toward the Mazda, toward the backhoe, toward **them**.

Reed radiated coiled energy. His jaw
brushed her cheek. His five o'clock shadow
felt rough against her soft skin. She could
hear the rasp of his breathing. The wide
contours of his chest felt as solid as a
stone wall. His arms around her had turned

to iron. Her cuffed hands rested against his abdomen, which was firm and flat and moving as he breathed. She could feel his every hard muscle and sinew as his lean body curved around her.

Her butt nestled against his crotch. It wasn't her imagination: he was hard there, too.

She couldn't help it: she went a little weak at the knees. Heat washed over her in a wave.

The lights found the dirt hill, and her attention immediately refocused outward. The lights touched on the dry brown surface, explored the slope of it, then pulled back a little. The narrow beams probed the field at the base of the hill, illuminating gently swaying weeds along with swarms of moths and other insects that swirled skyward against the black background of the night.

The lights swooped to within a few feet of the Mazda. Reed's arms tightened around her. She could feel him tensing, gathering himself.

Even if the officers see the car, Caroline found herself reasoning in an attempt to quell her rising panic, they won't know that it's us. They might think it's a random car someone abandoned in a field.

She was just registering that, to her aggravation, she was once again wrongly identifying with Reed when it occurred to her: if the officers did spot the car and were curious enough to come check it out, they would see her and Reed. There was no way around it.

Remembering that Reed was armed, she felt cold sweat prickle to life around her hairline.

The flashlight beams slid closer to the Mazda. Caroline held her breath.

Inches away from disaster, the stretching sabers of light were interrupted as they once again encountered the solid curve of the dirt hill. This time, the beams aimed at it directly instead of exploring its contours. That sent its shadow, big and black as a shroud, falling over the car. The Mazda was tucked just far enough inside the edge of the hill to keep the lights from reaching it, Caroline realized. The officers would have to walk into the field past the hill to discover the car—and her and Reed.

If they didn't see anything suspicious, they had no reason to do that.

Her pulse skittered. Her eyes stayed glued to the lights slicing through the darkness.

A moment later, the flashlight beams were gone.

Only then did Caroline breathe again. And only when she gratefully took in a sudden rush of air did she realize that earlier she had not been breathing at all.

"Whew." Reed's chest expanded against her back, which told her that he was taking a deep breath, too. She was suddenly supremely conscious of the feel of him against her again. He was bigger than she was, broader, harder—and to her own annoyance she liked that. A lot. "Let's give it a minute, make sure they're gone."

The slamming of two car doors sent a warm tide of relief surging through Caroline's veins. Then the headlights moved, slanted across the field, and vanished from her line of sight.

The squad car was gone. Reed must have thought so, too, because while he didn't release her, his hold on her eased.

"Steady," he said in her ear. Glad of his arms around her as her knees sagged a little with relief, Caroline rested back against his wide chest. He remained alert, listening, watching, for what seemed to her an inordinate amount of time. Finally his arms dropped away from her and he said, not quite whispering but quietly, "Let's go," while wrapping a hard hand around her bare upper arm.

Discovering that she was as eager to get away as he obviously was, Caroline didn't resist. She moved silent as a shadow at his side as they skirted the backhoe, then looked cautiously around the dirt hill to find just what she had expected to see: the fast food restaurants, convenience stores, and truck stop she had spotted earlier from her vantage point half a mile away.

The minute she had emerged from the Mazda to see the halogen glow of the lights beyond the hill, she'd been almost certain of where they were. Really, what were the alternatives, given the length of time they'd been driving and the relatively rural nature of the area?

Was Holly hiding over there somewhere? Or—and this was more likely—had someone been waiting there to pick him up?

There were a couple of big rigs parked

at the truck stop and a single car filling up at the service station across the street, but that was it as far as Caroline could see. No cops or cop cars anywhere.

"Come on." Moving fast, Reed pulled her through the weeds to the Mazda and opened the door that Caroline had expended so much effort exiting. Bundling her back into the car, he dropped the plastic bag he was carrying into her footwell, then leaned across her to pull her seat belt around her and fasten it, which, with her hands still cuffed behind her, promised to leave her trapped once more.

"Next time, I put you in the trunk." His tone was grim. His hands still busy fitting the seat belt into its latch, he shot her a condemning look. The dark gleam of his eyes was disconcertingly close. His mouth was just inches away from her skin. She could feel the warmth of his breath feathering her cheek. Defiant, Caroline narrowed her eyes at him—the only response she could make, with her hands cuffed behind her and duct tape across her mouth.

For a second their eyes clashed. Electricity sizzled in the air. The molecules between them seemed to heat.

She wasn't the only one to feel it, she could tell. His eyes flared. His mouth hardened. His jaw clenched.

He muttered, "Damn it," and his lids dropped over his eyes as he looked down, deliberately shifting his attention to the seat belt, which he seemed to be having more difficulty than usual getting to latch.

His arm and shoulder brushed her breasts, and all at once she was acutely aware of the accidental contact. With only the thin layers of her flimsy shirt and bra for protection, her nipples responded the way nature intended them to, and hardened into firm little buds. Surprised by the unexpected sensation, she caught her breath. To her dismay, the sound was audible, and when he looked a question at her in response she found herself glad of the darkness that she hoped made it impossible for him to read anything her face might reveal. The duct tape—she wanted it off. That was what her indrawn breath was all about, and there was no way he could know any differently. She made another inarticulate sound, deliberately this time, glared at him, and moved her mouth beneath the tape in hopes that he would get the message.

He did.

"Not a sound," Reed said, and carefully pulled off the tape.

"Do not put duct tape over my mouth again," she warned in a gritty undertone.

"Try to escape again, and I'll wrap you in so much duct tape you'll look like a mummy," he threatened, and closed her door with the softest of sounds. Watching his tall figure broodingly as he walked around the front of the car and got in beside her, Caroline was left to take a few deep breaths through her mouth, then run her tongue over her dry lips. She was angry at him. She was attracted to him. She was afraid for him, too. It made for a weird combination.

"Just so we're clear," she began as he started the car. He grimaced at the sudden rumbling of the engine as it turned over, which sounded very loud to Caroline's possibly oversensitized ears, too. "I wasn't trying to escape."

"Really? Looked like it to me," he replied, as, leaving the lights off, he put the transmission in gear and began to slowly

drive away from the establishments behind them, taking obvious care not to make
any excess noise or do anything that would
attract attention. "And since I need you, I
can't let that happen."

"I was trying to make a point," she said
with dignity. He gave her a disbelieving
look. "Yes, I got free, but I wasn't going to
go anywhere. I was going to sit on the
hood of the car and wait for you to come
back. To demonstrate to you that you can
trust me."

"Good plan." It was obvious from his
tone that he didn't believe a word of what
she was saying. The car bumped and rattled through the dark field. Weeds swished
past on either side, but the car was following tracks of previously flattened grass
that had probably, Caroline guessed, been
created by the advent of the backhoe.
Which was a good thing, because otherwise they would have left an unmistakable
trail come morning. He continued, "Worked
out well. I'm definitely feeling the trust, I
have to say."

"There's no need to be sarcastic," she
replied, nettled.

"There's no need to lie," he retorted. "I

get it. You were trying to escape. Fair enough. In your shoes I would have done the same."

"I was not trying to escape," Caroline snapped.

"And I'm not kidnapping you." His mouth twisted into a sardonic half smile. "We're on a date. I'm into bondage."

The image that conjured up actually made her blood start to heat again, which was beyond annoying.

"Aren't you funny?" The look she gave him was withering. "Here's the thing: I don't like having duct tape plastered over my mouth. I don't like having my hands cuffed behind my back. And I really don't like being kidnapped. So how about we come at this from a different angle, and you drop the whole kidnapping deal, and let me help you?"

"No can do, cher," he replied.

"Why not?" she demanded.

"For one thing, I don't trust you." His tone was brutal.

"Well, you'd better start." Her tone was equally grim. "Because from where I'm sitting, I'm the only hope you've got."

He didn't reply, and she thought it was

because they had reached the end of the field. Luckily, except for the glow from the cluster of halogen lights they were leaving behind, the night was dark, and, she judged, without its headlights on, the car would be almost impossible for anyone at any distance to see. Clouds had blown in to scuttle across the sky and obscure the moon, allowing only an occasional glimpse of the big yellow orb.

"Oh my God." As the car dipped into a shallow ditch before bumping up onto a narrow country road, Caroline glimpsed something out of the corner of her eye that caused her head to swivel toward it and riveted her attention: the expressway. It was well lit, so even from that distance she could see it clearly. It was almost devoid of traffic. No surprise, given the lateness of the hour and the fact that it was now Christmas Day. But what was so startling was the line of red revolving lights that stretched across all three lanes of westbound I-10. The lights were attached to squad cars, which had formed what appeared to be an impenetrable barrier.

It was a roadblock. Aimed at catching Reed, she was absolutely, 100 percent sure. One of dozens, no doubt, that had been set up to try to keep the escapees contained. All major exit roads in the vicinity of Old Metairie would be blocked. Cruisers would be patrolling the smaller streets. Ordinarily, given New Orleans' traffic, finding a single absconding vehicle was a Herculean task. Tonight, the absence of cars on the road made it infinitely easier.

Clearly her father, or whoever was in charge of the search, was no longer counting on them being on foot.

"I see it," Reed acknowledged, glancing that way, too, as the Mazda headed southwest, away from the expressway. "It's nothing I didn't expect."

"Where's Holly? Is he safe?" Caroline asked. The tension she was feeling put an edge on her voice. The uncertainty of not knowing what had become of Holly, or what Reed was planning to do, or any more than the very broadest strokes of what was going on was getting to her, she discovered. He glanced at her and seemed to hesitate. For a moment she thought he wasn't going to answer.

"Yes." His tone was clipped.

She waited. Nothing.

"That's all?" Annoyance colored her voice. "Just 'yes'? How about you fill me in a little, so I can judge for myself?"

"Yeah. No."

Caroline scowled at him. "He's an escaped prisoner. They won't stop looking until they find him. Just like they won't stop looking until they find"—she almost said **us**—"you." The mere thought of the ongoing search made her stomach knot. She couldn't see the truck stop or the service station or the fast food joints anymore, but she knew as well as she knew anything that the cops who'd searched the field with flashlights had not just given up and retreated. They were still looking, out there somewhere patrolling these country roads, and there were dozens more just like them out there hunting through the night, too. The uniforms might have overlooked her and Reed this time, but sooner or later they would be spotted: it was inevitable. Even if Reed fled across the country, which he currently showed no sign of doing, he would eventually be caught. Once added to the BOLO list that went out to every police department in the country, a fugitive's days on the run were numbered. The vast majority were caught within forty-eight hours.

"Thanks for the warning." His voice was dry. Of course, he was a cop: he knew that, too.

Caroline's throat tightened with anxiety. "You realize that you have no chance of getting away."

"I got out of Winfield's mansion," he pointed out. "With Holly, and you."

"That was pure luck. You have to know that. And you can't count on it holding."

"What I'm counting on is your father not wanting anything to happen to you."

She snorted. "That's a crock. I doubt he gives a flying flip whether or not something happens to me. You know that."

Reed shot her an unreadable look. "You're still his daughter. That counts for something. And a lot of eyes will be watching how he handles this. He'll do what he has to do to get you back safe."

Her eyes narrowed at him. "You ever think you might be wrong? Which, in this case, would be dead wrong?"

"I'm not wrong."

"So far, you haven't hurt anybody. I'm

betting he's going to be pretty confident that you're not going to hurt me, either."

Reed smiled at her, a slow and charming smile that was unlike anything she'd seen from him throughout this whole ordeal. Despite everything, she was instantly transported back ten years and he was once again the gorgeous guy she'd spent a summer crushing on. Her heart gave an unwelcome little flutter.

"Are you saying you don't believe I'd hurt you, Caroline?"

She realized that she had been all but certain of that for a while. "That's what I'm saying."

His eyes were once again on the road. He shrugged. "Believe me, your father thinks I'll do what I have to do."

"You know him, don't you?" she asked curiously. Ordinarily the superintendent would have minimal interaction with a homicide detective. "Outside of work, I mean?"

Reed flicked a glance her way. "You ask too many questions."

She frowned at him. "You could try answering some of them."

They were traveling fast now, way over the speed limit, booking it down the two-lane blacktop that curled away into the darkness like Reed was intent on putting some serious distance between them and the interstate as quickly as possible. Dread made her chest feel tight as she thought about the resources that were certainly being deployed to find them. Her father hated to be beaten at anything: he would go all out to bring Reed in. Although she couldn't see any at present, she knew there were helicopters up there aiding the search. The Mazda was still running without lights, which was a worthy attempt to disguise them both from the myriad squad cars undoubtedly cruising these back roads searching for them, and make them invisible to the searchers above. But it was dark, and anything could be on the road. Deer and other wildlife were a real hazard at night even under ordinary conditions. And if they should encounter a squad car while the headlights were off, the game would be up and the chase would be on with a vengeance.

Given those factors, she was almost relieved when they turned onto another,

even narrower blacktop road, and he finally switched on the headlights. This road
wound through a forest, and the foliage of
the tall trees crowding close together on either side formed a leafy canopy overhead.
She could no longer even see the moon, or
anything much, except what was revealed
in the blaze of the headlights: the rough
bark of ancient tree trunks, trailing gray
ropes of Spanish moss and swarms of insects, and the gleam of dark water curving
beneath the trees some little distance away.
She hoped the canopy would provide
enough cover to keep a helicopter from
spotting them. The road was twisty enough
and the woods on either side were dense
enough that the headlights should not be
visible to anyone who was not coming directly toward them, she was almost sure.

"Where are we going?" Caroline asked.

Reed was driving as if he had a destination in mind. As dark as the night was
there beneath the trees, she knew dawn
could not be many hours away and presumed he would want to be off the road
before then. Seen in profile, his handsome
face was hard and set. If he was tired, as
she guessed he had to be because she

was practically dead with fatigue herself, she could see no sign of it.

"You'll see."

Another nonanswer. She was getting sick of them. Her brows came together. "Do you enjoy being cryptic?"

He slanted a glance at her. "Makes my day."

"You can tell me where we're going, you know. Because, see, we're alone, and there's nobody I can tell."

Her sarcasm earned her a glimmer of a smile. "What, you don't like surprises?"

"About as much as I like having my hands cuffed behind my back and being trapped by a seat belt." Which was, not at all. Having her hands wedged in the small of her back was starting to get uncomfortable. So was not being able to move her arms.

"We'll be there soon."

"Is that supposed to make me feel better?" She glared at him. "This whole stupid trade-me-for-Holly's-little-brother scheme is not going to work, by the way. You're delusional if you think it will."

"It was the best stupid scheme I could come up with on short notice."

The trace of mocking humor in his voice did not sit well with her. "To hell with this. I want to know what's going on."

"No, you don't. Believe me, you don't."

"If you won't tell me, how about I try to figure it out for myself?" Caroline asked pseudosweetly, then frowned, thinking. Her eyes stayed fixed on his face as she continued. "What is it they say? Oh, yes: once you eliminate the impossible, whatever remains, no matter how unlikely, must be the truth. First thing to do is discard the most unlikely explanations, such as the slim but not entirely nonexistent possibility that you are completely crazy. Clearly you weren't after money, because you left the chance for a million dollars behind. Publicity? I don't think so. Here's what we're left with: you, previously a good solid cop, were fired yesterday for taking a bribe, which Holly swears was a setup. Holly was arrested for possessing drugs, which he swears was a setup, too. Who supposedly set you two up? A very generic 'the cops,' again sworn to by Holly. He's thrown in jail and thinks he'll be murdered by morning. You take New Orleans' top brass hostage, including, significantly, the superintendent of police and the mayor, in a spectacularly wrongheaded fiasco of a move that nevertheless succeeds in getting Holly out of jail and, not coincidentally, makes you both the object of a manhunt that's probably going to end with the two of you getting killed.

"So what is the common denominator here?" She paused, musing. Then her voice brightened with triumph. "I have it: the cops. Specifically, the NOPD." Her eyes narrowed on his face. His expression was guarded, but something in his eyes told her that she was on the right track. She continued slowly, piecing it together as she went. "I'm guessing you, or Holly—it would have to be Holly, wouldn't it, or else there's no reason for him to be involved—stumbled across something, some evidence of corruption, or a crime, which"—the look she was giving him turned speculative—"you reported to the superintendent of police, who either did not believe you, which accounts for the fight everyone says you two had, or did believe you and wanted to stop you from sharing what you discovered with anyone else. Bottom line, he didn't like what you had to say. The situation went to hell from there." At the telltale firming of Reed's mouth, she smiled. "Bingo, right?"

"Leave it alone, Caroline." The look he gave her was grim.

"Too late," she taunted. "Let's see, what could it be? What big bad could Holly have uncovered?"

"Goddamn it." He said it violently enough to make her eyes widen. But he wasn't talking to her, she realized a split second later. His eyes were fixed on something up ahead. His hands had clenched tight around the steering wheel.

Glancing out through the windshield, Caroline froze. Her heart lurched. Her stomach sank.

Although they were partially hidden by the trees, there was no mistaking the red revolving lights dead ahead.

A squad car was speeding right toward them.

CHAPTER THIRTEEN

Before Caroline could say anything, before she could make so much as a sound beyond her first instinctive indrawn breath, Reed doused the headlights. Darkness dropped over them like a curtain.

"Like that's not going to attract attention," Caroline scoffed.

"You have a better idea, I'm all ears."

She didn't.

"Oh, God, it's all over." Her voice sounded hollow. Her heart slammed against her ribs. There wasn't a thing she could do, except stare in horror at the oncoming squad car. While it was still hidden by the trees except for the brilliant flashing lights that could be glimpsed through the stockade of trunks, it was approaching at a fast pace. The siren wasn't on. If it hadn't been for the activated light bar on top of the car, they would have had no warning at all.

"We just now saw their lights. I'm hoping they didn't see ours." He had taken his foot off the gas rather than hitting the brakes. Caroline guessed that it was to prevent the telltale flash of red from the brake lights. She watched as he shifted down into neutral.

"Reed." He was pulling off the road. The Mazda bumped over gravel and then grass, going way too fast for a blind ride along the badly overgrown grassy strip at the edge of a forest. Trees flashed past Caroline's window, so close that she cringed a little. Thank God the car was slowing. Her voice went dangerously high-pitched. "What are you doing?"

The squad car came around a bend, and suddenly she could see it speeding directly toward them, a solid pale shape beneath the pulsing red light bar that lit up the night.

"Stopping." Even as he said it, the Mazda

bounced over a cluster of small bushes and, amid the sound of branches slapping the paint and scratching along the under-carriage, shuddered to a halt. Reed had already let go of the steering wheel and was reaching for her seat belt before it finally stopped. His voice sharpened as he leaned toward her: **"Duck."**

"What?"

She didn't get an answer. At least, not in words. Instead, as her seat belt released, a hard arm encircled her shoulders and he pushed her down so that she was lying across the console. He then covered her body with his own. The plastic console was hard and unyielding beneath her ribs. His torso on top of hers was heavy and suffocating. With the way he was twisted in the seat, her head wound up resting on the side of his muscular thigh.

"Oh my God, this would be the moment to take these handcuffs off me. Your best chance is to surrender to me before they—" Her voice broke off as the Mazda's interior lit up with pulsating red flashes. "—find us," she finished in a tiny voice.

The patrol car was clearly almost upon them. Once again, instead of welcoming potential rescue as any right-minded victim would, she found herself identifying with Reed. Her breath caught, her throat tightened up, and her cuffed hands clenched into fists. With Reed's big body resting atop hers, she could feel his tension. His arm around her was rigid, and his thigh beneath her cheek was taut. He was heavy as a sack of cement, holding her down below the level of the windshield so that neither of them was visible to the officers in the cruiser passing the car. Bent over as she was, with Reed's weight on top of her, it was hard for her to take a deep breath. His own breathing was even and slow, and she got the impression that he was deliberately controlling it.

He said, "I'm not surrendering."

As his forbidding promise registered, she realized to her dismay that she could not feel his gun where it should have been. All she could feel against her back was his solid chest and a ridged shape near his left pectoral muscle that she knew must be his empty holster. One hard arm curved across her body; his hand rested near her hip. The other—to her horror Caroline saw that he held his gun against his leg.

Cuffed as she was, there was not a thing she could do about it.

"If they see you with a gun they'll shoot you on the spot," she warned urgently.

Even as she said it the lights were upon them; the entire interior pulsed red as hellfire. Goose bumps raced over her skin. Her blood thundered in her ears. Bracing, she listened for the sound of brakes, of the siren being activated, of something that would tell her that the moment of reckoning was at hand.

He said, "Whatever happens, you stay in the car and stay down. I don't want you getting caught in any crossfire."

"We don't want any crossfire," she almost wailed. "Reed, **please** don't do this."

The whooshing sound of tires rolling fast over pavement was followed almost immediately by a lessening in the intensity of the lights inside the Mazda. A moment later, and the red flashes were entirely gone.

Caroline lay where she was, unmoving. Reed, too, remained motionless atop her.

Her heart continued to pound a mile a minute. She was sure that his did, too.

What was happening? Had the squad car stopped behind them? Were armed officers even now sneaking up on them through the dark?

Or had the cruiser simply passed them by and continued on?

Not knowing was driving her insane. Caroline felt like she was about to jump out of her skin.

Cautiously Reed lifted his head and looked around.

"Jesus Christ," he said, exhaling. "They're gone."

Oh. My. God.

"They're gone?" To Caroline's embarrassment, her voice squeaked. She sat up when he did, and they both turned to look out the back window at the same time. Sure enough, in the distance she could see the flashing red lights racing away from them. She felt shivery inside with the aftermath of fear, and took a deep, hopefully calming breath. "Thank God."

He looked at her. With both of them partially turned around in their seats, their faces were surprisingly close. His eyes gleamed in the darkness as they met hers. His mouth curved into the slightest of wry smiles.

"Hey, you're being kidnapped, remember? You want me to get caught."

"No, I don't," she said.

He must have heard the conviction in her voice, because his smile vanished and he looked at her searchingly. Then he leaned forward and kissed her.

At the touch of his mouth on hers, heat shot through her. His lips were hard and hungry, and the way he was kissing her made her dizzy. She closed her eyes and opened her mouth under his and kissed him back with all the pent-up passion for him that she'd been holding on to inside for ten years. Her heart began to pound and her body quickened and she shivered with a rush of absolutely unexpected pleasure.

Oh. My. God. In a whole different way.

When he pulled his mouth from hers, her lids fluttered up and she looked at him almost dazedly. Chemistry—that's what shimmered in the air between them. Potent. Explosive. The kind of inexplicable physical reaction that made getting naked and horizontal with the other person feel absolutely urgent. For a moment, as his gaze moved over her face, she went all melty inside in expectation of—something. Tender words. Another kiss. Feverish handcuffed sex. Until she realized that, although his eyes were heavy-lidded and hot for her, he was frowning, and the set of his mouth could best be described as grim.

Then he reached past her to grab her loose seat belt.

"Sit still," he ordered, pulling it around her. "I don't want to make this too tight."

"That's it?" she asked indignantly as he clicked the belt into place. "**Sit still**? That's all you have to say?"

"You wanting hearts and flowers, Caroline?" He sounded almost impatient. The look he flicked at her was impossible to read. "You got the wrong place, the wrong time, and the wrong man."

That stung. That made her mad.

"Obviously," she snapped, and glared at the road ahead because she didn't want to glare at him, since that would make how she was feeling just too damned obvious. "Instead of wasting time kissing me, you might want to try driving away. Because there might be another squad car. Or that last one might come back. The fact that he didn't see us is an absolute miracle anyway, and if I were you I wouldn't want to push it."

"I don't believe in miracles." Clearly ready, willing, and able to continue on like that kiss had never happened, he returned his gun to its holster then started the car again, while Caroline leaned back in her seat, rested her head against the head-rest, and tried to calm down. She felt limp with reaction, and 99.9 percent of it was from that blistering kiss. Her heart was still beating way too fast, and her blood still simmered.

"Then let me put it another way: God looks after fools and children," she responded caustically, turning her head so she could look at him.

He smiled. It wasn't much, a quick curve of his lips, but it was enough to make her go all sort of warm and fuzzy inside, which under the circumstances was absolutely infuriating. She might not be able to help feeling sexually attracted to him, but discovering to her dismay that she liked him, too, as the man he was now quite apart from her ten-year-old memory of him, was not a good thing.

In fact, it could be downright dangerous.

In sheer self-defense, she looked away. The Mazda was moving, jolting free of the bushes, its tires biting into gravel before finding the road. A quick glance back through the rear window found the squad car's lights. They were now no more than a distant flash of red through the trees.

"That was close," he said. "What do you want to bet they're rushing to hook up with the roadblock on I-10?"

It was possible, Caroline supposed. Thing was, she didn't care.

"You know, we can play hide-and-seek with the patrol cars all night," she said with a touch of acid as the Mazda accelerated to what she felt was a dangerous speed without turning on its lights. Fortunately just enough moonlight spilled through the overarching branches to make it not quite suicidal. "But I'd rather not."

"With any luck, we'll be off the road before another one comes along. Like I told you before, we're almost there."

She wanted to ask where, but knew there wasn't any point because he wasn't going to tell her.

"Yippee," she replied with a notable lack of enthusiasm, and to her annoyance that made him smile again.

Moments later, he turned the Mazda onto a dirt track that wove a considerable distance through the woods. Because by consensus they continued to avoid using the headlights, the deeper they drove into the trees the darker it got, until finally the car was practically inching along and Caroline couldn't see a thing. But he kept going, and at last they pulled into a clearing that, by comparison with the darkness they had just emerged from, seemed awash with moonlight. Caroline saw that it held a long, ramshackle-looking wooden structure with a tin roof. Reed stopped the car right in front of it, got out, and pulled open one of what looked like about three pairs of shedlike doors while she squinted at the words **Duck Tours** painted in big white letters above them. Then he got back in the car and drove into what appeared to be a rudimentary garage. Inside, it was so dark that she couldn't even see him sitting beside her.

"Duck Tours?" she asked.

"A guy I know used to run them through the bayous for the tourists. Went out of business when the price of gas went through the roof. It's been empty for a while."

"Oh." She understood that he was referring to the big yellow amphibious vehicles that she could actually remember seeing a time or two on the city streets. "This is where you're planning to hide out?" Her tone was doubtful.

"This is where I'm planning to hide the car." He killed the engine. "In a few minutes I need to make a phone call," he said. "And I want your word that you'll be absolutely quiet while I do it."

The threat of more duct tape, of which there was still a healthy amount on the roll in the backseat, was unsaid but there. It wasn't necessary.

"You know, I'd scream for help as soon as whoever you're going to be calling answered the phone except, gee, I'm guessing they're going to be too far away to come running."

"Does that mean I can trust you to be quiet?" His voice was dry.

"Oh, for God's sake, yes." She frowned as he reached past her to pull up the plastic bag he'd dropped into the foot-well. His arm brushed her leg, as did the plastic bag with its bulging contents, and then he was unfastening her seat belt and his arm brushed her breast, and there it was again, that jolt of sexual chemistry that made her toes curl and her body heat and that she absolutely was going to resist if it killed her. As he withdrew into his own seat she had to ask, even though she thought the chance of actually getting an answer was practically nonexistent. "Calling anybody I know?"

"Your father."

She was surprised by his answer, surprised that he told her.

"Why?" she inquired.

"To let him know I have you, in case there's any doubt. To arrange a trade." He got out of the car, opened the back door, presumably to retrieve items from the backseat, then came around to her door and opened it. A moment later she felt his hand on her arm. "Come on, get out."

Caroline got out. Reed closed the door, locked it with a beep, and then with his hand on her elbow urged her toward the grayish light that was the clearing.

As soon as they were outside, she saw that she'd been right: the backpack was slung over his shoulder. The plastic bag hung from his arm. He'd shed his jacket while he'd walked around the car to fetch her—she presumed it was now in the back-pack, although she supposed he could have left it in the car—and had rolled up the sleeves of his white shirt to the elbow. He was likely hot; even in her sleeveless blouse and short skirt she was feeling overwarm herself, which, since the tem-perature was relatively pleasant, she at-tributed to a hellish combination of reaction from their kiss and stress and the rain-portending heaviness of the air. Seen by moonlight, with his tall, broad-shouldered, supremely fit build and his shoulder hol-ster plainly visible against his shirt, he looked every inch the tough, seasoned police detective he'd been until the previ-ous day.

She faced, again, the mind-blowing puzzle of how he had ended up here, in this shadow-filled clearing on the run from the very institution to which he had dedicated his life. But she was too tired and jittery to analyze it any further at the moment, and so she turned her attention to her surroundings. The open area where they stood looked like it had once been a parking area, and from the texture of the ground underfoot she thought it might even have been graveled, although only a few scattered pebbles were left, embedded in the hard-packed dirt. The towering black walls that were, in actuality, the trees crowded the perimeter of what was approximately a sixty-by-one-hundred-foot rectangle. The sounds of the woods at night—a symphony of whirring insects, rustling leaves, scurrying creatures, and distant animal cries—were surprisingly loud, even there in the clearing. The air smelled damp, which wasn't a surprise: unless she was mistaken they were on the edge of one of the bayous. Lafourche, she thought, from the direction in which they'd traveled, although it was always possible that she was mistaken, that she'd gotten turned around.

Whatever, from the smell she knew there was stagnant water somewhere nearby.

She waited until Reed had closed the shed doors before saying, way more politely than he deserved, "Handcuffs?"

He turned to look at her. His face was impossible to read in the uncertain moonlight, but she thought she saw weariness in the set of his shoulders before he squared them.

"Yeah. No. I remember how you tried to escape earlier. I don't feel like chancing a repeat."

"Oh my God, I told you I wasn't trying to escape."

"You told me," he agreed.

"They're uncomfortable. My arms are aching."

His lips tightened. His eyes swept her face.

"Come on, Reed, take the damned cuffs off me. Please."

He made an indecipherable sound of disgust. She recognized it for the surrender it was.

"Don't make me chase you," he warned.

She huffed with indignation. "Like I'm

going to take off running here? Give me a break."

He looked her over again. Then he said grudgingly, "Turn around."

She did. A moment later his hand gripped her wrist to steady it and she heard the faint snick of metal on metal as he inserted the key into the handcuffs. Looking across the clearing at the impenetrable darkness of the woods in front of her, she realized that if she seized the moment, if the instant the cuffs were removed she did indeed take off running, she would have a fair shot at getting away. All she would have to do was make it into the trees—it wasn't far—and hide there in the pitch darkness until morning, when she could head for the road and wait for a car and flag it down. Of course, it was possible that he would catch her, but she had always been a fast runner—she figured her chances were pretty good, actually. If the man holding her had been anyone other than Reed, she realized, she wouldn't have hesitated.

That's when she knew for sure that she had no intention of leaving him on his own to face whatever fate awaited him.

She was going to do her best to make sense of what the hell was actually going on. She was going to do her best to help him to survive it, and even if it came down to it, get away. She was going to do her best to do her job, which was be a cop. Which meant protecting the innocent, bringing punishment to the guilty, and solving crime. **This** crime. Bottom line was, she was going to stay.

A second after she made peace with the truth of that, her wrists were free.

At last.

"That feels—" **better,** she started to say as her arms dropped and swung and the dull ache of the stiffness in her shoulders eased. Then she realized that the cuff on her right wrist was still in place.

"Hey." She turned toward him, lifting her shackled right wrist to show him what he'd missed, then broke off as she watched him take the open cuff and lock it around his own left wrist, shackling them together.

Lips parting in surprise, she stared at him.

Then she looked at their connected wrists. Then she got it. Then she got mad. All over again.

"Seriously?" she said.

"You better believe it." He tucked the key into his right pants pocket; she was careful to note where it went.

Her brows snapped together dangerously. "I am not going to run away. I'm going to stay, and try to solve whatever mess you've gotten yourself into, and do my best to help you live through this, which, incidentally and for your information, is not looking all that likely to happen. Regardless, you have my word I'm not going anywhere. So quit being a jerk and get this thing off me."

"Cher, you ever hear the phrase, 'Trust in God, but lock your car'? That applies here." Infuriatingly, he tugged the end of her ponytail before turning away from her. "Come on, we're walking. I'm going to call your father while I can still get a signal. A little farther in, and it starts to be a problem. You need to stay quiet while I'm on the phone."

"You are a total **douche bag,**" she hissed wrathfully, but he was already moving, which meant that she was, too. Captured hand leading the way, feeling like a dog on a very short leash, she found her-

self trailing after him whether she wanted
to or not. She was dragged even closer as
he moved his cuffed wrist so he could fish
something out of the plastic bag over his
elbow. A phone, she saw as he turned it
on and it lit up, one of the cheap, prepaid
ones that were impossible to trace. Because he had pulled it out of the bag he
had acquired when he'd lost Holly, she assumed it had been purchased from the
convenience store or truck stop or one of
the other businesses near the dirt hill.

Phone in hand, he cocked an eyebrow
at her and said, "What's your father's
phone number?"

She snorted. "Try 9-1-1."

"Look, I know the superintendent has a
personal, private number for family, but I
don't know what it is." His reply held a
touch of impatience. "I mean, I can fart
around going through the switchboard, but
there's a thirteen-year-old's life at stake
here and I'd rather there wasn't any mis-
communication."

"You know, that's so touching I can feel
myself getting all teary-eyed, but I still
don't know the number. It's not like I ever
call him." She matched him narrow-eyed

stare for narrow-eyed stare, then added, "You've got my cell phone. His number's in my contacts." His expression made her frown. "You do have my cell phone, right?"

It was new. It was expensive. It had pictures she didn't want to lose.

"I pitched it behind some furniture right before we ran out of the house. Those things are like a locator beacon."

Caroline thought about that. It could have been worse, she decided: he could have pitched it into the lake. "They would have searched the house, maybe even have tried to call me on it as a way to find me. The ringer was on. I'm sure somebody's found it by now. I wouldn't be surprised if my father has it."

"Good thought." Reed looked a question at her. "Number?"

She told him.

"Shh," he warned, and kept walking as he punched in the number with his thumb. She could quite clearly hear the phone connecting and then starting to ring on the other end as they reached the woods. With the phone held to his ear, he ducked beneath a curtain of vines, which meant Caroline did, too. Straightening, she found herself wrapped in a cocoon of darkness even as she was tugged willy-nilly forward. If it hadn't been for the glow of the phone, she wouldn't have been able to see Reed's tall form in front of her, or separate the towering black walls on either side of her into the trunks of huge oaks and honey locusts and sweet gums that crowded close to the path, or check that the spongy matter underfoot was—as she had devoutly hoped—no more than layers of decomposing leaves laid down like a carpet over marshy ground. Insects buzzed everywhere. Moths, gnats, mosquitoes, you name it. She felt something land on her arm, slapped at it, then felt something tickling her ankle, and brushed the toe of her sneaker over the spot. But the bugs were relentless, and there wasn't a lot she could do except resign herself to the ministrations of the bayou nightlife.

Caroline was trying not to freak out at the dozens of pairs of tiny glowing eyes that seemed to be looking at her from everywhere when she tripped over a root and, chain rattling, grabbed Reed's hand for balance. Glancing around at her, he closed his fingers around her hand. She was just registering how warm, strong, and really absurdly comforting his big hand wrapped around hers felt when the ringing stopped and, very faintly, she heard her father say, "Who is this?"

Just hearing his voice made her stomach twist. She was truly afraid that he was involved in the big bad, she realized, and the thought made her stomach tighten. Whatever his faults as a husband to her mother and a father to her and her sisters might have been—and they were many—she had always felt a grudging respect for his professional integrity. Despite everything, to have to question that made her feel—odd.

Issues, she told herself. **You have issues**.

Her father sounded wary, and she guessed that whatever had come up on her phone's digital display must have been something weird, like the number 000-000-0000. At this time of night, on this holiday, she shouldn't be getting any calls, so her phone would have been silent until now, with Reed's call. Even if the news of her kidnapping was all over TV, which it

might or might not be, no one would be
awake to see it.

"Superintendent." Reed's voice was hard.
"I have your daughter."

"Goddamn it, Ware, what the hell are
you doing?" Martin growled. His voice
sounded small and distant, but she was
surprised to discover that she could hear
him perfectly well. Because the path was
narrow, Reed was ahead of her; joined by
their linked hands, she trailed him closely.
She wasn't sure he realized that she could
hear both sides of the conversation.

"What I have to. You should know by now
that I'm prepared to do whatever it takes."

"Let Caroline go." Martin said it like any
concerned father would. Like her safety
was his first priority.

Reed replied, "I will—when I get what I
want."

"And what's that?"

"I want to make a trade—Caroline for
Anton Bayard."

"The little brother of that punk-ass kid
you just threw your life away for?"

"I see you know who I'm talking about,"
Reed said with a touch of menace.

"By now I know everything there is to know about you. I made it my business to. When one of my cops loses his mind and pulls a stunt like this, it's a reflection on me, and on the department." Martin's voice, which had been rough, gentled. "Ware, you need to come on in. I've been talking to some doctors here and they think that the loss of your family may have triggered some kind of mental breakdown. Come in and let us help you."

A mental breakdown triggered by the deaths of his son and ex-wife? The explanation seemed breathtakingly plausible, and for the briefest of moments Caroline was staggered by it. Could the big bad that Reed was reacting to really be all in his mind? Then she recalled Holly's fierce insistence that "the cops" had done him and Reed wrong, and did a lightning review of every interaction she'd had with Reed since she'd arrived on scene at the Winfield mansion. Conclusion: the man was absolutely sane.

Which meant that her father was full of shit. Or maybe, the tiny little voice of that part of her that still seemed to be the superintendent's loyal daughter suggested, maybe he was just wrong.

She found herself fiercely hoping that he was just wrong.

"Leave my family out of it." Reed's voice was ugly.

Martin continued without responding: "All that stuff you were talking about—those murders you thought were suspicious—I had somebody review them after you punched your way out of my office. They're no more than ordinary street crime, Ware, and that's the truth. I'm at headquarters. You come on in here, and bring Caroline with you, and I'll prove it to you."

Reed said, "Only way I'm bringing Caroline anywhere near you is to trade her for Anton Bayard."

Martin gave a short laugh. "Thing is, Ware, you may be having mental issues, but Dr. Cook—you remember him, he's the psychiatrist the department had you talk to after the accident and he's here right now, at headquarters, in fact—Dr. Cook doesn't see you as a murderer, and I agree with him. You held me hostage, and a whole bunch of others, too, and not one of us is dead. I don't see you killing Caroline. Worst you're going to do is keep her somewhere until we find you. Which we will. So I don't see that you have much leverage to make a deal. Why don't you just come on in?"

Caroline grimaced. Her father had zeroed in on the same thing she had: the issue of Reed's credibility as a dangerous kidnapper-turned-potential-murderer. If Reed hadn't killed any-one yet, what were the chances that he was going to start with her?

Reed said silkily, "You're right, I'm not a murderer. But then, I don't have to be. All I have to do is tell Caroline everything I know. Every little detail, Superintendent, just like I told it to you. What do you think about that?"

There was a short silence.

"You son of a bitch." Martin's volume dropped so that the words were barely audible, at least to Caroline, but the animosity in his voice iced the air. It told Caroline that Reed's threat had surprised him, that it had teeth, that it was something her father feared. It also signified capitulation.

Plus, she realized, it made it plain that

what Reed was referring to was something that her father really, truly wanted
kept secret. About suspicious murders,
Martin had said.

One more piece of the puzzle had just
fallen into place.

"I'll call you tomorrow—no, I guess that'd
be tonight—at 8 p.m. on that phone you're
holding to make arrangements for the trade.
In the meantime, you want to make sure
Anton Bayard is just as fine and dandy
when you pass him off to me as when you
picked him up," Reed said. "We understand each other, Superintendent?"

"Yes." The single clipped syllable was
like nothing Caroline had ever heard come
out of her father's mouth.

It made her throat tighten.

It signified that he was beaten. Martin
Wallace was never beaten.

"Good," Reed replied, and clicked off.

Caroline had been listening so intently
that when he stopped without warning she
almost walked into his broad back.

"Hell," he said. "Looks like we're going
to get wet."

As she edged closer than she would
have liked to a trailing vine in order to stand

beside him, she saw that he was staring out at the oil-black waters of an inlet sliding past only a few dozen yards away. It wasn't wide: maybe twenty feet. His hand held hers firmly, but she got the impression that at the moment he could have been gripping anything: the fact that it was her hand was incidental. His chiseled face was hard and set, and he appeared to be preoccupied with his thoughts. Just beyond where they stood the trees thinned out, and dense thickets of needlegrass clogged the marshy bank that led out to the water. A few stray beams of moonlight streaked through the canopy, gleaming darkly on fat drops of rain that had just begun to fall. Their ominous **plop-plop** warned of a downpour to come.

Before she could reply he glanced at her and added, "So. How much of that did you overhear?"

CHAPTER FOURTEEN

What was the saying? You can't go home again? Now that he was pretty much over reeling from the shock-and-awe onslaught of the past forty-eight hours, Reed was acquiring a bleak acceptance of the fact that it was true: his house, his job, most everyone he'd known, and everything he'd worked for his entire life were lost to him. Getting himself and Holly and Ant out of this alive was looking like the best he could hope for, and even that was a long shot.

The only way he was ever going home again was to prove that his suspicions were correct about the involvement of members of the NOPD in the murders of the four victims in the cemetery (those four would be enough, he judged; proving police involvement in the murders of Magnolia and the others would be gravy, but not essential to getting his life back), and that his actions in taking hostages at the Winfield mansion and in kidnapping Caroline were justified.

He had to stay alive long enough to do that. He had to figure out which cops were involved and thus actively wanted him dead in order to silence him, and which were merely out to kill him because they genuinely thought that he was now a dangerous criminal run amok. Then he had to be able to prove to the satisfaction of a judge or a prosecutor or a grand jury or a cabal of honest cops, depending on the scenario, that the results of his investigation were in fact accurate.

Yeah, and learning to leap tall buildings with a single bound would be a nice trick, too.

But because that seemed like the only path that did not involve him either dying or spending the rest of his life as a fugitive, he was going to try, to see what he could do, with the understanding that if things got too dicey he could cut and run at any time as long as he got Holly and Ant out along with him.

Caroline was a problem. The sweet seventeen-year-old that he remembered had turned into a beautiful, smart, resilient wiseass, and he flat-out liked her. She was also sexy as all hell. Kissing her had been a total error, an impulse of the moment that had been too urgent and unexpected to resist, and the best thing he could do for both of them was put it out of his mind. Unfortunately, that was way easier resolved than done: thoughts of taking her to bed were staking out an ever enlarging territory in the back of his mind.

But he wasn't going to do it. At this point, Caroline could still go home. Her life was still there waiting for her. She hadn't tripped and fallen down the rabbit hole like he had, and for her sake he was going to do his best to keep it that way. Add to that the fact that she was a cop, the damned superintendent's daughter to boot, with all kinds of loyalties and allegiances that he had no way of knowing about or understanding but that might ultimately come back to bite him, and that he had **kid-napped** her, for God's sake, and he would be a fool if he wasn't still having some trust issues where she was concerned.

And never mind the fact that every time he looked into her eyes he could see just how sexually aware of him she was.

Okay, sex was the last thing he needed to be thinking about right now. To have any chance at all of pulling this off, he needed to keep a clear head.

So he was putting bedding Caroline out of his mind, chalking it up as something to be followed up on later, maybe, as a lagniappe, a little special reward he would allow himself to explore if he could fix this, if he got his life back, if they had a chance for anything beyond a one-night stand. Which was a whole lot of "if." In the meantime, he was mentally consigning her strictly to the purpose he'd acquired her for: saving Ant.

It didn't help that thanks to their clasped hands, she was walking so close beside him that he kept feeling the soft curve of her right breast brushing up against his arm with every step she took.

"I damn well heard what my father said.

Don't tell me I misunderstood!" Caroline was practically yelling in his ear to be heard over the roar of the rain, which in the last few minutes had really started coming down, rattling its way through the canopy, rushing like a waterfall through the spots where the leaves were thin, splattering over them both in a cool, not entirely un-welcome shower. She sounded pissed—probably because she was. Reed would have been worried about the volume of her voice, except the only other living crea-tures likely to be found in this remote part of the bayou tonight were not human.

He would have replied, but he didn't see any point in it, because she wanted him to tell her about the "suspicious murders" she had heard the superintendent men-tion and he wasn't going to do that, so they were at a stalemate. Anyway, to say anything at all that she could hear he would have had to yell, too, which he didn't feel like doing at the moment, so he just shook his head at her and kept on walk-ing. Her hand jerked in his grasp, which he interpreted as signifying extreme annoy-ance on her part, but he didn't let go. In-stead he tightened his grip on her fingers, which were slender and fine-boned like the rest of her, as well as being, at the moment, slippery wet. The unmistakably feminine feel of her hand in his, the connotation of wetness as he couldn't help but apply it to her, immediately started to take his thoughts in a direction he didn't want them to go. He deliberately redirected them down a more productive path, to rehashing the phone call with the superintendent, and considering where it now placed him in this whole mess.

The conversation with the superintendent had confirmed what he had suspected: he was being painted as a head case, a lunatic on a rampage. Although in hindsight he supposed he should have seen it coming, what he had **not** expected was to have his supposed breakdown blamed on the stress associated with the death of his kid and ex-wife. The frightening thing about it was that it made sense, made his apparently inexplicable meltdown understandable and thus easier for everyone to believe. A lot of cops had witnessed what a basket case he'd been at the joint funeral, so for them to accept that he'd now gone off the rails wouldn't require that big of a stretch. Remembering the funeral brought a wave of pain with it. By now the feeling that his heart had gotten caught in a vise had become so damnably familiar that he knew how to deal with it, so he took a breath and forced all associated images and thoughts out of his mind as he counted backward from ten. Damn Martin Wallace for stirring up memories that he almost always nowadays succeeded in keeping securely at bay.

He was having more trouble than usual getting the picture of his little boy as he had looked lying in his small white coffin out of his head: he had to start the count again. Must be because he was bone tired. He was still wired, still running on adrenaline, but he could feel it starting to ebb. Once it was out of his system, he had a bad feeling that he was going to crash big time. Or maybe the unwanted image was hanging on because over the last few hours he'd been thinking way too much about the imminent possibility of his own death.

Whatever the reason, Reed knew one thing: dwelling on the past did no one any good.

"My father's involved somehow in those murders, isn't he?" Caroline yelled at him. This time, her eruption was welcome because it gave him something to concentrate on that wasn't as painful.

"I don't know," he replied, looking at her, breaking his silence just to get his head in a different place. It was the truth, he didn't, not for 100 percent sure, and he wanted her to know that there was still some doubt. After all, the man was her father. The slim oval of her upturned face was pale and shiny wet now, her eyes were squished up against the falling rain, and her pretty mouth was tight with irritation at him.

He found his eyes lingering on her mouth, found himself remembering that damned stupid kiss, and glanced away again.

"Who were the victims? When were they killed? Where?" Her questions were right on the mark. She would have made a good detective, he thought. If he had been trying to ferret out what had happened, he would have asked the same things in the same order himself.

"I could tell you, but then I'd have to kill you." Reed looked back at her with a glimmer of humor, careful this time to meet her gaze. "Or at least, somebody would."

"Ha, ha."

"I'm not joking. Leave it alone, Caroline."

"My father is somehow involved in what he himself called 'suspicious murders.' Holly kept talking about the cops doing this and that, which makes me think that the NOPD is also somehow involved in those murders," Caroline persisted. She wasn't letting it go, which didn't surprise Reed. When she wanted something she went at it full-throttle: he remembered that from that summer ten years ago. He deliberately wasn't looking at her again, but he could feel the intensity of her gaze on his face. She was doing a pretty impressive job with her deductions, which wasn't a good thing. She continued, "I'm right, aren't I? I can tell I am just from looking at your face. So how is the NOPD involved?" Her voice sharpened. "Are they covering up certain murders?"

"You ever hear, curiosity killed the cat?" he retorted, irritated at her relentlessness.

"Did you ever hear, two heads are better than one?"

"Not if one of them wants to live long and prosper."

"Fine. Once I'm back home, I'll ask my father what suspicious murders he was talking about."

That made his brows snap together. "That would be the stupidest damned thing you could do."

"So you tell me."

"No."

"Damn it, Reed, how can I help you if you won't tell me anything?"

"We've been over this before."

"Oh, right. I remember. You don't want my help."

"That's right."

"Because you don't trust me."

"Among other reasons."

"You can," she said, in a totally different tone, and her fingers curled tighter around his. "I give you my word that you can."

A promise like that might make like a little worm and try to chew its way into his heart, but he wasn't about to let it override his judgment. Neither was it going to make him change his mind about telling her anything, but he didn't say that. He didn't say anything else. He shut his mouth and kept walking.

She tugged impatiently at their joined hands.

"Reed."

He didn't reply. She was so close that her damned breast felt like it was smashed against his arm. Wet as they both were by now, the thin cotton of his shirt and the practically nonexistent silky stuff of hers were no real barrier: he could feel the fullness of her breast, feel the heat of her skin. His biceps were being nudged by the hard little bud of her nipple. Operative word there was **hard.**

Damn it to hell, her nipple wasn't the only thing that was suddenly hard.

She snapped, "What, are you going all strong and silent on me now?"

That earned her a derisive glance. Did she really have no clue what she was doing to him? He started to walk faster, head down against the rain, in hopes of escaping the contact. He would have let go of her hand, but given the fact that they were shackled together, which meant that she had no choice but to keep pace with him, and factoring in how treacherous the soaking-wet, mossy ground was underfoot, and how precise they had to be to stay on what wasn't really even a path, he figured that would be just asking for her to do something real useful like, say, slip and fall neck deep into a pit of slimy mud.

"You're pushing it, Caroline," he warned.

"Pushing what? You?" Her voice held a jeering note. Her breast didn't budge. She stayed right there with him, hanging on to him for what felt like dear life, which in her case, given where they were, he guessed it probably was. Hell, he didn't know if the increasingly uncomfortable tightness in his crotch had suddenly sensitized him to her or what, but now he could feel the whole intoxicating shape of her pressed against his arm. The soft roundness of her breast with its mind-clouding pebble of a nipple, the feminine slope of her rib cage, the firmness of her narrow waist and the way it flared out again into slender hips—

He opened his mouth, swallowed brackish drops of rain as well as air as he took a deep breath, then did his best to slam the door on the erotic images that had started flipping in an X-rated reel through his mind.

Thank God the water sluicing over him was cool.

"Good," she continued, although he had pretty much lost the thread of the conversation by then. "Maybe if I push hard enough you'll give up and admit you need help."

If he gave up, it wouldn't be to admit he needed help. It would be to turn and run his hands over the tantalizing curves that were making the water hitting his skin feel like it should be turning to steam. It would be to pull her against him and—

He grabbed onto his self-control with both hands.

"You want to get directly behind me now and walk right where I walk," he told her, careful to keep his voice neutral even as he pulled that out of his hat in pure self-defense. "The path's narrowing and starting to get treacherous. See those red eyes in the water over there? That's a big ole alligator just waiting for one of us to slip off the side."

He wasn't even kidding about the alligator: it was there, its shining eyes as visible as reflectors through the darkness. Course, the creature was just floating along, with no more interest in them than in catching a ride to town, because with all the nutria and muskrats and squirrels around they were fat as pigs and lazy from being well fed, but Miss Caroline from the city wouldn't know that.

She didn't. She quit riding his arm at last—thank God!—and fell in behind him.

Saved from both conversation and temptation, Reed set himself to cooling down.

Picking his way along this trail that wound deep into the bayou was second nature to him. He practically had muscle memory for it, which was a good thing because she was distracting the hell out of him and it was dark as a dungeon with the rain falling and the foliage bending close all around from the weight of the water hitting it. The smell of the swamp—a combination of decomposing vegetation, stagnant water, and mud—was strong. The bogs on either side were deep and unforgiving: over the years he'd seen the floating corpses of many animals, including several deer and on one memorable occasion a cow. Moving more or less parallel to the narrow, still-water tributary that eventually emptied into the Mississippi, they were heading south. The rain was now rattling noisily down through the canopy, falling so hard that it bounced as it hit the ground. The leaves overhead that had been providing them with some protection had pretty much given way, and they were being pelted mercilessly. Caroline was drenched despite the windbreaker that she had draped over her head. He was even wetter than she was, because he had the second windbreaker folded over his shoulder to protect his gun.

"Are we getting close?" Caroline yelled from behind him, sounding almost plaintive as the rain washed over them in sheets. When they had first started walking into the depths of the bayou he'd told her that they were heading for a place where they would take shelter for what was left of the night. At the time she hadn't expressed a whole lot of enthusiasm, but now he assumed she'd be more receptive as, instead of replying, he pulled her around a trio of towering cypress trees and waved a hand at their destination, which was right in front of them.

A worn-flat fallen log acted as a bridge over what was usually a finger of placid water but that tonight was swollen and rushing. He held her hand tightly as she followed him across, wary of slipping, then waited as she stepped down beside him onto a carpet of wet, muddy moss. Two strides after that, and he was climbing a trio of warped plank stairs and pulling her up behind him and onto the rickety porch of the fishing shanty that had been his refuge since he was a kid.

"Hallelujah," she said fervently, and he knew she meant for finally getting out of the rain. The rusty tin roof sounded like it was being pelted by BBs as the rain fell like a silvery curtain on all sides. Pulling the soggy windbreaker off of her head, she clutched it in one hand and stayed close to him as she looked cautiously around. Not that she could see much. The shanty's cypress siding was a deep, weathered gray even in the brightest daylight. Tonight the wet siding looked black, and the narrow, covered porch was dark with shadows. "Where are we?"

"I come out here to fish sometimes." Still with her hand in his, he unlocked the door and led the way into the absolute blackness that was the interior of the cabin.

It smelled faintly musty, like it had been closed up for a while, which was the case: he hadn't been out there in months. It smelled damp, too, but hopefully that was just the rain following them in through the door. Luckily he knew where everything was as well as he knew the path that had brought them there. Closing the door, sticking close to the outer wall so as not to trip over anything, he made his way over to the table on the far left side of the room. On it was a battery-powered lantern: working strictly by touch, he switched it on. Immediately the room was illuminated by a soft white glow that lit up the area around it while leaving the corners still deep in gloom.

"Is this where you grew up?" she asked.

He'd had to let go of Caroline's hand to turn on the lantern, and needing to make use of the arm she was tethered to had brought her closer to him than he would have liked. She stood right beside him again, no longer assaulting him with her breast but still warming up a good portion of his left side where their bodies brushed. He tried to see things through her eyes, taking in the one-room cabin with a glance:

rough plank walls and floor; rudimentary kitchen; the small wooden kitchen table with the lantern on it and two upright chairs at each end; a shabby brown tweed love-seat and a tan plush recliner with a coffee table in front of them, and a small, hope-lessly out-of-date television (useless for anything except watching DVDs because there was no cable) on a stand in front of that; a double bed, fully made up but with an old, flowered king-sized sheet thrown over it to keep out the dust and any sur-prise bugs between his visits; two plank doors that didn't quite hang plumb in their frames, one of which led to the small bath-room and the other to the equally small storage room, on the wall opposite the kitchen; between the doors, what in fan-cier surroundings would have been called an armoire that provided storage for the Spartan amounts of bedding and towels and extra clothing he kept on hand, as well as a few other more personal items. His gaze touched on it, skittered past. The furniture was old, the entire cabin not much bigger than the living room of most houses, but it suited its purpose and it suited him.

"No," he answered. He put the plastic

bag of groceries onto the table, then shrugged the backpack off his shoulder and dropped it beside the food. That long-ago summer, he remembered telling her tales of growing up in the swamp, and it was clear from her tone that she remembered. "I grew up over on Orange Cow Bayou."

Which was maybe an hour away as the pirogue paddled. After his mother had re-married and taken off when he was eight, with his father, having left when he was a baby, being by then long gone (both of them were now dead), he'd been raised in a similar but slightly larger shanty that had at least had a separate bedroom for his Granny, while he'd slept on the couch until he'd gotten too tall to fit. By the time he'd graduated high school and left for the Army a twin bed had been added to the main room which he'd slept on, although the lack of privacy had sucked. He had found his way here one day when he was out catching crayfish and sliders and had gone farther than he'd intended. The old man who'd lived here then had been out front in a fanboat cursing a blue streak as he'd tried to wrestle a heavy propane tank onto the porch from the boat tied up out front. A strong and sturdy eleven, Reed had stopped to help. From that day on until the old man—his name was Maxwell Sligo, he was a former cop, and it was he who had instilled in Reed the desire to become one, too—had died, they'd been fast friends. Reed had been twenty-one and just out of the military when Max passed, and the fishing shanty, left unoccupied, had just kind of become the place where he went to get away from it all. No one knew about it—well, no one who was left alive, anyway, his grandmother having died shortly after Max, and his son, well . . .

He shied away from finishing that thought.

In any case, when he'd had to alter his plans on the fly after finding out about Ant, this had been the hidey-hole that had immediately come to mind. He expected to be safe here, hidden away deep in the bayou as this place was, for a little while. Not for too long: he wouldn't chance that. But long enough to sleep, eat, regroup, and think hard about what he needed to do next to rescue Ant and save himself and Holly, who on the one encouraging note in this whole nightmare should be halfway to Mexico by now.

"So who does this place belong to?" Caroline's eyes were dark with worry as he took her dripping windbreaker from her, draped it over one of the chairs, and threw his own over the other one. Then he pulled his gun and did a quick check to make sure that it was still dry, which thankfully it was, although his left shoulder was about the only dry spot on him.

"As much me as anybody," he replied, and watched her long sooty lashes sweep down as she tracked what he was doing with his gun before he returned it to its holster. They were feminine, flirty lashes, and they cast shadows on her high cheekbones. Then they lifted suddenly, and her eyes gleamed at him. Until that moment, he had forgotten that in some circumstances her hazel eyes could look almost green.

"Will they know to come here looking for you?" She sounded genuinely afraid for him, which he had to remind himself he needed to mistrust. Her face was white with fatigue, and the strands of hair that straggled around it, like her once perky ponytail, were so saturated they looked as night black as his own.

Wet and bedraggled as she was, she was still so damned pretty that just looking at her made heat blow through him.

"No." As he thrust a hand into his pants pocket, digging for the handcuff keys, his eyes slid over the rest of her, which he realized instantly was a mistake, but still not soon enough to rectify it. That sexy, silvery blouse of hers was now a barely there, soaked charcoal layer that clung to her breasts like body paint; if she was wearing a bra—she was a cop, she had to be wearing a bra, didn't she? Didn't the department have a dress code about things like that?—he couldn't tell it. Her nipples looked like luscious little gumdrops pressing out against the thin fabric, and the sight completed the job of getting him hard again. With her wet clothes hugging her shape, he was reminded once more of how alluring her body was. Her slim tanned legs, mud-streaked beneath the short skirt, were damned alluring, too, but, he realized as he found himself covertly checking them out again, her firm round breasts with their **do-me** nipples were what did it for him.

They were turning him on to his back teeth.

She was turning him on to his back teeth.

He couldn't get the memory of that kiss out of his mind.

Goddamn it.

There didn't seem to be a thing he could do about it, though. Except grit his teeth and try to get over it.

"Where the hell were you, that you ended up coming out to a crime scene dressed like that?" he asked, because he couldn't help himself, because even before she had gotten soaked to the skin her bare arms and throat and short skirt still had been pretty damned sexy. Given the rain and the remote location, he didn't expect her to try to run, which was why he pulled the key to the handcuffs out of his pocket and reached for the chain that linked them. He sounded irritable, he realized. Hell, he was irritable. No, actually, he was tired and desperate and fiercely, stupidly, unbelievably **horny,** and one of those things was not like the others and it just happened to be the one that was driving him around the bend. What made it even worse was that he wasn't just horny in general, but horny in particular, for Caroline. Oh yeah, he was jonesing big time for Caroline, and that way lay trouble if he wasn't careful.

"I had a date." Face brightening, she watched him unlock the handcuffs, then as he pulled the bracelets off her wrist and his own she looked up to meet his eyes. "It was nice. I was having fun. You totally ruined my evening."

"What can I say? Shit happens." He put the cuffs onto the table, returned the key to his pocket, and watched sourly as she pulled the elastic off her ponytail and fluffed out her hair. A mass of tangled waves, it hung past her shoulders, wet and wild and— sexy. **Shit**. "Boyfriend?"

She shook her head and smiled faintly at him. He automatically tracked the curve of her mouth. Her lower lip was fuller than her upper one; both were the approximate color of raspberries. They tasted like—

Do not go there.

"Just a date," she said. Their eyes met, and what he thought he saw in hers—a

reflection of his own reluctant arousal—
made him grit his teeth. Sexual sparks
crackled in the air around him, and it was
all he could do to ignore how hot he was
getting and focus on what she was saying. She was looking at him and smiling
and saying something that he completely
missed, and then she paused and said,
"Reed," in this husky little voice, and **that**
he heard.

His heart started picking up the pace,
but before he could do more than register
how dark her eyes had suddenly gone she
put her hand on his arm. Her hand was
cool from the rain, he knew that because,
until a few minutes ago, he had been holding it, but still it felt like it was searing its
imprint on the bare flesh of his forearm.
He frowned down at her slim fingers, pale
against his darker skin, abstractedly curious about how they could be generating
such heat.

"You really can trust me, you know," she
said, and as he looked at her again she
rose up on tiptoe and leaned into him so
that her breasts brushed his chest and
pressed her lips to his.

Desire hit him like a freight train.

For a moment he just stood there, not reacting, practically turned to stone by the unexpectedness of **her** kissing **him,** letting her soft, warm mouth move on his without responding in any way. But then his lips parted as he breathed in, and the soft scent of her knocked him sideways, and she licked into his mouth, her tongue hot and wet and tantalizing.

The blaze of passion he felt then shot through his body like a blowtorch. It was primitive. It was intense. Hard as he tried—okay, that wouldn't be all that hard—it was impossible to resist.

Making an inarticulate sound under his breath, he slid a hand around the back of her neck and an arm around her waist and pulled her tight against him. Just before his eyes closed he saw that her lashes lay in feathery black crescents across her cheeks and a rosy flush had risen to stain her cheekbones. His mouth slanted across hers, careful at first, taking it slow, getting reacquainted with the taste of her—more rich-bodied wine than raspberries—and then turning fierce with hunger as she responded in a way that said she was dying to get naked with him. He parted her lips and claimed her mouth and kissed her like he was starving for the taste of her, which, as it turned out, he was. Her arms slid around his neck and she kissed him back just as greedily, and as their bodies clung together, generating so much heat that given the dampness of their clothes, he wouldn't have been surprised to see steam starting to rise around them. He felt the sweet roundness of her breasts and the hard little pinpoints of her nipples against his chest and the firmness of her abdomen moving against his crotch, and realized that he was in grave danger of totally losing his head. But he couldn't pull back, the choice was already out of his hands, she was driving him wild, making him so hot that it felt like fire was consuming him from the inside out. Every delectable inch of her was plastered right up against him, and his pulse jumped into overdrive and his heart hit about two hundred beats a minute, until his brain conveniently went somewhere else and his dick took the wheel and he was the bone-hard, blazing hot equivalent of putty in her hands.

Which were at that moment stroking over his shoulders, then sliding down the front of his shirt.

Those weird cases of humans spontaneously combusting? He was starting to get a handle on how that happened.

The table nudged his thigh. It was the right height, sturdy: that was the only kind of coherent thought that was getting through to his lust-fueled mind. Shifting around so she had her back to it, he tightened his arm around her waist and lifted her, positioning her so she perched on the edge, then spread her knees by stepping between them. Her thighs hugged his hips.

He was expressing his precise intentions toward her pretty graphically with his mouth and his body when something—a certain lack of focus in the way she was kissing him back, a sudden change in her breathing, or maybe **the feel of something being dragged across his chest,** broke through the haze of desire that was driving him and clued him in that something wasn't quite right.

He broke off the kiss for just long enough, as he thought, to lift his head and look down at her. Those long lashes lifted. She met his eyes and said, "Reed, I need you to take a step back."

Her voice was way cooler than it had any right to be.

Her eyes weren't the molten pools of desire he had been expecting to encounter at all. They were watchful. Calculating, even.

And that heavy thing he'd felt being dragged across his chest? Why, that would be his gun.

She was holding it. Two-handing it. Pointing it at him. Having pinched it from his damned holster.

Flushed with sexual heat, her mouth swollen with his kisses, her skirt hiked and her legs spread with him standing between her slim and sexy thighs, she nevertheless managed to look every inch a cop.

Her eyebrows lifted and mouth quirked up slightly in a Cheshire-cat smirk. "Back off, Reed," she said. "We're going to have a little talk."

CHAPTER FIFTEEN

"We both know you're not going to shoot me, Caroline."

The rough edge to Reed's voice was new. It was sexy enough to make her regret what she had interrupted—well, a little bit. The smoldering heat he was giving off notwithstanding, this was not how she wanted things to be between them. Getting her brains screwed out on top of a kitchen table by a man who obviously, until he'd looked down to see his own service weapon pointed at him, had been bent on having hard, fast, mindless sex with her wasn't the happy ending she had in mind.

It also wasn't why she had kissed him. Getting her hands on his gun was why she had kissed him, and it had worked, so now she needed to put every tantalizing thought of what had promised to be a session of really mind-blowing sex out of her head. To get what she wanted, she was going to have to fight the electricity that still charged the air between them, fight the heat and the urgent quaking inside her that had flared so fast that it had caught her by surprise. Knowing what her purpose had been going in, she'd been hoping to grab his gun without getting overtaken by the desire that had knocked her sideways when they'd kissed before. That hadn't happened, but she'd managed to pull out with her objective intact. Now she just needed to stick with the program.

Which she was determined to do. But he was making it way more difficult than she had thought it would be when she had come up with her plan. To begin with, the man was so mouthwateringly gorgeous that just looking at him made her want to start taking off her clothes. With his handsome face tight with passion and his white shirt wet and plastered to his tall body so that every sculpted muscle of his broad shoulders, wide chest, and strong arms were visible through the sodden cloth, he was the embodiment of every sexy dream she had ever had. She could see the shadow of a nice amount of chest hair through his shirt, and she found herself wanting to undo his buttons and check it out. His tux pants were soaked, too, and clung to his narrow hips and powerful legs like a second skin. His package—oh, God, she caught herself looking at it, and jerked her eyes instantly back to his face. But not before she registered that it was truly impressive, and felt her body tighten and quake deep inside in instinctive, atavistic response. His black hair was damp from the rain, his bronzed skin still showed faint marks from the fight with her father, and a visible amount of stubble shadowed his cheeks and chin. A dark flush rode high on his cheekbones. His mouth was set in a firm, tight line. His jaw was hard. His eyes as they met hers were absolutely black.

The gleam in them was—carnal. Superheated. Hungry. Well, no surprise there. She'd experienced for herself the intensity of the voltage the two of them had generated. The blazing desire in his kisses had been off the charts. They had made her dizzy, made her want him, left her—as she was still—all soft and shivery and melting inside. Even through the layers of their clothing (all right, the only layer she'd had in the game was her thin panties) she'd felt the absolutely incontrovertible evidence of his arousal pressing hard right up against her, leaving her in no doubt whatsoever about what he had in mind. She could have stopped him with a word, she knew, but for a few steamy minutes there she hadn't even thought about wanting to. One-night stands weren't her thing, and giving it up on a kitchen table in a frenzy of lust wasn't, either, but if they had been, if she hadn't been on a mission, if circumstances had been just a little different, well, she might have succumbed to Reed, and the hot urgent fire he'd ignited inside her. Despite knowing that unlike him, she at least had had a purpose to her kiss, she had still been responding to him as if he was everything she had ever wanted, still been kissing him back with abandon until she'd almost had to forcefully remind herself that the reason she had initiated the kiss in the first place was to get her hands on his gun. Even after he'd broken off their kiss to frown down at her with his mind clearly so fogged by passion that it had taken him a couple of beats to realize that she was holding his own gun on him, she'd still been so hot for him that calling their steamy little tryst to a definitive halt had been a close-run thing. It had taken every bit of resolve she possessed. She had actually felt regret when she had seen the sudden shock in his eyes and known that there was no going back and she was committed to the path she had chosen. Then he'd taken an involuntary step back and it had been game over—and game on.

She needed him to take another step back now. Actually, a few more, because he was still standing there between her spread legs and his hands were resting—not holding her but resting, big and warm and distracting—on the outside of her thighs. That meant he was still way too close, and their position still way too intimate, for her peace of mind.

"Back up." She gave the order in her cop voice, crisp and authoritative. He complied, slowly, his eyes holding hers, raising his hands to shoulder height with palms up as would any sensible person when facing a gun. As he stepped back, his eyes slid over her face, down her body. Suddenly all too aware of how she must look to him, soaked to the skin, disheveled, and—the word **exposed** came to mind, followed almost instantly by its more risqué sister, **wanton**—she frowned. Snapping her knees together, she slid off the table only to discover that her legs were a little wobbly. Leaning back against the table for support, she scowled at him—and kept the gun trained on the center of his chest.

Oh, God, what had she done? Though he was no longer touching her, his breathing was still clearly irregular. She could see his chest rising and falling as he tried to get it under control. The sensuous, seductive curve that had been his mouth just after he'd stopped kissing her had changed into something grim as reality started to sink in. His eyes bored into hers.

"Did you kiss me just to get your hands on my damned gun?"

He was quick. Well, she saw no point in lying about it. She put up her chin. "Yes."

He didn't swear, not out loud, but the look in his eyes did it for him. "They teach you that trick in the police academy?"

She shook her head. "I came up with it all on my own."

"Somebody ought to add it to the training manual." His tone had bite. "Making it work requires getting a little more hands-on than some officers might like, but it's damned effective."

"Glad you approve."

His eyes narrowed. "Like I said, we both know you're not going to shoot me."

She smiled, just to rub it in. "I've totally got the drop on you. I could."

His hands lowered, and he folded his arms over his chest. "You won't," he said firmly, confirming the silent message conveyed by his body language.

"But I could," she insisted. "You've got to admit it. You're right, to an extent: I wouldn't shoot to kill, but I could wound you, maybe hit you in the leg, incapacitate you. Then I could grab the cell phone out of your backpack and call for help."

"You might find yourself shit out of luck. Signal's iffy out here." His voice was sardonic.

"I might be willing to take my chances."

"You don't even know where we are."

"Southwest of the abandoned Duck Tours place. About two, two and a half miles in."

He looked her over for a moment in silence. "The way you were kissing me was damned hot. You weren't faking it. Just like you weren't faking it in the car earlier."

Was denying it even possible? They both knew how intense things had been. The aftermath still hung in the air between them, as combustible as gas fumes, as tangible as the sound of the rain beating down on the roof. "I guess we'll never know, will we? Anyway, just because you turn me on doesn't mean I won't shoot you. Or arrest you."

Arresting him was, actually, something she had thought about when she'd been plotting to take his gun. But given everything she now knew, which was nowhere near the whole story but, still, enough to fill her with doubts about the integrity of the local justice system, having him hauled off to jail was starting to seem like a really bad idea.

"You couldn't have waited ten minutes

to go for the gun? We both could have gotten off by then."

She frowned at him. "Now that's just crude. Also, overly optimistic. It takes me way longer than ten minutes."

The glittering desire was gone from his eyes. Now they simply looked hard. "Cut the crap, Caroline: what do you want?"

That was the question she had been asking herself for some good little while now. Finally, just before she'd hatched her kiss-and-steal plan, the answer had hit her like a brick to the head: what she wanted was more. More than just this single insane night with him. She wanted a chance to get to know the man she'd been wildly attracted to from the moment she had first laid eyes on him at age seventeen, the man who had been racked with grief at his family's funeral, the man who was risking his life to save Holly and Ant. The good, solid cop gone ostensibly bad. The hot, sexy guy who once had been a friend. There was something between them; a potent chemistry, the tiny embryonic seeds of an attraction that just might turn out to be something special. Forget a one-and-done, which was clearly what had been running through his mind. She wanted to let those seeds develop. She wanted to explore this thing between them. She wanted to have sex with him—boy, did she want to have sex with him!—but not as a prelude to parting forever. She wanted **them** to have a chance.

Which, since he was going to wind up shot dead, imprisoned for years, or on the run for the rest of his life, wasn't looking likely.

Unless, somehow, they could come up with a way to neutralize the big bad that had catapulted him into this situation.

"Did it ever occur to you that you don't actually have to tell me anything for me to be in danger?" she said. "All it takes is for someone to **think** you told me. And if what you know is really that explosive, I'm guessing that whoever it endangers won't want to take the chance that you kept your mouth shut." At the arrested expression on his face, Caroline pushed the point home. "I'm not safe no matter what you do. So why don't you just tell me the whole thing and let us try to figure it out together?"

The look he gave her was stark with sudden realization as the truth of her logic clobbered him over the head. She could almost see him thinking through the possibility.

"Here." She reversed the gun abruptly, and offered it to him grip first. "Take it."

His brows snapped together. Still, he wasn't slow to retrieve his gun. Taking it from her, he checked the safety, which she hadn't bothered to turn off, although she'd taken care to keep that fact hidden from him until now. Then, weapon still in hand, frowning as though he was in two minds about whether or not he might want to turn it on her, he looked a hard question at her.

"I was making a point," she explained.

"By taking my gun and holding it on me? Hell of a dangerous way to make a point," he said, tight-lipped, and finally restored the gun to its holster. Moving back a step, he rested his hips against the wide plank that served as a de facto kitchen counter, crossed his arms over his chest, and looked her up and down. The uncertain glow of the lantern light cast his shadow back against the rough board wall behind him and made him look big and tough and competent, like the seasoned cop he was. "Could have gone real wrong."

She made an impatient sound. "Don't you want to know what the point is?"

"Whether I do or not, I have a feeling you're going to tell me," he responded drily. She was definitely getting some antagonistic vibes from him.

"You can trust me," she said. "I'm on your side. **That's** the point."

"Kissing me and coming on to me like a house on fire before stealing my gun definitely convinced me of that."

"Oh my God, you're mad because I kissed you!"

"If I'm mad, it's because you kissed me **as a way to steal my damned gun**."

"I gave it back!" Straightening away from the table, she glared at him. "And kissing you was the only way I could think of to get my hands on it. Anyway, you kissed me first. In the car."

"Not with any ulterior motive."

"Just because you felt like it, hmm?"

"Because you're sexy as hell and you turn me on, okay? There, at least I'm honest."

"Like I'm not?" At the look he gave her, she made an impatient sound and added, "You are deliberately missing the point. I **didn't** shoot you, or arrest you, when I could have. That's because **you can trust me**. I believe in you. I want to help you solve this case. The two of us working together to pinpoint what's going on with dirty cops and suspicious murders and whatever else is involved has got to be a lot more effective than you doing whatever it is you're doing alone."

He gave her a derisive look. "I'm sure you think so."

"What does that mean?"

"It means that I'm a detective and you're not. So stay out of it, **pischouette**."

She knew enough Creole to translate that roughly as "little girl."

"Oh, wow. And how have your finely honed skills been working for you, Detective? About got the case all wrapped up?"

"That's not anything you need to worry about."

"I guess not. I mean, seeing as how I'm safe at home in my bed and all."

"You'll be safe at home in your bed again as soon as I can get you there, believe me. In fact, as far as I'm concerned, the sooner the better."

She bristled. "You're not going to tell me anything, are you? Despite the fact that I'm in danger whether you do or not."

"Nope." He pushed away from the counter and came toward her, not stopping until he was close enough so she had to tilt her head back to look up at him. She suspected that he was doing it deliberately, to remind her of how much physically larger and stronger he was, as a kind of payback for her threatening him with his own gun, which no cop liked, ever, and which Reed in particular, under these circumstances, must have found particularly galling. She stood her ground—well, the table was at her back so she didn't have a choice—but she met his hard gaze with a level one of her own, while at the same time doing her best to ignore her body's instinctive response to his renewed proximity. It was as if those kisses had flipped a switch inside her, and now she was physically aware of him in a way that she hadn't been before.

"I should have forced it out of you at gunpoint," she said with genuine chagrin, because, duh, she should have.

"Wouldn't have worked." The beginnings of a grim smile just touched his mouth. "You know, I'm not feeling the gratitude: I'm doing my best to protect you here."

"Forget gratitude. I don't want to be protected."

He gave a grunt of derision. "You heard how your father responded when I threatened to tell you everything I know, right? That's because what I know is dangerous. What I know is why Holly and Ant and I are in the spot we're in. What I know could get you killed. Even if somebody did suspect that I've told you everything, the fact remains that I haven't. You don't know squat, which means you don't even know where to start to look, which means that when you get back home you won't start poking around in things that can get you killed because you'll have no idea what you're looking for. I admit, you gave me a turn there for a minute when you suggested that whoever this is might kill you just because they think there's a possibility that I told you something. But the more I think about it, the more I think we can count on the fact that you being the superintendent's daughter will keep you safe unless you make some kind of overt move that says you're a danger to them. The kind of overt move you can't make if you don't know anything."

She scowled at him. "So when you let me go, when you and Holly and Ant are either dead or in jail or on the run, I'm just supposed to go back to work and resume my nonrelationship with my father and get on with my life like none of this ever happened?"

"Yep."

"No. Not going to happen. I'll start by looking at the last case you were working on, and take it from there. What do you want to bet I can figure it out?"

"Damn it, Caroline, let it go."

"Make me. Oh, wait, you can't."

That felt like checkmate. He gave her an exasperated look. "Anybody ever tell you that you're a total pain in the ass?"

"You think you're not?"

"There's a difference."

"What's that?"

"You're a beautiful total pain in the ass," he said.

Because that last comment was so unexpected, she wound up meeting his eyes for a surprised instant, but otherwise didn't react at all as he stepped closer and slid a hand around the back of her head.

Well, maybe she had a split second there when she realized where he was going with that and she sucked in air and her eyes went wide.

"I'm done arguing about it," he told her, so close now that his breath feathered her lips.

Before she could coordinate her brain and mouth enough to snap **Well, I'm not,** he kissed her. The touch of his lips on hers gave her the equivalent of an instant contact high. She was still hot from their last kiss, and this one immediately set her on fire. Her lids closed like they had weights attached; her head tilted helplessly back to give him better access to her mouth. He kissed her slowly, thoroughly, expertly, with all the heat but none of the hurry of the previous time, with a deepening eroticism that drove every rational thought out of her head, that had her melting inside, while her heart pounded and her blood turned to steam. His lips moved on hers like he meant to make this one kiss last all night. The hot, wet invasion of her mouth thrilled her down to her toes, and she kissed him back with a fierce passion of her own. She was just surging up against him, just starting to slide her arms around his neck, just starting to take things to a whole different level of intense, when he lifted his mouth from hers and let his hand drop from behind her neck and stepped back.

Her eyes flew open. For a moment they simply stared at each other. She felt— dizzy. Disoriented. Shivery with need. He was as turned on as she was, she could tell.

He radiated sexual tension like the sun's rays in a summer heat wave. And the only thing he was doing about it was watching her with that dark, sexy gleam in his eyes.

To kiss her like that and stop—

"What the hell was that?" she demanded. Okay, so she was breathless and it showed in her voice. Being breathless in no way detracted from her budding wrath. Because she knew, **knew,** that there absolutely had been an ulterior motive behind that kiss.

"I was making a point." He echoed the words she'd previously said to him as he reached past her toward something on the table. That brought him closer again, and she felt his nearness like a prickle of heat moving across her skin.

She looked at him suspiciously. "And what point is that?"

"You weren't faking it earlier." Snagging his backpack, he drew back, slung it onto one broad shoulder, and gave her a mocking smile.

"If it makes you happy to think—" She broke off with a quick frown. "Where are you going?" Her voice went sharp with anxiety. Because he was on the move, heading toward the door, and it was obvious that he was going somewhere. She felt cold suddenly, and folded her arms over her chest as she turned to watch his progress. The idea of being left alone in this small, primitive cabin in the middle of a swamp she couldn't negotiate while he went off to do God knows what elsewhere was, she discovered, more than a little alarming.

He could park her here and leave.

"To crank the generator," he told her. "It's out back. I'll get wetter, but we'll have power." She made note of the fact that he was taking the backpack with him, and presumed there was a reason. For one thing, she guessed that he wasn't about to give her an opportunity to grab the phone that was in there, and that would be because he still didn't trust her, because he had trust issues the size of Texas. "If you're hungry, groceries are in the bag on the table. Bottled water is in the lower left cabinet. Bathroom's through the door closest to the bed. There should be a towel in there. It'll be about fifteen minutes before there's any hot water." Having reached the door by that time, he paused with his hand on the knob to look back at her. "And, Caroline—you realize that if you were to do something stupid, like try to run away, if you didn't wind up hopelessly lost or drowned in a bog or eaten by alligators, I'd track you down and drag you back before you could get out of the bayou, right?"

"Oh, for God's sake," she said. "Get it through your thick head: I'm not going anywhere."

His eyes swept over her.

"One more thing: don't ever try to manipulate me by kissing me again," he warned softly. Then, without another word, he went out.

She was left to scowl at the closed door. Her plan to prove to him that he could trust her had clearly been a waste of effort, because he still didn't trust her. Worse, he was obviously still feeling all pissy because she had kissed him to get his gun. Which, in hindsight, had been a mistake on so many levels that she didn't have the energy to count them. Like opening Pandora's box, it had released all kinds of unexpected things into the atmosphere. First and foremost was sex.

Simple solution: sleep with him already, said a little voice inside her head.

The attraction between them was so strong that even while she was just standing there staring at the door, she caught herself having blazing microfantasies about screwing his brains out. If a relationship between them wasn't in the cards—and, given the circumstances, she had to face the truth that it was a long shot—what was wrong with settling for however many sessions of really mind-blowing sex they could squeeze in?

There were problems with that, and the reasonable part of her brain knew it, but the hot and bothered, I-am-so-turned-on part didn't want to know.

You've wanted him for ten years.

Carpe diem. Seize the day. This is your chance.

You might never get another.

That was the kick-in-the-teeth thought that was the equivalent of an icy shower.

Screw him until he was killed? Or arrested? Or forced to go on the run for the rest of his life?

That wasn't going to work for her.

That complicated her body's single-minded demand for a purely sexual thrill ride, because she realized that sex was maybe the smallest part of what she wanted from him.

There was no easy solution, so she turned her attention to seizing the day for more urgent matters, grabbing the lantern and heading for the bathroom, where she made use of the facilities, then grabbed the lone towel and used it to quickly towel dry her hair. The room was small, maybe six by eight feet, and gave the impression of having once been a shed that had been attached to the shanty as an afterthought.

The fixtures were basic, but they were all there: cheap white toilet and white sink with a standard mirrored medicine cabinet over it, molded plastic shower with frosted acrylic doors. All clean and fairly new. The floor was generic white tile, as were the walls up to about five feet from the floor. After that, the weathered cypress planks that made up the shanty rose to the ceiling. A blue plastic laundry basket in one corner was there presumably to act as a hamper. On the floor in front of the shower was a small gray rug. The bathroom looked like a do-it-yourself special, and she found herself wondering if Reed was responsible. She frowned a little as she thought about that: she had no idea if he was handy. She **wanted** to know, she discovered. She wanted to know every little detail about him.

The scary truth of it was, she was developing a real thing for Reed.

She'd had her fair share of boyfriends, but none of them had ever really gotten under her skin. **Ice, ice, baby** wasn't only her professional motto.

How ironic would it be if the exception to that turned out to be Reed? If the man she finally decided to give her heart to was the one person most likely not to make it through the next twenty-four hours?

There has to be a way out of this.

The problem was that he wouldn't tell her anything, and she was almost too tired and mentally fried to think.

A small overhead light flickered once, then blinked on, emitting a dim, pale glow. It distracted her. Glancing up at it, Caroline realized that the faint buzzing sound that now joined in with the rattle of the rain beating down on the roof was the exhaust fan, and that both amenities had sprung to life because, obviously, Reed had gotten the generator going.

Turning to check out the medicine cabinet in a quest for soap—there was none visible—she caught a glimpse of herself in the mirror over the sink. Her now damp and tousled hair hung in a darker-than-usual tangle around her shoulders. Her hazel eyes were shadowed with fatigue, which was no surprise given the hour. Her high cheekbones sported a hectic flush. Her ordinarily reasonably full lips looked several degrees plumper and rosier than usual, which she attributed to Reed's kisses.

Or, possibly, to the effects of the duct tape. Remembering the duct tape brought a frown to her face—she was still mad at Reed about that—and she was still frowning as her gaze fell lower and she saw, to her embarrassment and chagrin, how closely her wet blouse clung to the contours of her body. Something—probably the fact that she was soaked through and chilled now because of it, possibly her reaction to those blazing kisses—had caused her nipples to pucker and harden. They were embarrassingly visible through the wet silk, and she plucked the fabric away from her skin with dismay.

When she'd been dressing for the date that her call out to the Winfield mansion had interrupted, which would be her second one with Ben Paxton, a very nice, handsome, thirty-year-old accountant who lived in an apartment two floors below hers in a boxlike high-rise in Kenner, she'd been going for a little festive, a little sexy, but nothing too suggestive because, while she liked Ben, and she looked forward to a Christmas Eve dinner with him and a group of friends at the elegant Le Foret restaurant, she wasn't seeing the night ending with anything more than a good-night kiss at her door. The blouse had seemed perfectly appropriate then.

Of course, she hadn't foreseen that, before the night was over, she would wind up out of the chic little blazer that she had worn over it, or that she would get soaking wet. Just like she hadn't foreseen getting kidnapped, or casting in her lot with the villainous hostage taker—or, in a word, Reed.

That was it in a nutshell: she hadn't foreseen Reed.

Recalling just when the rain had started to fall, she realized that the only one who would have seen her looking like a contestant in a wet T-shirt contest was Reed.

That's what he had been looking at before she'd kissed him. She remembered his eyes on her, remembered the sudden sexy gleam they'd taken on, and the memory made her breasts tighten still more. It made her breathing quicken. It made her hot.

Face the truth: he **makes you hot.**

You've got it bad, she told herself with disgust, and opened the medicine cabinet to continue her search for soap. There were supplies in there, she was glad to discover. Besides a couple of unopened bars of—yes!—soap, which she immediately made use of to wash her hands and face, there were the usual first aid products, including AfterBite, which she happily grabbed on sight. She had a number of mosquito bites on her legs, which she had been dealing with by ignoring them in hopes that they would go away. This would be infinitely better. But as she looked down at her legs, she hesitated. Her ankles were gritty with the residue of the dirty water they'd splashed through, while her calves were streaked with mud.

She was just glancing speculatively at the shower when there was a tap at the door.

"You decent?" Reed asked through the crude panel. Like the rest of the cabin, it appeared to have been handcrafted from cypress, and it hung a little crookedly in the equally primitive door frame. It also lacked a lock, as she had noted when she entered.

How stupid was it that just the sound of his voice made her heart beat faster? "Yes."

He pushed the door open and walked into the bathroom. She was standing in front of the sink, and had to take a step back to let him in.

Despite her best intentions to remain unaffected, Caroline couldn't help but suck in her breath—inaudibly, she prayed—as Reed entered. His black hair was slicked close to his head, he had a towel hanging around his neck—and he was gloriously, completely shirtless.

CHAPTER SIXTEEN

For an unguarded moment, Caroline simply looked.

He was built like an athlete, all long, hard muscle. His chest was deeply tanned, silent evidence of a considerable amount of time spent outdoors without a shirt. Wide and muscular beneath broad shoulders, his impressive expanse of chest tapered down to his waist in a classic, masculine vee. His biceps bulged. His forearms were honed and powerful looking. In the center of his chest, a wedge of black curling hair, not too thick, traveled downward until there was no more of it re-

maining than a thin line snaking over abs
that were totally ripped. After that, the
waistband of his pants, slung low on his
hipbones, obscured her view. Realizing
where she was looking, she jerked her eyes
back up to his face, but not before she felt
a flush of heat and her pulse picked up.

It wasn't as if she'd never seen a man's
chest before. She had. But this was Reed,
Reed wearing nothing but black tuxedo
pants and a towel around his neck—in
other words, sexy personified.

In sheer self-defense she frowned at
him.

His eyes as they met hers were dark
and impossible to read. He'd definitely noticed her looking, and she waited for some
wiseass remark.

It didn't come.

"I brought you something," was what he
said, in a clipped tone that told her he
was still bent out of shape about the kiss.
Thanks to the feeble light of the overhead
fixture, she noticed fine lines at the corners of Reed's eyes, and deeper ones
bracketing his mouth, that hadn't been
visible earlier. He looked tense, tired, and
faintly grumpy.

He held up a new toothbrush, still in its packaging, which he waggled at her. In his other hand, he was carrying his gun, which was still in its holster.

"A toothbrush!" With a gift like that in hand, she didn't care if he was still mad at her. Caroline reached for it with genuine enthusiasm. A second one was in his hand, which she presumed was for his own use. They'd probably been in the bag of groceries on the table, which she hadn't taken time to look at before heading for the bathroom. She'd seen a tube of toothpaste in the medicine cabinet, she recalled. Turning back to it, she set the AfterBite down on the edge of the sink, and grabbed the toothpaste from the shelf with gusto.

"You're lucky I bought two." He pulled the towel from around his neck, which actually turned out to be two thin, cheap white ones intertwined, and slung them over the top of the shower, which lacked about two feet of reaching the ceiling. The display of rippling muscle that was involved sent her pulse fluttering. As she redirected her gaze in a hurry, he walked around her to place his gun on the back of the toilet, and she noticed that he was barefoot. Clearly her mind had been focused on something—somewhere—else, or she would have noticed sooner. As he turned back toward her his eyes slid over her, and Caroline was reminded once again of the revealing state of her blouse. Of course, he'd seen her accidental display before, but she'd just as soon he didn't keep seeing it. Casually she angled her body a little away from him. A quick glance as she squirted a dab of toothpaste on the brush found him looking at the AfterBite. He lifted his eyebrows at her inquiringly.

"Mosquito bites?"

"A few on my legs," she replied. It was, she discovered, perfectly possible to engage in innocuous conversation with a gorgeous, bare-chested guy who was biting his words off at her while he stood right beside her, seeming to take up way more than his share of the limited space. What was harder was not looking at his chest—or his muscular arms, or his taut abs—while she did so.

He glanced at her legs.

"That's the problem with showing so much leg: no telling what you'll attract."

"I was on a **date**. Sorry I didn't get the

memo on the proper dress code for being **kidnapped**." Okay, so much for friendly chitchat. The bathroom was feeling way too small. "Look, do you mind going away? I'd like to brush my teeth. And take a shower." She remembered the towels he'd been wearing around his neck. "Unless you want to shower first, of course."

"There's no showering first," he said. "Since I don't have anywhere to lock anything up, and I'm not prepared to leave you out here on your own with my gun and everything else, we're showering together."

At the idea of showering with him her heart gave a little hiccup. The picture it conjured up was so tantalizing that her mouth went dry. Which was why she had so many problems with the suggestion that she practically sputtered.

"What? Oh, no we're not. If you're thinking I'm getting naked with you—"

"Cher, we both know you'd love to get naked with me."

She was indignant. In spite of the fact that it just might be true. "In your dreams!"

"But I didn't say you had to get naked," he continued smoothly. "I'm going to strip down to my boxers, you strip to whatever you feel like stripping down to. Or not. You can stand fully dressed in the corner out of the spray for all I care. We get in, we get out, we hit the sack for a few hours. I've got a dry T-shirt you can sleep in. It's big enough so you'll be decent."

"If I was going to shoot you, I would have done it already," she pointed out astringently. Had she thought his trust issues were the size of Texas? More like the planet. "I didn't. I think that means you're safe."

"Yeah, well, I'm not prepared to chance you changing your mind."

"I don't want to shower with you," she said.

"Too bad. That's what's going to happen." He gave her an impatient look. "Come on, Caroline. Don't make it a big deal. I'm dead on my feet, and you have to be, too. Let's do this the easy way, then grab some sleep."

"You can't just say, too bad."

"I'm pretty sure I just did."

"Screw that."

He sighed. "There are two ways we can do this. You can get in the damned shower with me, or I can haul your ass in there."

"You can try."

"What's the matter, afraid you won't be able to keep your hands off me?"

"That," she said with dignity, "was low. I mean, I get it: you're mad. Believe me, if I'd known you were going to get so bent out of shape over a little thing like being kissed, I would have thought of some other way to get your gun. You don't notice **me** being all pissy because **you** kissed **me**."

His eyes narrowed at her. "You're not winning this one, Caroline."

They exchanged measuring looks. She could see from the obstinate set of his jaw that he meant what he said.

Well, as long as she didn't have to get naked she didn't really have a problem with the shower anyway. She just didn't like the way he was ordering her in there. Or the fact that he still didn't trust her. Or the fact that he wouldn't tell her anything, or let her help him. Or the fact that he was clearly perfectly prepared to trade her for Ant and just walk—run?—away.

At the moment, though, the shower was the issue at hand. The rest she would find a way to deal with later.

"Oh, fine," she capitulated ungraciously.

"First I'm brushing my teeth." For some reason, the idea of doing it in front of him bothered her: it seemed way too personal. That was one reason she had never lived with any of her boyfriends: she liked her privacy.

"So brush them. Here, I'll brush mine, too." Tearing his toothbrush out of its packaging, he came over to the sink beside her. Smearing toothpaste on it, he turned on the tap, warning, "The water's from a tank, so don't swallow."

Then he brushed his teeth. Watching white foam bubble around in his mouth, Caroline slowly followed suit. Rinsing her mouth in the sink alongside him felt disturbingly intimate. If he had any similar reservations about it, he didn't show it.

"Looks like your clothes are starting to dry. Lucky there's not much material to that date-bait skirt."

"So what is it that you have a problem with, exactly? The length of my skirt, or the fact that I was on a date?" She turned to scowl at him, and found her gaze riveted. His hands were busy undoing the top button of his fly, and as they moved on to his zipper she felt unexpected shimmers of excitement dance over her skin. Then she realized that she was **watching,** and abruptly glanced away, glanced down at her sneakers, found nothing of interest there, and was glad to get busy kicking them off as the sound of his zipper being lowered reached her ears.

"Neither. None of my business." Before she could reply to that, he added, "The good thing is, short as that skirt is, it should dry fast. I only mentioned it because, before you go getting in the shower fully dressed, you should know that the only clothes I've got here are a couple of pairs of jeans, which aren't by any stretch of the imagination going to fit you, and some underwear and socks and T-shirts. Which means you're probably going to want to put on the skirt again when you wake up, so I don't know if getting it soaked in the shower is the best idea. If I were you, I'd take it off."

Glancing up from nudging her shoes out of the way against the wall, she was just in time to watch him shuck his pants. He was wearing light blue boxers. They hung low enough on his lean hips that she could see even more of his washboard abs and the line of black hair that bisected them. His legs were muscular, masculine, and sported a nice amount of black hair. If he wasn't tan all over, she couldn't tell.

She'd been feeling cold before. No longer.

Wadding his pants up into a ball, he lobbed them into the laundry basket. "You're wearing panties, right?"

"Of course I'm wearing panties."

"That's right, I remember seeing them. So you can lose the skirt. Do what you want, cher, but we're going in the shower now."

Caroline gave him a trenchant look. Getting her skirt soaked did not seem like a good idea. "I'm not doing a striptease for you. Turn around."

One side of his mouth quirked up in a wry half smile, but even as she narrowed her eyes at him threateningly he turned around.

Lips compressing, she shimmied out of her skirt. Made of stretchy jersey knit, it was pretty wet, she discovered as she shook it out. So wet that getting it soaked in a shower wouldn't make a difference? It was a judgment call, but she decided that the shower could only make her sodden skirt even more waterlogged.

Off with it, then.

"You want to speed it up?" he said impatiently. "I'm growing old here."

Glancing at him—which she shouldn't have done, because she immediately got a close-up and personal eyeful of his wide shoulders and sleek, muscular back above a small, tight butt encased in trim boxers, all of which were sexy enough to make her breathing quicken—she draped her skirt over the side of the sink in hopes that it would be dry by the time she needed to put it on again. Then she hesitated. Her blouse was already wet through, and as revealing as it was going to get. And it reached almost to the top of her panties. If she took it off, she would feel naked in her panties and bra, which were flimsy, skimpy things that, wet, would be practically non-existent.

The thought of showering with him like that made her body start to quicken and throb, but she wasn't quite ready to go there. She didn't think.

"Caroline—" He glanced around at her. His voice was a growl.

"I don't suppose you have anything re-
sembling a shower cap?"

"No."

"I didn't think so."

Without another word, she moved to the
shower, pulled it open, and stepped in. Inside the cubicle it was shadowy, but not
really dark because the bathroom light
spilled over the top and filtered through
the frosted plastic door. She was twisting
her hair, which she really didn't want to get
all wet again, into a knot on the top of her
head when he stepped in behind her and
closed the door. Standing partially facing
away from him, she was suddenly aware of
him with every nerve ending she possessed.

"Short skirt, no bra: must have been
some hot date you had planned," he said
as he reached past her for the tap, which
was a single porcelain knob set into the
middle of the white molded acrylic that
lined the shower on three sides.

His comment reminded her that her nipples were plainly visible through the clingy
wetness of her blouse. Turning so her back
was to him and thus depriving him of that
particular view, she resisted the urge to fold
her arms over her breasts.

"My skirt is not that short, I am, too, wearing a bra, and my date was for dinner and that's it." Made for one, the shower was way too small once he was inside the plastic rectangle with her. She took an involuntary step forward, closer to the tap, but that didn't help: the warm firm muscles of his bare arm and chest brushed her as he turned the tap, which squeaked in protest. She felt the sizzle of the contact clear down to her toes.

"Sounds like a dull date."

"What, are all your dates orgies?"

"Always."

That was annoying. "No girlfriend?"

"Not lately."

She calculated how long it had been since his divorce, and then since his ex-wife had died, and found herself wondering if maybe he was still carrying a torch for her. Not that she meant to ask.

"Out trolling the bars, hmm?" was what she said instead.

"When I need to."

She was just registering the implication of that—translate **when I need to** to mean **when I feel like having sex**—when he added, "If you're really that interested in my love life, I can show you my little black book."

"I'm not at all interested in your love life," she snapped. "And you're crowding me." Because, with his big body brushing up against her back, he definitely was.

"You're crowding me," he replied equably. "I didn't build this shower for two." The tap squeaked loudly. "Come on, you cantankerous son of a bitch, work."

That last was clearly directed at the shower and not her. Other than that, his reply was interesting on a couple of levels: he'd built the shower, and most likely the rest of the bathroom as well, and when he came out to the shanty he probably wasn't in the habit of bringing a woman with him.

"Mechanical difficulties?" she gibed as the tap squeaked, a pipe groaned—and nothing else happened. When he didn't answer, she glanced around at him, and found herself eyeballing his wide, muscular, hunky chest. Standing foursquare and solid, he was broad-shouldered enough that he took up most of the space from wall to wall. His right arm still stretched past her, his hard biceps moved against her arm as he continued to wrestle with the tap—and there was no mistaking the fact that the reason he was slow to reply was that he was too busy checking out her butt.

She was wearing silky black bikini panties, which were damp and which she was quite sure were completely visible below the hem of her hip-length blouse. They were snug, on the skimpy side, and cut high on her thighs, but they provided perfectly adequate coverage for all her salient parts. She tried to imagine exactly what, standing behind her as he was, he might be able to see. Her blouse should just about meet the lacy waistband, which would give him a clear view of the silky cloth cupping her butt. Below them, her legs, long and tanned and slender, were bare.

She couldn't see his eyes, because his lowered lids blocked them. But she could see the sudden tautness of the skin over his cheekbones, see the sudden sensuous curve of his mouth, see the rise and fall of his chest as he breathed just that telltale degree too fast. She could feel her own blood heating. She could feel the sizzle in the air.

"Damn valve sticks sometimes. I had to jury-rig the whole system. No city water way out here." He glanced up, encountered her gaze, and frowned. She was looking at him over her shoulder. His arm rested right up against hers as he continued to twist the tap without, so far, any result except a whole lot of squeaking and the occasional groan: the shower didn't seem to want to work. She could feel the steely strength of his biceps as they turned and flexed. She could feel the heat of his skin.

She battled an impulse to duck her head and press her lips to that long, powerful arm.

Maybe she was ready to give one-night stands a try.

Maybe she was ready to give a one-night stand with Reed a try.

Maybe she was ready to take whatever she could get from him.

Just having him so close was making her shiver a little. Her lips parted with the need to take in more air.

He said, "You cold? Scoot around me, and let me try putting some muscle in it."

Not the response she had been expecting. If he was feeling the same sexual charge that she was, he didn't show it. She did as he asked, turning sideways as they edged past each other. They were both nearly naked, and the proximity of all that bare masculine flesh made her heartbeat speed up. It clouded her thought processes. Their bodies brushed—his arm against hers, the cloth of his boxers against the skin of her bare thighs—and she felt tiny electric tingles everywhere they touched. Sleek and powerful looking, his heavily muscled shoulders were at eye level, so she dropped her gaze, immediately encountering his wide chest with its well-developed pecs and wedge of fine black hair. Her breathing quickened and she could feel herself starting to go all soft inside. Then the tips of her breasts accidentally brushed his arm and immediately responded by tightening in a way that sent shivery little tendrils of desire shooting through her body. Catching her breath, she pulled back and looked up, checking to see if he had noticed. She could see the pulse beating in the little hollow at the base of his throat. She could see every whisker in the black scruff that darkened his chin. She could see the fine texture of the bronzed skin stretched tight over his cheekbones.

Then, because she was looking at him rather than where she was going, she stumbled over something—his foot, she thought—slipped, and automatically thrust out a hand to steady herself.

It landed right in the middle of his very masculine chest. Her fingers looked slim and pale splayed out in the wedge of fine black hair.

"Careful." He caught her arm, causing her to look up just as she was registering how firm and solid and warm his chest felt beneath her palm. She could feel the soft mat of his chest hair, and the beat of his heart, which was stronger and faster than she would have expected it to be under ordinary circumstances. Their eyes collided, held, and suddenly the memory of those hot kisses shimmered in the air between them. Just looking at his lean, hard-jawed, handsome face made her pulse pound. Her mouth went dry, and she licked her lips to moisten them.

His eyes zeroed in on the movement.

The electricity that surged between them made her dizzy. Her heart pounded.

Her pulse raced. Swaying toward him instinctively, she leaned her own warm curves against the solid, muscular length of him and lifted her face toward his. A surge of sizzling heat suffused her body at what she saw for her there in the dark, sexy gleam in his eyes.

"Reed," she murmured, her voice all low and husky.

He breathed in maybe a little too sharply and his hand tightened on her arm even as she went up on tiptoe, lowering her lashes, parting her lips in anticipation just before she touched them to his.

They moved against hers—and then they were gone. His now-iron grip on her arm was all that kept her from stumbling forward even as he stepped back so abruptly that he collided with the wall behind him.

For a second all she could do was frown at him in incomprehension. His eyes were ablaze with what she had no trouble at all in recognizing as passion—and at the same time were as hard as pieces of onyx.

"Reed," she protested in a far different tone, affronted, a little plaintive.

"Forget it, Caroline. I am not going there

with you," he said grimly. "We're not having sex. I may want to, you may want to, but it's not happening. We're going to take a shower, and we're going to get some sleep, and after that I'm going to see about getting you back where you belong. End of story."

Caroline's eyes widened. Her spine stiffened. He was still holding her arm in that unbreakable grip. Her hands curled into fists. Indignation swamped all her hot, sexy feelings like a tidal wave of ice water.

"What do you mean, forget it? Like **I'm** the one who has sex on the brain? Who dragged who into the shower? Who was just checking out whose butt? I— Let go of my arm." She jerked her arm free of his hold, turned, and thrust a hand out toward the shower door. "Forget the damned shower. I'm out of here."

"You're not out of here until I say you're out of here." He sounded like he was talking through his teeth—she wouldn't know, because she wasn't looking at him, or at least she wasn't looking at him until she shoved the shower door open and he hooked her with an arm around her waist, hauling her back toward him like a fish on a line. Then she looked at him, glared at him, but it didn't do any good because he wasn't looking at her. He was looking toward the tap while he twisted it hard.

The pipes groaned, a few drops of water spurted from the sunflower-size shower head, and then a deluge of hot water shot out, interrupting. With the initial drops as a warning, she just managed to close the door and jerk her head back out of the way in time to prevent her hair from being soaked by the rush of water that poured down like it was spurting from a giant hose. She scowled at Reed through the cascade.

"Jackass." Okay, the hot water felt wonderful. She had not realized how tired and sore her muscles were, or how chilled she was.

"The water will last for about five minutes," Reed yelled through the pelting torrent, and passed her a bar of soap, which she reluctantly—she was mad at him, but soap was soap—accepted. "You might want to get a move on. When it's gone, it's gone."

With that in mind, she put aside her outrage in favor of soaping up quickly, and then had the soap scooped out of her hand so he could do the same. The steam rising around them wrapped them in a welcome cocoon of soap-scented heat. With space as tight as it was, it was impossible not to have their bodies touch, their legs and arms brush, and it was maddening to realize that she was burningly aware of each glancing contact. Watching him rub suds over his face, then vigorously scrub his chest and arms, was way more intimate than brushing her teeth with him had been—and she discovered that she couldn't help but watch. As water sluiced the suds down the length of his powerful body, she found her eyes following the path of the suds and felt her heart start to beat faster again, as a delicious tightening sensation began to build deep inside her. With a silent curse, she deliberately averted her gaze.

It had been beyond infuriating when he'd told her to forget about sex. It was even more infuriating to discover that she couldn't.

The water stopped just the way it began:

the pipes groaned, and then the deluge slowed to a trickle, and then that was it. **When it's gone, it's gone,** indeed.

Soaked to the skin, not even allowing herself to think about how clingy and revealing her blouse must be at this point, Caroline found herself face to face with an equally soaked Reed.

His eyes slid over her. Her eyes slid over him. With his boxers now as thoroughly drenched as her blouse was, the hard bulge at the front of them was unmistakable. No matter how much he might want to deny it, there was the absolute proof that he was thinking about sex, too.

They both looked up at the same time. Their eyes collided. He knew where she'd been looking: she could see it in his expression.

"Caroline—"

"Forget it." Her voice held a note of malicious enjoyment. "I am **not** having sex with you. No matter how much you want it. Not even if you beg."

For the briefest of moments he simply looked at her with his eyes all heavy lidded and gleaming, totally confirming what she already knew: he was as turned on as she was. Then he reached up, grabbed one of the towels from the top of the enclosure, and handed it to her.

"Good to know we're on the same page," he said, and, taking the other towel with him, stepped out of the shower.

Caroline was left glowering after him.

Safely alone in the shower, she undressed, dried off, and wrung out her saturated blouse and undies, hanging them from the tap and the door handle in hopes that, by the time she needed to put them on again, they would be at least marginally dry.

Then, wrapping herself in the towel, which covered her from approximately the armpits to the tops of her thighs, she stepped cautiously out of the shower, shivering as she left the remnants of the steam behind.

Reed was nowhere in sight. Neither was his gun.

A T-shirt hung from the hook near the sink.

Caroline picked it up and looked at it. It was medium gray, had **Coors** written in bold black script across the front, and looked and felt clean. It was also big. As she pulled it on, she noticed that it smelled very faintly of some mild detergent, and it was indeed big. The sleeves reached to her elbows, and the hem reached halfway down her thighs.

Plenty of coverage. The only problem, of course, was that she didn't have a stitch to put on underneath.

It couldn't be helped. She took her hair down, quickly combed through it with the poor little pocket comb that was the only hairstyling implement she could find, made use of some lip balm from the medicine cabinet, applied dabs of AfterBite to the bites on her legs, and finally left the sanctuary of the bathroom, turning the light off behind her as she went.

Reed was lying on his back on the far side of the double bed, his head on a flat-looking pillow, one arm folded behind his head, his eyes already at half-mast with the need for sleep, clearly waiting for her to emerge. The only light in the room came from a small lamp on a table beside the bed. A red and blue pieced quilt covered him to approximately the middle of his chest. Above it, the rest of his chest and his shoulders were bare.

Hesitating in the bathroom doorway—which meant that she was standing almost at the foot of the bed—Caroline took a moment to assess the situation. He was looking impossibly hot, dangerously sexy, way tired, and slightly grouchy. Her heart beat a little faster and her body temperature rose just from the sight of him in a bed waiting for her. But he wasn't the only attraction. With Reed in it, or **even** with Reed in it—she wasn't quite sure which—the bed itself looked as appealing as an oasis in a desert. She was suddenly drooping with fatigue. Jelly legged. Fuzzy brained. Exhausted.

"Jesus Christ, you took long enough," Reed groused, and threw back the covers on the other side of the bed for her. "Get in here."

When she sent a questioning glance winging around the rest of the room—there really was no other place to sleep—he made an impatient sound.

"It's almost 6 a.m. With the day we've got coming up, we both need some sleep. Nothing else involved. So come park your ass."

Her brows contracted. By "nothing else,"

she knew he meant "no sex." "How could I possibly say no to that?"

But she was too tired to really argue, and too aware of the futility of it, too. If she didn't get into bed with him, she had little doubt that he would get up and physically put her where he wanted her. Anyway, besides the mild enjoyment she might get from annoying him, the only real reason she had to refuse was that she might find sleeping beside him too arousing, which he would instantly guess and mock her with. So, frowning, she moved along the narrow space between the mattress and the wall, then sat down on the side of the bed. Sliding in beneath the covers, she fell instantly in love with the too-thin mattress, just because stretching out on it felt so good. The pillow was thin, too, and flat, but it felt like the fluffiest down beneath her head. Her leg brushed Reed's; her arm brushed Reed's. Her whole body brushed Reed's. There wasn't any way around it: the bed was too small to avoid contact. Warm, sexy feelings abounded, but she was suddenly too tired to do more than experience them in the most pleasantly abstract way.

"Good night," she said, and was just snuggling down deep beneath the covers, just getting ready to roll onto her side with her back ostentatiously turned to him, when his hand, warm and strong, slid down her arm, leaving a trail of heat in its wake. She smiled a little as she flicked a look up at him, ready to taunt him by saying something on the order of, **wow, you really can't keep your hands off me, can you?**

Then she felt the cool slide of metal encircling her wrist.

Even as she heard the click and felt the thing lock in place, she knew what had just happened: he'd handcuffed her again.

CHAPTER SEVENTEEN

Shooting into a sitting position, Caroline twisted around to slay him with her eyes. Her sudden movement caused the springs to squeak. The iron headboard clanked into the wall.

"Really?" Lifting her shackled wrist—of course he had handcuffed her to himself again, her right wrist to his left one—as high as she could, she shook it at him. The chain rattled. His heavily muscled arm barely lifted off the bed. "Again?"

Reed didn't look particularly perturbed by her anger. Tucking his free arm beneath his head, he once more settled onto his back. His eyes gleamed darkly up at her. His mouth was an unrepentant line.

"Same thing as the shower," he said. "I'm not prepared to leave you in a position to get your hands on my gun or the phone or anything else, and I need sleep. So do you, which this arrangement means we'll both be getting. So unless you were hoping to get the drop on me again, or make a call or something like that, I don't see why you have a problem with it."

That was so infuriating that for a moment all she could do was blink at him.

"You—don't—see—why—I—have—a—problem—with—it," she repeated witheringly, spacing the words out. "You can just take it from me: **I have a problem with it**."

"Best I can do." Unfolding the arm from beneath his head, he reached out and turned off the lamp. They were immediately plunged into pitch darkness. "Go to sleep, cher. I'll still be around when you wake up. You can be mad at me then."

Glaring at him was a giant waste of time, because he couldn't see her. For a moment she sat there in the dark seething. She was acutely aware of the weight of his arm on the other end of the handcuff, the solid warmth of his leg brushing hers, and the steady rhythm of his breathing. It grew deeper and slower even as she listened. Clearly he was not letting her anger bother him. After a few minutes of this, she reached the conclusion that there was nothing she could do to free herself, so she might as well give her body what it was crying out for, and simply lie down and go to sleep.

She hadn't realized how mad she still was until he snored, a soft rattling noise that told her that he had fallen asleep in the face of her outrage. The sound made her fume.

It made her punch him in the arm.

Which did nothing to stop his snoring. Which told her that it didn't wake him up. Which told her how truly exhausted he was. Which did not make her any less mad at him.

It only made her realize that under the circumstances, being mad was a huge waste of energy. As he'd said, she could be mad at him when they woke up.

"Asshole," she threw at him.

A rattling snore was his only response.

Flopping down beside him because she was just too damned tired herself to do anything else, she was still listening to his snores when she fell asleep.

————————

When Reed awoke, the first thing he became aware of was that there was a woman sprawled on top of him. She was wearing something soft and short, and from the sound of her breathing she was dead asleep. Lying flat on his back with his eyes still closed, he smelled the soft scent of her hair, and felt its tickle beneath his nose as he inhaled. He felt the size and weight of her: with her head tucked beneath his chin, her bare right foot hit just above his left ankle, and she was slight enough that her weight was sexy rather than bothersome. He felt her unmistakably female curves pressing against him. Silky bare legs were entangled with his. Her face was pillowed on his chest, her hand was clasped in his, and her sweet little twat was pushed right up against some major morning wood. It felt as if a thin layer of cotton—that would be his boxers, the clean, dry dark green ones he'd changed

into after showering—was all that was pre-
venting them from going ahead and getting
it on right there and then.

His right hand, the one that she wasn't
holding, was curved around a tight, round
ass.

As he identified that warm satiny curve,
his pulse slammed into overdrive while his
fingers tightened on it reflexively. She
didn't stir, but he did. Almost painfully.

He was immediately afflicted with an urgent case of gotta-have-it. The word **horny**
suddenly felt far too mild to accurately describe the way he was feeling.

It had been a while since there had been
a woman in his life on any kind of steady
basis. When he saw a woman nowadays,
and they wound up in the sack, it was
usually at her place and he never stayed
overnight, because he wasn't into entan-
glements.

So who was sleeping . . . ?

He opened his eyes. He was in the
shanty, which was shadowy rather than
pitch dark, which told him that it was no
longer night. Grayish light was entering
through the two small windows set high in
the front wall. The pattering from the roof

meant the rain was still coming down, which would explain the quality of the light. He was guessing it was somewhere around noonish—he never slept longer than five or six hours at a stretch—but until he confirmed it by checking a phone he couldn't be sure. He slanted a look down at the woman in his arms. Ruffled coffee brown hair met his gaze. More than that of her he could not see: her face was hidden from him, and the pair of them were twisted up in a quilt that covered her to her shoulders.

Caroline.

She was lying half naked on top of him, he was squeezing her bare ass, and his erection was so big that it gave tent pole a whole new meaning. It was right on the verge of popping free of his shorts and going where nature intended it to go.

Whatever else she was wearing, panties definitely weren't part of the picture.

He breathed in, then wished he hadn't as the scent of her enveloped him. She was sleeping in one of his old T-shirts. He vividly remembered how she had looked crawling into bed in it, with her slender legs bare and her round breasts, which were the approximate size and shape of baseballs but infinitely more luscious, jiggling around inside it. At the time, he'd been dead tired enough where the need for sleep had trumped all but the most passing thought of sex.

He wasn't dead tired now. Far from it. And sex was just about the only thought in his mind.

He had handcuffed her to him. He could feel the metal bracelet around his own wrist, feel the short chain dangling between their clasped hands. At the time it had seemed like a good idea, but now that he was experiencing the result—her nearly naked body sprawled across his nearly naked body—it was starting to seem downright dumb.

When he had fallen asleep, she'd been mad at him. He was willing to bet that when she woke up, she would still be mad at him. Especially if she was still handcuffed to him. And if he still had his hand on her ass. That would probably get her furious.

He should move his hand. He should move himself, get up and out of bed while she was still asleep, before that part of him that was as stupid as it was hard won out. He was going to do both those things. He just couldn't bring himself to do either— quite . . . yet.

He wanted her so much that he ached with it. So much that it was all he could do not to roll her over onto her back and kiss her awake and fuck her into next week.

She wouldn't tell him no. In fact, she would enthusiastically welcome what he had in mind. He knew that as well as he knew there were alligators in the bayou. Caroline had been his to take since she was seventeen years old.

Hadn't done it then. Wasn't going to do it now.

Having sex with her would be a mistake.

He knew it, and could hardly keep himself from doing it anyway.

Add one more fucked-up thing to the whole fucked-up mess that his life had become: the woman he wanted like a starving man craved food wanted him, too, and the mess he was in meant that he'd be worse than a fool to do anything about it.

The problem with having sex with Caroline was, what was between them wasn't just about sex. He wanted sex, but even more than sex he wanted Caroline.

Last night, by the time he'd gone outside to start the generator, he'd been so consumed with the need to fuck her that he'd had to stand there in the rain for a while before he had cooled down enough to be able to think rationally.

The conclusion he'd come to once his dick had backed off and his brain was working again was that not fucking her was in his best interests. Getting involved with Caroline now, sexually or in any other way, would just give him that much more to lose. It would give him way too much skin in the game. If things went south— and he wasn't seeing very many scenarios in which things weren't going south—he would just be creating more pain. For himself, and for her, too.

Losing a kid had taught him to be wary of pain. Letting people get too close, letting them become part of the fabric of your existence, was a recipe for the kind of hell that he never again wanted to experience. Right now, the way things stood between him and Caroline, he could still turn his

back and walk away without any real dam-
age done to his raw and wary heart.

That was the way he intended to keep it.

With that decision firmly made, he had
turned his attention back to helping himself and Holly and Ant. At that moment,
having gone to ground in the bayou and
with Caroline a constant presence, he'd
made the only move he could make.

Punching in the only number he had,
which was for his former partner's old cell
phone, he'd called DeBlassis. DeBlassis
hadn't answered, and Reed couldn't quite
remember if the generic leave-your-name-
and-number-at-the-sound-of-the-tone response preprogramed into the phone was
the same one DeBlassis had had when
he'd lived in New Orleans or not. In the
spirit of a man throwing a Hail Mary, he'd
left a message anyway, updating DeBlassis on what was happening, and instruct-
ing him to take that file on the murders
he'd sent him straight to the Justice Department.

Which, even if the message got through,
even if the cell belonged to DeBlassis and
the man listened to his messages and still

felt the old partner bond enough to put his neck on the line, wasn't going to happen immediately: it was Christmas Day, and the government, like most everything else, would be shut down.

I'm counting on you, buddy, he thought, and disconnected.

He was on his own with the responsibility of keeping himself and Holly and Ant alive for at least another twenty-four hours. Right now, for him, the name of the game was delay. While Martin Wallace waited for his 8 p.m. phone call, while the pricks hunting him hopefully ran in circles chasing their tails, he was going to do his best to turn this around.

"Mmm." Caroline took a deep, sighing breath just then, and stirred a little, moving against him in a way that instantly reclaimed his attention and made him grit his teeth to keep from responding in the way he'd already made up his mind that he wasn't going to.

Was she waking up?

Time to move.

It took an enormous amount of willpower to get his hand off her ass, but he did it, reluctantly, sliding his palm over the firm warm silk of her cheek before dealing with the temptation to explore further by clenching his hand into a fist.

He had to concentrate on getting himself under control for a full minute afterward before he could summon the determination to reach down and fish the handcuff key out of his shoe, which he'd left beside the bed as a convenient storage/hiding place.

Before he completely lost every bit of his hard-won resolve, he needed to get up. He wanted Caroline so much that he gladly would have crawled over a nest of fire ants if he could have fucked her on the other side. Since that wasn't in the cards, the only thing to do was get himself out of harm's way.

His movements must have disturbed her a little, because she stirred again and stretched, long and slow like a sleepy cat. In the process she settled more fully on top of him, trapping his swollen and hungry dick beneath her so he was in real torment, so hot for her that he was surprised not to see flames licking at the covers. Breathing through clenched teeth and starting to sweat, he tried to slide out from under her a little as she stretched some more, luxuriously, extending her legs down the whole long length of his, bare skin to bare skin, stretching her arms upwards until their joined hands were extended all the way through the rungs of the iron headboard and his knuckles brushed the wall. He was pretty sure that the T-shirt she was wearing was now rucked up somewhere around her waist, and he was so turned on by the idea that just getting up and walking away seemed impossible. But he knew he had to move, forced himself to reach up and unlock the handcuffs, and that was what he was doing when she moaned, and squirmed, and pressed the warm wetness of her open mouth to his chest, and rocked against him in a way that froze him in place in the kind of agony/ecstasy arousal that just wasn't going to be ignored no matter how much he tried to reason it away.

Paralyzed by lust, mind fogged with steam, eyes barely open and teeth clenched as he did battle with a tsunami of torrid desire, he wasn't prepared for what happened next: she moved, fast.

He felt the coolness of her fingers grasping his wrist, heard a couple of clicks and the rattle of metal on metal, and was still processing the whole thing through a filter of intense lust when she sprang from the bed like a gazelle.

"Hah!" Landing barefoot beside the bed, breasts bouncing, legs flashing, and hair flying, she looked so sexy wearing his T-shirt and nothing else that it took him a second to get the significance of her expression, which was gloating, and her exclamation, which roughly translated as a triumphant **gotcha**.

Then he got it, all right: she'd handcuffed him to the bed.

CHAPTER EIGHTEEN

"Goddamn it, Caroline." Scowling at her, Reed jackknifed into a sitting position. His left hand was secured to one of the iron bars that made up the headboard, and the bracelet slid over the iron rattled as he moved. With the quilt puddled around his waist so his muscular chest was on full display, his black hair tousled from sleep and his jaw darkened by day-old scruff, he looked seriously sexy. And cranky. Oh, yes, definitely cranky.

Caroline found that she was loving cranky.

"Payback's a bitch." She was so pleased

with herself that she couldn't stand still. Careful to stay out of his reach, she practically did a little dance as she held up the handcuff key tauntingly. "Were you just feeling up my butt while you thought I was asleep, by the way?"

"Give me the key, Caroline." He ignored her question. Well, she didn't need an answer: she'd been fully awake from the time she'd felt a big, warm male hand tightening on her butt. If she hadn't had near instant recollection of the circumstances and identified the culprit as Reed, she would have been coming off that bed with a roundhouse punch for the perp in the space of about half a heartbeat.

But since it was Reed, the real difficulty had lain in her inclination to stay in bed and feign sleep and see where he was going with that. Of course, once he'd quit fondling her and come up with the handcuff key, she'd had the epiphany that had resulted in their current positions. As she'd told him, payback was a bitch.

She just hadn't expected it to be quite that easy.

At the look on his face, her already wide smile grew even wider. "What, don't you like being handcuffed? Unless you were planning to, I don't know, get up and be your usual bullying self, I don't see why you have a problem with it."

"Funny. Come on, Caroline. We don't have time for this."

She glanced around the shanty. Small, dark, cut off from the outside by the rain that was still falling, it smelled faintly of damp and old wood. The sound of the rain made a constant patter. Other than that, there wasn't much going on. "Looks to me like all we have is time."

"I have things I need to do."

"Like what?"

"Things, okay?"

"Not okay. You want me to let you go, you need to start talking to me. To begin with, I want to know about those suspicious murders."

He made a derisive sound. "Not going to happen."

"It will sooner or later. If you want me to unlock those cuffs."

"What are you going to do, torture me? Pull out my fingernails? Break my knee-caps?"

"All I have to do is leave you sitting there

chained to the bed. Sooner or later you'll have to go to the bathroom."

He snorted. "Cher, if you really think I won't piss in a corner if I have to, you don't know jack shit about men."

That thought was so appalling that she had to battle the urge to grimace.

"Your call. I'll ask you again when I get back." Directing another taunting smile at him, she headed for the bathroom, ignoring his bellowed **"Damn it**, **Caroline"** as the door closed behind her. She could hear the bed creaking and him cursing as, in a leisurely fashion, she used the facilities, washed her hands and face, brushed her teeth, and combed her hair, which, thanks to the humidity in the air, was waving around her face like a coffee-colored Little Orphan Annie wig. She felt fairly confident that the headboard would hold: it had felt sturdy enough. In any case, she was philosophical about the prospect that he might manage to free himself: even if he did, the point had been made. But she was hoping he couldn't, because he deserved to be right where he was for a while. Her skirt was still damp, she discovered as she checked it. So were her undies and her blouse. Deciding against putting any of them on in hopes that she might be able to wait long enough for them to actually dry, she headed back for the main room.

Having wedged the pillows against the headboard while she was gone, Reed was now leaning back against them, quilt still covering him to the waist, his expression surprisingly tranquil. Or at least, she would have thought his expression was tranquil if it hadn't been for the distinctly nasty gleam in the look he directed at her as she pushed through the door.

"Change your mind yet?" she asked. Stopping at the foot of the bed, she held the key up and waggled it at him as an incentive.

"Hell, no."

Okay, appearances to the contrary, he was obviously still feeling a little testy. Testy was almost as much fun as cranky. She smiled at him. He didn't return her grin; instead, his mouth tightened, and the gleam in his eyes got noticeably nastier.

"Fine." She headed for the table, where he'd put his gun, still in its holster. Since the table was out of reach of the bed, she presumed he'd left it there so that, handcuffed to his bulk while they slept, she couldn't get her hands on it.

Well, **surprise**. Putting the key down on the table, she picked up the gun, pulled it out of the holster, looked at it reflectively, then glanced at him.

"You know you're going to have to unlock these handcuffs eventually." He sounded like his patience was starting to fray around the edges.

"Probably." She restored the gun to its holster and put it back down on the table. It occurred to her that he absolutely knew that she wasn't going to shoot or arrest him, so he had no need to fear her getting her hands on his gun. Therefore, last night's handcuff act had not been about keeping her away from his gun. What then had he been trying to keep her away from? That, she decided, was important. The look she turned on him was speculative.

"No **probably** about it. You really want to try to find your way back through the swamp without me?"

He said that like he thought he was holding a trump card. Well, he was, but no need to admit it to him yet. "I could phone for help," she pointed out. "One little 911 call, and I bet half the cops in the state would be out here within—what?—fifteen, twenty minutes?"

"More like an hour or two. Anyway, we both know you're not going to do that."

She flicked him another look. He'd lost the tranquil expression in favor of a frown.

"Probably not," she conceded. "But I could. Not to rub it in, but this is the second time I've gotten the drop on you, and both times it was incredibly easy. You might want to be a little more careful in the future."

"Believe me, I will be." His tone bordered on grim. "Come on, Caroline, I get it: you don't like being handcuffed. Suppose I agree that I won't handcuff you anymore?"

She smiled mockingly at him. "I don't know. The thing is, now I'm finding out that I kind of like handcuffs—on you. Who knew I was kinky like that?"

"Don't make me break my bed to get free," he threatened.

"See, that's the thing about iron. It's hard to break."

"Think I can't do it?"

She shrugged. "You haven't yet."

He didn't reply. Which she thought made the answer pretty self-evident.

The bag of groceries was still on the table. She started pulling items out just to see what was in there. A loaf of bread. A jar of peanut butter. Some packaged trail mix. A couple of apples. A hunger pang assailed her at the sight of the food, and she picked up one of the apples and bit into it. It was tart and juicy. **Yum**. Looking at him, she took another bite.

He was watching her. "How about bringing me one?"

She laughed—she was **so** not falling for that—and tossed the other apple to him. He made a good one-handed catch and, with his eyes on her, sank his teeth into it.

She looked at the table next to the grocery bag and was surprised to discover not one, but two phones. One was the prepaid cell phone he'd used to call her father. She knew enough about them to know that when its minutes were used up, it was worthless. The other—she picked it up. Day-glo blue, it didn't look like anything that could possibly belong to Reed. It was connected to a charger, which was plugged into an outlet via an extension cord.

"You know what I'm asking myself right now?" She took another bite of apple as he chomped hungrily away at his. "I'm asking myself just what you handcuffed me to keep me away from. I don't think it was to keep me away from your gun." She paused to swallow.

"Yours?" she asked, picking up the blue phone.

His face told her nothing, which was interesting.

"Stolen," he replied, then when she lifted her eyebrows at him added, "Holly's got a bad habit of ripping off tourists." At Caroline's expression he shrugged. "Hey, I never claimed he was a saint."

"How did you get mixed up with him, anyway?" The phone was turned off. She turned it on, and the screen lit up: a picture of a fuzzy white kitten was the screen saver. Verdict: it most likely belonged to a teenage girl. Who hadn't bothered to password protect it.

"I've known him since he was a little kid. I knew his and Ant's mother."

"Knew?"

"She's dead." His tone changed as she started pushing buttons, calling up, respectively, e-mails and messages and texts and photos. "You know, there was a reason the phone was turned off. So nobody could track it."

"Hmm." She quickly pushed a button. The screen went black. She put the phone down on the table like it was hot. The last thing she wanted to do was to draw somebody to them who might be tracking the phone. "Why did you even bring it?"

"In case I needed to make a call that couldn't be traced back to my phone." He grimaced.

Throwing the quilt aside, he moved so that he was sitting on the side of the bed. The position left his manacled hand stretched behind him, but it was incrementally more dangerous looking than his reclining posture against the pillows. The only thing he was wearing was a pair of dark green boxers, and the sight of so much nearly naked male flesh was distracting. Stripped down, Reed was nothing if not eye candy.

Taking another bite of her apple, Caroline put the half-eaten piece of fruit down on the table and looked at him reflectively.

The thing was, she didn't think Reed

was worried about her calling for help, either. In fact, she was almost entirely certain of it.

So the question remained: what was he trying to keep her away from?

Gun. Phones. Groceries. Possibly his backpack? A glance around located it: it was right beside the bed. Even handcuffed to Reed as she had been, she could have reached it if she'd wanted.

So, no.

Why would Reed have a phone that Holly had stolen?

Unless Holly had given it to him. Reed almost certainly wasn't a fan of Holly's thievery. In fact, she could tell from his tone when he'd spoken about it that he wasn't. Holly wouldn't have given Reed proof positive that he had done something Reed disapproved of without a reason.

And Caroline was willing to bet the reason had something to do with why Holly had been arrested. The reason Reed had basically destroyed his life to get Holly out of jail. The reason she and Reed were at that moment looking at each other measuringly across maybe twelve feet of shadowy space.

The suspicious murders.

Watching Reed closely, she picked up the stolen phone again.

His eyes narrowed. His jaw hardened.

Unless someone knew that the stolen phone was in Reed's possession, no one would be tracking it to find him. That wasn't what he was worried about.

He was worried about her finding something on that phone.

She pressed the button to turn it on again. He stiffened. His shoulders visibly tensed.

She smiled triumphantly. "There's something on this phone that you don't want me to see, isn't there?"

"Put the damned phone down, Caroline."

"I take that as a big fat yes." She clicked from the fuzzy kitten to the menu.

"It's got a locator on it. Every minute you have it turned on increases our chances of being found."

"Bullshit," she said. "We both know you're not worried about that. What is it, Reed? What's on this phone?"

She clicked on the e-mails. The phone's rightful owner, she saw just from scrolling down through the messages, was named Elizabeth.

"Porn. Assignations with drug dealers. A Justin Bieber video. How the hell should I know?"

A jarring scraping sound brought her gaze back to him in a hurry. He was on his feet now, standing behind the bed, and the scraping sound had been him thrusting it away from the wall.

"You know what's on it." She was positive now. "It's something to do with those suspicious murders, isn't it?"

"Fine," he said abruptly. "You want me to tell you about the murders? I'll tell you about the murders."

Her initial rush of satisfaction didn't last much longer than it took her to look at him. His face was dark and hard. His cuffed left hand gripped the back of the headboard as if he wanted to crush it. His whole body radiated tension— Plus, his capitulation had come way too easily.

"You're going to lie to me." Her voice was flat. "Forget it, I'll figure it out for myself."

She clicked on the text messages, skimmed them. Nothing but things like, **where do you want to get lunch?** and **OMG, did you see that cute guy?**

"Put down the damned phone." He was starting to sound really angry. "I mean it."

"How to put this? No."

"This isn't some game we're playing, Caroline."

"The phone belongs to a teenage girl," she said. "What would she know about suspicious murders? Did she see something? Witness something?"

A loud scraping sound made her jerk a look toward him. At what she saw, her eyes widened, and she took an automatic step back.

Looking all dangerous and threatening, he stalked toward her, his hand gripping the headboard as he dragged the bed behind him. All dangerous and threatening, that is, except for the bed, which kind of took the intimidation factor out of play. The iron headboard was, as she had rightly calculated, apparently unbreakable. What she had not taken into account was how light the bed itself seemed to be.

"You look ridiculous," she said with a quick, condemning frown.

"Think I give a damn?" He was shoving furniture out of the way, clearing a path for himself plus the bed. She backed up some more, confident that she had some time. He might reach her, but it wasn't going to happen fast.

She said, "I'm right, aren't I?"

"Goddamn it, Caroline, don't do this."

"She witnessed something. I bet she took a picture." She clicked on the Pictures icon.

"Put the phone down, Caroline."

She glanced up again as, with multiple shrieks of metal on wood and wood on wood, he plowed through the obstacle course of the sitting area, shoving aside furniture as he came. Everything about him said that he was deadly serious in his mission to stop her from learning more, and she experienced a brief but measurable qualm. If he thought what she was going to find was really so terrible, maybe she shouldn't . . . But a picture was already filling the phone's screen, and she couldn't help herself: she had to look down at it.

It **was** terrible.

"Oh, my God," she said, staring at a close-up of the corpse of a boy of maybe thirteen or so, lying on the ground in the dark with a bullet hole between his eyes.

"Stop right there!" Reed roared, but she ignored him to click through to the next photo. Cursing a blue streak, he was making a terrific amount of noise with the bed as he struggled to get to her, but she was too transfixed by what she was seeing to pay any attention. A woman with a bullet hole between her eyes. Two more corpses killed the same way, both men. The yellow streak of a gun being fired through the darkness, less than a yard away from the head of one of those dead men, taken in what must have been his last split second of life. Those same four people alive, standing huddled together in a dark cemetery, obviously terrified. A man flashing a badge at them—

Her heart lurched.

"Goddamn it, Caroline!" Reed jumped her, grabbing her by the arm as he snatched the phone from her hand. His long, strong fingers bit into her flesh. Looking up at him almost blindly, still caught up in the hideous truth painted by the photos, she barely felt his grip.

"They were killed by cops," she said to Reed, who was looking down at her with a combination of fury and dismay. "Weren't they? That's what's up with the suspicious murders. That's what Holly meant when he said it was the cops. Police officers killed these people, and this girl—Elizabeth—witnessed it and took pictures."

She felt cold all over as she tried to assess what that meant. An isolated murder by rogue cops? But Reed had taken what he knew to her father and—

"The department's covering it up, aren't they? And my father's part of it." Then another truly terrible thought struck her. "What happened to the girl—Elizabeth?"

Reed tossed the phone onto the counter and gripped both her arms as if he never meant to let go. That was when she registered that he had somehow freed himself from both bed and handcuffs—right, she'd left the key on the table. He must have managed to reach it while she'd been looking, horrified, at the pictures.

"She doesn't know anything about those killings. If she did, she'd be dead. Holly stole her phone, was on the scene with Ant when this went down, and used it to take the pictures. He brought me in. I went to your father. And then the whole damned thing went straight to hell." He gave her a hard little shake that had her glaring at him. "I told you to leave it alone. Why the· hell didn't you listen?"

"Maybe because I don't have to listen to you?" Her voice dripped sarcasm. "Maybe because I'm a cop, too?"

"To hell with that. You should've listened."

His eyes as they stared down into hers were dark and turbulent. That look was because he was afraid for her, Caroline knew. If Reed was afraid for her—well, he wouldn't exhibit that kind of fear lightly. But the knowledge that he cared enough **to be** afraid for her made some small part of her that wasn't appalled and scared and sick to her stomach feel—good. Rallying, she took a deep breath.

"I needed to know what was going on," she said.

His mouth twisted and he pulled her right up against him. She felt the hard strength in his hands gripping her arms, the solid wall of his chest against her breasts, the warmth of his skin everywhere they touched, the sense of barely leashed power in his body. Being pressed so close to all those nearly naked masculine mus-cles made her heart beat faster. Her pulse rate speeded up. And she realized that no matter what, where she found herself was just exactly where she wanted to be: up close and personal with Reed.

"No, you damned well didn't." His voice was rough. His eyes were alive with anger and distress. "If they find out you know, they'll hunt you down just like they're hunting Holly and me. They'll kill you. The only thing you can do now is put the damned pictures out of your mind and pretend you never saw them and trust in the fact that you're the superintendent's daughter to keep you safe." Something in her face must have alerted him that she wasn't exactly with the program, because he blew out an exasperated sigh. "Goddamn it, Caroline, do you even realize how much danger you're in?"

"I'm glad I know." There was defiance in her tone, and somewhat to her own surprise she discovered that she meant every word. "There wasn't ever any chance I was just going to walk away from this without finding out what was going on, you know. There's no chance I'm walking away now."

His mouth tightened impatiently. His eyes flared at her. "That's the stupidest damned thing I ever heard. Of course you're walking away, just as soon as I can arrange it, and you're going to pretend like you don't know shit. I—"

He broke off because she was shaking her head at him. "Forget it. You dragged me into this. Now you're stuck with me."

"You're going back. You're going to tell everyone that you were my unwilling hostage this entire time, that you hate and despise me, and that you're glad for whatever terrible fate I may ultimately suffer. And you're going to keep your nose out of those murders."

"Not happening. You ever hear the saying **you can't unring a bell**?"

"The hell you can't. You're going to do exactly what I tell you. For your own damned good."

She met his blazing eyes with a level look of her own. "There's something we need to get straight between us, right now: you are not and never will be the boss of me. I go back if I want to go back. I keep my nose out of things if I want to keep my nose out of things. Otherwise, no."

Their eyes clashed.

"What is that supposed to be, your own

personal declaration of independence?" His voice was harsh, his face tight with anger and frustration. "Cher, this isn't the battle of the sexes. I'm trying to keep you alive here. Why would you even want to fight with me about it?"

He was glaring down at her. She glared right back.

"This is why," she said, and rose up on tiptoe to press her lips to his.

CHAPTER NINETEEN

The stubble on his chin as her soft skin brushed it felt . . . sexy. That she had to go up on tiptoe to reach his mouth felt sexy. The fact that he was nearly naked, and she was nearly naked, too, felt sexy.

Kissing him just because she could felt sexy. Even if he didn't seem to want to respond.

His lips were hard and tight beneath hers. Hard and tight and stubbornly resistant, just like his entire body felt hard and tight and stubbornly resistant. But as her mouth moved on his, plying it, coaxing, tracing the closed line of his lips with her tongue, two things happened: his grip on her arms relaxed enough so she was able to pull them free and slide them around his neck, and he kissed her back with a sudden fierce hunger that made her toes curl and her heart leap and her blood turn to steam.

Then with an inarticulate sound he pulled his mouth free of hers, lifted his head, tightened his hold on her hipbones—**that** was where his hands had gone—and as she opened her eyes to blink up at him in bemusement he frowned down at her and pushed her a little away from him.

Just a little away, putting no more than a few inches of space between their lower bodies, because she still had her arms wrapped around his neck.

For a moment they simply stared at each other. Electricity arced between them, so strong it practically singed the air. Her heart pounded. Her breathing was uneven. Her pulse went all haywire. Her body leaned toward his like the needle of a magnet leans toward north.

Then she snuggled into him a little more so that the tips of her breasts settled firmly against his chest—her nipples tightened instantly, making her body clench deep inside—and his head reared back and his body stiffened like she'd hit him.

"We're not doing this," he said grimly.

She might have been dismayed by his apparent rejection if it hadn't been for his voice, which was low and thick. And his eyes, which had a hard restless gleam that told its own story. And his hands, which were holding on to her hipbones like he couldn't decide whether to push her away or pull her right up against him again. And the very concrete (and **concrete** was the word) proof of his desire in the bulge she'd felt surging to life at the front of his boxers before he had pushed her clear of it.

"Fine," she replied in curt agreement, even though her voice was breathless and her breasts felt all prickly and tight and a hot sweet quickening had begun deep inside her body.

"You don't want to get involved with me," he warned. His voice was gritty and harsh. A dark flush had risen to stain his cheekbones. His eyes smoldered down into hers. "Not under these conditions. Not now."

"No, I don't," she answered with absolute truth, and watched his eyes narrow and his mouth thin and his jaw harden as if he didn't like that reply at all.

But what she didn't add was that it was too late, she already was hopelessly involved with him, having taken a header into the deep end of that particular pool during the previous night, a header from which she was still trying to surface, still trying to figure out if she was going to swim or drown.

And what she didn't do was stop leaning into him, or unwrap her arms from around his neck, or tear her eyes from his. And her heart didn't stop pounding and her blood didn't stop sizzling and her head continued to spin.

He was still looking at her as if he burned for her.

She couldn't see her own face, but she was pretty sure she was looking back at him the exact same way.

"Caroline." He seemed as if he wanted to say more, but he broke off instead to take a breath. He shook his head as if hoping to clear it and his eyes slid over her face. She could feel the tension in the solid, strong muscles of his shoulders and neck, feel the heat coming off his skin.

Her lips parted. They had to, if she wanted to breathe. He continued in a rough-edged voice, as if she was making some kind of protest, "It's you I'm thinking of here."

"Am I arguing with you about it?" Despite being tart, her voice was unsteady, because that's how she was feeling, kind of shaky and off-balance and wobbly and at the same time **on fire**.

She looked at him, at his dark, handsome face, at the sensuous curve of his mouth, at the jet-black glitter of his eyes, and felt a rush of desire so strong that she went weak at the knees. He was right. She knew he was right: getting involved with him at this juncture was an absolute mistake. Didn't mean she was going to walk away. Didn't mean she **could**.

"So let's break this up," he said, and from the way he moved his head and shoulders she knew what he meant: **let go of me**.

"Fine," she replied for the second time, still curt. Still breathless from wanting him.

Slowly she unwrapped her arms from around his neck and let her hands fall.

It wasn't her fault that he was nearly naked, or that his skin was so enticingly hot, or that her hands were reluctant to leave all those corded sinews. It wasn't her fault that they couldn't resist running over the heavy smoothness of his broad shoulders, or down the solid firmness of his wide chest. It wasn't her fault that the soft prickle of his chest hair beneath her fingers plus the honed masculine contours of his six-pack abdomen dazzled her into stroking all the way down to the low-slung waist-band of his boxers before her hands slid back up his body again with sensuous appreciation.

It wasn't her fault that her hands on him made him shudder, or made his eyes blaze.

Reed made a harsh sound under his breath. "Damn it, Caroline," he said, and let go of her hips to catch her wrists, stilling her hands against him just as they reached the firm, wide planes of his pecs again.

Their eyes collided. She forgot to breathe.

His eyes were as hot and hungry as she felt, and he didn't pull her hands away from his chest.

That told her everything she needed to know.

"Reed," she whispered. Then, because she just couldn't help herself, she went up on tiptoe and kissed him again.

He stood there as if he'd been turned to stone, not kissing her back but not pushing her away, either, while his fingers tightened on her wrists and his chest expanded beneath her hands and heat radiated from him in waves. Then he muttered a disgusted-sounding **"shit"** against her mouth and let go of her wrists to slide his arms around her and pull her tight up against him and kiss her back.

She caught fire. Just like that. Like her blood was flammable and he'd just set it alight.

His lips slanted over hers, hot and demanding, and his tongue took possession of her mouth like he owned it. He kissed her with a fierce passion that sent shivery little tendrils of desire spiraling through her body, that made her insides feel all shaky, that made her dizzy. She kissed him back with an answering hunger of her own, wrapping her arms around his neck again, plastering herself up against him because she simply couldn't do anything else, because she craved the feel of his hard body against hers, because she was swept away by need.

She could feel his arousal, feel his urgency, and she melted inside. She burned and quaked and wanted.

When his hand found her breast through the soft T-shirt that was practically no barrier at all, and cupped and caressed it, and then he ran his thumb back and forth over the already pebble-hard nipple, she moaned into his mouth, only to have the sound swallowed up by the intoxicating heat of his kiss. When his hand moved down to splay across her butt, to press her closer still to his telltale hardness, and then slid beneath the hem of the shirt to find her bare skin, she shivered and gasped.

"You've got the sexiest ass," he murmured against her lips.

"You **were** feeling me up earlier, weren't you?" she accused, although the lush devouring kisses he was dropping on her mouth were almost as distracting as his hand up her shirt.

"What if I said I was?"

"I liked it."

"Ah."

Then he was kissing her again like he could never get enough of her mouth and she was kissing him back the same way, and all the while her heart was hammering and her pulse was skyrocketing because his kisses were driving her wild and his hand was still up under her T-shirt and she still liked it there.

It was big, and long-fingered, and warm, and there was an abrasive quality to his palm that might have been faint calluses at the base of his fingers. It felt like a work-ingman's hand, capable and strong, and her senses were reeling because it was fondling her naked behind. He stroked her curves, traced the cleft that separated them, delved between her legs.

"**Oh.**" She made a soft sound of surprise as his exploring fingers found her most intimate place. They stroked, rubbed, then slid inside.

"**Oh,**" she said again, and her bones dissolved. Just like that. If her arms hadn't been locked around his neck, her knees would have given way and she would have collapsed.

"I want you." His hoarse whisper came as his mouth left hers to slide across her cheek and nuzzle the hollow below her ear. He had one hard arm wrapped around her waist now, holding her in place for him. His other hand was still between her legs. His fingers still moved on her, knowing and sure, tantalizing her, touching her where she most wanted to be touched, then slipping inside her and pulling out again, in an erotic rhythm that had her melting for him, that made her quiver, that made her dizzy with desire.

"Reed." It was all she could say. She was panting, moving against him, rocking into his erection, so aroused by the feel of it against her and what he was doing between her legs that she was gasping, trembling, so turned on that she could hardly think, let alone speak.

"Caroline." He bent her back over his arm, trailing damp hot kisses down the side of her neck. Then his hand left its playground between her legs, leaving her empty, leaving her wanting.

"Don't stop," she protested in a throaty little voice, clutching him tighter. Her eyes opened just as he swept her off her feet, picked her up in his arms, and started walking with her, and she saw that his eyes were ablaze with passion and his face was tight with it.

"Not till I make you come for me," he promised in a low growl that was so sexy she almost came there and then.

He put her down on the bed—it was wedged against the table, she saw with the tiny part of her mind that was still capable of noticing such things—and pulled her shirt over her head and shoved his boxers down his legs.

There was a moment there when he paused to look down at her, and the diamond-hard glint in his eyes was enough to make her heart pound and her pulse race. She tried to imagine seeing herself through his eyes: she was naked, leaning back on her elbows on a rumpled white sheet, her knees raised and slightly bent with one tipped inward so that at least the most essential part of her modesty was preserved. Her full round breasts and slim hips and long legs were on full display. Her face was tilted toward him so that her dark hair cascaded down her back. Her lips were parted. Her eyes were heavy lidded and sultry with desire. Her slender, creamy-skinned body throbbed with anticipation, and it showed in the arch of her back, in the rosy stiffness of her nipples, in the small, restless movements of her legs. In that same charged moment she registered his tall, athletic form, registered how big he was in every way that counted, and then she lay down and held out her arms to him and whispered his name.

She didn't know if he kneed her legs apart or she opened them for him, but he came down on top of her, letting her feel his weight, and the heat of his body, and the thick hot length of him, which he moved suggestively against her without entering her, provocative teasing that made her go up in flames. He kissed her mouth, hot, deep kisses, caressed her breasts and kissed them, too, pulling the nipples into his mouth until they were wet and quivering and standing straight up to beg for more, until her body writhed and burned and clenched. He kissed his way downward, running his mouth over her navel and the flat plane of her stomach until she was breathing hard, trembling with anticipation, dying for what she knew was coming next. Then he was licking into the cleft between her legs and she was clutching his head and moaning and coming in long luscious waves of pleasure.

After that, she thought she was spent, but that was before he stretched himself back over her and parted her legs again and pushed his way inside. He was huge with desire, hard and pulsing with it, and her body tightened instinctively around him. Then the sweet, hot quickening began again as he moved inside her, going slow and easy at first until she was moaning and arching her back and clinging to him like he was the only solid thing left in the world. After that he took her hard and fast, kissing her mouth, kissing her breasts, driving into her with a fierceness that awakened every primitive urge that she hadn't even known existed inside her, making her gasp and shudder and move with him and, finally, as she came with a shattering intensity that was like nothing she had ever experienced, dig her nails into his back and cry out.

"Oh, Reed. Reed. **Reed**."

He came, too, then, plunging deep inside

her body and shuddering at the force of his own release.

She was still floating in a dreamy, sex-infused fog when he rolled off her.

That made her open her eyes. Feeling all blissful and tender and ready to curl up with him and whisper chapter and verse about how wonderful she thought he was in his ear, she smiled and slid a look his way.

He lay flat on his back beside her. A comprehensive glance down his body objectively admired his sculpted muscles and long powerful frame, and that part of him which, even at half-mast as it currently was, was still impressively sized. But it was his face that drew her attention. One hand covered his eyes, and he was grimacing.

Not exactly the kind of après-sex reaction she was hoping for.

She wished, vainly, for the quilt, which had been lost along with the pillows and everything else in his bed-dragging rampage across the shanty. Then she spotted the top sheet, one corner of which clung to the foot of the mattress while the rest of it trailed onto the floor. Sitting up, she snagged it and pulled it up and over herself. She was still settling it in place when she glanced at him again and found that he was looking at her.

"Caroline," he said. He smiled at her, but the smile didn't reach his eyes. And there was something about his voice . . . He picked up her hand, carried it to his mouth and kissed the back of it. "You're beautiful."

There was still something about his voice. Something about his eyes. Something about his manner.

Something that didn't jibe with him just having had his world rocked in bed. Which she knew perfectly well was what had just happened.

She got the impression that he was mentally distancing himself from her as fast as he could. And she remembered that he had been adamantly opposed to having sex with her right up until the minute he'd been for it.

But when push came to shove, he was a gentleman. They'd had sex. So of course he would give her the obligatory smile, the obligatory kiss, the obligatory compliment.

Didn't mean a thing.

Under more usual conditions, his next step would be to get up, get dressed, and run for the hills, promising to call soon on his way out the door.

His reaction hurt. It made her mad. It also, she realized, should have been just exactly what she was expecting. He had warned her not to get involved with him, with the clear implication being that he didn't want to get involved with her, either. She had neglected to say to him, **As far as I'm concerned, too late**. But it was the truth. And now she was in it to win it. To win **him**.

Her only possible response? To behave as if it didn't bother her at all.

Curling her legs up beside her on the mattress, winding the sheet more firmly into place so it swathed her from her armpits to her ankles, she regarded him thoughtfully.

"Want to tell me why you're looking at me like the cat that captured the canary?" he asked. Sitting up, swinging his long legs over the side of the bed, he didn't seem one bit bothered by the fact that he was naked. She, on the other hand, having gotten an eyeful of his long, hard-muscled, bronzed-skinned body stretched out casually against the white sheet, was undeniably affected, but determined to ignore his au naturel state. Even if just looking at him sitting there like that did still have the power to make her blood heat.

Her lips compressed. "Just for the record, I think the cat ate the canary."

"Whatever." He stood up, reached for his boxers, pulled them on. Then he turned to face her. "What's on your mind, Caroline?"

She looked up at him. "What's on **my** mind? You just kissed my hand and told me I'm beautiful."

"So?"

"After we had sex."

"Yeah, I got that."

"**Not** what I would have expected from you."

He looked genuinely curious. "Want to tell me why you have a problem with that?"

"I don't know. I guess I expected better from you. You know, more finesse on the dismount. Not such an obvious brush-off."

"You looking for hearts and flowers again, cher?" His voice was wry. "I'm sorry about that. I told you from the beginning that us having sex was a mistake."

She shrugged. "I had a good time."

"So did I. Doesn't matter. It was still a mistake."

"I don't see why you think so."

"Because I know how your mind works. You went into it thinking hearts and flowers, like I said. But you need to understand: this is not a relationship. It was just sex."

"If that's your usual line during pillow talk, I have to tell you that it seriously sucks."

"I'm being straight up with you." He folded his arms over his chest. "This was a one-time deal."

She made a derisive sound. "You think I have a problem with that? I've wanted to have sex with you since I was seventeen years old. Now I can cross it off my list."

His brows contracted. "You have a list?"

"Yep. Places to see, things to do, men to fuck." She clambered off the bed.

He was frowning at her. "Caroline—"

"What?" She picked up the T-shirt from

the floor, pulled it on, and let the sheet drop out from beneath it. "Now that I've got you out of my system, we can get down to business. I want to know about the murders."

CHAPTER TWENTY

Watching her kick the sheet aside, toss her hair back, and fix that level stare on him, Reed found himself getting turned on all over again even as he digested her charming **more finesse on the dismount** and **places to see, things to do, men to fuck** comments with a combination of annoyance and appreciation. Annoyance because, generally, women left his bed with stars in their eyes, and her nonchalance bugged him; and appreciation because he had to admit that the attitude she was showing him was absolutely deserved. In fact, right at the moment he was kinda feeling like the biggest prick alive. The sex had been beyond hot, the woman was beyond beautiful, and he should be feeling pretty damned good right about now and going out of his way to make her feel pretty damned good, too. If things were different, he would in fact still be in bed with her, cuddling her, kissing her, telling her how gorgeous and sexy she was before easing her on into round two.

But he wasn't. He couldn't. There was too much standing in the way. Most important, this wasn't just some woman. He had feelings for her, liked her, cared about her, and going any farther down that road was a disaster in the making. Which was why he'd been far more abrupt with her than he ever was with any woman after sex, especially after truly phenomenal sex, and for all her cool dismissive front, he knew that she was bothered by it. He was sorry for that, but he wasn't about to change a thing.

He already had way too much skin in the game.

He wasn't about to set himself up to lose Caroline, too. And just about the only way he could see not to lose her was to not let himself have her in the first place.

Which was why sex had been a mistake, and why he had been backtracking just as fast as he could ever since he'd made that mistake.

It didn't help that she was looking smokin' hot in the T-shirt that she still wasn't wearing any panties beneath. It didn't help that she was clearly prepared to give him major attitude.

It didn't help that he knew she was crazy about him.

It didn't help that he was already dying to take her to bed again.

Fuck.

His eyes tracked her. She was on the move. Her (round, strawberry-tipped, luscious) breasts jiggled enticingly underneath his loose shirt, and the flash of her long, slim legs made him remember how good they had so recently felt wrapped around his waist. That made him hot, which he definitely did not want to be, so he gritted his teeth and forced himself to look away from her. The rain had stopped at last, and the sun was apparently trying to come out, brightening the place up a little. Given the shambles he'd made of the shanty—the table was now several feet closer to the kitchen counter, the bed was smack up against the table, and the rest of the furnishings were in a jumble against the wall—it was hard to be sure, but he thought that she was heading for the counter where he had tossed Elizabeth Townes' phone. Heading **for** Elizabeth Townes' phone, at a guess.

He felt momentarily cooled down enough to glance her way again. Yep, he was right. Heading straight for the phone. Of course she wasn't going to just let it go: it wasn't in her nature.

"What, are you going all strong and silent on me again?" she asked tartly.

It took him a second, but then he remembered: she wanted to know about the murders. He still wasn't sure how much he wanted to tell her.

"Caroline."

She shot him a look. Blistering, but not in a hot and sexy kind of way. Not anything like the look she had been giving him before he'd fucked her. That look had been sexually charged enough to melt his bones. Sexually charged enough to—

Whoa. Stop. Not going there. What are you, Ware, a slow learner? Reed chided himself.

"Would you quit saying my name like that?" She was being snippy. Well, he was willing to admit she had reason.

"Like what?" he said.

"Like I'm trying your patience."

"You are," he replied promptly. He knew it wasn't a smart thing to say, but the truth was he simply couldn't resist.

Reaching the counter, she raked him with a glance. "You know what you can do with that, right?"

She picked up the phone. He'd known that was what she was after. Then, phone in hand, she headed back across the shanty, bouncy breasts, sexy legs, bad attitude, and all. Watching, he felt his mouth go dry.

Jesus, he wanted her.

So focus on something else. Like the damned phone.

The thing was, he was perfectly capable of wresting the phone from her if there had been a reason to do it, but since she'd already seen the pictures he really couldn't see how she could get herself in more trouble with it, so he let bad enough alone.

"Where are you going?" he asked.

The glance she shot him was scathing. "You're a detective. Figure it out."

Shit. Okay, a beautiful woman with attitude turned him on. Under the circumstances, he should not be enjoying it.

A moment later she disappeared into the bathroom.

Ah.

He took advantage of her absence to step outside on the covered porch and reacquaint himself with the way life at the shanty had been before he had made the bathroom functional. He washed off with fresh rainwater from the barrel that always sat just off the edge of the porch for the purpose of gathering it, and the bucket and cloth and soap stored nearby. Now that the rain had stopped, the day was starting to get unseasonably hot and humid. The front of the shanty was right on the water, which was mud brown and moving faster than usual. An alligator lay sunning itself on the opposite bank. It turned its head to watch him as he baited a crayfish trap by puncturing a can of cat food from the cooler he kept on hand and dropped the trap into the water off the porch. The bugs were out in force, their high-pitched whirring as much a part of the bayou as the blue heron winging its way above the water or the big pines and oaks and cypress that crowded out most of the sky. It hit him that after today he probably wasn't going to get the chance to visit the shanty—which was one of his favorite places on earth and frequently had been his lifeline—for a long time, if ever. He felt the way-too-familiar bite of loss, which did no good whatsoever, and so he tried to dismiss it. He spared a thought for Holly, who he hoped was safe in Mexico by now, and a grimmer one for Ant, along with a promise: **Hang tight, kid, I'm coming for you**.

After placing one more unanswered call to DeBlassis—**where the hell are you, buddy?**—he then tried calling the Justice Department. He knew a couple of guys there, from a drug investigation he'd been a part of when he was working Vice. He wasn't exactly their favorite guy—clashing lines of command and jurisdiction didn't make for BFF status, same reason he was persona non grata with Dixon and some of the other JPPD guys—but time was growing increasingly short and he was growing more and more desperate.

Didn't matter. Government was closed. Fucking Christmas.

When he went back inside, Caroline was just emerging from the bathroom. As she crossed the room he was interested to note that her breasts didn't jiggle quite as freely as before, which made him think that she'd put on a bra beneath the T-shirt. And, probably, he concluded with way more disappointment than he knew he should feel, panties, too. At least, she was wearing her skirt, so he presumed she'd donned panties beneath it.

Thinking about what she was wearing under her clothes was the last thing he needed to be doing, so he tried redirecting his thoughts to something else instead. Like, for example, what his odds were of staying alive long term.

Verdict: dismal.

Even that didn't do the trick: he was still far too aware of Caroline. Who was, he saw, still engrossed in peering at the screen of Elizabeth Townes' phone.

Now there was something to send his thoughts in a different direction.

Grabbing a pair of jeans and a T-shirt from the armoire, he pulled them on, dragged the bed back into place, and, still barefoot, followed Caroline to the kitchen area, where she was opening cabinets. Her skirt wasn't a whole lot longer than the T-shirt, and he caught himself eyeing her legs as she went up on tiptoe to check the top shelf of the cabinet.

She had great legs. A great ass, too. And—

Damn it.

"Can I get you something?" he asked.

"Water. Please." Her tone was abrupt. As she came down off her toes, he caught the faintest whiff of soap, and toothpaste, which before he never would have considered any kind of aphrodisiac, although judging from his body's reaction, now that they were associated with Caroline they definitely were. Taking a self-defensive step away, he opened the correct cabinet and pulled out a few bottles of water, one of which he offered to her while trying not to let the very ordinary scents still assaulting his nose turn him on even more. She ac-

cepted the water with a nod of thanks, un-
screwed the lid, and drank, while looking
down at the phone in her hand again.
Opening a bottle for himself, he took a
swig, too, then pulled out a big pot and
plugged in the electric hot plate that served
as a stove. He filled the pot with bottled
water while watching her swipe her thumb
multiple times across the screen.

That bothered him. He'd never meant to
let her see the pictures, but she had, and
now she was thoroughly studying them,
and that made him edgy. Those pictures
put her in danger, and that thought frankly
scared him. But there was no taking it
back: as she'd said, you can't unring a
bell.

"What are you doing?" she asked, looking up from the phone as he added salt to
the water. He hadn't realized that she was
watching him, too.

"Cooking."

She raised her brows at him skeptically.
"You cook?"

"Yes, ma'am. See, I like to eat."

"What are you planning to cook? Peanut butter?" Sarcasm laced her voice. She
was still clearly pissed at him—and she

had also clearly inventoried the groceries. When he'd told Elsa what supplies he needed, he'd been anticipating a long truck ride with Holly. Thus the bread, peanut butter, trail mix, and apples.

"Crayfish," he told her, and, leaving his water to boil, went out to check the trap. Sure enough, the cat food had done the trick, he saw with satisfaction, and he quickly disentangled the dangling creatures and carried his catch back into the shanty. Caroline was sitting at the table now, poring over the phone, but she looked up as he headed toward the kitchen.

"Oh, wow, you can catch crawly things," she marveled when he held up his haul for her to view.

"One of my many talents," he replied, and she grimaced.

"Just so you're aware, not all of them are that impressive," she sniped with clear meaning, and as he grinned involuntarily he had to face it: **Caroline** with attitude was what was turning him on.

Suppressing the urge to go over there and scoop her up in his arms and make love to her until she ate those words required real effort.

"So, find anything interesting?" he asked, nodding at the phone, once the crayfish were added to the pot.

She shrugged. "I was checking to see if there's any way to identify the gunman."

"There's not."

"There might be," she insisted.

"Think I haven't tried?" He snagged a can of coffee and the coffeemaker from one of the two upper cabinets, both of which he had installed around the time he'd made the bathroom functional. The lower cabinets, like the counter, predated him. "Feel like coffee?"

The look she gave him then was friendlier than anything she had directed his way since they'd gotten out of bed. "Coffee? Really? Oh, yeah."

He plugged in the pot, opened the can, and put the coffee on, inhaling the smell like a drug. He **needed** coffee. He hoped the caffeine jolt would help clear his mind.

He needed to be able to think without getting all tangled up in X-rated visions.

"You know what they say about fresh eyes," Caroline said. It took him a second to understand that she was referring to fresh eyes looking at the pictures, which she was busy studying. The shanty kitchen didn't run to glassware, but there were some Styrofoam cups, which he got out, along with paper plates and packets of nondairy creamer, sugar, and plastic silverware, complete with napkins and tiny paper salt and peppers. "That's an NOPD badge, I'm almost positive, but the angle's not good: I can't see the number on it. Or the face of the man holding it." He knew which picture she was referring to. She continued, "In fact, all the pictures with the gunmen in them show them with their backs to the camera."

"Yeah, well, Holly was hiding across the alley behind some garbage cans at the time," Reed said wryly. The burbling of the coffee pot made a nice, homey sound, and the smell was enough to make him inhale deeply with anticipation. In the pot, the crayfish, bright red now, were just starting to pop to the surface of the water.

"Why would he take such a risk?"

Reed just shook his head as he got busy scooping out the crayfish. Piling them on paper plates, he carried them to the table, placing one in front of her and the other one in front of his chair.

"Looks good." Clearly no stranger to boiled crayfish, she was already snapping off tails and cracking shells with dexterity as he poured two cups of coffee, carried them and the rest of what they needed to the table, and sat down. She looked up at him, her expression several degrees softer than it had been before he had plied her with food. "Thank you."

"You're welcome." Grabbing a couple of slices of bread from the loaf, he passed the bread to her and began his own shell cracking. He was starving, he discovered as he wolfed down a mouthful of succulent meat. Obviously hungry, too, Caroline was eating daintily but greedily. With her fine-boned face washed clean of makeup and her dark hair tucked behind her ears, she didn't look a day older than the infatuated seventeen-year-old of that long-ago summer. Well, maybe minus a couple of degrees of infatuation. Looking at her, he felt a pang somewhere around the dangerous region of his heart. "Merry Christmas, by the way."

The arrested look in her eyes told him that she had at least momentarily forgotten what day it was.

"Merry Christmas," she replied. Then, in a clear effort at making neutral conversation, she added, "Did you have big plans?"

He shook his head. He'd quit celebrating Christmas, after—An instant vision of a little boy in blue-footed pajamas kneeling beneath a Christmas tree, chortling gleefully as he opened a pile of presents, rose up in his mind, and he almost winced. He closed that window down in a hurry, and focused on the present and Caroline. "Back when I was making plans, when I still had a job, I had today off. So, sleep in. Watch some football. Go out and grab something to eat."

The look she gave him was impossible to interpret. "Alone?"

"Yeah." He took a swallow of coffee, then went to work on more meat. "What about you?"

"I was on call, but I was supposed to have dinner with a group of friends."

"Not family?"

She shook her head. "My mother's in Florida with Emily. Sarah"—Emily and Sarah were her two sisters, as he knew—"is skiing with her boyfriend's family. So, no."

"No plans with the superintendent?"

The look she gave him answered that: no. Well, he wasn't surprised.

"Speaking of my father—" She picked up her mug and sipped at her coffee. "You're supposed to call him tonight. I presume to set up a time and place to trade me for Ant?"

Swallowing a section of crayfish, he met her gaze. It was cool and controlled. He was starting to know her expressions well by this time, and he interpreted that one to mean that she wasn't on board with the idea.

"That's the plan."

"Want to explain to me how that's going to work?"

He sighed. He couldn't see any harm in telling her. In fact, it was something that sooner or later she was going to have to know. "When I talk to the superintendent, I'm going to tell him to bring Ant to the Quarter tomorrow night at eleven, and that I'll call him then. When he's in the Quarter, I'm going to call and tell him that he has ten minutes to get Ant to Andrew Jackson's statue in Jackson Square and let him go there. There's a Boxing Day pirate festival scheduled for then in the square, where everybody wears costumes. I'm hoping to be able to grab Ant, clap pirate hats on our heads, and disappear in all the confusion."

Her face stayed composed in its careful mask of neutrality. "You know they're going to have the square surrounded and grab you the instant you set foot in it, right?"

He grimaced. "See, the thing is, I'm going to leave you somewhere else. Somewhere safe, but well away from there. The arrangement I'm going to make with the superintendent is that I'll call and tell him where you are when Ant and I are safely away."

Her brow furrowed, and he discovered that he liked watching her changing expressions as she thought it over.

"That could work," she said finally. "But it's chancy. They could just decide to grab you and torture my whereabouts out of you. Or they could know you well enough to know that you're not just going to let me die wherever you've left me, so they can feel pretty confident that if they grab you you're going to tell them where I am before I come to harm."

"But they can't be sure of that." Reed had already gone over all those arguments himself. "Plus, Jackson Square will be full of people, so they can't just shoot Ant and me out of hand and there'll be plenty of witnesses if I get arrested. And then there's Holly, who will still be on the loose, a wild card they'll also need to take into account."

"Even if it works—and that's a big **if**—you know it won't be long before you're caught or killed, right? Practically the entire planet will be looking for you. You'll probably make the TV show **America's Most Wanted**." She said it almost casually. But her eyes were clouded with worry for him. Registering her worry—damn it, he didn't want her to care—he felt his gut twist.

The last thing on earth he needed now was to be forming some kind of damned emotional tie with her. At the thought, what was left of the crayfish suddenly lost its appeal. He picked up his coffee mug, drank.

"I know that," he said as he set the mug back down. "That's why I scheduled my first phone call with the superintendent for tonight at eight, and the handoff for tomorrow night at eleven. I needed to buy some time. I'm trying to get the Justice Department on board, get them to launch an investigation into what's going on down here. Failing that, or even if that does work out, I'm hoping to be able to get a handle on who the bad guys are before I have to show up in Jackson Square. It can't be the whole damned department. There's got to be a limited number of cops out there killing people. If I know who they are, and I can figure out why they're doing it, then that'll open new doors for people to turn to for help."

Caroline looked away from him. Her hands were curled around her mug, but she didn't lift it to her mouth. Instead, she appeared to study the dust motes captured by a stray beam of sunlight slanting through the nearest window, while she frowned thoughtfully and bit down on her lower lip.

Reed found his eyes riveted on those small, square white teeth digging into that full lower lip.

When she looked back at him, it was with the cool, level gaze of a cop. Meeting her eyes, he was reminded that a lot had changed with Caroline in ten years.

"I've got a stake in figuring this out, too, you know," she said, her voice as level as her gaze. "What you seem to keep forgetting is that I'm a cop, just like you. Leaving out anything to do with our personal relationship, or lack of it, I can't just turn my back on murders when I've seen proof of them with my very own eyes. Could you?"

She had him there. He had to admit the answer was no. But still—he was afraid for her. That was the damned crux of the matter. He'd pulled her out of her nice, safe life without fully considering the consequences, and now he was scared shitless that he was going to get her killed. She must have been able to read his thoughts in his expression because her mouth twisted impatiently and, pushing her plate out of the way and planting her forearms on the table, she leaned forward to glare at him.

"Reed. Quit being an overprotective idiot and tell me what you damned well **know**."

"Hell," he said tiredly, after a moment. What she already knew was enough to get her killed, so he might as well fill her in on the rest in hopes that maybe she could shed some insight that had escaped him. "All right, fine. Maybe you can help. Remember I told you that Holly and Ant's mother was dead? Her name was Magnolia. She was murdered a few months back. Single gunshot wound through the forehead, just like the victims in those pictures. Official word was that she was the victim of street crime, but Holly's been telling me cops did it ever since. He's been trying to find proof, by doing things like hiding behind garbage cans and taking pictures of bad shit going down. Finally, a couple of nights ago, he did." He nodded at the phone in her hand.

Caroline sucked in air, her eyes widening. "Oh, my God."

"Yeah," Reed said grimly, and told her the rest.

"So what do you think is happening?" she asked when he had finished.

He shook his head. "I'm not sure. Some kind of protection racket? Cops horning in on the drug trade? I don't know."

"But my father knows about it?"

He hated to confirm it, but at this point there was nothing else to do but be honest.

"I told him everything I just told you. Took him a file full of evidence to back up what I was saying. You know the rest."

"Then he does." Her voice held no inflection at all. Her eyes held . . . pain. Skin around them contracted. Shadows at their backs.

He hated like hell to see her in pain. Hated it so much it told him something. Something he couldn't even bring himself to acknowledge.

"Maybe there's another explanation," he said, just to give her hope.

She shook her head: **no**. "So what's your best lead?" she asked briskly, no trace left of the emotion that had splayed across her face at the suggestion of her father's potential involvement.

"The cops who arrested Holly. They deliberately targeted him, planted crack on him. Somebody told them to do it. If I can identify them, and get them to tell me who sent them after Holly, then follow that up the food chain . . ." He didn't continue. He didn't have to. He could see from her expression that she understood.

"You have no idea who they were?"

Reed shook his head. "Holly said one guy was bald, one guy had dark hair. Both big, burly dudes." His tone was dry.

Caroline's mouth curved into a smile. For that, Reed thought, he owed Holly thanks.

"Very helpful," she said.

"What I need is the duty roster, to see who was working in that area that night."

"You think they were on duty and not freelancing?"

"I think so. Holly said they were in uniform and pulled up in a squad car. Plus they took him to the jail."

Just as he had, she appeared to accept that as fairly conclusive proof. "You don't have the duty roster?"

He shook his head. "Ever since Holly got arrested, I've been on the move. I tried finding it online, but I got shut down. My user ID and password wouldn't work. Apparently I don't have access to those files."

Caroline's brow knit. "Would my father?"

"The superintendent? I would imagine he'd have access to every file in the system."

"I know his user ID and password. He's

used the same ones for everything for years: hellraiser and grangier. Both with a **q** at the end. No caps."

"Holy hell," he said, staring at her, awestruck.

She shrugged. "Hellraiser was the name of his first boat, and grangier is his mother's maiden name. He puts a **q** on the end of both of them because he thinks nobody will ever figure that out."

"He may be right." Reed watched with some fascination as she started typing into the phone: Caroline continued to surprise him. "What are you doing?"

"If I can get Internet access—" She broke off, frowning at the small screen, then said **yes!** in a jubilant way under her breath before continuing—"which I just did, I think I can get into the files. I used to work part time down at police headquarters when I was in college. I spent a lot of time inputting information into the computer system."

Reed's respect for her knew no boundaries. "I'm impressed."

She flicked a look at him. "You should be."

Since there wasn't anything he could do

except watch, he got up and started to clear the table.

He had everything finished except taking the trash and the remains of the food outside when she said triumphantly, "Look at this. An arrest report for Hollis Bayard was filed by Officer Sean Stoller." She glanced up at him as he moved behind her and bent to look at the phone over her shoulder. "Do you know him?"

Her eyes were bright with interest. The green tinge in the hazel was pronounced, which he had noticed happening before when her attention was fully engaged. Framed by those long, sooty lashes, they were breathtaking eyes, and he found himself getting lost in them. Beautiful, sexy, smart: the woman was something special. Not that it made any difference to anything at all, he reminded himself sternly. He looked down at the phone, shook his head. "Good work. Does he have a partner?"

"Hang on a minute." A minute of flurried typing later, she said, "Officer Eddie Rice. Want to see their pictures?"

She held up the phone. Reed took it from her. The officers' ID photos were on the screen: Stoller had short dark hair. Rice was bald as an egg. Stoller was six feet, 200 pounds; Rice was six one, probably around 205 pounds. Big, burly dudes.

"Holly nailed it," he said. "Wonder who sent them after him?"

"I can find out the chain of command," she offered. "Plus do a search for associates."

"Cher, you are a wonder."

"Remember that," she told him, and, taking the phone back from him, starting typing again.

"Want more coffee?" he asked, and when she nodded he took her cup and refilled it. She was so engrossed in what she was doing that she barely looked up when he set it in front of her, and he smiled a little wryly as he glanced down at the top of her glossy dark head bent over the phone. Leaving her to it, he took the trash and the pot full of scraps outside. The trash he dropped on the burn pile, although considering that putting up smoke was probably a bad idea under the circumstances he didn't light it up. The remains of the bread and crayfish he dumped for the fish. There was a brief feeding frenzy, and then the scraps were gone.

The afternoon had grown downright sultry. The sun was out, shining down through a steamy haze as misty tendrils of condensation from the recent rain floated up toward it. The bugs were bad, and the smell of muddy water was strong, but still he was in no hurry to go back inside. Having Caroline's help was both a blessing and a curse. Without her, there was no way he could have gotten access to those files. Hamstrung as he was by not being able to physically go anywhere near headquarters or any police station, he might never on his own have discovered the names of the officers who had arrested Holly. At least now he had gotten hold of a string he could pull to unravel the skein of tangled yarn, which, thanks to his grandmother who'd been an avid knitter, was how he always visually pictured his more complicated cases. On the other hand, knowing that Caroline was now actively on board and working to help him figure this thing out felt good. Like he could count on her. Like she had his back. Like they were partners, almost. Which was bad.

The last thing he needed was to get any more involved with Caroline.

That thought was sliding through his mind when he walked back into the shanty to find her standing in front of the armoire. Above the massive piece of furniture's four bottom drawers were two doors that opened into a compartment that had been designed to hold something like a small TV. Caroline had opened those doors. As soon as he saw that, he stopped dead. His heart started to slam against his ribs. His gut clenched.

She turned to look at him. Her eyes were big and dark. Her face was utterly white.

In her hands she clutched a blood-stained blue plush teddy bear.

It was all he could do to breathe.

CHAPTER TWENTY-ONE

"I—I was looking for another shirt. I spilled coffee on myself." Caroline knew she was stammering, but she couldn't help it. The coffee had splashed down her right side: she had a ridiculous urge to point to the wet streak as proof. Reed stood immobile just inside the door. He looked big and tough and formidable, and he was standing absolutely still. The expression on his face was truly awful. He looked as if he'd just taken a powerful body blow. His eyes— she could hardly stand to look into his eyes. The raw pain in them was indescribable. "I'm so sorry, Reed."

Of course she shouldn't have touched the teddy bear. If she had realized sooner what it was, what she was looking at, she would have closed the compartment's doors and pretended she had never looked inside. But she **had** opened the doors, and there the bear had been, just sitting inside the upper portion of the armoire, a plump, pale blue toy with a white belly and a blue satin ribbon around its neck. Its presence in the armoire, in the shanty, was so unexpected that she'd succumbed to curiosity and picked it up before she'd thought it through. She'd just been noticing the pictures arranged behind it—maybe half a dozen framed photos of a chubby-cheeked little boy with curling black hair and a wide grin—when Reed had walked through the door.

In that horrifying split second as she'd turned her head toward him, she'd realized what the teddy bear and the pictures had to mean: she was looking at Reed's private shrine to his dead son. It was so personal, and at the same time so heart-rending, that she felt like she had been punched in the stomach.

"I'm so sorry," she said again, her voice

faltering. He hadn't moved, and his very immobility conveyed more than any words could have. That, and those anguished eyes.

She watched him take a breath. Watched his eyes flicker and some kind of protective shield come down, hiding the pain from view.

"It's okay," he said, and closed the door. He came toward her, treading lightly, his hard, handsome face as unreadable as if it had been carved from stone.

Caroline hadn't realized that she was still holding the teddy bear until he took it from her.

"Reed." She put her hand on his arm. "Can you talk to me about it?"

His eyes met hers. The shield was up, but she'd already seen past it. The teddy bear was like a spear thrusting through the barrier he'd erected around his emotions.

"There's no big secret. This was Brandon's." Brandon was his son, Caroline knew. She also realized that she had never heard him say the child's name before. His tone was conversational, almost casual. It didn't fool her for a minute. She could feel how much he was suffering with some kind of new internal radar that seemed to be attuned specifically to him. "He loved this thing. He called it Blueberry. It was tucked into the car seat with him when he died." He glanced down at the bear in his hands, and Caroline followed his gaze. His long fingers, tan and strong looking against the pale blue, were digging into the soft plush. She saw a few small brown stains marring the fur on one side, and wondered with a sickening feeling if they were indeed what they looked like: spots of blood. Her heart lurched as she made the connection: if the spots were indeed blood, they had in all likelihood come from his son. "By the time they gave it to me, it was too late to put it into the coffin with him, or I would have. But he was already buried."

Reed's voice didn't break. But Caroline's heart did. A lump rose in her throat. A knot formed in her chest. She could feel the sting of tears rising in her eyes. She didn't say anything. What was there to say? All she could do was listen to whatever he chose to tell her.

"I gave it to him the Christmas before he died," he continued. "After that, I almost never saw him without it. I brought it out here with me after the funeral. I stayed out here for a while, did some work on the place. I still come out here when I can. It seemed like a good place to keep it."

"I'm so sorry," she told him again helplessly as he put the bear back inside the armoire, setting it down with a tenderness that tore at her heart before closing the doors on it.

"I know." He sounded perfectly normal, perfectly composed. She knew he was not. "It's all right. It's been a few years now. I'm over it. At least, most of the time."

He walked away, heading for the opposite side of the shanty. She followed him, knowing that he was hurting, knowing that nothing she could do could change anything. When he stopped beside the kitchen table, gripping the back of the chair she had so recently been sitting in, looking down at her coffee cup and the phone on the table without, she was almost sure, seeing either, she took one look at the unyielding set of those hard shoulders and came up beside him and put a hand on his back in wordless sympathy. The softness of the well-washed T-shirt did nothing to conceal the rigidity of the muscles beneath.

"I don't imagine anyone ever really gets over something like that," she murmured.

"There are good days and bad days. Christmas is hard." Reed's tone was still just as emotionless as if he were discussing the weather. "His birthday's hard. He was killed three weeks before his fourth birthday. I was getting him his first bicycle, this little red thing with training wheels. He'd been begging me for one every time he saw me. His mother said he was too young, that we should wait until he was five or six, but I bought it anyway. It's still in my garage."

"You must have been such a good father to him." She rested her cheek against the firm muscles of his upper arm, offering what little she could by way of comfort. She could feel him fighting his grief, trying to reel it back into whatever closed-off place it must normally dwell in, and her heart ached for him.

The sound he made then might have been meant as a laugh, but there was no amusement in it at all. He shook his head. "Not really. I married his mother—Susan— because she got pregnant. We fought all the damned time. When she left me—she hated my hours, hated how little I got paid, basically hated me being a cop—I would have counted it as my lucky day except for Brandon. Not having him around all the time—it was tough. I'd been drinking quite a bit before we split up, and after that I started drinking more. I mean, it never in- terfered with my work, never really inter- fered with anything, but I could—and did—put it away upon occasion. Anyway, one night I'd had plans to take Brandon out—nothing special, basically McDon- ald's and the park—and when I showed up to pick him up they weren't there. Su- san was always doing that to me, 'forget- ting' when I was supposed to have him, making plans that conflicted with stuff he and I were scheduled to do together.

"That night, for some reason, it just re- ally pissed me off. There was a restau- rant down the street, so I walked down there and got something to eat and waited for Susan to bring him home. Of course, I knew she wouldn't answer her cell phone—by that time, she never would answer when I called—so I sat down there eating my burger and knocking back a few beers and getting more and more pissed until finally, around ten o'clock, I saw Susan's car scoot past the window. By the time I got back down there she'd parked the car in the driveway—she was staying with her mother, but that night her mother wasn't home—and was getting out. Well, she and I had the mother of all arguments right out there on the driveway. Brandon was still in the back, in his car seat, hugging Blueberry and watching us and listening to every damned word. Finally she said, 'I'm not going to talk to you anymore, you goddamned drunk,' and jumped back in the car. Hell, I was buzzed but I wasn't drunk, and that pissed me off even more, so I called her a few choice names and she peeled rubber out of there. I can still see Brandon waving good-bye to me as they left." His head dropped forward. Caroline could feel the tension in his long body, see the rigidity in his wide shoulders, see in the whiteness of his knuckles how hard he was gripping the back of the chair. "I was so mad at Susan, I fucking didn't even wave back. Twenty minutes later they were dead."

"Reed." Caroline slid a hand down his back. Her throat was so tight that it hurt to swallow. But she had to swallow before she could get another word out. "There wasn't anything you could have done to save them."

He slanted a look at her. There were lines bracketing his eyes and mouth that she had never seen there before, and his voice was harsh as he said, "It was my damned fault. If I hadn't waited around to have it out with Susan, she would have taken Brandon in the house when she got there and they would have been fine."

Her stomach twisted. Her eyes prickled with tears. She couldn't bear that he was taking such guilt on his shoulders. The pain on its own was bad enough. "It was **not** your fault. You had no way of knowing that would happen. You would have done anything to have made it turn out differently."

"You're right, I would have. Anything. But that doesn't make it any less my fault." He took a deep breath, grimacing, and she could feel him working to ratchet his emotions back down again. She watched

as he let go of the chair, slowly and deliberately, as if he had to consciously order
his fingers to release their grip. "You know
what I've never been able to get out of my
head? The last time my kid saw me I was
pissed and buzzed." His eyes were bleak.
"I haven't had a drink since that goddamned night, but that doesn't change a
thing."

"You loved him," she said, sliding her
arms around his waist and laying her head
on his chest, offering whatever slight solace might be found in a hug. Her eyes felt
hot with unshed tears. "That's what matters. You were doing your best for him. I'm
sure he knew that. I'm sure he knows that."

She looked up at him earnestly as she
spoke, and he cupped her face in both
hands. His fingers felt warm and strong
against her skin. His face was all hard
bone and angles with the intensity of emotion. The crow-black hair, the dark gleam
of his eyes, the high cheekbones, the
beautifully cut mouth, the lean jaw shadowed with stubble, were, she realized with
dismay, all etched on her heart now. What
pained him, pained her, too.

His thumb brushed her eyelashes. He

looked down at the glistening drops it captured, and frowned.

"Damn it, Caroline. Are those tears for me?" His voice was husky.

Without waiting for her answer—not that there was any answer she meant to give besides her tears, which spoke for themselves—he bent his head and kissed her. Urgently, thoroughly, his lips hard, his tongue exploring her mouth, as if kissing her was the only hope of salvation he had. She closed her eyes and kissed him back just as intensely, welcoming the steamy heat they generated as an antidote to grief, embracing the blaze of passion that flared between them as a balm for pain. The inside of his mouth was hot and wet, and the slide of his tongue against hers made her shiver and cling. His hand found her breast, closing over it, squeezing, caressing, and her heart pounded and her pulse raced and her back arched as she wordlessly offered herself to him.

"I want you. So damned much," he murmured, feathering kisses across her cheek as she ran her hands up under his T-shirt to stroke over the sleek warm skin of his back. His body was taut with muscle and his arms were tight around her. She could feel the unmistakable evidence of how turned on he was pressing against her, and in response her body caught fire.

"I want you, too," she whispered. At that he lifted his head to look down at her for the briefest moment, just long enough for her to see how heavy lidded and hot his eyes were. Then he was kissing her again, his mouth fierce and hungry. She could feel the urgency in him, feel his tension in the rigidity of the arms around her. When he pulled her shirt off over her head, she lifted her arms for him, then tugged his shirt up until he pulled that over his head, too. She had just a second to admire the breadth of his shoulders and his wide chest before he was tugging her skirt down her legs. As he crouched in front of her and she obediently stepped out of it at his command, he tossed it aside and then slid his hands up the backs of her legs to cup her bottom. She shivered as he pressed his mouth against the silkiness of her panties right at the apex of her legs. The moist heat of his mouth penetrating the flimsy barrier made her suck in air and clutch at his shoulders.

"Reed." It was the merest breath of sound, uttered as he moved his mouth on her and licked against the silk and the hot dampness of it reached the quivering little nub that burned for his attention. Her heart lurched, her body clenched, and her bones melted, but before she could collapse into a puddle at his feet he stood up, steadying her with his hands on her waist. She looked up to see that he was taking in her slender curves in the delicate black bra and panties. His eyes blazed as they ran over her body, making her mouth go dry and her insides go haywire.

"Caroline." He bent his head to briefly kiss each nipple through the thin layer of cloth, drawing them into his mouth until she moaned and slid her fingers through the crisp strands of his hair and held him to her.

When he let her go and stepped away from her, she had to steady herself by grabbing hold of the chair. Passion throbbed between them. The sizzle of it was in the air.

"Get naked for me," he said. His voice was thick and low. "I want to watch."

The mere idea of it excited her. Her lips parted because that was the only way she could get enough oxygen. Fiery little pin-wheels of desire shot through her blood-stream.

He stood there wearing nothing but his jeans, all broad-shouldered and muscular and hot. His eyes held a gleam she could only describe as carnal. His mouth had taken on a sensuous curve. Just looking at him made her toes curl. Her heart raced. Her body throbbed and burned. If he was using sex as a distraction and a solace, which she thought that he was, well, it worked for her, too. She was shivery with arousal, more turned on than she could ever remember being in her life. Burningly conscious of his eyes on her, she reached around behind her back to unclasp her bra. Holding it in place with one hand, she slid the straps down her arms before slowly, finally, allowing the flimsy garment to drop.

His eyes were narrow and glittering as they roamed over her breasts before rising to meet hers. At the look in them, her bones turned to water. The air between them sizzled and steamed.

"Now take your panties off," he said.

She did that for him, too.

His eyes moved over her, not missing

an inch, scorching her everywhere they touched.

"You are the most beautiful thing I've ever seen in my life," he said, and reached for her. She went into his arms, burningly conscious of how erotic it felt to be naked against his bare chest and the abrasion of his jeans, and wrapped her arms around his neck.

Then they were kissing again, hot and deep, and he was picking her up and taking her to bed.

Stripping off his jeans, tumbling her down on the bed, he came into her hard, setting the pace, taking what he wanted with an urgent need that had her writhing and clinging to him and responding with a fiery passion that was explosive in its intensity. He demanded and she gave, letting him take her to places she had never been, losing every inhibition she had ever had. In the end, when pleasure broke over her, as she arched against him and cried out his name and he thrust inside her one last time, she was mindless at the wonder of it.

Then they did it again.

The sex was wild, the climax shattering.

Lying there in his arms in the aftermath, she knew that everything had changed.

She had fallen in love with him. Hopelessly. Irretrievably. Terrifyingly. Not a thing she could do.

He lay flat on his back with her next to him. His arm was heavy and warm around her, and her head was pillowed on his chest. Her hand rested just above his heart. She could feel its steady beat beneath her palm.

For a moment she considered telling him.

Then she tilted her head and met his eyes.

They were absolutely unreadable.

She was just opening her mouth to say something, anything, except the one truly important thing that she was having instant doubts about revealing, when music began to play. Happy music. Young music. Bebopping.

For a moment the two of them lay there looking at each other in mystified silence as the opening bars of Miley Cyrus' "We Can't Stop" filled the air.

It hit Caroline first: "It's Elizabeth's cell phone. I left it on."

Glad of an excuse to get out of bed and

thus avoid any awkward postcoital chat until she had a chance to get her thoughts, and heart, in order, Caroline scrambled for the phone.

"Don't answer it," Reed said sharply, rolling out of bed behind her.

"I won't."

After everything she and Reed had done together, and not forgetting that at this point he had seen and more than seen every square inch of her, it was ridiculous to feel shy about being naked in front of him, she knew. But still, she did. She grabbed his T-shirt—hers was stained with coffee—and pulled it on as she went, which was why they reached the table, and the still-bleating phone, at almost the same time.

The name Julio Perez and a phone number blazed from the screen.

It meant nothing to her.

But apparently it did to Reed. He stared at it for a split second. Then, cursing, he snatched the phone up.

"I thought you said don't answer it," Caroline protested.

Hushing her with a shake of his head, Reed said a cautious, "Yes?" into the phone.

Then his brows snapped together in a ferocious frown.

"Hey, Dick—" Caroline could hear the urgent voice on the other end perfectly well. Her eyes widened as she recognized it. "I know where Ant is."

"Where?" Reed's voice was sharp.

"They got him at the Six Flags. In the theater. Where are you?"

"Never mind that. How do you know where Ant is?"

"I heard it on the street. I checked it out. He's there for sure."

"How the hell did you hear it on the street? In Mexico?"

"Umm . . ." There was a pause. Even Caroline, who was not that familiar with Holly, knew that his hesitation portended trouble. "Well—I'm not exactly **in** Mexico. I—uh— hitched a ride at a truck stop and came on home. Man, I couldn't just leave Ant."

"You're in New Orleans? Right now? What, did you steal the damned trucker's phone?"

"Yeah." Holly sounded a little shame-faced. "To both."

"Goddamn it, Holly, what the hell were

you thinking?" Reed exploded. "Are you **trying** to get yourself killed?"

"I found Ant," Holly said mulishly. "Are you going to come and help me get him out of there or not?"

"Fuck," Reed said. "Where are you? Right this minute?"

"Outside the main gate."

"Can anybody see you?"

"I'm smart enough to hide, so no."

Reed briefly closed his eyes. "It's going to take me about an hour to an hour and a half to get back into the city. Why don't I meet you someplace like, say, the skate park?"

"I'm not leaving here. What if they try to take Ant somewhere?"

Caroline could see from Reed's expression that he was mentally cursing a blue streak. But when he spoke to Holly his tone was abrupt, but calm. "Okay. I'll meet you in front of the main gate in about an hour and a half. Agreed?"

"Yeah."

"Holly—stay out of sight." Reed's voice was harsh with warning. "If they catch you, they'll kill you. And Ant, too."

CHAPTER TWENTY-TWO

"Goddamned stupid kid," Reed growled as Holly disconnected. His hand clenched around the phone.

"That was Holly." Caroline's tone didn't make it a question.

"Yeah."

The driving fear that filled Reed on Holly's behalf took a backseat for a second as his eyes slid over Caroline. With her dark hair all tumbled, her thick-lashed eyes wide on his face, her mouth still rosy from his kisses, and her killer body barely covered by his T-shirt, she was so beautiful that she took his breath away. She'd torn the bandages off the raw wound that was his heart. Instead of leaving it battered and bleeding, though, it felt more whole than it had in years. Maybe, he reflected, the wound had needed air to finally start to heal.

Maybe it had needed Caroline to finally start to heal.

He didn't have time to think about it.

"We've got to go," he said, and walked over to her to slide a hand behind her head and kiss her, a quick but thorough kiss that he couldn't let turn into anything more because he didn't have time for that, either. The kiss made him hot, which became pretty obvious pretty quick—because he was naked. As he let her go he saw her give him a once-over and watched her eyes widen as she registered that, which made him hotter still. "Damn Holly anyway. Kid never listened to anybody once in his life."

"If whoever is holding his brother has him at Six Flags, then he's not being held—at least not officially—by the NOPD, which means that the NOPD is not **officially** holding him to trade him for me. Could Holly be wrong?"

Six Flags New Orleans was the city's iconic amusement park that had been laid waste by Katrina and subsequently abandoned. It hadn't been operational since the hurricane despite numerous plans for its restoration, and lay dead in the Ninth Ward, fenced off and sealed against trespassers, like some giant urban wasteland.

"I don't think so. Holly's a pretty damned good detective. So far, he hasn't been wrong about a thing." He spoke over his shoulder as he headed for his clothes. "Cher, I'm pretty sure this stopped being about the official NOPD from the moment I got fired and walked out of headquarters. Whoever this is has enough clout to use the official NOPD as a weapon, but the real action is taking place behind the scenes."

"My father." Her tone held reluctant acceptance.

"I don't know."

"So what are you going to do?"

"Go get the little shit and see if I can pull Ant out of there."

"I don't think you should go," Caroline said in a constricted voice. A glance around at her as he picked up his shorts and jeans from beside the bed showed him that she was picking up clothes, too: that sexy underwear set that she had so memorably taken off for him, and her skirt. A fresh rush of heat coursing through his system made him grimace. He would have given a lot right at that moment to take her back to bed. She continued, "Like you said, if they get you and Holly and Ant, there's nothing to stop them from killing you."

"Which is why Holly should have kept his ass on that truck to Mexico," Reed replied savagely, already making plans as he pulled on his boxers. Bottom line was, he wasn't Rambo. Last thing he wanted to do was try to take on an unknown number of armed cops alone in an effort to get Ant out and safely away. But try as he might—and he had tried and would continue to try—he couldn't think of anybody he hadn't already contacted to bring in as backup. Terry had a wife and new baby; he was out. Besides, Terry, like any of his fellow cops who weren't involved in the murders or whatever the hell had led to them, would now consider him an armed and dangerous fugitive. Their duty was clear: they could either arrest or shoot him on sight, or else they'd be guilty of aiding and abetting at the very least. Even if a few of them might have been disposed to listen, he wouldn't be given time to make his case. Once he was taken into custody, he'd be accorded the same treatment that had been waiting for Holly: a back-door parole within hours.

Not a happy thought. Especially now that he was discovering that he really did want to live, when before he hadn't been entirely sure. He wanted to live, and have his life. He wanted a future.

Because of Caroline. Maybe even with Caroline. She'd given him something to hope for, to look forward to. In the process, she'd also given him way too much to lose.

Fuck.

He should've kept his pants zipped.

"You can't keep putting your life on the line for them," Caroline said. "You're going to get yourself killed."

Having pulled on his boxers, he was just getting ready to step into his jeans. He paused to look at her. Her face was pale and tight. With fear for him, he knew.

Hell, he was pretty sure he'd gotten to her just like she'd gotten to him.

"I can't walk away from them, and I won't," he said with finality. "They're my responsibility."

"Let me go get Holly," Caroline said. She was clutching her clothes in her hands, looking at him with an intensity that told him how serious she was. "Nobody's going to shoot me on sight. If I should get caught, I can just say I escaped from you. But I won't get caught. I can get Holly away from there, get him somewhere safe, and then—"

"Caroline," Reed interrupted. Having put on his jeans, he was zipping them up and fastening them. He was touched by this further evidence that she was now completely on his side, and even more touched by her apparent readiness to put her life on the line for him. But as he told her: "Me hide out while you go after Holly? Not gonna happen, cher. And you know it."

She must have seen that he meant it, because she didn't try to argue anymore. Her only response as she headed to the bathroom was a shake of her head and a tart, "You ever hear, stubborn idiocy killed the cat?"

He had to smile. "I think that was curiosity."

"Not in your case," she replied, and shut the door.

When she reemerged she was fully dressed, with her face washed and her hair brushed. She looked so pretty that he paused while loading and checking his guns—he had his service weapon, plus a backup he'd been hauling around in the backpack in case he needed more firepower, and enough ammo to fight a small war—to run his eyes over her appreciatively.

Under the circumstances, it was a sad state of affairs when just looking at her made him hot.

"I'll take this one." She grabbed his spare gun off the table. He was still frowning at her when she checked the magazine before expertly pulling back the slide. That reminded him once again that she was a cop, and because he really didn't want to see her thrusting a gun down the back of that sexy skirt, which was probably way too tight to hold it properly anyway, he simply slid his holster toward her with a terse, "Here."

Thing about it was, his plan was the mirror image of her suggestion. He was going to stash her somewhere safe before he went after Ant—going in there would be dangerous as hell, and the idea of Caroline in deadly peril made his blood run cold—but to save time and energy, he wouldn't tell her until the very last possible minute. Trading her for Ant was still a possibility, but if he could get the kid out first, before anybody was expecting him to try, that might be a better option. He wouldn't decide until he had secured Holly and scoped out the situation for himself.

"I found something on the phone earlier." She looked up at him from adjusting the holster's straps so that it fit her better. He caught himself wondering how she'd look in just the holster and gun and nothing else, and quickly shut down that line of thought. "While you were outside. I meant to show you, but—"

"You got distracted," he finished for her as her voice trailed off, and their eyes met. The memory of the sexy parts of that distraction hung in the air between them, making the atmosphere sizzle suddenly, and he watched with interest as her cheeks turned pink. But she jumped off Memory Lane to say, "Officers Stoller and Rice are in three groups together that I've been able to find so far. One's a softball league, one's a boating club, and one's a charity. There are pictures online."

"Show me," he said instantly.

"See, here's the thing," Caroline said once the pictures were opened. "These are all police-sponsored organizations. Two of them—the softball league and the boating club—are big, but they have only NOPD officers as members. But the charity—it's called Rescue New Orleans—is different. Look . . ." She pointed to the charity photo, which showed—he did a quick count— twenty-four officers, all labeled with name, rank, and police department. "Besides the NOPD, there are cops from Jefferson, St. Bernard, and St. Tammany Parishes. It's such a small group to have so many different departments represented."

"Where did you find that?" he asked, frowning at the picture.

"I did a search on Stoller and Rice's names. This came up in the department files."

"Hmm." He turned away, although the

picture stayed in his mind. "Something about the name kind of rings a bell." He thought about it, but whatever it was proved to be elusive. He added, "The point is, one of these things is not like the others."

"What?"

"It's a kind of yardstick I always use when I'm working on a case: what it means is, if something doesn't fit, there's probably a reason and it needs to be looked at more closely." He shook his head. "I'll keep thinking about it. You should finish getting together whatever you want to take with you. I'm going out to turn off the generator. Then we've got to go. If I know Holly, he'll find a way to get into trouble before too long."

He closed up the shanty with practiced efficiency, then placed one more call to DeBlassis—no luck—and the guys at the Justice Department—likewise no luck. After leaving messages with both identifying Stoller and Rice as suspects, he checked to see how many minutes he had left on the disposable phone, discovered he was down to just a few, and accepted it philosophically: he needed to be getting rid of it anyway. Even though it was supposed to be untraceable, keeping it too long made him antsy just on principle. He also wanted to get rid of Elizabeth Townes' phone, but the evidence on it made that impossible. Hiding it somewhere occurred to him, but that brought with it the problem of potentially not being able to come back for it. Unable to come up with a good solution, he dismissed that particular problem for the moment. At least he had a glimmer of an idea about how to get to Ant without getting caught or killed: he could call the fire department and report a fire at Six Flags, then go in under the cover of the fire trucks when they came. The plan had a number of flaws, but he thought it might be workable and, anyway, for now it was the best plan he had.

Having disconnected the generator, he paused beside it for a last look around. Dusk was falling, stealing over the trees and water in varying shades of purple. The bird-calls, the **plop-plop-plop** of fish jumping out of the water, and the vague rustlings of animals in the undergrowth were as familiar to him as the sound of his own breathing. The shanty had been part of his life for a long time, and in the weeks and months following his son's death it had been his refuge. The knowledge that he might not see it again would have depressed him if he'd let it. But he had become an expert in armoring himself against pain, and anyway in the whole scheme of heartbreak, places just weren't that important.

People were what mattered.

On the way back to the porch, his eye was caught by bushy clusters of rose-colored plants that he must have passed many times but never noticed before.

Now he did, because the deep pink flowers were shaped like hearts, and that made him think of Caroline.

Smiling wryly at his own idiocy, he stopped, picked several, and reentered the shanty clutching a handful of shaggy blooms like some lovesick swain on a TV show.

She was over by the table stowing away two bottles of water in his backpack. As he entered she looked up, and her eyes almost immediately zeroed in on the flowers.

He walked toward her, feeling like ten kinds of a fool.

As he reached her, her eyes lifted to his with a question in them.

"I thought I'd try for a little more finesse on the dismount this time." His smile felt crooked as he held the nodding pink blossoms out to her. "Hearts and flowers, cher."

"Oh." Voice soft, she took the flowers, looked down at them, took a breath, and looked up to meet his eyes. Hers were glowing, the golden hazel infused with green. The way she was holding the flowers, he knew the gesture meant something to her. He also knew that on the whole scale of relationships that were or were not happening, he'd just taken a big ol' step over the happening line. He didn't care. For what it was worth, he meant it.

"Oh," she said again, even more softly, then, "Reed," and slid the hand that wasn't clutching the flowers up over his chest and around his neck as she went up on tiptoe to kiss him. Her hand was slim and cool, and her lips were soft and warm, and he could feel every gorgeous, curvaceous inch of her pressed up against him like ink on paper, and he was instantly hard again. His mind went a little unfocused while his body zeroed in on the one thing he was trying not to focus on, which was taking her to bed. The kiss that had started out all gentle and tender immediately turned fiery hot, and it was all he could do to break away.

"We've got to go," he said again, hating to cut the moment short. Electricity crackled between them, and for a moment she simply looked up at him with her eyes as unfocused as he was feeling and her lips parted and damp from his kiss. Then she sank back on her heels, and stepped away.

"Thank you for the flowers," she said simply. Reed knew she wanted to say more. He didn't press her, instead nodding and turning away to snag the backpack, before sweeping the shanty with one last look. After that, they were out the door. The thought of Holly doing God knows what as he waited for him quickened Reed's step.

"I've been meaning to ask you something," Caroline said as she followed him down the steps. "I thought, watching you with my father when you were holding him hostage, that you knew him better than

most detectives would know the superintendent of police. Was I right?"

He looked at her, considering. Some
things were secret, not to be talked about.
But he knew better than most what Caroline had been through. And maybe this
was something that she ought to know.

"I went to a few AA meetings after the
accident. I found out that I'm not actually
an alcoholic, so I stopped going." He
paused to wait for her to catch up to him.
"Your father was there. We started talking
some. He told me that he'd been attending
weekly meetings for the last five years."

"He drank," she said slowly. "Some of
the worst times—"

She broke off, and he could tell from
her expression that she didn't want to finish the thought. He respected her privacy
enough to let it go if that was what she
wanted.

They'd reached the fallen log that served
as a bridge across the finger of muddy
water by that time and he was reaching for
her hand to help her up onto it when he
noticed that she was still carrying the
flowers.

"I didn't mean for you to bring them with you," he said with a quick frown. "You should have left them."

She shook her head, and her hand tightened protectively around the stems. "No way."

Their eyes met, and what he saw in hers made his gut tighten and his heart beat faster. But this was no time to explore it, no time to say the things that maybe he might want to say.

Later. If there was a later.

CHAPTER TWENTY-THREE

With darkness falling, the bayou had turned ghostly and full of shadows. The earth let off steam in the form of mist, which wafted skyward in pale, vaporous fingers. Long tendrils of Spanish moss hung over the path. Its touch was dry and feathery as they brushed through it. Luminescent eyes glowed everywhere, following their progress. An alligator swam slowly past. A cacophony of insect sounds filled the air. They walked back the way they had come, with Caroline mostly following in Reed's footsteps to navigate the trail. He held her hand, partly to make sure that she didn't fall into anything hideous, but also because he wanted to. Her hand felt like it belonged in his now.

Leaving her was going to be hard.

Once they were in the car and on the road, he could feel his tension building. It was dark enough so that they needed headlights, dark enough so that no one passing could see inside the car, but because it was Christmas Day, there were very few cars on the road. After the isolation of the shanty, he felt exposed, and he didn't like it. He was afraid of I-10 because of the search efforts that were likely still concentrated on it, so kept to the back roads as he drove toward the city.

"Are you still going to call my father at eight?" Caroline asked. She'd been quiet since they'd gotten in the car, and he guessed that she was feeling the strain, too. Her face was pale and drawn, and she'd been letting her head rest back against the seat.

"Yes." He'd been thinking about that, and the conclusion he'd come to was, he would go ahead and set up the exchange. He hoped not to have to use it, but it would be better to have it in place just in case. It would also serve as an effective way of fooling whoever was holding Ant into a false sense of security. If the kid was to be exchanged later, no one would expect anyone to try to rescue him beforehand.

"Still going to make arrangements to trade him for me?"

"Yes. If for no other reason than to buy time." The back road they'd been on changed character as they headed into the city, and he drove carefully, minding the traffic lights, sticking to the speed limit. After a few minutes he pulled onto 61 and headed for Mid-City. There was still very little traffic even as they cruised through well-lit, densely populated areas, and that made him nervous. His worst fear was being spotted by some eager patrol officer.

"Makes sense," she said.

"There's something you should know." His tone was deliberately low key. He didn't want her to guess that he was telling her this because, if he was able to get Ant out, he would immediately be taking off with the Bayard brothers and leaving her behind. DeBlassis and the Justice Department might or might not come through for him, but what was looking pretty certain was that they were not going to come through in time. If he survived, he was going to have to run, and he couldn't—wouldn't—take Caroline with him and put her any further at risk. Before he went, he wanted her to know who these other players in the game were, and what they knew. In his judgment, she would be safe if he left her, far safer than if he took her with him, but just in case she needed help he wanted to give her an idea of whom she might be able to turn to outside of New Orleans. Besides, any Justice Department investigation that ensued—and he was pretty sure one would follow; in his experience the feds were slow but thorough—would almost certainly sweep her father up in it. He wanted her to be prepared for that. "I've sent copies of everything I have on the murders and the investigation I conducted into them to a good friend and old partner of mine, Elliot DeBlassis, who lives in Boston now. I told him to take them to the Justice Department. I also contacted some people I know in the Justice Department. At some point, I'm hoping the Justice Department will open an investigation into—"

The muffled ringing of a cell phone interrupted. It was just an ordinary ring, no music, which he knew must mean it was the disposable.

Caroline was already reaching into the back, scrambling to pull it from his backpack. He could smell the faintest of sweet scents from those heart-shaped flowers as she jostled them while getting to the phone. When she handed it to him, he automatically glanced down at it, but it told him nothing. The name and number of the caller did not come up.

Unless this was a wrong number, there were only two possibilities. His heart started to beat a little faster.

"Hello," he said into it. Careful, just in case.

"All right, you've got me back down here in the cesspool," DeBlassis growled in his ear. Just hearing that familiar voice conjured up the man in Reed's mind's eye: light brown hair buzzed the last time Reed had seen it, bright blue eyes, pugnacious features, six feet, stocky build. Who would have thought that Reed ever would have considered that combination the most beautiful sight he could possibly lay eyes on outside of Caroline? DeBlassis continued, "Where the fuck are you?"

A wave of relief washed over Reed so strongly and suddenly that he might have closed his eyes from the impact, if he hadn't been driving.

"In the wind," he replied, and glanced Caroline's way to find that she was sitting up and looking at him with sudden hope. He gave her a quick, encouraging smile even as he said to DeBlassis, "You're here? In New Orleans?"

"You called, I came. Been on a fricking plane all day. Brought the troops."

"What troops?"

"The feds, who do you think? On the way down we were looking into that shit you sent. It doesn't paint a pretty picture of the local yokels."

"Yeah, I know."

"So where you want to meet?"

Reed calculated, and named a little restaurant about a mile from Six Flags. He didn't want to get any closer to the abandoned amusement park in case the sight of swarming federal agents should spook

Holly, or anybody inside, into doing something stupid.

"Give me about twenty minutes," he
added.

"That long?" DeBlassis groused.

"I've got to drop off a passenger first."
Out of the corner of his eye Reed saw
Caroline stiffen. He refused to look at her,
but then, he didn't have to—he could feel
the killer beam of her eyes on his face.

"A passenger? We talkin' the punk kid
you busted out of jail or that smokin' cop
you abducted?"

"The cop."

"Okay. Twenty minutes," DeBlassis
agreed abruptly.

"DeBlassis," Reed said before the other
man could disconnect. "Thanks for coming."

DeBlassis grunted in reply. The buzz in
Reed's ear told him the conversation was
over.

"DeBlassis is here with the feds," he
told Caroline. There was an edge of excitement in his voice as he dropped the
phone down into the console. She'd heard,
he knew, but it bore repeating. He felt his
mouth stretching into a slow grin as the

reality of it hit him. "Looks like we may be going to get through this after all."

"Thank God. Oh, thank God." Her response was heartfelt. She'd curled one leg beneath her and leaned forward as she'd listened to his conversation, and now she slumped a little in the seat with relief. "They'll go after Holly and Ant **and** get you out of this?"

"I hope so. I'll know more once I meet with DeBlassis."

Then her brows twitched together and she frowned. "You're planning on dropping me off somewhere before that?" Her tone was way too polite. She was watching him steadily.

"Cher." They were close to the little dive hotel that was his immediate destination, maybe two miles from the restaurant where he'd arranged to meet DeBlassis, and about three miles from Six Flags. "There's a hotel right up the block here. It rents rooms by the hour, it's a dive, but it takes cash, doesn't require ID, and nobody sticks their nose into anybody else's business. I'm going to give you some money, and I want you to go in there and get a room and hole up and wait for me."

The laugh she gave did not bode well for his plan.

"No," she said baldly.

"'**No**' isn't an option here. That's what's going to happen."

"Reed. I'm a cop."

"Yeah, well. Bullets kill cops, too." That's what was scaring him, he realized. He was starting to get tantalizing glimpses of a future, of what was possible. DeBlassis was in town with the feds to help him solve this damnable case and get his life back. And he'd found Caroline. The black hole that had been his life for so long that he could hardly remember it any other way was suddenly starting to light up with twinkly little stars.

He was afraid of being plunged right back into darkness again. Once burned, twice shy had nothing on him. He knew from personal experience just how fast a man could lose everything.

"I'm going with you." Caroline had that stubborn expression on her face. "I'm in on this. No way am I not in on this."

By that time they had reached the hotel, a four-story pink stucco building with its unsurprising name, Pinky's, emblazoned in neon on the side. He knew it from his days in vice, because, at twenty-five dollars an hour, it was a popular spot for hookers in the area to take their johns. Multicolored Christmas lights, garish against the pink, outlined the double glass front door and lower windows. He could just glimpse a lighted Christmas tree through the big front window. The parking lot had only a few cars in it. Pulling in, he parked in a shadowy corner. Then he cut the engine, unfastened his seat belt, and turned to look at her.

It was dark where they were, but he could see her perfectly well in the glow of neon lighting.

"Come on, Caroline," he began impatiently. She glared at him. She was making no move to unfasten her seat belt, her arms were folded over her chest, and if ever an expression said **wild horses aren't getting me out of here,** hers did. He reached for his wallet, pulled out all the cash he had left. "I've put you in enough danger. This is going over to the feds now, and then I'll be out of it, too. I want you to take this money and go in there and get a room. I'll be back just as quick as I can."

She eyed the cash. She eyed him.

"Screw that," she said. "And screw you, too. This overprotective crap you do is sweet in small doses, but it has got to stop. I'm an adult, I'm a cop, and I decide what I am or am not going to do. And I am going with you."

He dropped the cash in her lap and leaned over to unfasten her seat belt.

"The hell you are," he said perfectly pleasantly. The seat belt strap slackened across her body, but she immediately grabbed the buckle and clicked it back down into place. The look she gave him was nothing short of belligerent.

"Try to stop me," she snapped. "Go on, give it your best shot. What are you going to do, tie me up in the backseat? Leave me handcuffed somewhere? I don't think so. Not anymore."

"Goddamn it, Caroline, would you please just give me a break here?" The hideous thought occurred to him that if she was bound and determined not to go into the hotel there wasn't a whole hell of a lot he could do. He could drag her out of the car, but if he physically carried her into the building they'd call the cops. Pinky's minded its own business, but not to that extent. He narrowed his eyes at her in frustration. "If I'm being overprotective, it's because I don't want to take a chance on you getting shot. And that's because I damned well can't stand the thought of losing someone else I love."

He hadn't even realized what he was going to say until the words were out of his mouth, and then they stopped him cold.

Caroline stared at him, her eyes wide.

"**What** did you say?"

He was mute. He had nothing. He was still chewing over the words, and the feelings behind them, himself.

As far as getting her out of her seat belt was concerned, what he'd just said worked like a charm. She unfastened it with a click and curled both legs beneath her and leaned toward him.

"Reed Ware, did you just tell me you loved me?"

It was too dark to see the green in her eyes as they searched his, but he was sure it was there. Those long lashes cast shadows on her cheeks. Her delicate features, her kissable mouth, every beautiful inch of her was right there in front of him, his to claim.

His heart shuddered a warning. Life was about as predictable as a hurricane, and if he did this, if he went there, he was once more going all in, pushing all his chips to the center of the table, with everything to lose.

"Yeah," he said. "I did."

The smile that beamed back at him put the neon lights behind them to shame.

"I love you, too," she said, clear as a bell, no hesitation for her. Then she leaned across the console and put her hands on his shoulders with the obvious intention of kissing him, but he didn't wait.

He picked her up and pulled her over the console and into his lap, scooting the seat as far back as he could so she wasn't squashed against the steering wheel and kissing her at the same time. Then her arms were twined around his neck and she was lying back in his arms and her mouth was driving him insane and he was kissing her like she was everything he'd ever wanted in his life, which she absolutely was.

"I love you," he said against her lips,

because she deserved to hear it and he needed to say it, to plant his stake in the future with those words.

"Reed," she murmured, sounding as dazed and dazzled as he felt. Then she surfaced just long enough to fix him with a militant look. "Don't think you're changing my mind. I'm still going with you."

Something to argue about later. But he didn't say that. Instead he kissed her again, hot and hard.

He was still kissing her when someone tapped sharply on his window.

Instantly wary, he jerked his head up. Caroline, who'd been lying back in his arms with her head brushing that selfsame window, sat up on his lap. She blinked at the window, her arms still looped around his neck.

At the familiar face that peered back through the glass at him, Reed let out a relieved breath then broke into a grin.

"DeBlassis." He identified the intruder to Caroline, and giving her a quick kiss, lifted her back onto her own seat.

A moment later, he was out of the car and shaking hands with his old friend. Reed didn't think he'd ever been as glad to see anybody in his life.

"Here we got all this serious shit going down and I find you making out in a car," DeBlassis said with mock disgust.

"Wait a minute. We were supposed to meet in Shuman's parking lot," Reed replied, naming the restaurant. "What are you doing here?"

"We were headed that way when we spotted this car turning in here. I was pretty sure I recognized you behind the wheel. We pulled in after you, but by the time we got parked it looked like you needed a minute."

"Thanks for continuing to hang back," Reed said drily.

DeBlassis shrugged. "Couldn't wait all night. And didn't think you wanted to put on a show."

Considering where things had been going with Caroline, Reed thought, **Fair enough.**

DeBlassis' eyes slid to Caroline, who was getting out of the Mazda on the other side while a stranger in civilian clothes whom Reed presumed was a fed held the door open for her. Just looking at her was enough to make Reed feel really, foolishly happy; recognizing that his face was threatening to ease into an idiotic smile, he glanced away. DeBlassis was wearing civilian clothes, too, a sport shirt and slacks, as were the other two men standing back in the shadows near the white SUV they'd arrived in. Reed had known DeBlassis for a long time: he recognized the gleam of appreciation in the other man's eyes as they moved over Caroline.

"Caroline Wallace, Elliot DeBlassis," Reed said, introducing them.

"Nice to meet you." DeBlassis acknowledged her with a nod.

Caroline smiled."**Really** nice to meet you," she replied.

As she came around the front of the car toward them, DeBlassis, who from his long association with Reed of course knew Holly, peered into the Mazda and asked, "Where's the punk kid?"

Reed was just about to tell him when one of the guys standing in the shadows moved a little, enough so that the pink neon light hit his face, and Reed realized that he knew him: Sergeant Glenn Wyman, from Vice. NOPD.

Reed's brows snapped together as he flicked a lightning look at the second man in the shadows. It was too dark to be sure, but he looked familiar, too: Something Purnell, Major Crimes. NOPD.

His internal radar went on instant high alert. His gut clenched. His heart leaped. His blood ran cold.

Shit. Shit. Shit.

His eyes crashed into DeBlassis', and he knew.

Reed grabbed for his weapon, which he'd thrust into the back waistband of his jeans. DeBlassis grabbed Caroline at the same time, ignoring her surprised gasp and deftly dodging the elbow she reflexively threw as he yanked her back against him and shoved his gun hard against her temple.

"Don't move," DeBlassis snarled at Reed, whose gun was by then up and aimed at him. For a split second the years of friendship stretched out between them—Reed had lightning recall of everything from DeBlassis' first day as his partner to them being best man at each other's weddings to

DeBlassis' unflagging support at Brandon's funeral. The gun at Caroline's temple never wavered, and Reed became aware, too, of the other three men closing in, their weapons pointed at him.

Betrayal was a bitter thing.

"You **fucker**," he said to DeBlassis.

DeBlassis replied, "Drop your weapon. **Now**."

CHAPTER TWENTY-FOUR

The parking lot was deserted. No one on the street. Heart hammering, Caroline realized that screaming was useless with no one to hear, even as the SUV slammed to a halt directly in front of them. Trying to run or fight with three guns trained on them was suicidal. She was handcuffed; her weapon had been taken.

Two absolutely unproductive thoughts chased each other through her mind: Reed loved her. They were going to die.

"So, where's the punk kid?" DeBlassis asked Reed, his tone almost conversational.

"Mexico," Reed answered as, hand-cuffed and tight-lipped with fury, he was shoved through the SUV's rear door. "Good luck finding him, too."

The guy who was already in the SUV, the one who'd been hauling Reed in even as a second guy pushed him from behind, struck Reed a glancing blow in the back of the neck with the butt of his pistol, making him stumble. He then shoved Reed into the middle row seat that was farther from the door.

"Hey," Caroline protested sharply as she was shoved in after Reed. Grimacing as SUV guy—average height and looks, a weight-lifter's overly muscular build—locked the seat belt around him, Reed shook his head at her. Their eyes met. His were hard: cop's eyes. His unspoken message: save it. Stay cool. Then she was shoved roughly down into the seat beside him, and she saw murder blaze in the depths of Reed's gaze, which was trained on her unwaveringly.

Caroline's stomach turned over as SUV guy yanked a seat belt around her, too, before sinking back into the third seat as the door beside her was slammed shut. A moment later, the guy who'd shoved her into the van got behind the wheel. He was a little taller than SUV guy, and slimmer, too. She thought she'd heard DeBlassis call him Wyman. He looked vaguely familiar, but she couldn't really place him. She had the impression that he was a cop, and that she'd seen him around.

Her first faint hope that DeBlassis and the others were participating in an official arrest of Reed had dissipated even before they'd clapped handcuffs on her. No "You're under arrest"; no identifying themselves as law enforcement. No Miranda. Nothing like that.

These guys might be cops or feds, but what they were doing was strictly off the books.

The threat of violence hung in the air, as tangible as the humidity.

"So, Mexico," DeBlassis mused, getting into the front passenger seat and turning to look at them as the SUV got under way. Having so recently had a gun held to her head by the guy, who looked like a cross between a football player and a choirboy, she wasn't a fan. After an assessing glance at Reed, he nodded at the guy behind them, then looked at Reed again. "You want to rethink that?"

The guy in the third seat leaned forward. Caroline felt his arm brush hers, felt his breath on her cheek. Then she felt something cold and sharp on her bare thigh. Looking down in surprise, she saw a small, wickedly sharp, silver-bladed knife pressed into the skin just above her knee.

Her heart leaped. Her breath caught. Her muscles tightened, making the point of the blade dig into her skin. It was all she could do not to jerk away, which would have made it cut her.

"Since when are you into hurting women, DeBlassis?" Reed growled. She could feel his anger and his fear for her from where she sat. It was coming off him in waves. His body was taut, muscles straining against the seat belt. Not that it did any good. She deliberately didn't look at him, knowing that the growing panic that she was fighting to keep contained would be evident in her widened eyes, her dilated pupils, and send him right over the edge with rage. Stay calm, she told herself. Think.

"We need to find the kid." DeBlassis' tone was almost apologetic.

"This is beige upholstery," Caroline pointed out in as calm a tone as she could manage while cold sweat prickled to life around her hairline and her palms grew damp. "If you start cutting on me in here, you'll ruin it. You'll never get the blood out."

DeBlassis stared at her, laughed. "Good point," he said, and nodded at the guy with the knife, who withdrew the blade and sank back into the third seat with a grunt. Caroline felt weak with relief. Reed had visibly tensed; as the immediate threat to her was removed, she saw some of his tension ease, too. "We can wait."

Then her eyes were caught by something else, and she found herself watching in horrified fascination as a bright red bead of blood formed on her leg where the knife had been. Her stomach tightened. Her pulse drummed in her ears. Watching it start to trickle down her leg, she heard a ringing in her ears.

She took a deep, steadying breath.

"Holly really is in Mexico," Reed told DeBlassis. She thought he was unaware of the steady thread of blood creeping down her thigh. "I put him on a truck for the border first chance I got."

"I guess we'll find out." DeBlassis seemed to settle in more comfortably. He was turned sideways in the seat, watching them, his gun pointing at Reed almost negligently, not really aimed at him, although Caroline knew that could change fast. The implication in his words was obvious: once they got where they were going, they would torture her until they were convinced Reed was telling the truth.

Caroline thought of the pictures she had seen of the corpses with the bullet holes in their foreheads, and went cold with fear. The goose bumps on her arms and legs had nothing to do with the temperature, and everything to do with the danger that she and Reed were in. These men were ruthless. They were killers.

There was not a doubt in her mind that they meant to kill her and Reed.

And right at the moment, she wasn't seeing any way out.

She went all shivery inside as her mind cast frantically about for possible avenues of escape, and kept coming up empty.

"How's Helena?" Reed asked. The question sounded almost idle, but DeBlassis stiffened.

"My wife's fine. She's not in this."

"When you get back home, give her my love."

DeBlassis glared at him. Then he grimaced. His hand holding the gun jerked, and for a moment it pointed down. Then DeBlassis seemed to pull himself together, and the gun came back up again.

"What'd you have to go and raise such a big stink for, anyway?" DeBlassis sounded genuinely angry. "Taking a bunch of VIPs hostage. Getting yourself all over TV. Trying to contact the Justice Department, stirring things up. All over that goddamned punk kid? I always knew he was trouble."

Reed said, "They killed Holly's mother. You remember Magnolia? Holly found her body, shot in the head. Course, you didn't do that. Happened after you left." His eyes never left DeBlassis' face. "They brought you back down here strictly to lure me in. Because they knew you were my partner, my good friend."

A muscle beside DeBlassis' mouth twitched. "You think I like having to do this? I'd put this shit behind me, started fresh in Boston. Now we got no choice but to make you disappear."

"You've always got a choice." Reed's voice was hard. "Look, Caroline's got nothing to do with any of this. I abducted her, for God's sake. Look at her. She's young, she's pretty, she's a woman. Like Helena. You don't want to hurt her. Let her go."

"Like I could. Hell, I got orders."

"Orders from whom?" Reed asked as the SUV stopped and the driver got out. Caroline looked out the window with a stirring of hope that maybe they were in a populated area where it might be possible to do something like, say, press her face to the window and mouth the word **help** at passersby, but what she saw immediately dashed it: they were at a side gate to the abandoned amusement park. The headlights picked up a bright yellow metal sign affixed to the gate: Service Vehicles Only. It was dinged up, battered. The ten-foot-tall chain-link fence that surrounded the entire 225-acre property was crowded with scraggly weeds that had grown almost as tall as the fence. In the distance, the skeletal remains of the Mega Zeph roller coaster and a Ferris wheel curled against a dark, star-studded sky. Watching the driver drag open the gate, she thought of Holly. He was supposed to be waiting for them outside this very amusement park. Only he would be outside the main gate, where they were not.

A knot formed in her chest at the realization that there was probably not going to be any help coming from anywhere. She wet her lips, trying to keep her breathing even.

"The big boys." DeBlassis glanced at Caroline as the driver got back in the car and drove through the gate. He addressed his next words directly to her. "You should know. Your dad's one of 'em."

That didn't come as any big surprise. Still, the confirmation felt like a weight settling on her chest.

"My father won't want me to be killed," she said as if that were a certainty, although secretly she was far less confident.

DeBlassis looked at her steadily. "Probably not, but he'll do what he has to do to save his own ass. Just like we all will."

"We taking them to the theater?" the driver asked.

"Yeah," DeBlassis replied.

Caroline remembered Holly saying that Ant was being held in the theater. The really bad stuff was going to start once they reached it, she guessed, and the thought brought fresh butterflies to her stomach. Right at that moment they were driving along a dark, deserted street in what could have been part of Small Town, USA. Or, rather, Small Town, USA, as assembled by Tim Burton. The brightly painted buildings were crooked and covered with graffiti. Dark stains that looked like mold were everywhere. Weeds grew through the concrete. Debris lay on the sidewalk and in the street. The effect was macabre, ghostly. She remembered this section of the amusement park: it had once been called Easy Street. The theater was not far ahead. Her heart started to pound again. Her throat went dry. The only plan she could come up with was, as soon as her feet touched the ground, to run like hell.

It was not a good plan.

"Rescue New Orleans," Reed said abruptly, naming the charity from the picture with Stoller and Rice. Caroline glanced at him in surprise. His gaze was steady on DeBlassis' face.

DeBlassis frowned. Caroline could see the driver, too: he stiffened. And she thought, **Ah. We're onto something with that.**

Then she realized that unless they somehow managed to survive, it wasn't going to matter.

"What about it?" There was no mistaking the defensiveness in DeBlassis' tone.

"I came across a picture of the group in the department files while I was looking into a rash of murders with the same MO as Magnolia's," Reed said. "The charity's name seemed familiar at the time, but I just now placed it. I remember you being a part of it. I remember you talking about it, saying something like you were helping yourself by helping New Orleans. I remember that big Lexus you bought, and the vacations you took, and the size of Helena's engagement ring. I kept wondering how you were managing to afford all that, given the amount of money we made. Then again, I was supporting a family, and you were single. That's what I chalked it up to, anyway." He smiled at DeBlassis. It wasn't a friendly smile. "You were getting paid to do something on the side, weren't you? I'm guessing, from the way this has gone down, that it was kill people."

"We need to go ahead and shut this guy down," SUV guy said. His tone was ugly, and the tension in the vehicle was suddenly so thick that the air practically vibrated with it. Caroline's nerves jumped. Her breathing quickened. SUV guy's reaction told her that Reed had hit the nail right on the head.

"Who's he going to tell?" the driver scoffed.

"Feeling smart, Ware?" DeBlassis asked. "Enjoy it, because it's temporary."

"The victims were all street people," Reed continued. "Dealers and druggies, hookers and pimps, gang members. I know the superintendent knows about what's going down, because when I took my suspicions to him the shit hit the fan." He stared at DeBlassis. When he continued, there was a note of incredulity in his voice. "Hell, did the city hire you to get rid of some of the bad actors?"

"Not the city," DeBlassis said, and the driver barked, "Shut the hell up, DeBlassis."

"What difference does it make?" DeBlassis snapped back. "He's not going to be around to tell anybody." To Reed he added, "You know how bad crime's gotten since Katrina. It's taking over the damned city. Pretty soon nobody's going to be safe. Some of the bigwigs put together a freelance team of off-duty cops to clean up the worst of it. To get rid of the worst of the scum. We got recruited, told what needed to be done, and got paid. We were killing people but they were bad people, lowlifes, and it was actually a good thing for New Orleans. I looked at it like it was our civic responsibility, like we were taking the city back from the criminals one dead drug dealer at a time."

"Jesus, DeBlassis, you use jails for that, not murder," Reed replied, and for a moment the two men stared each other down.

"We're here," SUV guy said. With a small start Caroline realized that he was talking into a phone.

Her blood turned to ice as they pulled up outside what was left of the ornate Orpheum Theater. Just like all the other buildings along what had once been a re-production of a French Quarter street, it was brightly colored and marked with graffiti—and totally creepy looking.

"Just FYI, I sent a copy of that picture of the Rescue New Orleans group to the Justice Department, along with an e-mail detailing my suspicions," Reed said. Caroline knew it was a lie: he hadn't had time to do any such thing. She also knew that just as she was, he was desperate to come up with some way out for them. They were running out of time. The thought made her so scared she was sick with it. She wondered if he was, too. If so, she couldn't tell it. He looked utterly composed. He continued steadily, "I also sent them a copy of the same file I sent you. And I've been calling them with regular updates, just like I was calling you." He smiled that less-than-friendly smile at DeBlassis again. "They're going to come looking for me, and Caroline, and Holly and Ant. They're going to investigate. You can probably come up with some sort of plausible deniability for what you've done to date. You kill two cops with the feds closing in, and you'll be putting yourselves on the line for murder one."

"Get him the hell out of here," SUV guy said. The driver had already turned off the ignition and was getting out of the vehicle. Caroline's heart slammed in her chest as she contemplated the possibility of running. Would she get a chance? Would there be cover? If she went for it, she could get shot right there and then . . . She tried not to think about what taking a bullet in the back would feel like.

DeBlassis was aiming his gun now, keeping Reed covered. As the door beside Caroline opened, SUV guy stretched an arm past her to unlock her seat belt. Then the driver reached in, grabbed her arm, and hauled her out. As her feet hit the crumbling pavement and the hand on her arm tightened to keep her from falling flat on her face, she knew this was it.

Darting glances all around, she made an instant, panicked assessment. The night was dark, but not so dark that she couldn't see and be seen. The full moon was already riding up the sky, and numerous stars were out, bathing the scene in an otherworldly glow. The street was wide. The buildings across the street looked to be made of one solid piece of plywood, with no alleys or gaps of any kind between the facades of various shops. To the left and right were long expanses of empty street: no cover there. No cover anywhere. **There was nowhere to go if she ran.**

"Dick!" a boy cried. She shot a look in the direction of the voice and saw the shadowy figures of a man and boy close together, emerging from beneath the over-hang. Even as she spotted them the boy somehow got free from the man who'd ob-viously just brought him out of the black hole that was the entrance to the theater and bolted toward them. He was a young teen, thin, dark haired. He ran like a sprinter with the finish line in sight.

"You! Stop!" the man yelled. Caroline's heart leaped into her throat as she watched his gun snap up.

"No!" she screamed, and jerked away from the driver's grip to spring toward the kid, who streaked past her like she wasn't even there. Reed was just stepping down from the vehicle with SUV guy at his back. At the same time DeBlassis emerged from the passenger door to keep Reed covered. They all pivoted toward the oncoming kid.

"Don't any of you fucking move!" the driver screamed, dancing back a couple of steps, then everybody converged and Caroline found herself, Reed, and the kid who could be no one but Ant hemmed in by four men with guns.

Oblivious, Ant threw himself against Reed, wrapping his arms around his waist, making him stagger back a step. The fact that Reed was handcuffed and that multiple guns were pointing at them didn't seem to deter him one bit.

"Hey, Ant," Reed said to him, very low key under the circumstances.

"They're gonna kill us," Ant cried. He was so scared his teeth were chattering. "I heard 'em talking. They were just waiting for you to get here and—"

"Shut the fuck up." SUV guy slammed the rear door and shoved Reed, with Ant still attached, toward the center of the street. Her chance to run lost, Caroline gravitated toward Reed, too, so that the three of them stood together in a wary little knot.

Looking at DeBlassis, Reed said furiously, "Kid's fricking thirteen years old and—"

Gunfire cracked, the sound a loud **pop pop** in the night. The driver screamed and fell to the street. Time seemed to suspend for a split second. Even as Caroline realized what had happened everyone was crying out and jumping and scattering, and she was, too, falling back toward Reed and Ant as a voice bellowed, "Get your hands up! Federal police!"

A jumble of thoughts exploded through

Caroline's brain at once: a jubilant **we're saved,** followed by **where are they?** and finally, a questioning **federal police?**

DeBlassis and the others were just starting to put their hands in the air. Growling, **"Run,"** in her ear, Reed nudged her into movement with a shove from his shoulder. Pulse leaping, awash with the icy conviction that **all was not well,** she ran, bolting after Ant, who was streaking back toward the theater, with Reed maybe a step behind her saying, **"Go, go, go."**

"Federal police! Keep your hands up!" the voice yelled again. An instant later more gunfire cracked, an **exchange** of gunfire now, Caroline realized even as she pounded after Ant into a sliver of space that ran along the side of the theater. It was an alley, a tiny, dark alley. The gunfire was coming from a sheltered position nearby. She could see the dark silhouette of a man rising above a large concrete planter to snap off shots. A glance back showed her that DeBlassis and the others no longer had their hands in the air, that they had taken cover and were returning fire. A bullet zinged past, so close she could hear the sound of it whistling by her ear. With a little gasping cry she cringed and dodged and kept running. At the same time, out of the corner of her eye she saw a dark shadow run into the alley behind Reed. She saw bright flashes as this newcomer snapped off shots, too, not toward them but the other way, toward DeBlassis and crew. She heard Reed bellow, **"Move your ass,"** and on the wall saw a shadow of a figure in a hoodie and jeans and finally understood: **Holly.**

Holly with a gun, yelling **Federal police. Oh my God. It was a bluff.**

Steps behind Ant, she reached the end of the alley and was just bursting out into a landscape littered with toppled fiberglass statues and derelict rides and what looked like an entire roller coaster lying flat on the ground when a scream behind her made her look back.

Her heart clutched.

Reed had been right behind her. He was no longer there.

CHAPTER TWENTY-FIVE

Caroline felt like she was dying inside, bleeding to death from a thousand tiny cuts.

Reed and Holly were on the street in front of the theater. Reed lay on his side on the broken pavement. It was too dark to reveal much about his condition, but from the restless movements of his legs Caroline knew that he was still alive. Holly knelt near his head. His very posture conveyed abject fear. DeBlassis and one of the other men—he was clasping his shoulder, so Caroline assumed he was the driver, whom Holly had shot—stood over them. Moonlight glinted on the barrel of DeBlassis' gun. She had no idea where the other two men were, although she was as sure as it was possible to be of anything that they were hunting her and Ant.

At the thought, her heart shivered with fear.

"We got to do something," Ant whispered. Crouched beside her, he sounded as anguished as she felt. They were hiding behind the half wall of the bumper car ride at the far end of the street. With the roof and three walls enclosing them, they were enfolded by darkness, sheltered and protected by it. Derelict bumper cars dotted the space behind them, providing plenty of camouflage, or at least so Caroline hoped, for their own shapes. The smell of damp, of mildew, was unmistakable. The smooth metal floor felt slightly slimy beneath her feet.

"There's nothing we can do except go for help," Caroline whispered back, ignoring her own nearly irresistible need to rush to Reed. He was wounded, and she had no way of knowing how badly, no way of knowing if he was still bleeding, no way of knowing anything, and it was tearing her up inside, but the hard truth was there was nothing she could do. She was hand-cuffed and weaponless. To allow herself and Ant to be taken would only ensure that they all died. She had to place her faith in the thought that they wouldn't kill Reed and Holly until they had her and Ant, and continue hiding as they made their way toward the fence in hopes that they would find some way to get through.

Please, God, keep them safe, was the prayer she sent winging skyward, and pre-pared to move.

"Come on," she whispered to Ant. "We're going now."

"He's my brother." Ant sounded on the verge of tears. "I can't just leave him."

"If we don't, they don't have a chance," Caroline replied, knowing it was true.

With another long look at the captives, Ant nodded, and they cautiously started to move. Bent almost double, they were hur-rying along the wall toward the opening that permitted access to the ride when a big black car rolled past with a sound scarcely louder than a whisper. Caroline heard it before she saw it. Freezing so fast that Ant bumped into her, she watched its progress over the top of the wall with her heart in her throat.

Its headlights lit up the scene at the end of the street: she was able to clearly see Reed and Holly, and the men standing over them.

She was so riveted, and she guessed Ant was, too, that the first inkling she had that anyone was behind them was when she heard a gloating, "Got you, bitch," and her heart leaped and she turned her head to find herself looking into the mouth of a gun.

SUV guy was taking no chances this time: he marched her down the street toward the others with a fist in her hair and his gun nestled below her ear. She was so frightened she was dizzy with it. Her heart pounded. Her pulse raced. Ant was being towed along behind her. She couldn't really see him, but she could hear the ragged gasp of his breathing, feel his fear.

Her mind worked feverishly to find some way out, but there didn't seem to be any. Bottom line was, they were caught.

As horrible as the corollary thought

was, as much as she shied away from facing it, that meant they were all four probably going to die.

The black car had stopped and cut its headlights. Whoever was inside the car had gotten out. Three people walked toward where Reed and Holly lay on the ground.

Moonlight touched a man's white hair. Caroline's eyes widened. Her heart leaped.

With hope? With dread?

Whatever else he was, he was her father.

"Dad," Caroline cried even as SUV guy pushed her past the car so she and Ant and their captors became part of the group around Reed, too.

Martin Wallace's head whipped around so fast that she knew he hadn't been aware of her presence until she had called to him.

"Caroline."

His tone made her go cold all over. It was—full of pain.

What had DeBlassis said? **He'll do what he has to do.**

She could see the glint of Reed's eyes, see that he was looking at her, and one

tiny part of her brain rejoiced that he was
in good enough shape to be awake and
aware. She was being marched over to
stand beside him and Holly. Ant was, too.
Her father watched, but made no move to
interfere.

"You can't just let them kill us," she
begged him, shattered that it appeared he
was willing to do just that. **"Dad."**

His stony face and lack of reply sent her
stomach plunging clear to her toes.

"Please," she begged, and then SUV
guy said, "Shut up," and, with his gun still
pointed at her, shoved her down to the
pavement so her knees scraped painfully
against the concrete. Kneeling beside Reed
now, she heard him say something to her,
but she was still focusing so intently on
her father that she didn't understand the
words.

"You don't have to be here for this, Martin," said the man at her father's side. Caroline really looked at him for the first time
and recognized the man as the mayor,
and finally felt like the world as she knew
it had truly spun out of control. She had
known Harlan Guthrie for years, had liked
and respected and supported him. And

now—the cold truth was that he was a murderer. The mayor put a comforting hand on her father's arm. "I'll handle it. You go on home."

"You ever thought that maybe we should end this?" Her father's voice grated on Caroline's heart. It was heavy, sad—and resigned. "Maybe this has gone far enough. Maybe we never should have started it. Maybe we were wrong."

"Hell, Martin, it's a damned war and you know it. The scumbags are taking over our city. Putting 'em in jail is a waste of time—they just get right back out. They prey on innocent citizens. The tourist industry—it's our lifeblood, and we're going to lose it. What we're doing here may be outside the law, but it's not wrong. We put our own private team together, and we pay 'em to take out the people who need to be taken out. It's either that, or let them have the city and run everybody else out." He looked at SUV guy and gestured. "Get these folks on out of here, Purnell. Then get the place cleaned up."

"Yes, sir," Purnell replied. Reaching down, he grabbed Caroline by the arm and jerked her up. Holly was being pulled to his feet, too, while Ant was already up-right and DeBlassis was leaning over Reed. Caroline realized that what she had just heard was Mayor Guthrie giving the order for them to be killed.

The taste of fear was sour in her mouth.

"Dad." A whole lifetime's worth of feel-ing was in that cry. Caroline jerked free, ran toward the man whom she had both loved and hated, admired and feared in equal measure, in one last desperate ap-peal. Her eyes widened as his gun hand came up and he aimed. She heard Reed yell a hoarse, "Caroline," and her father fired his gun and she screamed, all at the same time.

But she wasn't shot, it wasn't her whom he had hit, and there was another scream behind her. As she collided with her fa-ther's chest she realized it was Purnell who had been shot, that he must have been targeting her as she ran, and then her father was taking her to the pavement with him as gunfire erupted around them and what seemed like dozens of men swarmed out of the darkness with weap-ons at the ready screaming, "Freeze! FBI!"

Half an hour later, having been given rudimentary treatment at the scene, Reed was being loaded into an ambulance. He'd been shot in the leg, nothing life threatening, although the EMTs had described it as a serious enough wound, and was being taken to the hospital. Ant was being taken to the hospital, too, for observation after his ordeal. Holly, who refused to be separated from Ant, was already in the ambulance with him. Caroline, who refused to be separated from Reed, was going, too.

Having just released Reed's hand, she was standing by the ambulance's wide back doors as Reed's stretcher was lifted through them when her father came up to her. She hadn't spoken to him since he had gotten up from the pavement and been engulfed by the onrushing tide of FBI agents. She'd been shocked to learn from the FBI agent who'd asked some questions of her and Reed shortly thereafter that her father had been wearing a wire and that the FBI had been using him to take down the mayor and the whole Rescue New Orleans operation even as they had stealthily infiltrated the amusement park's grounds to rescue her and Reed and Holly and Ant.

Looking at her father, she realized that she didn't know what to say. Their relationship had always been so fraught with tension and mixed emotions. But in the end, when it counted, at least he hadn't been prepared to let her die.

On the whole scale of father-daughter relationships, it probably didn't count for a lot. But it counted for something.

"You doing all right?" he asked her, and she nodded.

"You?" she countered, and he nodded, too.

"Dad—" She broke off, unsure of what she wanted to say. Finally she went with a simple, "Thank you."

"You know, tonight's the first time you've called me Dad since you were a little girl," he said, and because it was true she didn't reply. Then he shook his head at her. "You didn't really think I was going to stand by and let them kill you, did you? As soon as Ware called me, that night after he'd kidnapped you, I realized that there was no way you were coming out of this alive if I didn't do something. Guthrie wouldn't have wanted to take the chance on leaving you alive: he had too much to lose. Orders would have gone out, and you would have been caught in the crossfire of a rescue attempt, or something similar. I wasn't about to let that happen, so I did the only thing I could think of: I contacted the Justice Department and agreed to turn state's evidence and wear a wire and do whatever I had to do to bring the whole operation down. I'm not coming out of it too badly—I won't be prosecuted as long as I testify against the others—but I did it for you."

"To tell you the truth," she responded, because the time for a little truth was clearly at hand, "I wasn't sure what you'd do."

For a moment he simply looked at her.

"I know I haven't been much of a father to you," he said heavily. "I know I put you and your mother and sisters through some terrible things. I was under a lot of stress back then, and I was drinking heavily, as I'm sure you remember, and I was out of control. But now, I'm asking you to forgive me. You're my daughter, and I love you. I've always loved you."

Love, Caroline decided as she looked

at him, was a strange thing. Like a persistent weed in a sea of pavement, it could survive in the nooks and crannies of the heart, and just when you thought it had been completely ripped out by the roots, it would shoot right back up.

"I've always loved you, too," she said, and knew that despite everything it was true.

Then she patted his arm and he covered her hand with his. Their equivalent of a hug, she supposed. It wasn't a whole lot, but it was something. For them, maybe, a new start.

Miracles happened sometimes, didn't they? It was Christmas, after all.

CHAPTER TWENTY-SIX

Four days later, Reed was in his house in Bywater. He was in his small kitchen, kicked back in the wheelchair he was relegated to until his leg healed enough for him to graduate to crutches. Dinner was cooking, and the smells of a dozen good things hung in the air. The kitchen was white with touches of blue, with pots bubbling on the stove and the counters crowded with the desserts they would enjoy later, and with everything Caroline needed for baking. Because Ant had been sad about missing Christmas, they were having Christmas today.

Him and Holly and Ant and Caroline. All four of them, together.

It was Holly and Ant's first Christmas without their mother.

It would be the first Christmas he had actually celebrated since Brandon's death.

They had him chopping things: bell peppers and garlic and onions for the Shrimp Courtbuillon Holly was making. According to Holly and Ant, that was the dish Magnolia had made for the holiday meal every year, and it meant Christmas to them. Holly swore she'd taught him everything she knew, and Reed had told him to have at it. Caroline, on the other hand, was a big proponent of Christmas ham. She had one baking in the oven at that moment, while she did something that involved braiding bread dough on the counter near where Reed sat with his wheelchair pulled up to the well-scrubbed wooden table that anchored the center of the room. Since he couldn't stand for longer than a few minutes at a time, the consensus of the other three had been that chopping was all he was good for, and so he had a knife and a cutting board and was chopping away.

"You ain't doin' that right, Dick." Holly

eyed Reed's handiwork critically. He was at the stove, stirring tomatoes into a roux. Ant, who sat on the opposite side of the table busily deveining shrimp, looked over at what Reed had done and nodded agreement with his brother as Holly added, "You got to make it real fine."

"Nobody likes big ol' chunks in the sauce," Ant concurred.

"If I chop it any finer, it's going to be mush," Reed retorted, pausing in his work to frown down at the vegetables he'd already reduced to slivers. He had to blink to see them clearly: the onions were making his eyes water.

"Keep on chopping," Holly directed. "Tiny little pieces. Even-sized."

Reed started chopping again, more vigorously, blinking with every other stroke of the knife.

"Like Mama used to say, you need to learn to wield your knife with finesse." Coming from Ant, that pronouncement both touched Reed's heart and sent his gaze shooting toward Caroline, who made a little choked sound that he saw was her trying to stifle a laugh.

Her eyes twinkled at him as she said, in

the tone of someone who was stoutly defending him, "I think he wields his knife with a great deal of finesse."

To Reed—although thankfully not to Holly or Ant, who appeared oblivious to the double entendre that suddenly made his blood as steamy hot as the kitchen—that was so suggestive that he barely missed cutting off his own thumb with the knife. What he did, instead, was hit a particularly large chunk of onion in such a way that it sent a spray of juice directly into his eye.

He yelped, clapped a hand to his eye, and immediately made a bad situation worse.

"Here, use this." Caroline was beside him, thrusting a damp cloth into his hand. Reed pressed it to his burning eye.

"That's good enough, Dick," Holly said. Through the blur of his watering eyes, Reed watched him head for the table. "I need to put them in now, anyway."

"Yeah, they don't look too bad," Ant agreed.

As Holly scooped up the vegetables, Reed said to Caroline, "Wheel me out of here for a minute, would you? I need some fresh air."

"I'll be right back," Caroline said to the boys. Then she wheeled him into the small hall that connected the living room.

The moment they were out of sight of the kitchen, Reed dropped the rag, tilted a look up at her, and growled, "Just wait till later. I'll show you some finesse."

As Caroline gurgled with laughter, he caught her hand and dragged her down for a kiss. His hand slid beneath her hair to cup her head, his fingers threading through the silken fall with sensuous pleasure. Her mouth was hot and luscious and sexy as hell, just what he'd always wanted. In fact, she was just what he'd always wanted. The best Christmas present ever.

He was just about to tell her so when Holly yelled from the kitchen, "Caroline! Timer's going off on the oven! You want me to do something?"

As he vaguely became aware of a tinny beeping that he recognized as the oven timer, Caroline pulled her mouth from his to yell back, "No, I'm coming." Then she looked down at him.

Her eyes had that green gleam that he loved and her cheeks were flushed and her mouth looked like it had just been thoroughly kissed, which it had.

"I've got to go cook," she said, and dropped another quick kiss on his mouth. "I love you."

"I love you, too," he answered. She gave him a dazzling smile and then was on her way back to the kitchen.

Luckily he didn't actually need her to push his chair: he could manage just fine on his own. Making the executive decision that he needed to give his eyes time to recover from the onion assault before he returned to grunt duty in the kitchen, he rolled on out to his living room, stopping just over the threshold to look at the scraggly Christmas tree that Holly had hauled in from somewhere (Reed didn't want to know) and decorated because Ant had been sad about missing Christmas. There were piles of presents under the tree, including the engagement ring he'd wrapped that morning and meant to give Caroline later. Well, actually he hadn't wrapped it. He had swaddled the small velvet box in tissue paper and stuck it into a red gift bag, but the idea was the same. Getting away from her for long enough to buy it had been a trick—they had been practically inseparable since he'd woken up from surgery in the hospital—but he'd managed it. Later, when they had some time alone, he meant to propose.

Maybe she would think it was too soon. If so, then he was willing to wait. For however long it took her to make up her mind. But as for himself, he didn't want to waste a minute. One thing he'd learned through all this was that no one knew what would happen in the next hour, let alone the next year. Unexpectedly, against all the odds, he had found love, and hope, and happiness, and he was grabbing on to them with both hands. He meant to hold on to them for as long as he could.

He had his job back. He was getting his life back.

His boy was tucked away in his heart, and would be there forever.

But there was room in there, too, for Holly and Ant. He'd already been talking to Holly about finishing school and maybe someday considering becoming a cop. Given Holly's sleuthing skills, that career path seemed like a no-brainer. And he meant to do his best by Ant, helping to see him through his teen years with some degree of stability.

And Caroline? Caroline was his to love, and, he hoped, to keep. To build a future with. To build a life with.

The three of them were his family now.

Thanks to them, he'd found the road home again.

ACKNOWLEDGMENTS

I'd like to thank Elana Cohen, Faren Bachelis, Steve Breslin, Liz Psaltis, Ellen Chan, and Jean Anne Rose, for all their great work on this book. Your contributions were invaluable.

I'd also like to thank my agent, Robert Gottlieb, for being so supportive, and Mark Gottlieb for doing such a good job with my ebooks.